Chapter 1

5 days

Sid Vicious is under the table waiting to see if there's any dropped food. When Nana isn't looking, I kick him. Right in the belly.

'That poor dog must be bursting,' Nana says. 'Will you no take him out, Janey?'

She says this every day but I can't, not any more. It's Sid's fault that I found the dead body.

A BAD, BAD PLACE

www.penguin.co.uk

A Bad, Bad Place

FRANCES CRAWFORD

bantam

TRANSWORLD PUBLISHERS

UK | USA | Canada | Ireland | Australia
India | New Zealand | South Africa

Transworld is part of the Penguin Random House group of companies
whose addresses can be found at global.penguinrandomhouse.com.

Penguin Random House UK, One Embassy Gardens,
8 Viaduct Gardens, London SW11 7BW

penguin.co.uk

Penguin
Random House
UK

First published in Great Britain in 2026 by Bantam
an imprint of Transworld Publishers

001

Typeset in 12.25/15.5pt Minion Pro by Six Red Marbles UK, Thetford, Norfolk.
Printed and bound in Great Britain by Clays Ltd, Elcograf S.p.A.

The authorized representative in the EEA is Penguin Random House Ireland,
Morrison Chambers, 32 Nassau Street, Dublin D02 YH68.

A CIP catalogue record for this book is available from the British Library

ISBNs
9780857508003 hb
9780857 508010 tpb

For Mammy

Chapter 2

The police want to interview Janey again. The wee soul has told them everything, so what in God's name do they want from her?

My nerves are shot so we sit upstairs on the bus so I can smoke. It's full fare at this time of day and no doubt Tottie-Heid will dock my wages when he finds I'm away. It was nice of Cathy to take over, especially with all that mess in the Gents. She's been one of the good ones through this. It's funny because I've never liked her much. Same with Mrs Khan on the tenth floor, no a word between us in years then this happens and she's bringing food and wee treats for Janey. Funny.

Janey's sitting cooried in tight beside me, the way she used to as a wean. Every now and then I feel her twitch, like Sid Vicious dreaming about rabbits. It's been happening since the day at the old railway and I'm no even sure she notices it.

'Look at this one sitting behind us, the shoes on him,' I say to try and give her a laugh, 'like those clowns with the big banana feet.'

'Clowns,' she says, no even bothering to look. 'Do you think it'll be the baldy policeman again, Nana?'

'I don't know, sweetheart. He's no so bad, is he?' Janey looks at me from under her fringe. It's desperately needing cut and

I'm embarrassed no to have noticed. 'This Saturday, Miss Eveline's. Shampoo and set for me, and flicks like the blonde lassie in Abba for you. What do you say?' The electricity bill can wait.

'It was ages ago I wanted flicks. I can't stand Abba.'

It doesn't seem that long since she and the Callaghan lassie were showing me their Abba routine. What was the song again? They had all the dance moves. Couldn't sing for toffee right enough but I clapped and cheered and said they were stars. 'The Dance Queen', is that it? Christ, what's wrong with me these days? This past two weeks seems to have brought back memories I don't want and shoved everything else to the side.

I reach over and move the fringe from Janey's face, thick black hair like her poor daddy. There's a smell from the back of the bus, the heat's making it worse, and I feel bad about leaving Cathy to deal with the toilet. Somebody must've emptied their whole stomach last night. Stuart's likely serving slops on the fly again. Tottie-Heid pretends that doesn't happen in his pub. Turns a blind eye to everything that man, except the staff. He's got it in for the Catholics and likely I'm only there to offend with Pope jokes. What can I do though? No many people want pensioners and it's cash in hand.

Janey stares out the bus window. Since her first class at school, every single teacher has complained about her constant talking. Oh, they all say, she's bright enough and popular too, but she needs to stop chattering. Stopped now all right. Breaks my heart to sit here and no a word.

'Here, is that no him you like?' I try again. 'What's his name from *The Star War*? Mr Kirk, is it? The one with the ears. See there, outside Woolworths.'

'Everything about that's wrong,' she says and even that teeny smile makes her face shine. 'It's *Star Trek*, it's Mr Spock and no way would he be in Glasgow.' She tells me about the actor and where he lives in America and about the film they're making.

But then the silence again and I know she's back thinking about the murdered woman.

I had to collect her from school and she's still in her uniform. I worry whether sending her back was the right thing.

For a week after it happened, the two of us stayed home in that dark place that comes after a death when time stops and you can't see to anything any more. Then Tottie-Heid sent word that if I wasn't back on Monday morning, he was getting a new cleaner. I thought it would help Janey to be at school with her pals. But I don't know, I just don't know what's for the best.

The heat is going for my ankles and the strap on my sandals has burst again. It'd be just the thing if it came flying off in front of these police and me with big sausage feet. Need to stop in at the Red Shop for glue when we get back. I wonder if I've enough in my purse to get Janey an ice lolly.

'Give me your jacket off, hen, and I'll carry it. You must be sweating.'

'I'm cold, Nana. Freezing.'

Janey takes my hand outside the police station and I'm glad of it because it's no just the police making me sick with worry, it's this feeling.

A day or two after finding the body, she asked if I'd ever done anything bad.

'Jeez-oh, aye. Plenty. But see most bad things? Most of them are just mistakes, daft mistakes that people make. You're no meaning to be bad, no often anyway.'

'Even big sins? Are they just mistakes?' she said, and I thought she was talking about the murderer.

But here's the thing, the thing I can't shake. She's been to Confession three times since that day. What does a twelve-year-old have to confess?

Chapter 3

13 days

The police keep us waiting for ages on plastic seats that smell of pish. Nana's nearly finished a whole packet of Embassy Regal and the smoke curls round her head, the same wispy grey as her perm. There's a tramp walking up and down, muttering and swearing, and Nana gives him her last fag. She's like that with tramps and jakeys, talking to them about dead normal stuff like the weather and the terrible price of pies these days. He's got fingers missing and I don't want to look at the stumpy bits but I keep staring. Same with his trousers.

A policewoman comes to get us. My legs are sweat-sticky and there's a farty noise when I stand. Nana nudges me but I don't laugh.

The policewoman is the one who tells me to call her Val.

'How's things, Jane?' This is the third time we've met and she still can't get my name right. 'You must be excited about going up to Big School after the summer,' Val says.

Big School, what a diddy.

I walk close behind Nana who's doing a weird shuffle with one of her feet. Val takes us up a lot of stairs to a room with no windows. Two days after I found the body, they came to our flat to ask their questions, so maybe now they know. Maybe this is the bit where they say they know.

Baldy's sitting at a table, waiting. He doesn't wear a police uniform, just ordinary man clothes. Not really ordinary, more posh, with a tie and shirt. He shakes Nana's hand and says he appreciates us coming in.

'I don't know how yous can't give us peace,' Nana goes. 'The wean told you everything.' She knows I'm no a wean but I see what she's doing.

'It's routine, Mrs Devine. Just in case she's remembered something.'

'Witnesses often recall details at a later date and our Jane is a very smart girl,' Val says and smiles like she's my friend or something.

That day, I call it Dummy Railway Day cos that's where it happened, Val had taken me into a cubicle at the police station to clean up cos I'd wet my pants. I heard her outside, talking to a man who wanted to know if the witness was any use. 'Doubt it,' Val said, 'she's from Possilpark. Bloody lucky if she can remember her own address.'

'My name's no Jane. It's Janey,' I tell her and she makes out she's writing that down with an invisible pencil. Diddy.

We sit across from Baldy and he tells us he's going to record the interview. I suddenly need the toilet and maybe that's why all the chairs in here stink.

'Recording started fourteen-thirty hours, Friday, 27th April 1979. Case number . . .' blah blah blah '. . . Janey Rizzo Devine, date of birth 9th March 1967, residing at Flat 8B . . .'

Rizzo was my da's name, Vincent Rizzo. It's my real name and I prefer it but I guess Devine isn't too bad. Miss Cox has the worst name a teacher could have.

'Also present, Mrs Margaret Mary Devine, grandmother—' There's a bit of palaver and Baldy has to switch off the tape. 'It's just for the record, Mrs Devine.'

'Aye, well, now it's on the record. I'm no Margaret. Always Maggie. And God help anybody that Peggy's me.'

Baldy sighs and drags his hands across his huge shiny head. He's probably got hair but shaves it off cos he thinks he's Kojak. His name turns out to be Detective Alistair Baxter. He lights a cigarette and gives one to Nana. Val is standing behind us, guarding the door. She must be pure melting in that heavy uniform. I touch my pinkie and blink twice, the trick we did as wee kids when we made a wish. But she doesn't faint.

'I want to start at the point where you go to Martin Gillespie's door, hen,' Baldy says at last.

Everybody's ready. There's a scab on my knee that's exactly thirteen days old. I pick it just enough for a tiny blob of blood to appear. And now I'm ready too.

Martin opened his door. He was in his pyjamas, proper *Star Wars* ones, not fakes from the market. He gets nice clothes cos his da works on the rigs.

'I can't come, Janey. We're going to the Botanics.'

I was raging cos I got up early. 'You're going to miss the Spitfire then.' The firework was a belter. I found it near the bins, all nicely wrapped in toilet roll and poly bags. Somebody must've planked it and forgot.

'Can you no wait? It'll be a mental explosion in The Screke,' Martin said.

'It's no my fault, you're the one messing up.' I was kind of wanting to go with them, the Gillespies are nearly my family, but he didn't ask. He'd brought a bit of gammon out for Sid Vicious and was making him give a paw. I was pure huffy but Martin still did the chant, 'Sing like Johnny Rotten, sing like Johnny Rotten.' I joined in and Sid howled. Martin was knotting hisself when he closed the door.

The Dummy Railway used to be real and the tracks stretch for miles. Even though it's all grass now with places to hide and climb, hardly anybody plays down there. When you get down the embankment, there's a weird quietness, like the air is too thick or something. There's stuff lying about that nobody wants to look at, manky nudie magazines and mattresses with stains that give you the boak. Nana's likely the only person that remembers when the trains ran and sometimes I worry about her being so ancient.

I followed Sid through the gap in the railings. The jaggy nettles there are murder but Sid goes mental off the lead and crashed through them, bouncing all the way down the embankment to the tracks. It hadn't been raining but my shoes still squelched in the mush between the rotted sleepers.

The plan was to light the firework in The Screke, an old tunnel that's top secret. There's a bend in the middle of The Screke that takes all the light away and the echoes are loud enough to ache your teeth. The big dare is to scream all the way through it but without running. Nobody ever manages because even if you don't believe the stuff about ghosts and evil skeletons, you still have to watch for glue-sniffers and drunks. I was thinking I'd wait for Martin after all.

Sid was way ahead and I had to run to catch up. He was making growly noises behind a rosehip bush, itchy-coos we call them because of the way the buds stick to your skin. Maybe I would pick some to shove down stupid Martin's stupid pyjamas. But there was a stink.

'You better not be rolling in keech again,' I said out loud.

I wasn't scared when I saw her, not at first. She was lying face up and her legs were apart but at a weird angle. You could see right away that she was dead. There was a droning sound but I think that was just inside me. I didn't stop, just kept walking towards her like it was any ordinary thing. Her feet were bare and dirty and I looked around but couldn't see her shoes. I don't know why her shoes mattered. Then I knelt down beside her. That's when the wee bit of broken glass went into my knee.

'Why did you kneel down, Janey?' The police always ask this.

'I don't know. I just thought . . .' I thought she wanted somebody with her, I thought she was maybe lonely. But I don't say this because it makes me sound a bit mental.

'This is the point that you touch Samantha Watson's dress.'

My face goes bright red. 'There was blood all over her tummy and her, her, down there. She had no pants on.' I feel Nana's hand on my shoulder. She reaches forward and wipes my knee with her hanky. I've gone too far picking the scab.

'And you don't know how long you waited?' Baldy asks. I shrug. Long enough to see a big fat bluebottle crawl out of her mouth.

'Have you remembered seeing anyone walking near the embankment?' Val asks. I shrug again, and she makes a tutting noise. I really don't like Val. 'Could you try to describe how Miss Watson looked?'

My leg starts shaking and blood from the scab plops onto the floor. Red, shiny blood. The blood on Samantha was not red. Her dress was sodden in thick dark sludge, oozing over the bright polka dots. And it smelled. Why did her blood smell? Why was it so dark? Black puddles of blood all round her body.

'No,' I say, way too loudly. I stand and the plastic chair makes a big clatter and they are all staring, but I'm no talking about that. No way, no for anybody.

'Right, that's it,' Nana says. 'Yous already know about the taxi driver who called your mob. So there's nothing more to be said.' Nana's wee and a bit fat but when she's angry, she looks pretty hard. She lifts her handbag and shuffles over to square up to Val. Sometimes Nana is better than all the mums and dads in the world. All the time, really.

'Mrs Devine, please,' Baldy says. 'Janey, hen, sit down and tell us about the taxi. You absolutely sure it was moving? Gonnae talk us through that bit again.'

'I don't— I don't really remember how I got to the main road.' It's like one of those dreams where the bits don't join up and you know there's a chunk missing.

'But you are sure it was Balmore Road?' asks Val. She reminds me of the snobby Andrea, always putting up her hand in class.

'The taxi,' Baldy says. I hope he's angry at Val for showing off.

'It nearly hit me. That's how I know it was moving. The driver got out and shouted at me to get off the effin road,' I say effin because Nana doesn't stand for swearing unless it's about Orangemen, 'but then he was staring at me, and he took my hand and sat me on the pavement. He pulled his taxi over and brought me one of those tartan blankets. He said he was Alex, Taxi Alex, and did something bad happen.'

'Did he mention the body first? Think hard, hen.'

'No,' I say, 'it was me that told him about, about—'

'Did Alex Finlayson look clean to you?'

'Clean?'

'Any mud or stains on his clothes?'

I close my eyes to remember better. Taxi Alex was chewing Wrigley's Juicy Fruit. He had very rubbery hands and his voice was high, not like a man talking. He talked a lot, on and on and on, but I can't remember what about.

'I think he was clean. Maybe some dirt on his shoes.'

Baldy is writing all the time, the words like toaty blue earwigs crawling over his notebook. I want to go home.

'Did the taxi driver leave you alone at all?' he says, adding more earwigs.

'Just a wee while. He went to look over the bridge at the Dummy Railway. When he came back he gave me a Wham.'

'He gave you a what?'

'It's a sweetie,' Nana says, and does a look cos taking sweets is not on.

'It was for shock, Nana.'

'This Alex character. Yous looking at him?' she asks, her mouth doing that tight thing where it looks drawn on. 'Is this no supposed to be gangland related? The papers are saying Samantha Watson's father has connections to the Eggman and—'

'We can't discuss that, Mrs Devine.' Baldy sits back on his chair and tugs at his trouser knees. Men do that, even priests and they don't really count as men. Maybe they think it makes them look important. Or maybe their trousers just don't fit right. 'OK, Janey, last question. Can you tell us anything else about that day? Anything at all?'

He's looking right into my face now.

'No,' I lie.

Chapter 4

Tottie-Heid is in the snug with a *Daily Record: Murder and Crime Family Pull-out Special* spread on the table. He's like a wean with a comic.

'Stuart, 'mere,' he shouts to the barman. 'Check these pictures. See what a lovely-looking lassie she was.'

Stuart catches my eye. He's in a bit of a state.

Of all the staff at The Glen, without a doubt Cathy's got it the worst. Behind the bar, Tottie-Heid squeezing in tight, making out that he's only touching to move her out the way. Cathy can't afford to say a thing, no with three weans and one of them not right. But I feel for Stuart too, forced to listen to this shite just because he's a man. As long as there's hair on your chin, you're always one of the boys, always part of the team. Stuart sits, a big skinny-malinky with a glass of Irn-Bru, wishing he was miles away. Poor soul, AA and working here. He doesn't stand a chance.

I start thinking about my three brothers sent to war and only Finn, the youngest, came back, bringing that ear of his. Some men never stand a chance. I need to wipe my eyes but my hands are manky.

'Always a waste when they're gorgeous,' Tottie-Heid says and lowers his head. It's nowhere near opening time but his teeny eyes are already clouding from the drink, his spongy nose shining. What gives that dung-heap of a man the right to drool over Samantha Watson, making judgements, as if she was nothing more than a nice vase that somebody took a hammer to?

'Of course, Ah'm well quoted with Billy Watson, well quoted,' he says. 'If you ask me, the murder wis come-back. Billy Watson's messed wi the wrong people.' As if he knows anything.

'Is it right Watson works for yon Edgar brothers?' Stuart says. 'Sees to their money?'

'Aye, so Ah've been tolt. Duncan Edgar, the Eggman, he owns that Ashfield Cabs up the road there. Billy does his accounts, his dirty accounts if you get ma meaning. Right-hand man to the Edgars, so he is.' Tottie-Heid turns a page in the *Record* and points to a photograph, taken from miles away. 'See that big cunt in the hat? Top man in the MacQuarrie family. He's got it in for the brother, Jimmy Edgar. If the MacQuarries are in a war wi the Edgars, Billy's lassie wis just collateral. No doubts.'

He sees I've stopped to listen. 'Away and see to the mopping, stupid face.'

My husband used to speak to me like that, and after Donald Devine, I swore I'd never let another man order me about, yet here I am, kowtowing to Tottie-Heid.

I move to the bar and start. It wasn't too many years ago that The Glen had sawdust on the floors and I still find it lodged in cracks in the lino. It's no a popular pub, and the hard wood chairs, decrepit tables and mean wee strip lights seem to match Tottie-Heid's personality. There's a gloom that stops the young yins coming in and most daytime customers are the two-bob mob who smoke dowts off the street, the dedicated drinkers who wouldn't even notice if the place was on fire.

When I empty the ashtrays, I find the Snotterer has been in again. Cathy maintains he doesn't come in to drink, just to fill ashtrays with phlegm. She keeps an eye out but has never caught him in the act, and without a doubt it'll be a him. I was dealing with one of the Snotterer's messes when the police told me about Janey finding the body.

Must be near four weeks now, and when they came in I thought it was for the usual free pies and pints. Tottie-Heid, supposedly well quoted with gangsters, is right cosy with the police. But I heard them ask for me and my insides shrank.

Tottie-Heid brought them over and I had to sit before my legs went.

'Mrs Devine? It's about your granddaughter,' the woman policeman said, her face sour with the information.

'It's all right, missus. Your wean's no harmed,' said the other one, an older policeman that I wanted to throw my arms around and cuddle, 'but you need to come and get her at the station.'

'Her lassie in trouble, then?' Tottie-Heid asked, no doing much to hide his delight.

'Nothing like that,' the policewoman said. 'She was walking your dog—'

'Oh, surely no Sid Vicious? Has he been knocked down again? Ach, Janey'll be—'

'It's not the dog, Mrs Devine. Your granddaughter found a corpse.'

They had a panda car waiting outside The Glen, and it was when the policewoman took my arm to help me in that I realized I was still holding an ashtray full of snotters.

There's a big laugh from the snug. What can Tottie-Heid find funny about Samantha Watson's story? Another dead woman. Woman. Samantha was only twenty-two, no much younger than my Marie when she died. And wee Donna just eight. All just lassies. What is there to laugh about?

When they leave to do the barrels, I sit to read. I don't like bringing the paper home because this stuff would just upset Janey. Upsets me but I can't stop myself. Is there a name for that – when you don't want to know about something but go out your way to find out? Probably just stupidity.

There doesn't seem to be anything new apart from the approximate time of death on Saturday morning. Oh, Mother of God, it's terrible close to when Janey got there. Bile fills my stomach but I can't stop reading. The rest of the article is the tripe they've dredged up on the father. Samantha's hardly mentioned and no a word about the murderer or what they're doing to find him. I'm demented knowing he's walking the streets, demented. In my mind's eye, I see him down the old railway, having a laugh as well.

Chapter 5

23 days

Twenty-three days since I found the body.

Last year, I drew a Countdown to Christmas on my bedroom wall. The woodchip wallpaper made it look rubbish and Nana was annoyed when it wouldn't clean off.

Now, I'm marking the days since the Dummy Railway in my secret scrapbook. Miss Cox let me bring the binder home and the front cover still says *My Ancient Egypt Project*. There's stickers of Tutankhamun and the first page has a rubbishy drawing of a pyramid. But the rest is all about Samantha Watson.

Nana said nobody would know it was me that found her. But the neighbours in our flats knew, and Ali in the Red Shop, and likely everybody in the whole of Possil. Probably Nana's boss that spread it about. Or Nana.

And everybody at school knew. On my first day back, they all crowded round.

'Was it all blood and guts, Janey?'

'Were you screaming? Did you shite yourself?'

'Was the dead woman a nudie?'

I just stood there looking at the ground till Miss Cox came out and made them line up. She took my hand and we went in the teachers' entrance and she was all nice and kind. That made it worse and I wished she would just shout like normal.

Now, they leave me alone but there's still loads of talk about the murderer and how it's somebody they know – him with the funny eye, or a guy who works with their da, or that Rangers supporter with the big van. Even my best pal, Lorraine Callaghan, goes on and on about it. She likes freaking out the wee yins, saying the murderer's hiding in the school toilets waiting to get them alone and then . . . the kids usually run away screaming at this bit. But maybe me and Lorraine are no best pals any more. Since Dummy Railway Day, I hardly go out and nobody comes up for me. No even the Smelly Kellys.

This morning at playtime, Lorraine's all pally with that Jackie McPhee. Don't care.

'What you standing behind the bins for?' Jackie says, slinking up beside me. 'You trying to hide your new trainers? You get them at The Barras?'

I look at my feet and think about my old shoes crashing to the ground. Wearing them was giving me the shivers so I chucked them out the window, along with the other clothes from Dummy Railway Day. Even my cracking new Harrington. Nana went down and binned them but she missed the pants and some wee boys are still using them for scabby-touch. Nana wasn't angry when I told her why, but I had to wear my gym sannies till she saw Big Des. He's got her Family Allowance book.

'Look what we got,' Lorraine says, opening a packet of cheese and onion. There's a bottle of nail polish in there. 'Boots No7, Jackie knocked it off her sister.'

'Want us to do your nails?' Jackie asks. 'You'll need to hide your hands in class but. Check mine.' She wiggles Frosted Pink in my face.

Wiggling and wiggling till all I can see is Samantha Watson's nails, broken and filthy like she'd been scrabbling in the dirt to get away. And I feel it again, the smashed hand in mine, too cold and too heavy.

'Just, just get lost,' I shout and push Jackie. I didn't think she would fall.

Mr McColl hasn't looked up yet. There's a folder open on his desk but I don't know if it's about me.

'So, Miss Devine, what are we going to do with you?'

Behind him is the cupboard where he keeps the headmaster belt. It's black and made of special thick leather and everybody says he broke a boy's wrist with it. Lucky he doesn't belt girls.

'Violence against a classmate cannot be tolerated,' Mr McColl says, 'no matter what the circumstances. I always find myself surprised when I have to confront a girl about this issue. You've certainly let yourself down.'

It was just a toaty wee shove.

'I think it may be of immense spiritual assistance if you speak with one of the Franciscan Sisters,' he says. 'Sister Agnes Benedicta is wonderfully sympathetic with girls.' It's hard to concentrate on what Mr McColl's saying because of the way his moustache moves when he's talking. 'Yes, wonderfully sympathetic.'

I start thinking about Sister Agnes and the way she calls everyone Rosie Rainbow or Sandy Sunbeam. I think about her soft white hair that matches her knitted cardigans, and her smiley crinkly face and shaky old-lady hands. And I imagine telling her about the black blood on Samantha Watson and the places where she was ripped open. I don't even know the real words for women's private bodies. On our class bookshelf, there's a *Ladybird Book of Bible Stories* with all the swear words scribbled over Adam and Eve's nudie bits. That's the words I know.

'Here you are, Miss Devine. Phone this number and make an

appointment for a chat.' Mr McColl manages to pass the piece of paper without looking.

Martin Gillespie is waiting to walk me home.

'Did you get the belt?' he asks. When I show him the phone number, he studies it then shoves it into his mouth. 'The nuns, the nuns,' he laughs, chewing and gagging, 'you've no even got a phone. What a joke.'

Me and Martin are in the same class and everybody thinks we are cousins. I call his mum Aunty Angela because she was my mammy's best friend. I don't mind pretending I've got family but I don't hang about with Martin in school. He's not one of the boys that fights or goes on about Celtic, and he's only got one pal, Logie, and he's weird too. They once had a three-day argument about whether Judge Dredd keeps his helmet on in the bath.

Even though he was supposed to be with me that morning, Martin has not said one word about Samantha's body. No one single word.

What he did do, though, was sit in my room.

Right after me and Nana came home from the police station on Dummy Railway Day, I went to bed and slept. Not even like an early night, I slept all the time, for four days. Nana had to wake me for food and the toilet. She brought the kitchen chair into my bedroom and sat beside me. And sometimes, Martin was there too.

He spits the last piece of the nun number down a stank. 'Think we could teach Sid to pogo?' he says.

'Taupe?' Nana says.

'Taupe.'

'Taupe? Taupe?'

'Aye, Maggie, bloody taupe. I've no clue what colour it is either.'

Nana and Jean Jarvis are looking at the catalogue. Jean is Nana's best pal and it's mad that old people still have friends.

'Just put me down for black. It'll no show the dirt,' Nana says, pointing at something in Ladies' Underwear. 'And better make it a double D, they're making cup sizes awful tight these days.'

'Right. With the four pack of pants, that takes you to, eh, £1.12 a week. Twenty-two shillings in real money,' Jean says.

I hear Sid scratching at the kitchen door, desperate to see the visitor and maybe bark to show what a good boy he is. For a minute, I almost go to him.

'Janey,' Nana says, 'come and we'll look at the school skirts. Grey for Secondary, am I right?'

'I don't want anything.' Jean puts the catalogue away and gets her jacket on. Monday is one of their domino league nights and this'll be Nana's first time back since Dummy Railway Day.

'Are you sure you're fine with me going out?' Nana asks. I want to say that I'm never fine but I nod. She's wearing beads and her nice cardigan. Angora she calls it, but I don't think that's a real word. Jean wears trousers so she's likely younger. I thought Nana was maybe about eighty or ninety but the police read out her date of birth and she's sixty-six. Nana never wears trousers.

Jean's out at the lifts. 'There's a big dog keech on the landing again,' she shouts in. 'Wait now, it might no be dog. Mon see.'

'A wee minute, Jean.' Nana rolls her eyes up to Heaven and I smile. Sid's pulling on the lead, he likes The Standard Bar but he probably wants to examine the shite too.

'Lock the door behind us, lamb,' Nana says. When she kisses my cheek, I smell her hairspray. 'We don't want robbed again.'

I used to think it was funny that somebody sneaked in and stole the broken hoover. But now I put the snib on and shove the footstool against the door.

*

Later, I hear Nana making tea and singing about the wild colonial boy. She never used to get drunk except at The Bells. I need to say my prayers cos it's my fault. My scab is still nice and fresh and doesn't need any picking. I do an Act of Contrition for the bad thing, and then my God Bless list.

God bless Nana and all the Gillespies. God bless Uncle Finn's bad ear and Dad's family in Italy. Eternal rest grant unto Mammy, Dad and Donna. And dear God, please please look after Samantha, even if she was a Protestant.

I feel saddest when I say Samantha's name but I know that's daft.

I must have been making a noise when the nightmare came because Nana's here. She's holding me, telling me it's OK, safe now, wee chooksy. The streetlight makes the room orange and my eyes are sleep fuzzy but I can see the flab on Nana's arm and the wee hole in her slipper. I see my Snoopy books and Paddy Panda, and the radio-cassette that Aunty Angela said I can keep. And I see Samantha, sitting on top of the wardrobe, her bare bloody feet dangling. I wave and she waves back.

Chapter 6

The sky's started to lighten. I'll no be worth a button at work but it's pointless going back to bed. The living room is freezing so I pop the fire on, just the one bar or they'll be cutting us off. I notice the redness on my hand where Janey was gripping it. What am I going to do with her? Angela Gillespie says there's officials that could be helping, social work and the like, but I'm no sure. Janey needs her own people round her. And you hear stories. A woman in Cadder had her weans taken away when she asked for help. Poor soul was struggling with the baby blues, likely just needing a hand for a wee bit. They came for the weans in a minibus and the whole street was out giving them dog's abuse. A tragedy, an absolute tragedy. What if they come in a minibus for my Janey?

I shouldn't have had that third bottle of stout last night, my stomach isn't what it used to be. Maybe a bit of toast will help. The dog wakes and I scrape out the last tin of Chappie onto his plate. Poor Sid Vicious.

'Your pal won't stay angry at you forever,' I say and rub his ears, 'she'll love you again.' He finishes the food in seconds and licks the lino in case he missed any. God, he's an ugly brute of a thing. Only Janey and her wee kind heart could have chosen Sid Vicious. He paws at his empty bowl then moves awkwardly to face me.

I used to have a right big kitchen. My tenement in Maryhill had high ceilings and long sash windows that let the light stream in. It was from one of those windows I could see the wreckage that had buried my family. The entire tenement came down but the Rizzos were the only fatalities. Even the workmen sent to fix the gas leak survived. It was a blessing it was a working day, a blessing the family with the six weans were on holiday, a blessing the couple in the ground flat were out collecting their pension. All those blessings and all that luck. Just none for me.

When I put in for a move, the Corporation were quick with an offer, I'll give them that. But now I live with windows suited to jail cells and a kitchen without space for a dog to turn around. Ach, I need to stop this feeling sorry for myself. Possil's a good place.

'Sorry, son, that was the last of it,' I say to Sid Vicious. He has a more expressive face than most people I know and looks as if he's about to weep. 'Ah, don't. I'll check the bins at work for a pie and bring— Oh, wait a wee minute, wait a wee minute.' I suddenly remember there's half a steak-pie supper in my handbag. Jean can never resist Romano's, even after a night on the sweet sherry.

When we were waiting in the chippie queue, this man came in.

'Here's somethin you'll want to know, missus,' he said, sticking his face right next to mine. Reeking of cheap wine he was, bits of tobacco stuck in his teeth. 'You'll want to know this. That deid wummin your wean found? That deid wummin was a whore. Her bastardin faither whored her out and it wis him that killt her.'

'Away you,' I said and shoved him, 'and take your filthy mouth with you. Talking about the dead like that. Mrs Romano, Mrs Romano,' I was shouting because I'd had a few myself, 'sling this eejit out your shop before I set my dog on him.'

Just thinking about it makes my stomach go again and I run

to the toilet. What gives these people the right? And it's no just the drunks, I get them all, even at Mass, desperate to tell me what they've heard about Samantha or about her father. He's just another poor soul that'll never see his daughter smile again.

'Mon, Sid Vicious, we'll have a walk round the block before Janey's up.'

The May sunshine's vanished and the rain is slopping in through the double doors of the flats. Somebody's put cardboard down but it's no helping. Thank God I didn't put my shoes away.

Mrs Khan gets off the early bus, she must be on nights. What is it she does again? She told me but it's gone. It's in a hospital or an office, she carries a clipboard so it must be a good job.

'Mrs Devine,' she says, stopping a bit away so she's no too close to Sid Vicious, 'are you well? I wonder if you have been ill?'

'Ill?' Christ, did she see me vomiting on Saracen Street last night?

'You did not come on Saturday. The clothes for Janey? Remember? You said Saturday. Lovely clothes, Mrs Devine, my daughters are growing so fast. Denims from C&A.'

When did I agree to this? 'Ah, well, now, it was Janey. I'm awful sorry, hen, she—'

'No, no, I understand.' She nods and softens her voice. 'Janey will recover from this, I promise you.' She side-steps the dog and wades through the puddle. A vigorous-looking woman, the kind you could ask to help shift your wardrobe. Handy to know a woman like that.

'C&A,' she shouts from the lobby.

Imagine me forgetting Saturday. I'm usually on the ball with this kind of thing, and this is sore. Like a smack in the face.

Chapter 7

26 days

Nana walks me to school like I'm six years old again. She starts work at half eight and I'm first in the playground but it's better than walking on my own. This morning, there's a van sitting at the gates with the engine running. The driver, in dusty clothes and woolly hat, gawps at us. I used to be brave – the only girl to climb out the trapdoor at the top of the flats – but now every stranger makes me shake. Samantha's killer hasn't been caught and I can't stop thinking about it. To keep Nana here, I ask stupid questions like who is her favourite saint, and what's happening in *Crossroads*.

'And, and what about Aunty Angela's new rug? When that's coming, Nana?'

'What's that nosey so-and-so looking at?' Nana's noticed the van too. 'Can I help you with something?' she shouts, all annoyed. The driver sticks two fingers up at her, then opens a newspaper.

The playground is getting busy and Nana has to go to work. She squeezes me tight when she leaves. The Primary 7s are all buzzing, it's the visit to St Augustine's, the Secondary where we'll go after summer. Everybody's wearing real clothes and I feel daft in my uniform. I forgot and Nana forgot, so I don't have a permission slip. Lorraine's wearing her new blue cap-sleeve and she's raging.

'We were supposed to be partners, Janey. You need a partner. Fuck will I do without a partner? Eh? Eh?'

I can't even think up an excuse and walk away. When the bell rings, Lorraine's in the line with Jackie, who's got a new cap-sleeve too. I would've worn my Damned t-shirt, Martin's Damned t-shirt. It would've looked way better than them, Lorraine's style is rubbish and that Jackie is a pure copycat.

In the hall, Miss Cox is shouting about best behaviour and reputation of the school but nobody is listening. Jamesie Doherty is telling everybody you get to see the girls' changing room, and if you are dead lucky, they are in it.

There's a Protestant Secondary school near our Primary, but St Augustine's is away up in Milton and we'll need to get the 47 bus. Today, a special bus has come. Jamesie turned up in a Celtic top so he's no getting to go either and the two of us watch everybody piling in. Lorraine and Jackie push on to make sure they get the back seat. That's where I would have sat. Then one of the boys slings a jumper to Jamesie, and now he's allowed to go as long as Miss Cox doesn't see even a glimpse of those football colours.

Just me left and I get told to wait in class for Sister Agnes Benedicta.

I'm nearly crying when the bus leaves, which is daft because Secondary's just another school. For a minute, I think about sneaking away, I've got house keys, but that van is still at the gate. It's probably just a workie or something but I run back inside.

Everybody talks about the mad stuff they would do if they got left alone in the classroom, like changing their test marks or drawing a big willy on the blackboard. I just put my head on the desk.

Sister Agnes comes in very quietly. 'Where's my Rosie Rainbow?' she says. Everything about her is quiet, except her nun outfit, which rustles like brown leaves. 'Oh, it's yourself, the girl with the lovely smile. Will we find somewhere cosier to wait, just the two of us?'

The cleaners are busy in the Staff Room but the office is empty and I sit on the treatment couch where you get disinfectant on your playground injuries.

'Isn't this the very thing, now?' Sister Agnes says. 'We'll have ourselves a grand time of it.'

It is quite nice. She gives me a KitKat and diluting orange in a paper cup and I'm glad I didn't go with them. Starting Secondary was all I'd been thinking and talking about, and now it's nothing.

'I've been hearing something happened to yourself.' Sister Agnes sits with her hands folded as if she's saying a prayer. 'A bad, bad thing. Would you like to have a little chat about that?'

A little chat? Well, it was effin terrible, Sister Agnes. I found a corpse all ripped apart and I did something that was definitely wrong, and I can't remember a big chunk of what happened next, and I have nightmares and pish the bed, and I'm scared to go out in case the killer gets me. How about that then, Sister?

But what I say is, 'I'm fine, thanks, Sister Agnes.'

She closes her eyes and nods and nods, and tells me to remember my prayers at night especially to the Blessed Virgin Mary, who takes a special care of all little girls.

Nana's working late so I pull my Special Box from under the bed. My secret scrapbook is hidden under old newspaper cuttings, a Wombles pencil case and the Ramones badge from when me and Lorraine got boyfriends.

In my pocket there's a page from a newspaper. Since Nana stopped buying one, I get the papers out the bins, or from the Witchy Sisters who leave theirs stacked outside their door. No way are they witches and they're likely no even sisters but they scare the shite out of everybody and if you go to their door at Halloween they give you teeny poisoned cakes. Lorraine ate one but wouldn't tell anybody if she got sick.

I unfold the page and smooth it out nicely.

. . . the last known sighting of Miss Watson (22) is leaving a party in the Hillhead area. The police believe Miss Watson got into a dark-coloured Hillman Avenger which was masquerading as a minicab.

I dig out the map of Glasgow showing where the new health centre is getting built, and draw a red line from Hillhead to the Dummy Railway. It's no very far. Masquerading means kidding on, I looked it up, so Samantha would've thought she was going home. I try to picture her, happy and excited after a party, waving to her pals, then running to get in that fake minicab. But in my picture, her face is a battered black balloon.

I look at newspaper Samantha, the usual photograph on a beach in Yugoslavia. Her bikini is lime green with swirls and she's in a pose like a beauty queen. Samantha has a nice figure. Had. That's what Aunty Angela says, 'A nice figure.' For ages, I wanted a nice figure, any kind of figure really cos I'm the shape of a lamppost. But now it just reminds me of Samantha's soft bits all torn apart.

The report's got another smaller photo and I like it better. I don't even know why they use the bikini one, it was taken ages ago when she was seventeen and had long hair. This new one is from one of those photo booths and Samantha's hair is short like the day I found her. She's pure beaming and I imagine a kind of story where one of her friends is standing outside the wee curtain doing funny noises to make her laugh. Maybe werewolf howling, or diarrhoea. Martin does brilliant diarrhoea sounds but that makes me remember good times and I don't want to.

I cut out everything and stick it into a new page and underneath I write my made-up story about the photo booth. I'm writing everything down – stuff from TV, newspapers, what the neighbours are saying, even all the rubbish they talk in school. Then maybe, maybe if I know about her, Samantha won't be just a mess of skin and blood and holes.

Chapter 8

The bang is right behind me. Gas. A tray stacked with empties drops from my hands and there's another explosion when it hits the floor.

'Sorry, Maggie,' Stuart shouts, 'cellar door. Forgot to put the catch on.'

The cellar door.

Tottie-Heid buys cheap pint glasses that break if somebody looks at them the wrong way and I'm surrounded by a puddle of tiny diamond splinters that reek of Tennent's.

'Stay where you are, Ah'll get the brush,' Stuart shouts.

He clears a path and sits me at the one table with padded chairs, then rushes back to finish sweeping before Tottie-Heid arrives.

I light a cigarette and there's a wee tremble of the match. I need to give myself a shake, it took me a long time to get over living with fear and I'm no going back. Gas. Imagine my first thought being gas.

No doubt that was down to Janey, last night.

She was sitting at the big table, drawing or colouring in or something, and she says, 'Did you have to look at my mammy's body?'

'What? What you saying?'

'After the gas accident. Did, did you have to go and identify them?'

'No.'

'Did you see any of them aft—'

'I said no, Janey. Not another word. Put your pens away and get yourself washed.'

That's why Stuart's on his hands and knees gathering shards of glass, and why 16th July 1969 is replaying in my mind.

I worked in Bryant & May on the machines in those days, and the foreman called me to the office. I thought it was something to do with the picketing – three police standing there, hats in their hands, and I thought it was union stuff. My God. When they told me there had been an accident, a gas leak, I was having none of it. No, that's no my family. Aye, that is their address and aye that is my daughter's name but she's home. She's home because they're decorating and her man Vinnie has got the week off and they've just moved and Donna and baby Janey will have their own bed-room now. The hard-nosed sergeant grabbed my arm and he squeezed it and it was sore and I looked at his face and I knew. I knew that my family were gone because of the excitement in his eyes.

They took me home, and at some point a woman from the Immaculate Conception came to stay. That woman and the way she washed, fed me, put me to bed, and I don't know even her name or how long she stayed.

So, no, I never saw the bodies. It was Vinnie's brother who went to the morgue. He came round after it to give me Marie's wedding ring but no a word about how they looked. The pic-tures you make in your own head . . .

*

Stuart has finished clearing my disaster and is hiding the glass so my wages don't get docked. He's a nice man. I get back to cleaning the two Babycham deer, the wee things are the only brightness in this whole grim place and I don't like leaving them to cigarette filth for too long. When Cathy arrives she launches into a long story about Tottie-Heid demanding a written list of who's barred, but the only thing in my mind is Marie's wedding ring, small and gold and dented.

Chapter 9

30 days

I was late leaving school today cos I was waiting for Martin. He was taking ages to come out the toilet, then the jannie said there was nobody in there and to get myself home. Stupid Martin, he probably got caught up in a discussion about Dr Who's trousers or some mad thing.

I run most of the way but stop to watch a game of Kick the Can starting on Balglass Street. Some of the big girls are playing and probably cheating. Definitely cheating.

One time in the winter, we played Kick the Can all night. Everybody joined and there was no out-of-bounds. It was brilliant. Some kids from The Jungle came and made flaming torches with clothes poles and petrol. Me and Lorraine were doing great, sneaking around behind the old dookit, till stupid Stevie Baw-Jaws from the sixteenth got us caught. The game stopped when somebody's mum came out, raging in slippers and nightie. I was sorry for being narky with Stevie because his dad got him on the stairs and leathered him, right across his wee chubby cheeks. But it was the best Kick the Can ever. When I went in, Nana was sleeping in her chair. She's pretty strict about coming-in time so

I put on my pyjamas and woke her, kidding on I'd been in bed for hours.

One of the McGuires sees me and comes running over.

'I'm no playing,' I tell her.

'No, Janey, it's no that. Your uncle's wanting to talk to you,' she points towards my block, 'he's got a motor.'

My uncle? Uncle Finn lives miles away and is too old for driving. Maybe it's Martin's dad. I don't call him Uncle George because he works away most of the time but they've got a colour TV so he's likely rich enough to buy a car. Then I get a bit excited thinking it could be my real uncles from Italy, come to visit at last.

The wee McGuire girl takes my hand to lead the way. Her lips are Mr Frostypop green and her hand is sticky but I don't pull away. She's all proud and puffed up about bringing me the message.

'What does my uncle look like?' I ask Sticky-Hand.

'He's a man,' she says.

'A man? What kind of man?'

'Normal man. No a weirdo like Donnie Harelip or Black-Hood No Face.'

'Donnie's no a weirdo. And who's No Face supposed to be?'

'Black-Hood No Face is new,' she talks really fast, like she'll explode if she doesn't get it all out, 'Black-Hood No Face is maybe a ghost and he's wanting wee lassies. And dugs. You better watch your big dug.'

'You talk rubbish,' I say. 'Which McGuire are you? You Diane?'

'Diane's my sister.'

'Sandra?'

'Nope.'

'Peter? Are you Peter?'

'Don't be daft. There's no Peter McGuires.'

'Are you, ehm, Scooby Doo? Scooby Doo McGuire?' She's laughing, but something pops into my head and I stop walking. 'Is my uncle's car a dark-coloured Avenger?' I ask, thinking about the newspaper report and the fake minicab. That just makes Sticky-Hand laugh even harder. ''Mon we'll go round the back way,' I say, 'and you can point to the car out my window? OK?'

Suddenly, there's a crash and we turn to look. Kick the Can has got a bit mad and the can's gone through a window.

'There. Look there, that's Black-Hood No Face,' the wee girl goes, tugging at my arm, 'see? See? Tolt you. He's after us.'

There's girls laughing and Gibby from the flats is rolling a tyre along the street, but no weirdo.

'You talk shite,' I say, but a shiver goes through me, strong enough to make Sticky-Hand pull away.

When we turn back, a ginormous guy in a leather jacket is belting along the road. He's coming right at us but I can't move. The McGuire girl hides behind me and I feel her wee hands holding me tightly and I wish I had someone to hold because the killer is here and I'm going to get stabbed and—

'You Janey Devine?' he asks and grabs my arm. I can't answer, my breathing feels too fast, my tongue too big. Will he chop my body like Samantha's, will he take my pants off?

'You Janey Devine?' he asks again, leaning down to my ear and I feel a bit of his spit on my cheek.

Sticky-Hand lets out a wail and starts running.

Don't leave me, don't leave me, get somebody, get a grown-up. My mouth is open but none of these words come out, just a toaty wee moan.

The big guy laughs and shouts after her, 'Don't say nothing to nobody you. Ah know where you live.'

A car pulls up beside the kerb, a fancy dark-coloured car. The sight of it unfreezes me and I start wriggling. My arm nearly pops out the socket trying to get free but the guy just laughs again and yanks open the back door. Is this the way he shoved Samantha in? Did her head clonk against the door too?

I roll into a tight ball and try to scream but all that comes out is a whine. Two men are talking, maybe to me, but my hands are over my ears and my eyes are shut and I'm moaning and moaning. The car door opens again and somebody sits in the back beside me, a rough hand takes mine. He's saying my name. He opens my fist and puts something in my palm and I can't help looking.

It's a photograph of a girl in a funny homemade hat, all ribbons and bows with cardboard chicks. An Easter bonnet. It's Samantha Watson in an Easter bonnet. She's smiling and the man beside her has a giant chocolate egg and he's smiling too. For a minute, I think I'm sleeping and this is part of the Dummy Railway dream. Somebody took my hand in that dream too.

But then the voice is suddenly loud. '. . . her dad. Samantha's dad. You're OK, Janey, you're OK.' He is patting my head and when I turn, I see the man in the picture. He's older and his hair is white but his eyes still look like Samantha's. And now I'm thinking about her one dead eye like a marble and the other one swollen shut, and I start to cry.

'You don't need to be scared. Christ, I wouldn't scare you for a million quid, hen. Here, now, c'mon now.' Samantha's dad puts his arm around my shoulder and gives me a big proper cloth hanky that smells of aftershave. He takes the photo, touches Samantha's face, and puts it in his pocket.

'Ho, Lulu,' he shouts at leather jacket guy, who's in the driver seat now, 'Lulu, say you're sorry.'

'Aye, sure, Billy. Didnae mean nothin, hen.' Lulu's looking at me in the car mirror but he sounds annoyed, no sorry.

'That daft big bam's face would scare anybody,' Samantha's dad says and smiles, and that helps. 'I'm Billy Watson, and I know you're Janey Devine.' He holds his hand out for me to shake, like a grown-up, and I start to feel a bit normal again.

'I just wanted to come and say thanks. Thanks for, for finding my daughter.' Mr Watson stops speaking and looks away, his breathing weird and broken. Then he goes, 'I wanted to make sure you're doing all right. Are you, Janey, are you doing all right?'

'I'm fine,' I say in a quiet voice.

'Time's getting on here, Billy,' Lulu goes, pointing to his watch, 'he's phoning at half-past and if—'

'Aye, I know the fucking time,' Mr Watson says. 'Sorry, hen, sorry. Listen, do you think you could tell me about what happened when you found Samantha? I need to hear it. But, but only if it'll no upset you, mind.'

The police never even said that.

'I'm OK, I can tell you,' I say.

Mr Watson asks if we can chat at his house, just for a wee while and he'll bring me right back after. You're no supposed to take a lift but I feel dead sorry for Mr Watson. And I kind of want to see where Samantha lives. Lived.

Chapter 10

It's a good sign really, Janey being a bit late like this. She'll be away home with Martin, likely getting her dinner with the Gillespies. There's something very touching about Martin and her being pals, just like their mammies.

Marie and Angela. Did everything together those two, even getting married the same year, although Marie definitely got the better deal in husbands. Shame the way George turned out with the drink, but you can't blame Angela. He was a right nice lad when they met, how could she be expected to know? With Donald Devine, I was supposed to be getting a decent hard-worker, somebody that would make a good father. When I think how that turned out, fear rolls over me like a black cloud. The old fear. What am I doing letting him into my head?

I need to get busy. I'll go for the milk, then drop in on Angela. If Janey's annoyed that I'm checking up, I'll pretend I'm in to borrow the hoover.

Ali makes me leave Sid Vicious outside, even though his shop is in no way hygienic and yon loudmouth from 17B is in with her terrier.

'How's your granddaughter, hen?' 17B asks. Hen. She's at least five years younger than me.

'Janey's doing fine. Thanks for asking, hen,' I say.

'She'll never be the same. A sin for her, so it is,' 17B says, shaking her head and paying in coppers.

It takes Ali a full five minutes to count it. 'Everyone is talking about Janey Devine,' he says.

'What do you mean?'

'Everyone is talking. Every day. They ask what I know about Janey Devine. What can I get you?'

'Just a pint. Ali, what are they asking?' I don't like this, not one iota.

'They ask if she comes in the shop, what she looks like, where she lives. They ask about the murder, they ask if she saw the murderer. Did she see the murderer?'

'No, she did not. Who's asking, Ali?'

'Women. Men. Weans. I don't know who they are. The woman from the church. The man who drinks Vimto. I don't know names. Who around here tells me their name? Who asks my name, who asks "how's the family, Ali?" Another two pence, please. Milk is up again, bloody Mrs Thatcher.'

Flaming nosey devils round here, sticking their nebs into our business. I'm so angry, I nearly forget Sid Vicious. See, if I catch anybody asking about my Janey, there'll be a strange face in Heaven.

There's a group of lassies playing outside our block and I stop to let them pet the dog. Poor Sid Vicious doesn't get much affection these days. I wish Janey could understand that it's no his fault he stopped to smell the corpse, you can't blame a dog for behaving like a dog.

None of the lassies have seen Janey, no that she's been out playing these last weeks. No doing much of anything really.

I'm just putting my key in the front door when Mrs McGuire

steps out the lift, a couple of her wee yins in tow. 'Hello, how's things? How's your—'

'Aww, Maggie, see and wait a minute,' she's out of breath and the wee yins are whiney, 'I'm right sorry it took me so long to get to you. Lorna waited till she had her dinner before cracking a light about it. But soon as I knew it was your lassie, I got my coat—'

I take hold of her. 'Tell me, for God sake.' My heart is going like the clappers and I know I'm holding Mrs McGuire too tight, but if I let go, I'll fall.

'Janey went in a motor. Wi a man. Lorna says it was her uncle but he wasn't nice. Maggie, I'm sorry.'

Chapter 11

30 days

The only criminals I know are the shoplifters who sell stuff round the doors, and Jed the druggie. Nana says Jed is just to be pitied, even though it was probably him that stole our hoover. The newspapers say Mr Watson is a criminal money launderer who works for the Eggman. On the drive, I wonder if he might mention that, or the Eggman. I really want to know if his nickname has anything to do with eggs.

He doesn't talk about any of that, he's mostly just sad.

Mr Watson is not posh but his house is. It's in Bishopbriggs and it's got a nameplate on the gate, *The Sheiling*. No idea what it means but way fancier than *Flat 8B*. The big guy, Lulu, opens the car and tells me to get out. There's a slash on the back of his hand, like Uncle Finn's scars but much newer, and it gives me the willies.

The path and garden are totally huge, and it's the same inside. I'm scared to touch anything cos it's all so fancy – staircase, wallpaper, tables, lamps, even the carpet is clean. This must be a life of luxury that Nana says royal parasites have.

We go in the big living room and I wish Nana was here. She always knows what to say to new people and I feel babyish cos I don't know where to sit or what to do. There's other men here too, three in the hall and another talking to Lulu, and I'm never anywhere with men and that's making it worse.

'Sit down, sweetheart,' Mr Watson says. Lulu brings him a can of lager and a lemonade for me. The glass has sheep and daisies round it. I guess it was Samantha's. There's a big photo of her on the mantelpiece and Mr Watson hands it down to me. I look at it for a while cos it seems that's what he wants.

'I like her necklace,' I say, which is probably a rubbish thing to say.

'Oh, aye? A special present from her mum on her sixteenth. See the wee stone inside the heart? That's aquamarine, the birth-stone for March.'

'I'm March as well,' I go, and suddenly want to cry. Whenever I learn anything about Samantha that matches me, it makes her murder feel worse. On the radio, one of her neighbours said she had loved animals and I locked myself in the toilet to cry for ages.

Mr Watson tells Lulu to wait near the phone and I'm glad it's just me and Mr Watson now. He brings out a photo album and there's some older pictures with Samantha's mum but I don't know how to ask about her. Mr Watson talks about how clever Samantha was at school and how she was studying at college to be a social worker. The Smelly Kellys have got a social worker and I think he's a bit like a teacher. A nice teacher though.

Then, Mr Watson asks me about Dummy Railway Day.

'Remember, Janey hen,' he says, 'if this is hard, you don't need to tell me. I just miss my wee girl so much.'

'It's OK, Mr Watson, you're her daddy and that's different.'

It isn't different, and when I start, Samantha's bright photo smile turns into dead Samantha's open mouth and smashed tooth. But Mr Watson's no even breathing as he listens and his eyes are all red and sore, like you get if you rub them with dirty hands. So I keep talking, about the railway and the firework, about Sid running on ahead, and about Samantha. When I mention holding her hand, he cries a bit and I do too.

I don't tell him about the mess of her body, and I don't tell him about the thing I did.

When I'm finished, he walks up and down, rubbing his face and shaking his head. Then suddenly he kneels in front of me and grabs my hands.

'Anything else?' His voice is tough now and I don't know why. 'Anything else?'

'Nothing, Mr Watson,' I say and it comes out shaky. There's no way he could know about the bad thing, no way.

'Gonnae think hard? There must be something.'

I start crying again cos he's squeezing too tight.

The living room door opens and Lulu is there. 'Billy, man. Ease off.'

'Ah, Jesus, what am I doing?' Mr Watson looks at my hands and rubs them softly and he isn't scary any more. 'I just thought, I thought she might have said something to you, Janey.'

'She was deid, Billy,' Lulu goes. I nod and nod to show that's right and wipe my nose on my sleeve. 'That's your call, by the way,' Lulu says.

When Mr Watson goes to talk on the phone, Lulu asks if I want to see Samantha's bedroom. It's up two flights of stairs and it's huge with a slanting roof like *Little House on the Prairie*.

'Polis made a right mess when they searched but Ah sorted it. Everything's back exactly how it was,' Lulu says, sounding pleased with hisself.

I'm rubbish at guessing ages for grown-ups but I think Lulu is about twenty. His hair is in a quiff like Joe Strummer and blond like Samantha's.

'Are you Samantha's brother?' I ask.

'Fuck gave you that idea?'

'Just, just cos you're here.' I feel stupid and wonder if Mr Watson got angry cos I said the wrong thing to him too.

'Billy's no got any other weans. Ah work for him, we aw do and we're aw here for him.' He sits on the bed, a big proper bed with a headboard, and picks up the nightie from the pillow. I wonder how he knew where to put everything back when he tidied? Maybe he was Samantha's pal.

I love other people's bedrooms and start to feel a wee bit excited. How great if Samantha had been my friend or cousin or something, and I was visiting and she was showing me round.

There's a lot of posters, not bands like Martin's, just boring politics stuff about marches and freeing people. I want to look in the wardrobe, but feel all dizzy imagining her shoes in there.

Her missing shoes and her bare feet and the puddles that weren't rain.

I stand still for a bit before moving to her dressing table. It's messy with make-up and fancy jewellery, and sellotaped all round the mirror, there's photographs from one of those cameras where the photo comes out in seconds. On the floor there's a book, *The Passion of New Eve*, with a bookmark sticking out, and now Samantha will never ever find out what happens to New Eve. Suddenly, I feel dead sorry for her things, for the denims draped on her chair, the sparkly bangles, the green plastic hairbrush – all waiting for Samantha to come back. For the first time since Dummy Railway Day, I'm raging.

How could anybody just stop Samantha from coming back to her room, to everything ordinary?

I slump down next to Lulu. He's lying on his back, looking up at the skylight. I would really really love to have a skylight, even if all I'd see is Mr Burns in 9B stomping about in his work boots.

'Know something?' Lulu says. 'Sometimes at night, you can see Venus up there. Mercury an all.'

'How come you know that?' I say, and it sounds totally snide. But I didn't mean he's too stupid, I just wondered why he was in Samantha's room at night.

'Samantha tolt me,' he says, then makes a noise that's maybe crying. I don't want to look in case he's mortified, so I hang over the bed for a dekko underneath. That's where I keep all my good stuff. Behind a pile of magazines called *Spare Rib*, I find a jewellery box with pink and purple butterflies on it.

'Can I open this?' I ask, pulling it out to show Lulu. He sits up and shrugs, so I lift the lid. Inside are different-sized drawers and compartments and a teeny ballerina. When I was wee, I was desperate for one of these for my birthday. Nana got me a torch. When the ballerina starts to spin round, I wish this was mine. There isn't much inside, a couple of silver rings and a Kissing Cousins necklace, but in the secret drawer I find a blue envelope and open it.

'Gies that,' Lulu says and snatches it. He kicks me off the bed, which is pretty sore cos his trainers are massive. 'Stop being so fuckin nosey you.' He shoves the envelope in the pocket of his leather jacket but I already got a look. It's photos, and the top one had a woman's bare legs.

Then, Lulu throws the nightie on the floor and says we need to get moving. That's when I find a sticker. There's loads of them on the bedside cupboard and one's fallen off. Lulu doesn't even notice me pick it up.

It's time to go home, and at the front door there's three different cars on the driveway. I don't know any houses big enough for even one car to sit outside.

'This is for your granny,' Mr Watson says and gives me a bundle of money, 'tell her to buy something nice. Thanks again for talking to me, Janey, and I can't say how sorry I am for losing my temper. And for scaring you on the street. I'm no mysel right now, no mysel.' He gives me a kind of half-hug and I feel sad for him again. Then he says Skinny Jimmy will drive me home and the nickname is funny because the guy's dead plump.

When I open the front car door, Lulu runs over and whispers to me to sit in the back. Then he leans in and says, 'Mind what age this lassie is, Jimmy. She's no one of your usual pick-ups. Right?'

Skinny Jimmy swears at him, then laughs.

On the drive home, Skinny Jimmy gives me two Curly Wurlys and I eat them both even though it's nearly dinner time. Then I remember I didn't tell Nana where I was going and now she'll be angry too. It was bad enough Mr Watson shouting at me.

Before I go into our block, Skinny Jimmy rolls down his window to tell me to stick the bundle of pound notes up my juke.

'Mugged for 2p round here,' he says, which is pure cheek. The money makes a big bulge under my school jumper and I wonder if it all came from Mr Watson's criminal business.

Stupid Mrs McGuire-Peed-in-the-Fire is at our door, and Nana is up to high doh, shouting about getting the police. Wee Sticky-Hand is here too. Her name is Lorna and Lorna's lips are still green.

Nana pulls me inside then makes me promise never ever ever to do anything like that again, or she'll come to my legs. Nana doesn't smack but I know she's serious cos she says bloody.

Then she sends me to my room. I don't care that Nana's upset, I'd do it even if she was standing watching. It would be horrible to get pushed in the car again though. Still a bit freaked out about that, I thought it was the murderer grabbing me . . . But I'm glad I spoke to Mr Watson, Samantha would be pleased.

I get my scrapbook out. The sticker from Samantha's room needs glue because it's got bits of fluff on the back. It's bright yellow with a red star that says *Rock Against Racism*. I try to draw the bedroom but it looks more like a Dairylea cheese triangle. I'm rubbish at drawing. I add a picture of Bugsy, the rabbit Samantha used to have. When I asked Lulu what happened to Bugsy, he said it went in the pot. Men always think they're funny and they just aren't. It's hard to work out if Lulu was Samantha's friend or no. He did look really sad, but when I found that envelope, he was definitely angry. There's a stoater of a bruise on my leg where he kicked me.

Wonder why those photos were planked? And I'm wondering if I should have told Mr Watson the bad thing. He's no the police. If I had a dad, I might know what matters to them. Will things be better for Mr Watson if the police catch the killer, or is he heartbroken forever?

With Nana, it would make no difference if the Gas Board took the blame for the explosion. 'It'll no bring them back,' she says.

Chapter 12

'You sure this is it, son?'

'You're no in Possilpark now, missus,' the taxi driver laughs and leaves me standing in front of a nice semi-detached. I don't know what I'm expecting but certainly not festoon blinds.

Two days it's taken me to decide what to do about Billy Watson. Getting the police in was my initial reaction but Janey was no having that, and even with my dander up, I need to be careful no to add to her distress. Two nights lying awake to decide, and now, standing at the door of a serious criminal, I feel afraid.

Afraid of a dangerous man, and it's sad that feeling is so familiar.

I open my handbag and the sight of the money makes me angry enough to keep going.

'What can I do for you, missus?'

I'm taken aback when a lad opens the door. Tall and blond with hands like shovels. What do they feed youngsters these days that makes them grow? In my day, a tall man was five foot eight.

'Eh, well— I'm— I'm looking for Billy Watson.' Janey was certain but I'm starting to wonder if she misremembered the address.

'He's no here,' the lad says, closing the door. I stick my foot in.

'Tell him I want a word. It's about my granddaughter, Janey Devine. And if he doesn't—'

'What? What will you do?' Billy Watson stands in the hall. I recognize him from a clip on *Scotland Today* where he's leaving somebody's trial. 'Let her come in, Lulu,' he says.

Lulu? I have to fake a cough so the boy doesn't lamp me for laughing. And then, for God sake, all I can think about is yon time I saw the real Lulu when she opened the shopping centre. Lovely skin she had, and beautifully groomed. Teeny right enough.

Billy Watson stands in his living room. He's ages with myself, his hair gone to white but nice features and no belly on him. The papers call him The Ghost and he puts you in mind of a newsreader rather than a gangster. He's still wearing the black tie and I appreciate that.

The room is immaculate, like a page in the catalogue. On a white marble mantelpiece, there's a candle burning beside a big photograph of Samantha. That'll no help, that's for sure. A picture can't fill that space where your child should be, all it does is remind you of the photos you'll never see. Samantha in a wedding dress, with a baby on her knee, with grey in her hair.

Billy Watson says nothing, just looks straight at me, waiting. I'm shaking and I'd be kidding myself if I said it was the anger. It takes all my strength to pull out the bundle of notes and throw them in his face. They scatter over the fitted carpet.

'You can have that back, Mr Watson. Every damn penny of it.'

I'm hoping he doesn't count it because I used some for the taxi. And two nice chops for our dinner and a bit of tripe for Sid Vicious.

'If you ever, ever speak to my Janey again, let alone bring her here,' I can feel my cheeks burning and there's a bit of spittle flying, 'by Christ, you'll be sorry. I don't care who you are or . . .'

He drops into a chair that looks like real leather, a lovely cream colour. To be honest, I was ready for him to get tore into me. I'm no ready for the look on his face.

'Christ, Mrs Devine. I didn't mean any harm. I just, I just—'

'You OK in here, Billy?' The big Lulu pops his head round the door. Maybe he thinks I've a knife tucked under my headscarf. Oh God forgive me, that's no funny.

'Fuck off,' Billy Watson says.

'You mind your language,' I say, forgetting who I'm talking to for a minute. He points to the couch and I have to flick the pound notes off before sitting. There's enough at my feet to buy chops for a month.

'Will you no call me Billy? You want anything? A drink, cup of tea?'

My hands tighten on my handbag. 'You can stick your tea, and your Billy. What do you think you were playing at? Twelve years old, and you, you lifting her off the street like that.' I take a deep breath because I know from experience there's only so far you can push a man. 'Look, I am sorry for your loss. Awful sorry. But what happened to your Samantha—'

He holds up his hand and I see it's trembling. He wants to say his piece, so I keep quiet for now.

'If your Janey hadn't found my daughter, she might still be lying there,' he says. 'And what she did, holding Samantha's hand like that, talking to her.'

Talking to her? This is news to me.

'I know she was already gone but, but I can't tell you what it means to know the wean was nice to her. That's why I gave her the money. I didn't know what else to do, missus.'

He picks up Samantha's photograph. She is right bonnie-looking, even with a man haircut.

'We'd given up on a family, both of us over forty and babies lost. Samantha was our wee miracle.' Billy smiles slightly. 'I remember . . . I remember when she was a wean, me and her had a mad game. She'd squeeze her nose to make a pig snout, and I was the wolf chasing her. When I caught her, I'd throw her up in the air. She'd be squealing but I never let her fall, never. Oh, Jesus, her nose, all smashed to fuck. How did I let that happen to my wee miracle?'

He stops to get himself together and I recognize his emptiness, that big terrible nothing when you lose everything. And suddenly Marie rushes into mind. She's never far from my thoughts but these last weeks have been crowded with her.

'Ten bob? Ach, Mammy, that's too much.'

'Will you just stick it in your purse, Marie? My bonus came in. You and Vinnie go to the pictures.' She was on her way to the steamie with their washing and her lovely blonde hair was tied up tight. Apart from height, there wasn't a trace of her father in Marie's looks and I thanked God for that on a daily basis. 'Yous haven't been out in ages, go and see that new Michael Caine one. It's meant to be a rare laugh, and you know I'll take the wee ones.'

'Are you sure?' she said. Didn't like to ask for anything, my lassie, didn't want to inconvenience a living soul.

It was then she squeezed my hand. I can still feel it, the warmth of her skin. And it'll never come again.

'I know exactly what it's like to lose a daughter, but even that's no an excuse for what you did to my Janey.'

'I'm sorry, but I don't know what I'm doing any more. See all this,' Billy Watson kicks a pile of notes, 'what's the fucking point of it all? What good is it? It was all supposed to be for Samantha. When her mother—' He stops, and shakes his head. 'Ach, I don't know. But I had to speak to your Janey. Do you get that? I had to know what she saw. They're telling me nothing, no a fucking thing. But it matters, know, every single detail matters to me. I didn't mean to scare her, Mrs Devine—'

'Maggie. And it was me was scared. She said it was fine talking to you, better than the police.'

'The polis? The fucking polis?' he says, his voice sharp now. 'See at first, I thought it was a wind-up. They've done stuff in the past to get at me, and when they came to inform me, oh, fuck, I laughed. Even at the mortuary, I was still being wide. Then they pulled back that sheet, the state of her.' He covers his mouth like he's about to vomit and I feel sick even imagining it. 'Pain and fucking terror. That was the last thing my daughter experienced in this world. Do you have any idea, any fucking idea what it's like to know that?'

'I do,' I say quietly. I hadn't a minute's peace till a fireman who'd come to their funeral told me my family would've died instantly. 'I do know what that's like, but it doesn't give you the right to—'

He's not really listening, he just needs to tell it.

'You know what they did? Those fuckers read out a list of the injuries to her body. The polis've never been able to get me, never found anything to charge me with, and now they had me. They read the list as I stood there looking at my daughter's face. I've seen a man being beaten and it's no like in films. There's a point when the begging starts.' His face tightens as his fury spills out. 'See if I had the bastard that did this to Samantha, I'd tear him apart with my bare hands. Tear him into tiny fucking pieces.'

He gets up and goes to a drinks cabinet. A real drinks cabinet, no in Possilpark right enough. He hands me a half and I take it, not to be sociable but because my whole body is quivering.

'Know what they're saying? The fucking polis say it was because of me that my wee girl was slaughtered. Slaughtered. Some rival getting back at me. Do you believe that?'

The speculation about turf wars is all anybody's talking about.

For a minute, I consider telling him how interested the police were in Taxi Alex, but I might have picked that up wrong. It's no enough if somebody's going to be ripped to pieces.

'Surely not,' I say because I don't know what else to say, 'surely it can't be about all that nonsense.' I can see he thinks it might be. Guilt on top of everything. Ah, God help you, Billy Watson.

I sit with him for a while and we keep everything civil. He remembers the gas explosion so he knows I've been where he is. He shows me a photo album and talks about Samantha training as a social worker, which isn't what you'd expect given her background. No that it would make any difference if she'd been selling herself up Blythswood Square. Except to the papers, and maybe the police. Definitely the police now that I think about it. But it's obvious Billy wouldn't care, and that makes me warm to the man.

Janey feels a connection to Samantha that I wish she didn't and has been asking about the funeral. Billy says it'll be no bother for us to come, as soon as they release the body.

Another big lad comes in and nods, and it's then I'm reminded who Billy Watson really is. His whole self shifts, the way he stands, the set of face, even his voice drops. It's like a different man striding out the room, shouting names, telling them all to get into the effin kitchen.

Lulu comes to sit with me and I ask him to show me the toilet. It's a terrible thing having an old woman bladder. As I'm going up the stairs, Lulu hands me a bin bag.

'Billy says you can take all the stuff in there for Janey. All the perfumes and shite.'

I feel slightly embarrassed to have reached sixty-six without ever being in a house with three floors and enough space for a family of ten. My father would spin in his grave to know I'm intimidated by wealth, 'you're as good as any one of those rich fuckers,' he'd tell us. I give myself a shake and stop admiring the depth of the shag pile. The bathroom was Samantha's own, an en-suite the size of our living room. The lassie's bottles are everywhere – fancy creams, sprays, lotions – and I put some shampoo and soap in my handbag. I'll hand the rest in to Mrs Khan. She's got four daughters, poor soul.

Lulu pushes in when I unlock the door. He grabs the black bag and takes a bottle out, passing it from hand to hand and saying nothing. He's early twenties and good-looking, a young Burt Lancaster maybe, nice skin for his age. But there's something very hard in his eyes, a look you see in weans who aren't looked after, and his fists show the marks of a fighter.

'Can I squeeze by you, son?' I say, just to make him stop.

'She wisnae as nice as everybody is making out, you know.'

'Who's that?'

'Samantha,' he whispers.

'That's a terrible thing to say.'

'You didnae even know her.' He slips the perfume bottle into the pocket of his expensive leather jacket then spits into the bathroom. I'm left with a feeling of something not nice, something a bit dirty maybe.

Billy comes back and it's getting on when we finish blethering, and a good hour back to Possil. He convinces me to take some of the money, no all of it mind, but enough to see us through this bad patch. I wish I hadn't seen him swaggering around, playing the hardman, waiting for the trouble to start. I wish it had just been the talk about his daughter because then I wouldn't have doubts about him.

A friendly wee toerag with an earring is driving me home and Billy comes out to the car. He shakes my hand and says we'll get a chance to speak soon. But I never want to be near this man again in my life. Grief and guilt and horror pour out of him and I've got enough of that of my own.

Chapter 13

35 days

The van comes up and Nana goes to the window.

'Janey, will you nip down for cigarettes?'

'Can you go? I— I've got a sore tummy.' Being out on my own is even worse since Lulu shoved me in that car.

'Ach, you're havering. You're just saying that cos it's mince night. Here,' she opens her purse, 'ten Regal and a couple of cones. Make it three, Sid Vicious loves a pokey-hat.'

A pound note. It's nearly pension day and she's usually scrabbling about with half-pences. I bet it's from Mr Watson. She was raging when I gave her it, 'What does he think I am, sending me his filthy money,' and was going to tell him where to stick it but looks like she kept some. Maybe all of it. I think it was nice of him, nobody ever gives us money.

'Take the dog, hen. And you don't need to walk him, just let him do his business.'

The lifts are broken and Sid drags me down the stairs, all happy at being out. How come Sid's allowed to just be normal and happy? If he hadn't stopped at Samantha's body, I'd never have seen it. I'm no getting him a cone, I'll tell Nana he ate it.

Gibby is hammering at an old motor, he's always messing with broken stuff. Nana thought Gibby was a bad devil till he fixed her iron and wouldn't take any money.

Right after Dummy Railway Day, people came to see if they could help. Mrs Khan brought dinners and biscuits and juice, and Gibby brought two stale rolls. But he did ask if Nana needed anything done and he started taking Sid out for walks.

He sees me and takes off his manky work gloves.

'How you doing, wee yin?' He claps Sid, who jumps up to lick his face. That would knock most people over but Gibby is solid and muscly. 'Ah heard yous had to see the polis again. Bastards. They still going on about the dead lassie? Making you talk about it?'

'A bit,' I say.

'You don't need to think about any of that shite, OK? And see if they polis keep hassling yous, give us a shout. Bastards. Ah'm heading up Ruchill, want me to take the dog?' I hand over the lead. ''Mon then, Sid, ma man. Find some rabbits,' he says, tucking the hammer into his belt.

I don't know where they'll get rabbits in Ruchill but I'm glad to see Sid go.

At the van, Stevie Baw-Jaws is paying with ginger bottles.

'... and three chocolate tools and a two red laces,' he goes. 'Hey, Janey, you coming out?'

'Nope,' I say.

'Gonnae come out? Gonnae bring your ball? You can have some chewing gum.' Stevie holds out his Wrigley's and the smell ... the smell of Juicy Fruit.

I'm no at the van any more, I'm sitting in the taxi with Taxi Alex and he's chewing and chewing as he wails, 'That woman, what a mess, what a mess. What will her poor maw think?' His crying is funny and high-pitched like a baby doll.

Takes me ages to order the cones, the guy is getting annoyed and wee Stevie asks if I've got a stutter now. Another bit of Dummy Railway Day crashing in. But it means the stuff I told

Detective Alistair Baxter about Taxi Alex was wrong. I said he just looked over the bridge but he must've seen Samantha too. When? I can't get it right in my head, can't make these memories connect up.

Chapter 14

There's somebody hammering at the door but the daft dog's just lying in the hall chewing something that might be a table leg. God knows where he got that.

'Bark like Johnny Normal,' I tell him, but that's no it. 'Woof like Bad Boy Billy.' Not a peep. 'Janey, what is it you say to make Sid Vicious bark?' She's been in her room since Mass.

'Sing like Johnny Rotten,' she shouts and the dog brings the place down. 'Is that Aunty Angela? Is she coming today?'

I open the door a wee crack, holding Sid Vicious's collar and letting him keek out. Angela would never thump the door like that. And after Billy Watson lifting Janey, I need to be wary.

It's Big Des Grey's wife.

'Can you take that thing away?' she says. 'Ah need a word.'

I shut the dog in the kitchen but don't ask her in. 'Tell your man I'm paying as much as I can.'

'No, no, it's no that. In fact, here. You've, ehm, you're all square.' She opens a shiny clutch bag and pulls out my Family Allowance book and I wonder how much of it went on that peroxide beehive of hers. Mutton dressed as lamb, right enough. Big Des said it would be near Christmas when I was paid up, but I grab the book sharpish. She fake smiles and turns to go, then stops. It's likely no her fault that Des is a dirty thieving loan shark but I can't stop myself from drawing back when she leans in close.

'Listen, Mrs Devine,' she says, with fry-up breath, 'you're a nice wummin so Ah'm gonnae tell you something. You've made friends wi the wrong people. Des is no angel but these guys, these guys are the real deal.'

'Wrong people? Who you talking about? And what gives you the right to say anything to me about anybody—'

Just then, Angela Gillespie and wee Kirsty step out the lift. 'OK, thanks, pet. See you soon,' I say quickly.

'Aunty Maggie, have you got any biscuits?'

'Kirsty, that's rude.'

'She's no rude, Angela. She's my wee blessed lamb. Come and I'll give you a big swing then we'll get a biscuit.' The wean squeals as we spin, but we knock Our Lady of Lourdes over and I make myself dizzy.

Angela takes my arm and sits me down. With her square build and big feet, Angela always looked horsey beside my Marie and now she's putting on the beef. Same with the wean, four years old and heavier than Janey. And the get-up she's wearing, like a walking pompom. What's her mother thinking?

Oh, God, when did I become such a crabbit old midden? Angela Gillespie's nearly forty with three weans, she's every right to be hefty, and she's a grand girl. Ten years on and she still visits, still watches Janey and she's one of the last that still talks about Marie. Didn't even hold it against me when I mentioned her George's drinking. Aye, Angela's a grand girl and I'm awful fond of her. Awful fond.

She hands Janey a comic. 'Martin sent *Smash Hits*, it's got The Skids in it.'

'Och, the names for the groups these days,' I say, 'that's something you'd see the doctor about.' Angela laughs and I can see the pair of them – her and Marie giggling, best pals, heading up the dancing. 'Can I get you a cup of tea?'

'I'm no stopping. Going to see my wee daddy, change his curtains.'

'How is your dad?' Kirsty's biting Sid Vicious's tail and Janey's no even bothering.

'He's no bad, pain comes and goes,' Angela says.

'Let me know if yous want me to come and sit with him, your mammy's got a lot on her plate with that leg of his.'

'Thanks, Maggie. He's got a student nurse coming in now to dress the wound – Kirsty, leave that dog alone, he'll bite you in a minute. Fiona something the nurse is called, posh but awful nice. And guess what? She was at school with Samantha Watson. I'll need to tell you what she said about the ex-boyfriend—'

'Take Kirsty to play in your room, hen,' I say because Janey's stopped reading her magazine to listen.

'Can we get Spirograph, Janey? Can we get bouncy balls? Can we? Can we jump on your bed, can—'

Whenever I see Kirsty I wonder if Marie might have, a grandson, maybe. When you lose a child, it's no just them you mourn, it's the ones that might've been. Something else that will hit Billy Watson one of these days.

'Is Janey still no sleeping right?' Angela asks when they're away. 'Ach, I'm no surprised. Member me and Mum saw that man getting run over on Argyle Street? Four year ago that was, and we're both of us still upset.' She takes her jacket off and settles herself. 'When Martin's going to the pictures, I'll see if Janey'll come with him, keep her mind off it.'

Coffee runs right through me but I keep a jar for visitors and

Angela has a cup to tell her Samantha story. Four sugars, but I say nothing.

'It seems the nurse was Samantha's pal at school,' Angela says, 'one of these snobby places where they stay on for Highers and the rest of it. Samantha was fifteen and right flattered when this lovely big seventeen-year-old showed interest in her. Daft about him, the nurse says, and it got right serious quick. These are gorgeous fig rolls, Maggie, are they Galbraith's?'

'Just the Co-op, hen. So what did Billy say about her having a boyfriend? Where was he in this?'

'That's the thing. This guy was Mr Perfect with the dad, and he went on to the university so that was in his favour too. But with Samantha, well, different story. Poor lassie couldn't do a thing without his say-so, always checking up on who she spoke to, what she wore, where she went.'

'Did he hit her?' A terrible chill runs through me, memories pushing in that have no business here.

'Nurse never said, so who knows?' Angela lowers her voice. 'But apparently he wanted Samantha all to hissel. That's the age you need pals as well, all hanging about together. Member the great wee crowd me and Marie had at school? Christ, sometimes I wish I was back then, I really do.'

I notice now how tired Angela looks. 'What's this article's name? Has anybody told the police about him?' I ask.

'Actually, you'll likely know him—'

'Mum. Mum, look what we made.' Kirsty runs in, shoves a wobbly stack of bricks under Angela's nose and knocks the fig rolls onto the carpet. Sid Vicious moves in like a cheetah. 'Aunty Maggie, look. I made a Lego robot and Janey made a Lego robot.'

'Oh, they're brilliant, so they are.'

'Be careful, Kirsty. Aye, Maggie, you'll know the boyfriend to see—'

'Mum, who made the bestest robot? Is it mine? Is mine the bestest?'

'It's great, sweetheart. And yours is great too, Janey. Anyway, the ex works in Possil library. You'll have seen him, hippy-looking sort, John Lennon specs. Wish I could remember his name, cos by Christ, it's right daft.'

Chapter 15

51 days

'Ninian? Ninian Hogg?'

It was near Christmas and Asha and me were watching the librarian hanging tinsel in the Reading Room.

'Is that really his name?'

'Not so loud, Janey,' Asha said and slapped at my arm.

'Ninian,' I said, 'what's that about? Did his ma and da hate him?'

'I heard they got it off the gravestone where they—'

'Did the dirty?'

'Stop it, we'll get slung out.' Asha pulled her jumper over her face to muffle the laugh. She pretended to be angry but really she thought I was dead funny. We watched Ninian move his ladder, being careful no to wake a man sleeping under the big table.

'His pals call him Nino. I get to call him Nino,' Asha said, all smiley, 'he's really nice.'

'Oh, man, you fancy him. Asha and Ninian, up a tree, K. I. S. S.—' I sang and this time she gave me a proper smack.

'Shut up, I don't fancy him. And just shut up anyway cos I don't want chucked out.'

'I'm going to tell,' I said, walking towards him. I wasn't going to, I was just winding her up. It was good hanging out with Asha especially when Nana worked late and the flat was freezing, and empty.

After hearing Aunty Angela talking about Samantha's old boyfriend, I go straight to the library and Asha's sitting at her usual table.

She's in the library nearly every day. Sometimes she does homework and sometimes just reads, but mostly she wants peace from her sisters. Everybody does that, moans about their brothers and sisters. I wish I still had Donna so I could moan too. The Khans live in my block and Asha's already in secondary school. Nana says it's rude to talk about people's religion or colour so I don't really know what a Muslim is, but it seems a shame she has to go to Proddy school.

'Want to do a *Mates* quiz to see which pop star is your secret twin?' she asks. 'I got Debbie Harry.'

I shake my head, I'm waiting for Ninian Hogg to finish sorting toddler books. There's a new Tintin book open on the table in front of me but I've no looked at it.

'Janey,' Asha says in a toaty voice, 'Janey, I'm sorry I didn't come down to see you after, after the thing. My mum told me to but I didn't know what to say.' She reaches over and touches the sleeve of my school shirt with one finger. 'Wish it wasn't you, wish it happened to somebody else.'

She's got tears and maybe I'm going to cry too so I pull my arm away and slam Tintin shut. It makes Ninian look and he comes over.

'Loud,' he says, but he's no annoyed. He wears round glasses, has a nice cheesy smile and long brown hair and he might look OK if he had better trousers. How could Samantha go out with somebody who wears purple cords?

'What's on your homework schedule today?' he asks. Asha doesn't answer, she's a bit shy sometimes. Ninian lifts her pigtail and twirls it like a skipping rope and she giggles.

'Did you used to go out with Samantha Watson?' I ask. For a wee minute he does look annoyed but then he bows his head.

'Samantha is, I mean was, the love of my life. My heart's broken. Truly broken.' He talks in a low voice and it's weird hearing a man saying stuff about love. Then he goes, 'Oh God, your knee's bleeding.'

I've been picking my scab without paying attention.

'We'd better get a plaster on that.'

Ninian takes my hand and I follow him into the library store room. I've never been in here and it's darker than I expected and kind of stuffy. He gives me a paper towel then looks for the first-aid box.

'So, why're you asking about Samantha? Who told you I was her boyfriend?'

'It was me that, that found her. Down the Dummy Railway.'

Ninian closes the cupboard he's been searching and turns really slowly.

'You're the dog walker? Fuck,' he says and it sounds wrong, like if you hear a teacher swear, 'that must've been, traumatic.' There's a wee ladder and he sits on a step so we are the same height. He looks at me so closely that I blush.

'You got a bin?' I hold up the paper towel to stop him staring, but the sight of the blood makes me feel boaky and I drop it.

'Give it here. Sorry, I'm sorry, honey. It's just, just, how are you even getting out of bed with memories like that?'

'I don't really remember much,' I say and hope he doesn't start asking.

'What, like amnesia?'

'I don't know what it's called, but, but after seeing, seeing, Samantha, the next thing I remember is a man finding me.'

'A man found you?' Ninian's voice is low and soft.

'A taxi driver, on Balmore Road.'

'Yeah, right, OK.' He nods. 'I've heard about people suppressing memories, the brain's defence mechanism or something. But, hell, poor you. Even imagining what happened to Samantha has wrecked me. What kind of warped animal could do that to a beautiful girl?'

Ninian stares at me again. The glasses make his eyes bigger but not frog-eyes like Speccy Kathleen. It feels like he's waiting, then he stands and puts his arms round me. Apart from once when Martin's dad was steaming, this is the only time a man has ever hugged me. It gives me a funny shiver. Ninian feels solid and, and, I don't know, mannish? Is that a word? And he smells dead clean.

'I can see why Samantha's on your mind. Sit down there and go ahead, ask me anything.'

He tells me they were boyfriend and girlfriend at Secondary. They loved going to the pictures, to restaurants and on long walks together. He got on dead well with Mr Watson and went on their family holiday to Yugoslavia. Once, at the Shows, Samantha was sick on the Waltzers, so he spent all his money at Hook-A-Duck just to win her a giant gonk. They were always together and he always took care of her. Nino, I can definitely call him Nino, had even started planning their wedding.

When I ask why she chucked him, he looks annoyed again.

'When Samantha started a degree at Glasgow Tech, she got into politics, marching up and down shouting about justice and women's rights. Women's rights, for Christ's sake. Her new friends didn't like me and sadly turned her against me. But I always knew we'd get back together. Hey look, I found the Elastoplast.' He kneels and lifts my leg onto his. 'What happened to your knee? Did you fall?'

'It was Dummy Railway Day. I mean, it was the day I found Samantha. It happened at the railway.'

'Well, that's a coincidence. I hurt my leg that day too.' He rolls his trouser leg up to show a big white bandage. They are very bad trousers. 'It's a burn,' he says, 'my uncle spilled tea. He's not very well and I look after him.'

'Where's your mam and dad?' I ask.

'They work in Saudi Arabia. I see them sometimes but I'm happy here with my uncle. Poor Uncle Callum, the police upset him badly when they wouldn't let me sit in the interview room with him.'

'I hate talking to them,' I say, thinking about that big policeman shouting in my face. I bite my lip to stop crying in front of Nino.

'It's OK,' he says, 'they bully everyone. And I know what it's like to be bullied. Look, I need to get back to work but come and chat again. Maybe it'll do you some good to hear nice things about Samantha. And I'll have a wee think about how to stop the police bothering you.'

Before I leave, Nino gives me an old library leaflet with a picture of him getting an award, 'Glasgow Storyteller of the Year'. You can see younger Samantha in the crowd, all proud. The leaflet will be good in the scrapbook with all the things he told me. I might try drawing the giant gonk, I really love those gonks. Maybe Samantha's new student pals didn't like Nino but I do. He didn't treat me like a wee kid and you can see how much he misses Samantha.

Chapter 16

It's one of those days where you don't know what to wear. The sun's out but the wind's biting and this daft jacket is just not warm enough. It was Janey persuaded me I'm no too old for an anorak, I never feel right in it though.

The meeting is in a café on Maryhill Road near the Barracks. Stuart the barman made the arrangements. The memories of raising my daughter in this area are among my best, from her first day at school to her wedding at St Columba's. But now I would rather walk through the Gates of Hell than through Maryhill.

At least I don't need to pass the spot where my family were blown to pieces.

There's a lot of changes round here, the sandstone of the tenements has been cleaned and some of the closes have these new security doors. But Terry's Snacks is exactly the same. When I walk in, the warm blast of lard and vinegar takes me right back. It's the same wood panelling and Italian crooners on the walls, the same stained lino on the floor. A big-bosomed, narky waitress points at the last empty booth. It seems my shape's changed a bit though because I have to squeeze in. I wonder if it's the same family running the place, the cook certainly has the Italian good looks. He puts me in mind of Vinnie.

The Rizzo men were all very handsome. And being tailors

they were always immaculately turned out, apart from Vinnie, who was dishevelled even on his wedding day. A right artistic boy he was, thoughtful and kind, and he could fairly make Marie laugh, which I loved about him. Sometimes he suffered what Marie called 'his doldrums' but she was exactly what he needed to get through it. Vinnie was a painter and decorator by trade and his father had plans to set him up with his own business. The Rizzos were a big supportive family. I was happy that Marie became part of their closeness.

None of Terry's customers seem to mind when I take a good look round, probably assume I'm just a nosey old besom. Must be nearly two months since I last met Taxi Alex. He was going into the police station as we came out and he stopped to speak to Janey. It was just a minute or two but I'm sure I'll recognize him. Funny-looking wee man.

Stuart was desperate that I meet with him.

'Please, Maggie, do it as a favour to masself,' he said, passing me the note. He'd waited till Tottie-Heid was in the office, none of us want him knowing our business.

'I'm no sure, son. I'm no sure I should be repeating anything that was said.'

'I know, I know, but he's up the wall. Look, I'm no supposed to tell anybody this, but he's my AA sponsor,' Stuart was whispering and I struggled to hear, 'and he's a gem of a man. Never lets me down, day or night he's there. C'mon, Maggie, he's no wanting much, just to see if the polis were saying anything about him.'

The fern cake's no as nice as it used to be. Nothing's ever the same as when you were happy.

It would've been the fifties when Marie and I would come to Terry's Snacks. Always a fern cake and a banana boat on my day off, always raspberry sauce right down her front. We were still living with my mother in those days so I was able to work full-time. After Donald Devine, everything was a struggle and it was Mam set me back on my feet. Marie and my mam. Oh, they loved each other, those two. The day the jukebox arrived in Terry's, the three of us were bursting to see it, and Marie adamant that Granny was to get first choice. It must've been winter, because Marie had on thon red knitted cardigan. My eyesight was still good enough for Arran patterns and it was a lovely thing.

Here I am picturing exactly what my daughter was wearing twenty-odd years ago but I have no idea what my granddaughter had on yesterday. Likely one of those punk rocker t-shirts she borrows from Martin. They're no very pleasant some of them.

Taxi Alex has arrived, said hello, sat in the booth, been to the counter, and the toilet, and now he's showing me the menu, talking ninety to the dozen. One of these busy characters that can't stay still.

'Mrs Devine, I'm late. Sorry, sorry. Let me get you something to make up for it. Will you take another tea? Ham and eggs? How about a bridie?'

There's a hint of somewhere else in his accent, East Coast, Highland, I'm never sure. With some men, you see the boy they were, and Alex's young self is written all over him. The ginger hair, the freckles, the solid wee frame. He looks forty going on eight. He's smartly dressed for a taxi driver, shirt and tie under a light V-neck jumper, and he doesn't look like a drinker. You can see it on Stuart, the sweats, the shakes, the desperation.

I order eggs. He's having his lunch and it's no nice letting somebody eat on their own.

'That last fare changed his flaming mind halfway to Denniston.

I didn't mean to keep you waiting, it was fair good of you to agree to this.'

It wasn't goodness, the only reason I'm here is to see if he can shed light on the thing with Janey, to see if he knows what it is making her so worried.

Nearly an hour later and I've been treated to Alex's entire life story. Or, 'two life stories' to be accurate. A bad lot when he was a young man, a heavy drinker who hit rock bottom. His second life started at the age of thirty when an uncle dragged him to AA. Now, he couldn't be happier with his taxi, and his gorgeous wife and boys. He showed me the sons' photo – two wee ginger nuts in football strips, two wee Jimmy Johnstones.

'. . . and away they went, leaving bloody great holes every-where.' I have no idea how he got onto it, but Alex has started describing every detail of a dodgy builder scam on last night's *That's Life*. 'Esther promised action but what's the poor old guy supposed to do if it rains, that's what I want to know? How do these scunners get away wi it, Maggie?'

The man could talk the hind legs off a donkey.

'Look, I don't mean to be rude but I need to move soon to be back for Janey,' I say, looking at my watch. She comes home to an empty house on Tuesdays and that's more than enough.

'God sake, I didn't realize the time,' he says, calling for the bill. 'Let me run you home, my taxi's outside.'

The taxi slows to a crawl near Firhill as a big procession walks behind a hearse outside the stadium. Must've been a Partick Thistle fan. When Alex pulls the taxi into the side, I'm think-ing it's out of respect but he comes right out the cab to sit in the back next to me. Then the real talking starts.

'Did the police mention me at all?' he says. 'I didn't want to ask in Terry's, I know my voice attracts attention and I've this terrible feeling the police are watching.'

'Watching? You're havering, Alex.'

'I've got a record, ken. It's from years ago but they knew about it.'

'What did you do?'

'Bag snatching. From old women. I know, I know, you're right to be disgusted but it was the drink. I swear on my maw's grave I wasn't a bad boy, just desperate. The police caught me the one time and when the old wifey couldn't testify, it was dropped. It didn't stop me getting my taxi licence, but it must be on file somewhere. That bald policeman mentioned it and, like a stupid clipe, I started owning up to more. Once I start blabbing, I can't stop.'

'That's no enough to connect you to a murder, son. You're being daft.'

'You think so? Honest?'

I tell Alex exactly what was said at the station. He bites his nails as he listens, and whether it calms him or not, I don't know. But he nods and pats my knee and goes back into the driving seat.

'Listen, Alex, did anything happen with Janey while you were with her?' I say.

'In what way?'

'Just anything that might have upset her, made her worry. Feel guilty maybe.'

'You don't think seeing a dead body was enough to upset the bairn? It fairly upset me.'

'Aye, well, obviously, but did anything else happen to her? Or anything she maybe did?'

'You should be asking her that. My laddies, they would tell me anything. Anything, because I'm a good dad. But let me think.'

He's quiet for all of three seconds. 'The police were angry that she touched the corpse. You ken that, aye? Really she shouldn't have done that, everybody knows that from TV. Do yous not watch *The Sweeney*? Or *The Rockford Files*? That's a cracker of a show, there's an episode in that where—'

'Just drop me here, this is fine,' I say. He's getting right on my nerves now. After me doing my best and telling him everything.

'Thanks again for coming, Maggie. And you're right about the gang thing, these crime families are notorious. I'm sure we'll all sleep better when this is over. It's just this business with my shoes that I don't understand.'

'Your shoes?'

'Did I not say? The police came to our house and took my shoes. The ones I was wearing that Saturday. Forensics, they said.' Alex waves then, and drives off.

Forensics.

Holy Mother of Christ, did I just have scrambled egg with the killer?

Chapter 17

73 days

School's finished for the summer holidays and Lorraine and me are walking home from the chippie. Being out is getting a wee bit easier.

Lorraine's telling me what happened at the final Primary 7 disco. '. . . and that Andrea, thinks she's something just cos she wears a bra now, flashing it in the bogs . . . Can you believe Jackie getting off with Jamesie Doherty? . . . and then Martin did his pogo and crashed into Miss Cox and sent her flying. You could see her knickers . . .'

Sometimes I listen.

We meet Gibby, pushing a pram full of lead. He strips it off the roofs in Carbeth Street, and that's why the rain comes in and why Jean's clothes always smell damp.

'Mind tell your granny Ah'll pick the dug up the night, back of seven,' Gibby says.

Lorraine makes a face when he's passed. 'I hate the Gibsons, my whole family hate the Gibsons. One of them was in jail.'

'Which one?'

'Gibby. But maybe no that Gibby. You shouldn't let them watch Sid.'

'Maybe,' I say, but I don't care who's got Sid.

'You going to the murdered woman's funeral, then?' Lorraine asks, and now I'm interested.

'Uh-huh, me and my nana got invited. You need to wear black, and cos she's a Proddy, there won't be any Mass.'

'That's rotten for that poor woman.'

'Have you got any black clothes I can get a loan of?'

'Yuks, no. What's wrong with that t-shirt you've got on?' Lorraine says. She can be a bit of a tube sometimes.

'It says The Stranglers on it. Have you been to any funerals? It's supposed—'

'Know what?' she goes. 'I bet Jackie just got off with that Jamesie cos she's jealous. When can we go to your uncle's again?'

At half-term, before Samantha, Lorraine was allowed to come to my Uncle Finn's and that's when we got the boyfriends.

Uncle Finn is Nana's brother. He works at gutting fish and even though he's nearly Nana's age, they still let him. Visiting is a bit like a holiday and it takes us ages to get to Fraserburgh. Sid Vicious always pukes on the bus but is pure happy the rest of the time. He should probably live near a beach so he can run mad every day.

This was the first time I had a pal with me and Lorraine was a bit freaked out by Uncle Finn's ear. It looks like a wee red bum. When she got used to it, she thought it was cool he got it in the war. The war is probably why Uncle Finn didn't get married and why he lives in an ancient old cottage with weasels in the cellar. And a real fire. He and Nana sit at the fire with whisky and talk about the olden days. It's hard to tell if remembering makes them sad or happy because they cry and laugh. And sometimes Nana sings.

If you look deep into the fire, you can see the future, but it only works for the person who brings in the coal. Uncle Finn said that when I grow up, I will do something very special. Don't know what because I got fed up going out to the coal bunker.

Usually on visits, I look after the weasels – they eat mice and chopped pork, and definitely not Wagon Wheels. Uncle Finn lets me use knives and hatchets, and probably run with scissors if I wanted, and I built a cracking den behind the cottage. And since I got Sid, I'm allowed to walk him to the sand dunes by myself.

But Lorraine didn't want to do any of that. She wanted to hang about at the swings. It's the only park in the town and pretty rubbish with no rocky-boat or chute. That's where we met the boys.

There was a bunch of them and they were laughing at our accents. We were laughing at theirs too, and the weird words like 'ken' and 'quine'. Even weirder, they didn't know if they were Catholic or Protestant. Lorraine guessed Proddys because Catholics always know. They were nice anyway. Andy's only eleven, but I chose him because of his spiky hair and badges. Lorraine fancied the one with the good bike, then decided his chin was too square and changed to Fergie, who's nearly got a moustache. I got kind of bored with them, apart from when we played Truth, Dare, Double Dare. Andy and me had to kiss for Double Dare. I told him it was winching, he said it was smoorching and I liked his word better. It was my first smoorch and our teeth clonked. Before we left, we all said we would write letters but nobody did. Andy gave me his Ramones badge though.

'I'm dying to see how Fergie's moustache is doing but. Gonnae ask your nana to take us soon?' Lorraine says. I tell her I will, but I won't.

An angry mum comes out on her veranda and shouts down at Lorraine, 'If you scare my bairns one more time, you'll feel the back of my hand.'

Lorraine waves and does a thumbs up, then says to me, 'Mental old bampot and her stupid wee lassies.'

'What'd you say to them?'

'I just telt them about the maniac. Telt them no to hang about by their self or they'll get sliced up like Samantha Watson.'

'Shut up about her,' I say.

'It's true but. The maniac's no caught and everybody knows he's in Possil. Check this.' Lorraine has her wee purse from Dublin hanging round her neck, and inside there's a holy medal. 'Specially blessed by some big-deal bishop. It's for protection.'

'Shut up,' I say again. My heart's speeding, and in the distance I think somebody is shouting my name. It sounds weird, like listening to a seashell, and the panic starts building in me again. Lorraine just keeps talking.

'You should get something holy an all, Janey,' she says. 'A guy in The Brothers bought my brother and his pal a pint, and asked about the dead body and who found it.'

'What guy?' Fear is making me too loud. 'What'd he look like? Did your brother tell him about me? Why—'

'Gonnae calm down,' Lorraine says. 'I only heard him and his pal talking about it. And I'm no gonnae ask him about it either cos I'm never talking to him again. Know he wore my simon to his stupid football? My good white simon, all stretched.'

Lorraine goes on about her brother till I definitely hear my name. There's somebody behind us, somebody walking far too fast and breathing too heavy. I need to run, I need to—

'Wait, hold on, girls.' At first, I don't recognize her because of the clothes, it's like the Pink Panther puffing along the street.

'Goodness you two, I've been trying to catch up since the Cross.' She holds out her hand to Lorraine. 'Hello, I'm Constable Val Wilde, one of the police officers looking after Jane.'

Looking after me?

'Nice trouser suit,' Lorraine says, 'lovely and bright.' I can see she's dying to laugh.

'Thanks, and you are super cool in your wedges. Now, I need a few words with your friend. I'm sure she'll see you later.'

Lorraine looks at me to check it's OK. I nod and give her what's left of my fritters. Behind Val's back, she mouths, 'Fanny,' and now I'm dying to laugh.

Val follows me right into the flats. Her and Baldy went to Nana's work last week to get us to come for another interview. Nana told them it was too upsetting and that the Legal Aid man advised we are not obliged to attend. Nana laughed and laughed telling me that because there is no Legal Aid man.

'Nice to see you out having fun, you must have loads of plans for the summer,' Val says. 'Is Gran home?'

'She's on overtime,' I say, 'helping the barmaid.' Don't know why I'm explaining anything to Val.

'Oh, right. Never mind. It's you I want to talk to anyway, Jane, it's you who can help.'

Chapter 18

Hollywood Dancer is trying to sell me a camera. Oh, I wish to God I didn't have to work the bar, but Tuesday is Cathy's day at physiotherapy with her lassie and Tottie-Heid won't let her go unless one of us covers. What's the name of Cathy's wee mite again? Is it Cherry? Berry? These fancy modern names are right confusing.

'What do you say then, Maggie?' Hollywood Dancer holds the camera like it's a holy offering. 'Russian. Best make there is.'

'It's no really for me,' I tell him. 'I've never owned a camera and this thing looks like it might've been used to spy on the moon landing.

'Tell you what,' he says, desperation making his voice boom, 'see us a few pints and you can have a shot of it. Keep it till Saturday, let your wean have a go. It's got the film in it, aw ready. Just the three pints, or even—'

'I'd get my jotters for that. But see him over there? Head to toe in denim? Been at a loose end since he had to get rid of his snakes. A camera might be right up his street.' Hollywood rushes over and launches straight into his sales pitch again.

Tottie-Heid is watching. Just as well I didn't give away any drink.

''Mere a minute,' he says, and points to the spot where he wants me to stand. 'When did you get made boss in here?'

'Eh, is this one of your funny jokes?'

'Don't get wide. Some cunt in the snug just tolt me – tolt me – to come and get you.'

'I don't know who that might be,' I say.

'Him. That big cheeky bastard.'

'Oh, that's Lulu. One of Billy Watson's boys. He's likely come with funeral details. I'm awful sorry, I'll—'

'Billy Watson, is it?' Tottie-Heid's whole manner changes. 'Well, in that case there's no problem. No problem at all, away you and talk and Ah'll cover the bar. You make sure and pass on my condolences. To Billy hisself, mind.'

Lulu doesn't look too pleased about being a message boy.

'Billy's waiting outside in the car,' he says, face like a well-skelped arse. I take my overall off and while I'm tidying my hair, he says, 'Gonnae tell him yous cannae come to the funeral?'

'Why is that?'

'Janey,' Lulu says. 'She's, she's no good for Billy.'

'What's that supposed to mean? And while I think about it, I've got a few things to say about the way you shoved her into Billy's car and scared the bejeezus out of the McGuire wean. Does that make you feel like a big man, eh? Do . . .' I stop talking because Tottie-Heid has positioned hisself to hear every word. It's a lovely feeling walking past him though, knowing he'll no say a thing about me skiving.

'The stuff Janey was tellin him,' Lulu says as we go out the door, 'it's making everything worse. Tell her to shut up about Samantha and forget what happened.'

Lulu has got no right to say anything about my granddaughter, but truthfully I wish she would stop. I wish she would just forget.

Billy's holding the car door open for me. 'Maggie, good of you to come, we went round to yours and Janey says you work the—'

'She's no supposed to open the door when I'm no in.'

'She didn't let us in, she told us over the buzzers, don't get angry with the wean,' Billy says. He sits in the back beside me and it must be grand to be chauffeured around like this. It's six weeks since we met, and by Christ, Billy's no looking any better. There's a nasty rash on his face and a wildness in his eyes that's a sure sign he's no sleeping. My heart goes out to him, it really does.

'How are you, Billy? You coping?' I ask.

'Coping? That's a question.' He seems to be considering this very seriously. 'Aye, I suppose I am coping. You know yourself how dark the hole is.'

'I know you'll hear this over and over but try to get through one day at a time. That's all I can offer you.'

I could offer him what I've learned about Taxi Alex and police forensics, about his dodgy past and that nervous anxiety he's got. But this is murder, Janey's already too involved and I need to be careful no to drag us in any further.

'It's no any easier with the polis on my back,' he says, 'these interviews, interrogations, are wearing me down. Getting so bad that sometimes I'm thinking maybe I did have something to do with the murder.' He's rubbing at the rash now, making it rawer, like Janey with that scab on her knee. 'I've had to get my lawyer in, and I fucking hate my lawyer.'

'You'd think the police would have better things to do with their time,' I say but can't help wondering if they have their reasons.

'Thanks for that. No everybody accepts my innocence as quick. They've pulled in every cunt I've ever had dealings with, but they're still getting nowhere.'

Then something strikes me. 'What about Samantha's boy-friend?'

Billy sits up straight, his voice sharp. 'You heard something? Something about Ninian Hogg?'

'Is that his name? Oh for Heaven sake, that's a wee shame. No, I've not heard a thing, honestly, just that she had a lad.'

'Aye, she did. And I liked Nino,' he slumps again, 'a nice boy with safe plans for his future. Got a lot of good memories of those times. Helen, the wife, wasn't sure about him but you know mammies and daughters.'

It certainly took me a while to come round to Vinnie, I admit that, till I saw how he made Marie laugh.

'Nino was a decent lad,' Billy says, 'stood by us when Helen went into hospital, driving Samantha to the ward every day. To be honest, I was sorry Samantha gave him his marching papers cos that's the point she went a bit mad with the nights out and the drink and, ach, you know, usual stuff. A quieter life with Nino, that I liked better for her.'

'Aye, but you can't interfere, they need to live—'

'That wee cunt keeking out the door, is that your boss?'

'It is. I'll need to get back in, sorry.'

'No problem. Listen, they finally released Samantha and I wanted to bring the funeral details since you've no got a phone.' He gives me a card, which he could have told anybody to shove through our door.

As I'm getting out the car, he says, 'See if you ever want to work somewhere other than that dive, give us a shout, Maggie.'

'Thanks, Billy. And once the funeral's out the way, you'll notice a difference.'

Hollywood Dancer has had no luck with his sale and is seconds away from getting slung out. I nip into the back and take a pound note from my purse.

'Here you go, Hollywood,' I say, 'I'll take the camera till the end of the summer, then you can get it back. Is that a deal?' You'd think I was giving him the crown jewels.

'You're a darling lady,' he says and kisses my hand. God sake. After sinking a pint, he treats the pub to a demonstration of the Paso Doble. He's very nimble and gets a nice round of applause. But Tottie-Heid comes out his office and shouts at me to 'tell that auld poof to stop prancing about'.

I wish to God I could walk out this place. And I wish to God I wasn't going to the funeral of another young woman.

Chapter 19

73 days

Val's got nice hair. I didn't notice it before because it was in a daft granny bun, but it goes straight down her back and it's fair. I've never seen a colour photo of my mammy but Aunty Angela says she had shiny blonde hair.

Val's not sitting down, just walking around, doing her nosey.

'Does your gran often work late?' she asks, picking up the castanets some neighbour brought us from Tenerife. For a laugh, Nana clacks them and we hoof around together shouting 'Olé'. We used to anyway.

'Just on Tuesdays when she helps behind the bar. She's always back before dinner,' I tell her and that's nearly true. 'Do you want a cup of tea? Or a cup of coffee?' I'm only asking to make her stop snooping.

'If you're allowed to use the kettle, coffee would be great. Will you make sure your dog doesn't get out the kitchen? Pet fur makes me sneeze, unfortunately.'

Then she starts asking stupid questions about Nana's working hours and do I ever have to cook for myself or get left alone overnight. She wants to hear that Nana's no looking after me. I want to tell her about Nana letting me sleep in her bed when I'm scared; about the way she pretends she's no hungry so I get the last sausage; how she sings the wrong words just to make me laugh. I could tell her that if Nana died in another gas explosion, I would die too. But I don't tell Val any of that, I just open the kitchen door and let Sid jump all over her.

When Val finally calms down, she sits and I pass her the coffee, dribbling some on her pink trousers. I might have gone too far because she goes all quiet.

'I'm having some trouble at work, Jane,' she says at last. This is not what I'm expecting. 'The men I work with exclude police-women from everything. I'm only allowed to assist on this case because a child is involved, and when I am invited to briefings, I have to put up with constant comments about my looks. They are so rude, Jane.'

I want to say that I'm not Jane but she looks kind of upset and is fidgeting with one of the crochet covers. Nana says the covers are to make the couch look bright and special but they're just hiding the worn bits. I know what Val means about the police-men being rude, there's boys who shout that manky shite at all the girls, even wee toaty ones.

'That's a shame,' I say, but don't have a clue why she's telling me.

'It is. It is a shame. But perhaps you and I could do something about it. Team up, girls together.'

'Team up?'

'Look, I don't mean to patronize you,' I'll need to look up that word, I'm no asking her, 'but you are very bright and I have an idea. It's to do with the piece missing from your account of four-teenth April.'

A bit of sick sloshes into my mouth and I taste Romano's frit-ters. Val's probably got handcuffs in her horrible brown bag. She comes to sit on the arm of Nana's chair, putting her hand on my shoulder. God, I'm shaking.

'Hey, it's OK, don't worry. You aren't in any trouble, not at all,' she laughs, 'isn't it funny how people get so worried around the police?'

No, it's no funny, no funny at all, Val.

'This is just a small thing, something I've been reading up on. Your account of that morning has at least one hour missing, an hour that you don't want to remember but which is possibly hidden inside your mind. Have you had any little flashes, a fleeting image in a daydream, perhaps?'

The minute she asks, a 'little flash' pops into my head. The long grey intestine-thing hanging out Samantha's side, the way it curled like it was moving, like it was alive. Val's no got a scooby.

'I told yous everything,' I say.

'Never mind,' she goes, 'I'm sure we can shake something awake in your mind. Actually, I'm very keen on psychology, it was my first choice of career.'

I know what psychology is because Nana watches *Dallas* and somebody is always lying on a couch talking about problems. 'Why didn't you do it, then?' I ask. 'Everybody hates the police.'

'What? No. Do they?' Val says. 'No, no, I joined up because of my dad. A family tradition. And I don't think the police are hated, in fact most people—'

'Everybody round here hates yous. Really really hates yous. They all say—'

'Yeah, OK, fine. Anyway, this idea. There's a proven method to retrieve repressed memories. It involves revisiting the site of trauma and I was hoping that you and I might—'

'You want me to go back to the Dummy Railway?'

'Well done, I knew you'd understand.' Val claps as if I've just done a magic trick. 'If we trigger something from that morning, anything, it might impress my boss. Who knows, you may even remember something important about Alex Finlayson and that would really show the men.'

Taxi Alex helped me, I'm no saying anything about him.

*

101

I didn't tell Val about the jaggy nettles and now she's rubbing a dock leaf on her ankle.

She thinks I've come back to help her, but it was all her questions about Nana. If you aren't getting watched right, the police take you away, put you in an orphanage or something. And maybe they'd put Nana away too. If I remember something useful, maybe it won't matter that Nana has to go to work. Even if I don't remember, it'll look like I'm no hiding anything.

On TV when there's been a murder, even when it's meant to be like weeks later, you see police vans and tape and men with notebooks and cameras. The Dummy Railway is deserted. Except, except there might be a shadow on the opposite embankment, like somebody watching. But there's no person, just straggly bushes rustling about in the wind. I hope it's the wind.

We're standing at the old dyke above the tracks. The grass here is scrubby and black where it's been set on fire, and that sets something off in my head, a story or a nursery rhyme maybe. Somebody burning their trousers or their feet and, and . . . is it a story? I'm scared again and start wailing, I want to go, I can't be here—

'Jane,' Val is patting my back, 'slow your breathing. It's just a panic attack, just a wee stooshie. Big deep breath, that's a girl.'

Val puts her arm round my shoulder and we sit on the dyke. A group of boys with a football go by, staring as they pass. I feel stupid about being so scared and I hate Val seeing me like this.

'Time to go,' she says, 'and to exactly the same spot where you found Samantha Watson.'

As we scramble down the embankment, the smell comes back. Nana had let me use her Christmas soap but the stench of Samantha was on me for ages, just under the lemon. And the noise is back too, angry wasps echoing inside my ears. I see the place where Samantha's purse was lying and then I see her place, behind the itchy-coo bush. It's just dirt now with footprints in the mud.

Just dirt.

'My first murder scene,' Val says, crouching to examine nothing. 'I wish I'd been here that morning, even on the most basic assist. Or first on the scene, checking the corpse for signs of life, that would—'

'Shut up,' I say. My t-shirt is wringing with sweat and my shorts are damp from sitting on the wall. Or it might be pish again, I can't even tell.

'I'm being unprofessional here, I apologize, Jane. Let's just close our eyes and try to remember.' Our eyes? What's she got to remember? Maybe how she was lying in her bed that Saturday, deciding what horrible clothes to wear? 'Think about that morning, don't force it, just step by step.'

Samantha's hand is cold. I wish I had some mits with me, or a wee blanket. A blanket would cover all the— no, no, don't look there, don't think about those slashes. Think about, about her purse. It's one of those hippy purses and there's nothing in it, not even a half-pence. Poor Samantha must've been skint. And there's Sid Vicious, snuffling about, his tail wagging. Somebody is singing. It's me. Shut up, Janey. Lean a bit closer, tell Samantha no to be scared of Sid.

I open my eyes here, to skip past what I did next. Val is wiping something from her shoe, but is still repeating in a soft voice, 'Step by step, Jane, let it all come back.'

I see the bluebottle, busy busy on Samantha's lip, and I'm crying and running and, and then I'm near The Screke. I need to find a grown-up but all I can think about is the safe secret darkness of The Screke.

'I was hiding,' I say loudly, 'in The Screke. I went in there.'

'A breakthrough,' Val says, looking happy. 'Let's go then, show me where you hid.'

'But, but I remembered. I told you. That's us done, time to go home.'

'Now, listen to me, miss. This isn't a game. You can't simply decide to leave, not when you might hold crucial evidence. Now get moving and take me to this place.'

Val is angry. I imagine her writing a letter to some official about a poor wee Possil girl being neglected by her bad grandma and I start walking.

The bushes and weeds along the tracks are huge in the summer and the squelchy ground has gone crispy and dry. When we reach the stretch where houses overlook the embankment, I hear kids out playing and wish I was up there with them. Val is interested in everything and has her notebook out. I keep my head down and concentrate on the shite lying about. Bed springs, beer crate, petrol can, Action Man's head—

'Are we going under the bridge?' Val's voice startles me.

There are quite a few tunnels along the track and this one's got a platform on either side. It's short and bright and under the gigantic 'No Surrender' graffiti, you can still see 'British Railways' stamped into the brick.

Val stops to examine a mouldy car seat till she realizes what the brown stains are.

'Go up onto the platform,' I tell her, the echoes and water running down the stone walls making everything sound like the swimming baths, 'use that bit to stand on there, then feel along the wall for the opening.'

But she can't get a grip to climb, she's useless, and I have to lead the way.

The gap in the tunnel wall is slimy with moss and Val's pink get-up is like camouflage now. She looks like she might cry. We follow a bit of a path, half-hidden in overgrown bushes, till we reach The Screke. I don't really know plant names but I recognize ivy from Christmas, and the way it covers the entrance makes it look like Dracula's tomb. The reek here is of the olden days, wet dirt and mould, and you can tell The Screke was built way before the Dummy Railway. It's too narrow for a train to go through, but nobody can guess the length because time in there is different, walking end to end feels like hours. Nobody can guess what it was built for either – secret experiments on convicts, mining for gold, burning witches. Nana says it was a farmers' tunnel to take sheep and cows under the canal but that's the maddest idea of all. As if there was any farms round here.

'You know that screke is an old word for scream?' Val says. God, what a know-it-all. At least she isn't so full of herself looking into the total absolute darkness. She takes a wee torch out her bag and the beam bounces around like mental. Again, I get the creepy feeling that somebody's behind us. I take Val's hand, and for once I'm glad she's the police.

'You go first and I'll follow,' Val says and gives me a shove.

I take slow baby-steps but when I reach the bend, everything shifts and tilts.

A girl is huddled tight against the wall, her whole body shuddering. Her hands are muddy and her knee bloody. She's wearing a new Harrington and gym shorts because her denims are in the wash. Other Janey lifts her head, her eyes like golf balls. She's listening to the breathing.

I was hiding in The Screke and somebody else was in there, breathing hard.

Val tries to grab me as I run out.

'Taxi Alex,' I shout because I have to tell her something, 'he saw Samantha. I was in his taxi and he was talking about the state she was in.'

It's the memory that came when Stevie Baw-Jaws was eating Juicy Fruit. It's nothing to do with The Screke but I'm never going back in there. Never, ever, ever in your long-legged-life.

We are back on the street and Val can't wait a minute longer to call her boss. I'm sitting on the pavement because everything inside me is twitching. Window panels in the phone box are missing and I hear what she's saying.

'. . . thank you, Sir. With regards to the time discrepancy, she was hiding as you thought. She showed me where. It's an older tunnel which wasn't mentioned on the search report . . . Not that I could see, but with decent lights it might be worthwhile. I'll mark the location on my report, with the new information on Alex Finlayson . . . Agreed, very interesting indeed. And, Sir, you were right about the girl's reaction. Once I had her sympathy, I didn't have to wait for permission from the old dear . . . Yeah, too right, very glad. Oh, for goodness sake. Hold on a second, Sir. Hey, where are you going? Hang on and I'll take you home. Jane, wait.'

I keep running and shout, 'My name's not fucking Jane.' Don't care if that is ten Hail Marys.

Chapter 20

It's no been the best of weeks. Janey's been struggling since that hatchet-faced nonentity took her back down the old railway. That bloody woman won't know what hit her if she ever shows up here again. There must be some law against taking a child without asking, even for the police.

Thank God for Mrs Khan's lassies. Three of them, I remember Asha's name but no the others, found Janey sitting on the stairs, and seeing the state of her, took her home. They got her nice clean clothes to put on, and something to eat that was 'way better' than my cooking apparently. When Janey wouldn't stop shaking, they woke their mother. Janey said Mrs Khan was 'gentle', which sounds a lovely thing, and the right way to treat a wean who's upset.

It was Mrs Khan herself who came to get me when I finished work, and aye, she was certainly gentle when telling me what happened. She invited me up, and it was a blessed relief to find Janey in the girls' room, all of them giggling about something.

'Nana, look,' she said, 'Asha's lending black clothes for me for the funeral. And Reeta's going to cut my hair.' Reeta is the oldest lassie and she asked my permission, so polite those girls. It was very enjoyable to be surrounded by family noise and chatter and we stayed till I remembered that Sid Vicious hadn't been fed. I wanted to give the sisters a couple of bob, especially the one that did the haircut, which is smashing considering she's a typist. But Mrs Khan wouldn't hear of it so I'll need to get them a box of biscuits.

Janey didn't want to go over what happened with that scunner policewoman, but the rest of the week, she was in a terrible narky mood. Nothing I did or said was right, and I even caught her smacking poor Sid Vicious. Then, last night while I was marking a hem on the funeral trousers, the trouble really started.

'How come we've got no photos? How come?' she said and I could hear anger in her voice.

'What do you mean, sweetheart? Wait, stand still, you're—'

'You never even put up any of my school photos.'

'Will you sit down, lassie, and tell me what all this is about?' She was storming about, pins flying all over the carpet. She started talking about the Khans' home and the family photographs: parents, grandparents, daughters, nephews, nieces, aunties.

'There's even one of a house, Nana. A house in India from long ago. Can we not even put up one family picture?'

It's years since Janey's thrown a tantrum, so I was a bit lost. And of course, I didn't know if it was due to what happened to her, or just her age. Marie could be a right wee madam when she hit her teens.

'You're making yourself upset about nothing,' I said. 'Come and have a wee cuddle and—'

'Stop talking to me like I'm a stupid baby that's just, just shat on the carpet,' she shouted. Then the tears started.

So, today we're having a special day, the three of us. Right after Mass, we collected Sid Vicious and got the 54 to Cadder, and it's thanks to Billy Watson, and whatever his criminal activities are, that we had bus fare. It's a while since we've been to the cemetery, which makes me ashamed. When Janey was young we visited every Sunday, and she had a wee song, 'Goin to see my mammy, goin to see my daddy, goin to see Donna too. They're away up to Heaven, yoo-hoo, yoo-hoo, yoo-hoo.' She'd sing it as we walked, with a special skip and hop to match the tune. And with every word, I'd shatter inside.

I've brought chrysanthemums, a bottle of ginger and crisps. Now that we've cleaned the headstone and Donna's marble angel, we're sitting on the grass having our picnic. One thing I will say for the Rizzo family – they paid for beautiful graves. The perfect spot too, at the end of a row in the quieter side of Lambhill Cemetery. The Campsie Hills are in the distance and it's a comfort to know this'll be my resting place one day.

I watch a teeny sparrow land on the head of Donna's angel. Generally, I've no time for birds, with all their pecking and droppings, and I've certainly no time for the poems about their fancy swoopings that are supposed to be about a different thing altogether. But there's something about that sparrow, something of Donna and the way she watched the world . . . Ach, I'm away with the bees.

Sid Vicious has wandered off with a scabby-looking stray but I keep my eye to make sure he doesn't toilet on any graves. Janey's making a daisy chain to leave for her sister, and it's nice to hear her humming as she works.

'We could go to Grandpa's grave,' she says, 'put some of the flowers on it.'

'Who?' I'm puzzled, then it hits me. 'Oh, you mean, aye, well, no. It's, he's, the grave's no this cemetery, hen. Look at Sid Vicious, run and catch him, sweetheart, he's nearly out on the main road.'

Christ. Grandpa. Never in a million years.

*

Tonight, we have a fine roast chicken dinner with Angel Delight for afters. Again thanks to Billy. While Janey washes the dishes, I hunt for the tin with the photographs and of course it's at the very back of the hell-hole cupboard. I'll need to clear that out one of these days.

'Leave the dishes and mon see the photos,' I shout, emptying them over the table.

That table, rammed in behind the couch and the window. Nobody has big tables these days, Angela and her lot eat in front of the telly, plates balanced on their laps. All the things I had to leave when we moved, I don't know why I insisted on the table. Those poor men that had to hump it up eight flights when it wouldn't fit in the lift. Of all the things.

'Look. Here's one with Mammy,' Janey says, shoving the photo under my nose. She has certainly brightened up.

'It is. And that's Donna she's holding. It's the backcourt at Hotspur Street, and see that window? That was my bedroom. Donna's in her Baptism gown, so, let me think, 1961.'

'Who are these, Nana?'

'That's my mother and father, your great-granny and great-grandfather O'Connell.'

'They look a bit moany.'

'Ah, well, right enough,' I say, 'but that's the way pictures were taken in those days. They were good people, hard-working and decent. Maybe they were a bit moany but life was terrible hard for the working class in those days. Especially if you were Irish.' But she's too busy for one of my lectures on oppression.

'Who's in the pram in this one?' She's studying every picture like a scientist with a microscope. What's she looking for, I wonder?

'It's you, my lamb. You can just see your wee face keeking out. One of the professional photographers on the seafront at Rothesay took this. 1968 it is, the only holiday yous had together. Oh, Janey, how happy your mammy is, and look at your dad and Donna in their funny straw hats. Dear Lord, I'd forgotten about this photo. Ah, it's all right, sweetheart, I'll be fine in a wee minute.'

I'd also forgotten about my wedding picture.

'I never knew you were skinny, Nana. So, that's my grandpa, then. How come you never talk about him?' Janey asks.

'He died in the war,' I tell her, the same lie I told Marie.

I look at Donald Devine's dour expression, the simmering rage that I mistook for thoughtfulness, and I shudder. If only he had died in the war, at least I'd have the pension to show for those hellish years. No idea how that photo survived, I was sure I'd destroyed every trace, but it's going straight down the rubbish chute tonight.

'Oh, see this one,' I say quickly, 'your class photo from Primary 2. Mon tell me the names of all your wee pals.' Janey squeezes onto my chair, pointing out the good ones and the bad ones.

The photographs remind me about Hollywood Dancer's camera and Janey is delighted when I give her it.

'It's just a loan of, mind,' I tell her, 'and I'm no buying a new spool. But there's twenty in it, and we'll get the chemist to get them developed.' I finish the dishes myself while she takes photos from the window. It makes me smile because from this height, everything will look teeny.

We settle to watch the late film together. I love a Western and thankfully this one isn't as bloodthirsty as these modern ones.

'Remember you wanted to be a cowboy?' I say.

'Did not.' She's spread out on the couch, and sits up to look at me like I've lost my marbles.

'Aye, you did. Yon teacher told me, her that was always sniffing. She asked everybody in class what job they wanted when they grew up. There was the usual footballers and shop workers, but then wee Janey Devine boldly announced she was going to be a cowboy with a big horse called Champion. Miss Kennedy, that was the sniffer's name. Miss Kennedy said your classmates were very impressed. Do you no remember?'

Janey's laughing hard now. No heard that sound in a while.

'I remember Miss Kennedy and her sniffing, but a cowboy? That's mental. Do you think I've still got a chance? Think Champion would fit in the lift?'

Before bed, I give her the Rothesay photograph to keep. She's going to stick it up on her bedroom wall, where it'll break my heart over and over again.

Chapter 21

82 days

C an't believe I'm excited about a funeral. It will likely be horrible and sad and I'll be crying, but I'm looking forward to it. Maybe, when I get to say a proper cheerio to Samantha, everything will go back to normal.

This morning when I got dressed, I was different. The black clothes and new haircut make me look older. Usually, people think I'm a daft wee ten-year-old and I was pure jealous when Lorraine got her bra and secretly hoped it would snap and everybody would laugh. But now my head is full of Samantha and it makes me sick to think I ever wanted a woman's body. Sick, and worried it'll happen anyway. I close the wardrobe door so I can't see the mirror any more.

I asked some of the Proddy kids about crematoriums and Keith from 12D said that when they burn the bodies, you can smell it. He said there's smoke everywhere and at the end they give you a box full of the burnt person. Keith also says *Blake's Seven* is filmed in a real spaceship so he's probably talking shite. I hope so.

Nana's wearing lipstick and a hat and her special funeral coat even though the sun's out. She says the coat is 'quality' but it smells like old wardrobes. Nana isn't excited, she's serious and narky. Gibby was late coming to collect Sid and she gave him a right shirikin. He did a crabbit face behind Nana's back and I burst out laughing. I don't know what's up with me.

We get a taxi to the crematorium and it's a surprise to see a crowd waiting. I thought it would be just Samantha's family. Suddenly, I feel like I am ten years old and I take Nana's hand. We stand at the edge of the crowd, I don't know what everybody is waiting for. I only recognize Mr Watson and some of the men from his house. Lulu notices us and does a quick wave. He looks funny in a suit.

'Maggie. Maggie Devine.' A woman in a furry coat comes hurrying over. This always happens. Wherever we go, somebody knows Nana.

'Oh, it's, it's . . . yourself,' Nana says.

'Rose. Rose Wodehouse. Apple turnovers.'

'Of course it is. It must be, what, seven years. And look at you, Rose, you've no changed a bit.'

The woman is taller than Nana and fatter. Her perm is blonde and doesn't match her eyebrows, which are black and bushy like the kind you get in a joke shop.

'Come, let me shake your hand, Maggie. It's you that hasn't changed a bit, my dear. And who's this with you?' Rose Wodehouse's mad eyebrows go up as she checks me out. 'Is this your poor orphan granddaughter? No, it can't be. All grown up already.'

They start blabbing about old times at some bakery and the people who worked there. Especially the ones who are dead or had tragedies.

Then Nana says, 'So, tell me, what are you doing here? Did you know Samantha Watson?'

'I was just going to ask you the same. I'm related to Samantha's mother, my husband is Helen Watson's cousin. Not that we saw much of the poor girl after Helen went into hospital but Samantha used to call us Uncle Hugh and Aunt Rose.'

I thought Samantha's mum was dead like mine, so that's something to write about later. Nana asks if Helen Watson will be here today.

'She won't, no. I'm not even sure if she knows her daughter is gone. I can't visit Helen myself, even the smell in hospitals makes me ill, but Hugh saw her in January and the poor woman was being spoon-fed. Spoon-fed, Maggie. A head injury is a shocking thing.' Rose lowers her voice and signals for Nana to huddle in. 'Of course, there's still questions about how Helen came to be knocked down. I mean, what's a married woman doing alone in town on a Saturday night? But you know me, my dear, I don't repeat gossip.'

She switches to a story about the factory foreman who went to Peterborough and ended up with an artificial leg. It's boring, so I ask Nana if I can go and say hello to Mr Watson. Hopefully, Nino will be here, or Fiona who was her school pal, but I'll only know her if she's wearing a nurse uniform.

The big doors have opened and Mr Watson has already gone inside. The crowd is moving now so I decide to wait here for Nana. I hope Rose Wodehouse has gone, her coat smells even fustier than Nana's. Someone taps my shoulder, I turn and it's Taxi Alex. He's no wearing a black suit or coat, just his grey jumper and a bunnet like old men wear.

'How's things, Janey Devine?' he says, quietly for Alex.

'I'm OK.'

'Aye, well, I'm no so OK. This business. This buggering business.' He shakes his head. 'You still getting questioned? Police are hounding me.'

After what I told Val, it's likely my fault they are hounding him so I don't want to hear anything about it.

'You can sit beside us,' I say, 'my nana's just coming.' She's still yakking with Rose but they are moving slowly forward.

'No, no, I'm just going to slip in at the back. Just want to pay my respects since I'm part of this. You feel that an all? Linked to Samantha Watson?'

But before I answer, a woman in big glasses comes over.

'Do you mind if I stand with you?' she asks. 'I don't know anyone and I don't want to intrude in family grief.'

Alex pulls his bunnet low over his face and walks away, which is rude, so I tell her it's fine. You can talk to strange women but not men. It's hard to guess anything about people if they're wearing funeral clothes, but she has the same clever snobby accent as policeman Val.

'How did you know Samantha, if you don't mind my asking?' the woman says. This must be a usual funeral question. I really don't want to tell her, so I copy Rose's thing about being a cousin.

'I'm very sorry for your loss,' she says and shakes my hand. 'My name is Gayle Banks and I knew Samantha at college.' I think she must be one of the pals Nino mentioned but she's a lecturer. She tells me that Samantha was a wonderful hard-working and bright student.

'You seem like a clever girl too,' she says. 'I expect you're planning university in a few years.'

I haven't even got a clue what people do at university except rant about politics and see bands, but I'm kind of proud that Gayle called me clever. When she asks about Mr Watson and how he's managing, I tell her that he's got lots of friends staying with him and she's very interested to hear about them.

Nana arrives with Rose and a man who is taller and fatter than everyone. He's blowing his nose loudly and his eyes are watery. He nods but says nothing, he must be Uncle Hugh. We all go in together.

The crematorium has benches like a church but it's grey and

empty. They should get some lovely statues like the Sacred Heart of Jesus, or stained-glass windows which are good to look at when the priest is boring. We sit in the middle and I see Mr Watson at the very front with two old ladies in black hats. They've got their heads bowed and I wonder if I should do that. When Mr Watson turns to shake hands with some man, I wave and mouth 'hello'. Nana nudges me and looks angry. Not knowing what to do is making me feel stupid and all the sad faces make me try to calm down.

I concentrate on Samantha. There's no altar, just a kind of a stage, and that's where her picture is. It's a happy photo, she's smiling, which makes me happy. I know it sounds mental cos she's dead and I never met her, but I bet I know more about Samantha than some of the people here. I'd like to shout, 'Samantha, it's me,' and that's so weird, I giggle. Nana nudges me again. I don't know why I'm carrying on like this. I try looking at all the flowers but one bunch is green with wee red buds and it looks like the itchy-coo bush. I can't be thinking about Dummy Railway Day so turn away quickly.

Gayle is watching something going on at the back. Standing there is Detective Alistair Baxter with another two men, and that bam Val. They probably made her a sergeant or something for all her psychology work on me. I know the police are trying to find the killer, and that's great, but I'm no helping them again. I'm never telling about the bad thing and never remembering anything else.

Val probably doesn't see me but I put on my dirtiest look just in case. Gayle asks if we recognize any of Mr Watson's friends who are talking to the police.

'I certainly know Duncan Edgar,' Rose says, pointing, 'and his lowlife brother, Jimmy.'

Finally, it's the Eggman. He looks pretty tough with his Crombie, shaved head and thick neck, but he doesn't look like an egg.

Skinny Jimmy is talking non-stop, which reminds me of the drive home when he wouldn't shut up about Crunchies being way better than Curly Wurlys.

'It beggars belief those Edgar thugs were invited today,' Rose says. 'Helen would be mortified.'

Everybody has turned to watch now. One of the policemen is poking at Skinny Jimmy's jacket and their voices are getting louder. Then everybody turns back to watch Mr Watson walking down the aisle, his shiny shoes clicking and his head bowed. I can't see Mr Watson's face when he speaks into Detective Alistair Baxter's ear, but his hand is screwed into a fist. Lulu pushes past Val and flings the door open. The police leave and Skinny Jimmy laughs. Maybe he's excited like me.

'Can you believe that? Throwing policemen out,' Rose says to Nana, who isn't talking much now. 'What a nerve.'

But I want to cheer. I hope Val has a big brass neck.

The funeral starts when they carry a wooden coffin down the aisle and it looks far too big for just Samantha. I must've seen the coffins at my family's funeral but I don't remember. Somebody that isn't a priest appears on the stage and the talking starts.

Uncle Hugh blows his nose loudly when the coffin goes through the wee curtains. That's where it gets burned but there's no smoke or smell. Stupid Keith in 12D. Nearly everybody is crying especially when 'Amazing Grace' starts. Rose keeps dabbing at her eyes, even though they're totally dry. When Nana cries, she makes no sound and the tears just slide down, and I don't want to see that.

I don't even think about Samantha until it's time to go. Her photograph is still on the stage and it feels like she's watching everyone leaving without her. Just like I left her in the Dummy Railway.

Uncle Hugh passes me tissues from his Man-Size Kleenex box.

Chapter 22

What does Janey look like with that coconut haircut and those tight trousers? She could be going to see one of those lamentable bands rather than a funeral. And that Gibson no turning up till the last minute, then asking for money for dog food. Dog food? It'll be a bloody bottle of Thunderbird.

Ach, I'd like to go back to bed and stay there for this whole damnable day.

The wrong weather for a funeral, sun splitting the streets, and the taxi fare double what I expected. Now to cap it all, who's among the mourners but that busy-body Rose Wodehouse. It was bad enough years ago when I had to work beside that woman, but at a funeral . . . dear Christ, as if there's no enough death and horror today without somebody who knew my husband. But sometimes just pretending to be yourself makes it happen. Having to make conversation with Rose helps me calm down.

Even inside the crematorium, she's still blethering with some young woman who's far too excited about the unpleasantness with Billy's team and the police. And who do I see slinking out a side door but Taxi Alex. There's something about that man, I can't put my finger on it, but showing up then no staying for the service – that's no right.

Oh, God help us, they're bringing in Samantha's coffin. Every head turns, every breath held. And when they place it at the front, all I can see are three coffins. Marie and Vincent and Donna.

There was a long wait before my family could be laid to rest because of the Gas Board inquiry. In the end, they were exonerated because engineers were on site the day of the explosion. The two workmen had been trying to isolate a leak and were on a tea break when the fireball erupted from a mains pipe. It roared through the kitchens of all four floors. Marie, Vinnie and Donna would've been sitting at their smart new Formica table to eat lunch, baby Janey sleeping in the back bedroom. And when the walls came crashing down, a fallen wardrobe protected her cot. A miracle, everybody said, but a miracle would have saved them all.

It was the Rizzos who organized the funeral, they were big in the St Vincent de Paul, so the service was in St Andrew's Cathedral. You've never seen such a turnout. To this day, though, I could not name any one of those mourners, it's just a fog of condolences. I was shown to the front pew with Janey and my brother, Finn. He'd come down to try and help but when the three coffins were carried in, it was too much and he left. There was a full Requiem Mass, far too long for a toddler, especially one with a sore hand, and eventually I had to take Janey outside.

When I think about that funeral, it's never the bishop, the choir, the fancy tea at The Rogano afterwards, it's always Janey and me alone on the street outside, crying together.

*

When Samantha's coffin slips away, Billy Watson folds in on himself. The memory of that despair knocks the wind out of me and I have to hold Janey's arm. She's been wriggling about like a bag of rats, smiling and waving and it's no right. It's just no right. I should've put my foot down and said no to coming today.

When it's finally over, I make straight for the gates but lose Janey in the crowd. When I spot her, she's deep in conversation with some elderly women. So much for a quick exit. If Janey keeps this nonsense up, I swear to God I'm going to—

'Nana,' she shouts, ''mon talk to Samantha's gran.'

I've no option now.

They're all relatives on Helen's side and I wonder about Billy's family.

'I'm awful sorry for your loss,' I say to the grandmother. 'Samantha is in our prayers.'

She's in her eighties, with grey skin and a good hat. Two of the women support her frail frame but I feel the newness of grief in the strength of her grip.

'Will you pray for us too, Mrs Devine? For Helen and William and I?' Her voice trembles and she squeezes my hand to the point of numbness.

'Always,' I say, 'and tell Billy—'

'Oh, but surely you'll come to the hotel and talk to him yourself. Bring this wee lovey,' she takes Janey's hand now, the two of us like anchors against her pain, 'William speaks so well of you both.'

I look over at Billy, all his hardman confidence gone, trying to accept sympathy when the only thing in his head is his daughter's coffin. And then Rose Wodehouse barges in and offers a lift and Janey is asking to go and there's nothing I can do, no matter the misery burning deep into my heart.

Rose has lost a glove so I go help her look. Janey waits in the car with Hugh, a nice man with at least a touch of dignity.

The glove is lying near the side entrance, you could spot it from space. Red gloves to a funeral, for crying out loud.

'Take your bloody hands off me.' A woman's voice. Christ Almighty, what now? Rose turns like a bloodhound picking up the scent. Two of Billy's lads are frog-marching that young woman in the glasses towards the car park.

'I'll have the police back here in an instant,' she's shouting, digging her elbow into Lulu's stomach. They're trying to put her in the driving seat of one of these wee teeny cars but she's no going quietly. 'I know who you are. Every damned one of you will be named in tomorrow's *Record*.'

A reporter. Just what the poor Watson family need.

It feels like a very long drive to the Wake. I've heard of The Western Hotel and apparently it's expensive.

The business with the woman reporter has left me even more unsettled, and when we're seated at a table, I gladly accept a glass of wine. It's no something I've drunk very often and this one is sweet and pleasant and it's the third glass before I know it.

I'd hoped to be far away from Rose Wodehouse but I'm next to her and another cousin, a woman with the complexion of grated cheese, who is telling everyone that Billy Watson needed special permission to have Samantha cremated.

'He didn't want the authorities coming and digging her up. Knows more about the death than he's letting on,' she says.

I envy Janey, escaping to sit with the young ones.

Working at Balmore Bakery, Rose never missed a chance to remind everybody that she and Donald Devine were childhood sweethearts. And now, she's at it again.

'One of life's funny coincidences that Maggie and I ended up working together. Donald and I were courting, and it's just unfortunate he was a Pape, or I would have undoubtedly been

Mrs Devine. No offence, Maggie, but I'm from a good Protestant family. Donald was such a lovely chap. No offence, Hugh.'

A lovely chap. Eejit doesn't know the escape she had.

On top of all the damn emotions of this funeral, the guilt that goes with Donald Devine nearly overwhelms me. I go to find Janey to walk me out for fresh air but the lad at her table says he hasn't seen her for some time, then Rose, face red with urgency, telling me there's no sign of her in the toilets. Where else could she be? Has she been taken?

Chapter 23

82 days

I was waiting in Uncle Hugh's car when Nana and Rose came back with news that Gayle Banks got chucked out. Just like the police. Turns out she's a reporter and the stuff she was asking about was for her newspaper. How mad is that? On the drive to the next bit of the funeral, Nana and Rose talked about it the whole time. Nana was raging about Gayle's damned nerve and lack of respect, while Rose was worried she'll end up in *News of the World*. She kept repeating that she meant no disrespect to Mr Watson or Mr Edgar, and asked if we'd noticed a camera. Uncle Hugh and me shared his Polo Fruits. I'm glad I didn't tell that Gayle who I really was.

The hotel seems fancy. It might not be, it might be rubbish, but it's the first hotel I've been in. There are tartan carpets, tartan curtains and the staff wear tartan waistcoats. The gathering to remember Samantha, which Nana is calling a Wake but nobody else is, is in Glencoe Suite. It's a huge room with windows that go to the ceiling, round tables with white cloths and, at the front, a big long table totally covered in food and drinks.

It's called a buffet and you get a plate and walk along, picking whatever you want. I'm worried about taking too much but

Nana's piling her plate high, and filling a napkin with chipolatas for Sid Vicious. When I see everybody else going back again and again, I do too. I'm no even hungry.

It's mostly old people at our table. A wee lady is asking everyone if they can still bend, and Nana has relaxed, chatting about terrible diseases and bad menfolk. Everybody seems cheerful now, there's loud laughing and even Mr Watson is talking and shaking hands. When I go to check out the toilets, he calls me over and pats my head and gives me a fiver. A fiver. That's more than birthday money so I have to say no thanks. Nana's rules are so annoying. He smiles and says I'm a wee doll and he's proud to know me. My face goes a bit red but it is nice.

'How about you take, let's see, £3.74? Will that suit you?' Mr Watson gives me all the change out his pocket. Probably enough to buy straight black trousers like the ones Asha lent me.

When I get back, Uncle Hugh tells me to help myself to something off his three plates and I hear Rose whispering to another woman. About the murderer.

'The police must have a reason for all that questioning,' the woman is saying, and she sounds exactly like the freaky scarecrow in *Worzel Gummidge*.

'I've been thinking the same, my dear,' Rose says, 'no smoke without fire.'

'If she knew too much about his criminal activities, he would have to shut her up. First his wife, then his daughter. Am I right? Am I right?'

They're talking about Mr Watson. Samantha's daddy. I pretend to reach for Uncle Hugh's plate and knock a can of beer over the woman with the scarecrow voice.

Nana is helping to mop it up and I'm about to ask if we can go home when one of Samantha's friends comes over and invites me to sit with them. I'm the youngest here, apart from a baby and nobody in the whole world would want a baby near them.

Nana goes to their table to check them out before letting me move.

Samantha's college pals are all about her age, and are nice and kind and you can tell they all liked Samantha. Really liked her. I'm OK about them knowing who I am, and when I tell about Dummy Railway Day, the girls hug me, and they say Sid Vicious is the best dog name ever.

At the crematorium, I didn't listen to the vicar, or whatever he was, rambling on and on about the youth of today and Samantha Watson being a shining example of her generation. It didn't sound like he was talking about a real person but I'm paying attention to what the pals are saying about Samantha.

Most of them are wearing something that belonged to Sammy, who was really great about lending her stuff. They call her Sammy, which makes me think of a friendly snake. Tony opens his shirt to show her 'No Nukes' t-shirt, and Heavy-metal girl jingles a load of shiny bangles. Heather makes us laugh by flashing Sammy's bra and it's a surprise to see that bras can be red. They take turns to talk about Samantha's kindness, and I secretly write some of these on a napkin.

1. S paid rent for Maryam who was going to get evicted. Think that means chucked out her house.

2. Audrey borrowed college books off S. Said she's heart broke cos she can't give them back.

3. S bought Frizzy-perm girl a ticket for David Bowie at Apollo. Best night of her life ever.

4. Tony owes S for millions of nights out. Went on a bit much about beer and dancing.

Heather makes a joke about keeping them all in Red Lebanese which I don't understand but they all lift their glasses and shout,

'Cheers, Sammy.' Probably won't add that one to the scrapbook. There's also quiet talk about the night of the murder. Tony and Heather were both with her, and I need extra napkins to write it all down.

Heather is my favourite, she's the funniest and talks to me more than the others. And she tells me some things about Samantha that aren't so nice.

'I'm going to be honest with you, Janey,' she says, 'because it's not right the way the dead are made out to be saints. It's not right because it puts pressure on the living. Sammy had faults like everybody else.' Heather has her arm around my shoulder and her breath smells of the wine. 'Sometimes she'd boast about her dad's reputation, and she used his connections. All that "I know the Eggman, and if you don't let us in your pub, he won't be happy." Not the best thing about Samantha Watson but still part of who she was. You get what I'm saying?'

I get it fine. Jackie tells everybody her uncle plays for Dundee United just so she gets picked first in Games, and any time Speccy Kathleen is in trouble, she goes, 'My brother's got no legs,' and she gets let off. It's good to hear Samantha was a closet sometimes, everybody is.

Heather asks me to show her the way to the toilets, and on the stair she stops at a long window.

'Can you believe that?' She's pointing to a big pond behind the hotel. 'Swans.'

'I'm going out to try and touch one,' I say, 'want to come?'

'Nah, I've got business that I know Sammy would approve of.'

Then she tells me about her secret boyfriend. You wouldn't think a secret boyfriend is a thing for a grown-up woman but it's because of Samantha.

'A couple of days after it happened, I went to Billy's to . . . I want to say offer condolences but really I needed to check that it was true,' Heather says. 'Nothing about Sammy's death seemed real. It still doesn't.' She wipes at her runny mascara and I wonder if I'd be so sad if Lorraine died. 'Anyway, Billy couldn't see anybody, and Lulu offered to drive me home. You know Lulu? Tall with the blond quiff? Gorgeous so he is. It sounds bad to say it out loud but we just hit it off. We're not telling anybody because, well, imagine getting together right after your best mate is murdered. You, Janey Devine, are the first person to know,' she shakes my hand, I think she's a bit drunk, 'and that's because you've got a dog called Sid Vicious. This weekend will be our six-month anniversary. But not a word, eh, Janey?' She winks and then says if I see Lulu, to tell him she's waiting at the upstairs bar.

Heather must be drunk cos it's only three months since Samantha died. But I can see why Lulu fancies her, she's got purple streaks in her hair and Doc Martens.

The swans and ducks check me out but don't come close, they're all gathered round a mum and wee kid who are throwing bread. I head back to the hotel to get some of the tiny triangle sandwiches.

As I'm cutting through the car park, Lulu's standing behind a car so I go to give him Heather's message. The sun is beaming down and when I shade my eyes, I see he's tucking his shirt into his trousers. His hair is messed up, and his red cheeks give me a bad feeling and I stop waving. Then I see legs, and Lulu kicks them.

Samantha's legs were manky with blood and spread like a broken Tiny Tears. And her poor bare feet. But it's man's legs Lulu is kicking. I suddenly realize that I'm still walking, close enough now to recognize Skinny Jimmy on the ground. Jimmy's eyes are closed and there's wet blood on his nose. Lulu boots into him again and I don't want to be here.

But it's too late.

Lulu and me look at each other, frozen like we're playing Still Statues. The wee kid at the pond is laughing and the ducks are quacking but there's nobody else in the car park, nobody to see. Skinny Jimmy does a snorty-cough thing and I let my breath out, relieved he's no dead. Then Lulu rushes forward and grabs me, slinging me over his shoulder. A fireman's lift, Nana calls that.

'You're always in the wrong fucking place, hen,' he says. He takes big calm steps, but his voice is fast and excited. 'Bastard was saying stuff about Samantha. Cannae get away wi that, no the day. Deserved a fuckin doin but Ah dinnae stab him.'

When he says 'stab', I shiver and his hands tighten. Right at that minute I picture his hands tightening around Samantha and I'm trying to find my scream before he takes me away to the Dummy Railway too. But he suddenly dumps me on the stairs outside the hotel.

'Tell nobody nothin, and when the polis come, say you were in the lavvie or something. Hear me?' Lulu makes out he's zipping my mouth shut and I smell Skinny Jimmy's blood on his hand. Then he starts shouting, 'Eggman, Eggman. Where the fuck are yous?'

I run into the hotel as men barge past me. They all have the same wound-up, buzzing look as Lulu. They're shouting too and I cover my ears to block them out.

The tartan hotel people are rushing around and a waitress at the door of Glencoe Suite grabs my arm as I pass.

'Nobody's allowed in,' she says and I can't tell if she's angry or scared. I can't tell if I'm angry or scared either, I just want to go home.

Behind the waitress, a wee crowd is gathered. I twist easily out her grip and push through the circle of mourners. There's another somebody lying on the ground, with a black coat laid over them. A quality coat with pockets full of chipolatas.

'Nana,' I whisper.

Chapter 24

Two days and Janey hasn't said a word about the funeral. Suits me just fine. I've been trying no to even think about the damn day till Jean came to the door, waving *The Daily Record*.

'It's no disgrace, Maggie,' she says, helping herself to one of the hotel's sausage rolls, two days old but still edible. 'Anybody can faint at a funeral.'

'I know that, but with all the fuss, I just wanted the ground to open and swallow me.'

Rose Wodehouse had the damned cheek to infer it was the wine caused me to pass out. Maybe the drink didn't help but she doesn't know the damage it causes to hear your wean is missing.

'So, did the ambulance come for yourself, or for that Jimmy one that got a doin?' Jean's a good soul but with things like this it's hard to know if it's genuine concern or downright nosiness.

The buzzer goes, making us both jump, but there's only static on the intercom.

'Nobody there,' I say. 'Happening too often these days.'

'It'll be weans. So, what happened after the ambulance?'

'I know weans sometimes press it and run away, but this is getting beyond a joke and if I catch whoever's—'

'The ambulance, Maggie.' Jean needs every detail. She'll be

wanting to get the story straight before taking it to the rest of Possil.

'Aye, well, the hotel manager phoned when he thought I'd had a heart attack, but it was Jimmy that they took away. Handy for him, I suppose.'

'The paper is saying serious assault,' she says, putting her reading glasses on to check the facts.

'It did look like a right sore hammering,' I say, trying hard no to actually picture it. 'I was still in the ambulance getting my blood pressure checked and the medical lassie shouted, "Stab wound," when Jimmy was carried over. She got a rare laugh when his pals claimed that he fell on broken glass. But you know the worst thing about it?'

'Your Janey?'

'She wouldn't leave my side, Jean. After everything she's been through, to see Jimmy Edgar all beat up. Terrible quiet again and just when she seemed a bit more like her wee self.'

'STV news says the attack's another pointer to the murder being connected to organized crime.'

'Ah, well, I don't know about that but I'm thinking the police were expecting trouble. They arrived right on the tail of the ambulance, probably watching the hotel.'

'About time the police paid attention. Somebody should've put a stop to this nonsense years ago. Crime clans, or hooligan families, or whatever the hell they're calling them, running wild. Bits of Milton are no-go, even in the afternoon.'

'They're no talking about the Young Team here,' I tell her. 'It's no your Tongs or your Fleet chasing about with their mammies' kitchen knives. This is the big men, the ones with the money.'

'Aye, but we know them an all. MacQuarries that own yon pub on the Balgrayhill Road. Remember the domino quarter-final?' she says, dipping the sausage roll in her tea.

'I wasn't there. That was the day Janey found the dead lassie.'

'Oh for the love of Christ, so it was. Well, that youngest Mac-Quarrie was storming through the bar. Storming. Anybody so much as look at him, kicked out the door, and I do mean kicked. Then, when his wife took him into the back to calm him down, we heard the bottle smash across her face. You never heard a scream like it—'

'You've told me this before, Jean.' I can't let myself think about that broken wife and her screams. Or about my husband shoving a cloth into my mouth to make sure there were no screams.

'Now, if I don't take that dog out, there's going to be mess all over the floor,' I say.

'You should be taking it easy, Maggie. You're always pushing yourself.' Jean pops the last sausage roll in her pocket. 'I'll walk you as far as wee Mrs Clark's to collect her catalogue money. Imagine, eighty-seven and a new mattress. She'll no get the best of that.'

'That son of hers will have it earmarked.'

Sid Vicious is tied to the lamppost outside the library. He'll be fine as long as no cats pass. I've books to hand back but I wouldn't mind a look at Samantha's ex-boyfriend, him with the funny name, because I can't place him. But it's the nice lassie with the dandruff, and she lets me off with the overdue fines. Lassie, she's fifty if she's a day.

The Reading Room is quiet so I sit to check what the newspapers are saying about the Wake. There's no sign of Gayle Thingamy's name on any of the stories, although the *Herald* has 'by our Crime Correspondent', and it does have a couple of snippets that might have come from Rose Wodehouse. There can't be many people know how poorly Helen Watson is. I had no idea. The mention of protection at Billy's house might've come from myself actually and I hope I've not said the wrong thing. Thankfully, the quotes are credited only to 'a mourner'.

What I find hard to read is a supposed history of the Edgar family. Their father was a known robber, jailed for stabbing a bookie. According to this, Duncan 'Eggman' Edgar is in charge now. Even though they've never been jailed for more than a few months, the brothers are linked to all sorts – protection, stolen goods, armed robbery and, what really troubles me, drugs. I know these reporters can say what they like about criminals to sell newspapers, but I feel foolish that I'd assumed Billy and the Edgars were just selling dodgy fags and running minicabs.

The *Record* and *Evening Times* both make the connection between Samantha's murder and the attack at the funeral. According to 'police sources', the murder investigation is now 'concentrated on organized criminal groups in the Glasgow area'. The MacQuarrie family are named too, and this shower sounds even worse.

There's a lot of certainty about the gang connection but it makes me uneasy. I know these hard cases do horrendous things, but surely just to each other? Surely not to an innocent lassie? And if the police have got it wrong, who's going to find the real murderer?

Just as I'm leaving, the ex-boyfriend appears carrying a bundle of *National Geographics*. With the long hair and wee round glasses, he does look like John Lennon, but when he smiles and waves over, it makes my skin crawl to think how he treated Samantha.

Chapter 25

86 days

My scab is infected. I've been picking it a lot because the funeral didn't help one bit. It wasn't what I expected and the whole thing was like Circus Day.

One time, we went to Edinburgh with Nana's trade union pals. I'd been excited for weeks but everything about the day was weird. We went on a train and got sandwiches that were brown bread, I wore a new tank-top and there were kids with us that I didn't know. And when we got to the circus, it was way too much. There was a smell of wetness and dung that was too smelly, and loud trumpet music that was too loud. Beside me, two wee boys were going mental and one had pink candyfloss in his hair. I hardly watched any of the acts and the only one I remember is balancing poodles.

Now, instead of Samantha being laid to perpetual rest, all I'm left with is more mess in my head. Skinny Jimmy lying battered, Nana passed out on the deck, all that horrible gossip about Mr Watson. And a new secret that's no even mine, it's stupid Lulu's. Everything's piling up inside me and the only way to make it stop is digging into my scab with the end of a biro.

No wonder my knee stinks.

*

Nana had to ask for the morning off work to take me to the doctor and her boss is raging. We were late for the appointment cos Gibby was telling us a mad story about Sid jumping on the 54, and while he was chasing after it, Sid was watching him out the bus window. Dead funny so it was and it cheered us up a bit.

The doctor's name is Dr MacTavish. She wears farmer clothes and has plump cheeks and a whiskery chin. You'd think she would be jolly but she's really not. Getting the pus cleaned out of my knee is sore, but it's worse when she tells me I'm a silly girl to have made such a mess of myself. My face is pure red.

Nana has a special polite voice that she uses with doctors and teachers.

'One other thing, Dr MacTavish,' she says, 'is there anybody that could maybe help Janey? I mean, help to get over all the terrible things she's witnessed. Someone she could talk to?'

'To speak plainly,' Dr MacTavish is scrubbing her hands at a teeny sink, 'your granddaughter needs to buck her ideas up. She's young and healthy and there's no reason in the world why she shouldn't put such experiences behind her. Get some exercise, Janey, fun activities with friends,' she says, smiling. 'I'll write a prescription for antibiotics: two weeks, three times a day. And, Mrs Devine, for goodness sake feed the girl. She is wholly underweight.'

Walking home, we hardly speak and I can guess what's worrying Nana. If that doctor got together with Val, they could make up a report saying I get left alone and no fed right. They'd take me away for sure. We stop at the chemist and the antibiotics are the size for a horse to swallow.

Martin is waiting at our door to see if I want to go to Springburn Baths. Nana mutters about exercise and makes me go.

We walk for ten minutes without saying a word. This isn't right, Martin's never quiet. And he never walks fast. He's deliberately staying ahead so I don't see his face. Then he blurts out Samantha's name and I understand. He's ready to talk about Dummy Railway Day.

'See if I went with you, bet none of it would've happened,' his voice is low and serious like a normal boy, 'we'd have went right to The Screke and you'd be OK.'

'It's no your fault,' I say, 'it was stupid Sid's fault. It was him that found her.'

'How did you no just run away, Janey?' he goes, stopping to look at me. 'How did you stay to look at a dead body? I'd fucking freak out, get right off my mark.'

'Nobody knows what they'd do. I wasn't even thinking about her being dead.' Martin's eyebrows are scrunched together and he's chewing his knuckle like it's a bar of toffee.

'Just as well you weren't there, you'd have shat yourself,' I say. He's no sure whether to laugh, no sure whether he deserves blame. 'Member how you crapped your scants the night of the Yeti?' I try.

Martin does the Yeti then and I shove him in a hedge and we're OK again. I can't let him feel guilty about this, nobody should feel guilty except me. And the killer. Then he says, 'Hey, did you watch that one with the murdered body in *The Professionals*? You see this guy, Mickey somebody, finding a body in an alley, it's been shot about five times and it's fucking gross, and Mickey nicks something out the dead guy's pocket that's important to the government. And Bodie and Doyle get called in cos the dead guy's a politician or something. And then, Bodie gets in a fight with this security guy—'

I grab his arm. 'What happened to Mickey that took the evidence?' Martin's still yakking away. 'Martin, what happened to the guy?' I say, much louder.

He stops. 'How? You steal something? You a spy or something?' He's laughing but it's no funny. No one bit. 'Mickey got slapped about to make him talk. Then he got the jail. And there's this bit when Bodie and Doyle chase the killer in their motor, and they run him over and . . .'

When he's older Martin's going to be a punk drummer, and to stop him talking I ask about the new U.K. Subs single. He switches to a demonstration of the drums on 'Stranglehold' and even adds the hi-hat, whatever that is. But all the time, I'm thinking about Mickey that got slapped and jailed.

One good thing about Martin, he plays mad fun games that your pals would slag you for and we have a laugh in the pool. Swimming is about the only thing I'm good at and we mess around, kidding on the gunge leaking out my knee is turning everybody into toxic zombies. The lifeguard starts shouting at some big boys diving in, they shout back and it makes me think about the men shouting at the hotel when Jimmy was all bloody. I start shaking and snivelling and Martin takes my hand to pull me out. I push him away and sink to the bottom of the deep end till the lifeguard blows his whistle and tells us to get out.

Martin has enough money for one hot chocolate. He takes a swig, then hands me the paper cup and pats my arm. You never know what's going to upset Martin – when his wee sister got knocked down, he shrugged and said she'd be OK; when Sid got knocked down, he cried for a day. If Martin starts acting all sad and worried around me, everything will be a million times worse. I tell him I'm fine, that I just swallowed too much chlorine and he takes the hot chocolate back. That's way better.

Nana is back to ranting. I prefer shouty-angry because quiet-angry makes me worry. She makes me eggs-beat-up-in-a-cup, blabbering about good working-class food.

'The damn cheek of that big lump casting aspersions like

that. All the women on our side are thin,' she says. 'What's yon thingamy when you inherit your shape or hair colour, like being ginger? And see this?' Nana pats her big belly. 'This is four years on a jam doughnut machine. Exercise. I'll exercise her, the lazy so-and-so, sitting on her backside behind a desk all day.'

She smacks a plastic bag full of fruit in front of me, like I'm the one that mentioned it. 'There. Fruit,' she goes, still all moany. 'I had to walk right along to the Cross. No even an apple in the Red Shop, and the old fruit shop turned into a bookies. Then, that Sid Vicious nearly had me over when Colette let her cat out.'

Sid hears his name and trots over, wagging his tail. He whines a bit when I poke his nose with my spoon. He's lucky I'm no holding a fork.

Nana plumps into her chair, feet on the footstool, ready for her forty winks. All the mums I know go out to work, do the shopping and cleaning, and still aren't tired. I wish Nana wasn't old, I wish she wasn't old enough to die soon.

I make her tea and put some of the teeny sandwiches on her saucer. The news is on Radio Clyde, and she's switched from complaining about the doctor to ranting about Mrs Thatcher.

'Shush a minute, Nana,' I say loudly, and turn up the radio.

'. . . in connection with a recent attack at The Western Hotel. Police have taken the unusual step of naming the wanted man as Louis McLure, last known address in the North of Glasgow. Police are warning the public not to approach McLure but to contact the nearest police station. Meanwhile, protestors gathered in George Square today for the arrival of—'

'Louis McLure,' I say, 'that's Lulu.'

'It must be him stabbed Jimmy.' Nana is pure shocked and crosses herself. 'And if this is the crime gang feud they're talking about, they might link him to Samantha's killing,' she says and now I'm pure shocked.

Another secret that I shouldn't have kept.

Chapter 26

My feet are laupin and only an hour into the shift. Old age doesn't come alone, as my mother used to say, and it's bringing the whole flaming gang for me. It's hard enough cleaning but Tuesdays doing my barmaid are hellish. My tablets are supposed to help with the swelling but now I wouldn't trust that Dr MacTavish to treat a dog. Thank God Cathy's back on at five.

The bandy-legged postie has been on the Guinness since opening. He's three sheets to the wind but still manages to light his damned pipe. I move to the end of the bar to escape the stench but the memories come anyway.

My husband had two passions in life – smoking, and throwing his weight about. The factory work wrecked his lungs and he had to give up fags, but every night he treated himself to a pipe. And every weekend he treated himself to a spot of wife-battering. The first time he slapped me was for being 'too fucking moany'. I was so surprised that I laughed. Laughed. Then the fear and embarrassment took hold. Like a lot of these bad men, Donald never hit me where it would show, and never hard enough that I needed a doctor. At the time, these things made me grateful.

'Here, you,' Tottie-Heid shouts, 'gonnae hurry and serve them wummin in the snug? Fuck sake, my wan-legged granny could work faster than you.'

One of these days, one of these days that man will push me too—

'Maggie,' Stuart arrives to restock the gantry, 'meant to tell you, there was a lassie in asking for you last night,' he says, 'went right out my heid.' He's obviously not himself, needs a shave and a wash, and there's a new despair in his eyes. I have a feeling he's off the wagon.

'A lassie? A wee lassie?'

'Big lassie. Twenties maybe. Ordered a half-cider and took her time wi it even after you-know-who tolt her women are no allowed to drink at the bar. Left her phone number and Cathy put it in the wummin's lavvie so he wouldnae see it.'

'Wonder who that might be? Thanks, Stuart. And listen, son, if you're struggling, remember I'm here.' He nods and looks at his feet. It's hard for men to talk, and daft that they don't.

I'm on the way to get the phone number when Tottie-Heid shouts me into the office, and there's the Edgar brothers standing there. More trouble. I silently pray to the Virgin Mother that it's nothing to do with Janey or the murder.

'All here now,' Tottie-Heid says. 'Right, gents, sit yourself down.' He's arranging chairs and fussing to clear his desk. Puts me in mind of a wean trying to be teacher's pet. 'Maggie, bring us a bottle. Whyte & Mackay suit yous?'

'Bring it yoursel, man,' Jimmy Edgar tells him. 'Want to sit, missus? We need a word.' Jimmy's dressed in one of these tracksuits although I doubt he's ever played sport in his life. Duncan Edgar would look like any other toerag in a Rangers top if it wasn't for the beautiful baby in his arms. A sleeping angel in a lace shawl and frilly blue bonnet, just weeks old. I nip my cigarette.

Tottie-Heid comes back with whisky and four glasses.

'Fuck you waiting for?' Duncan says, shifting the baby to pour himself a drink. 'Beat it.' Even under the drinker's red of his puffy cheeks, Tottie-Heid blushes and I can't stop my smile.

'What's the baby's name?' I ask.

'Duncan. Three lassies, and a boy at last. Want a go?'

I hold out my arms to welcome the warmth and breathe in his goodness. Ach, there's nothing nicer.

'No the best circumstances Ah know, but it was good to meet you at the funeral, Maggie, and we've been tolt you can help us out, know,' Duncan says quietly. We're all quiet, wary of waking wean Duncan. His father downs one whisky and pours another.

'It's about Lulu,' Jimmy says. 'You know he's done a runner? Dirty lanky big cunt. Now, we're no getting you mixed up in any of our business here and we're no explaining why we want him, but we want him before the polis get him.'

'No doubt yous do, but what's it got to do with me?' I ask.

'He's got family in Possil,' Duncan says. 'His da and ma are The Jungle, cousins in Hamiltonhill. We're asking everybody up your way to keep an eye. Big Des Grey's on it but you've got different pals, especially the ones at your chapel—'

'Lulu's mob are bastarding left-footers like yourself, man,' Jimmy puts in cheerily.

'Keep your ears open at Mass, at the shops, this dive.' Duncan waves around Tottie-Heid's pride and joy. The office is just a bit of the store room separated with chipboard walls and it's a certainty that Tottie-Heid is hearing all this. 'Even your lassie might pick something up from other weans. Will you do that for us?'

'We're no spying for anybody,' I say, loud enough that the baby stirs.

'Here, Ah'll take him, he likes to be on the move,' Jimmy says, moving with the care of an old man. That'll be the stab wound playing up. No wonder he wants to get a hold of Lulu.

Duncan waits till they're out the room, then leans across the desk. Up close, I notice the white seam of an old scar on his cheek and his nose has been broken so often it resembles misshapen dough.

'This is no a case of spying,' he says. 'What if this bastard killed

Samantha? For your wee grandwean's sake, would you no want him out the way?'

'Dear Christ, I didn't think of that.' But in my head, Taxi Alex is talking about forensics, and that librarian is smiling his sly smile. Would it be right to mention them? Instead, I ask, 'What makes you sure it's Lulu? Is it the newspapers?'

'Fuck the papers. And fuck the polis. All Ah know is there was no reason for Lulu to chib Jimmy, but he did. And that's enough to get him in a room and find out if he did the same to Billy's lassie. Now, will you let me know if you hear anything?' I nod and tell him I'll do my best. Tottie-Heid's desk is as untidy and smelly as the man himself and Duncan has to rummage for something to write on. 'That's Ashfield Cabs' number, phone anytime, even if it's only a whisper. OK?'

I nod again but I honestly don't know any McLures. They certainly don't go to our Mass but I could ask if they're St Agnes'. It's just one damned thing after another with this whole terrible business. I wish to God it hadn't been Janey in the old railway that morning.

Jimmy puts his head round the door to say the baby needs feeding.

'One last thing, you keep this between oursels. No a word, especially if you see Billy Watson, that poor cunt's got enough on his plate,' Duncan says, then slides some fivers across the desk. 'For your trouble.'

'Put that away, Maggie Devine is no for sale,' I say, then realize how it sounds. As if anybody would be interested in buying my old body. I nearly laugh.

'Fuck sake, it's only a wee bung.' Duncan forces the money into my hand. 'Take it and get new specs.'

My glasses broke when I fainted and I've got them taped up with an Elastoplast. Wish a plaster could help my big black-and-blue backside too.

Tottie-Heid has already swooped in to suck up to the Edgars so I don't get a chance to return the money. Thirty pounds. In what world is that 'only a wee bung'?

'Hello? Hello? Is that Heather?' I hope to God this is the right number. It was written on a beermat so it could be anybody, up to anything.

'Hold on,' some man says and I hear him shouting her name. She'd better no take too long, whoever she is, I've only got a two pence piece and the phone box has been used as a toilet.

'Yeah? Who's this?' She sounds young but everybody's young to me now.

'Em, I heard you were looking for me in The Glen.'

'Is that Mrs Devine? Hi, hello. I'm one of Samantha Watson's mates, we met at the funeral. Don't know if you remember me, Mrs Devine?'

'Are you the brown one? Or the one with the hair?'

'I was the one standing with Janey when you woke after the faint.'

'Aye, I know you. You had workie's boots on with your dress.' I liked this lassie because she had her arm round Janey. 'What can I do for you, hen?'

'It's nothing really, it's just, after you left the funeral, I found a watch. It's small with a pretty strap and I thought it might be Janey's. She said you worked in The Glen, so I brought it in.'

'That was nice of you but she's no got a watch.'

'Oh, right.' Heather's quiet for a minute. 'Do you mind if I give it to her anyway? If I hand it in, the staff will just keep it. My mate works in hotels so I know what goes on. It might be good for Janey to have a watch for Secondary.'

'Aye, you give her it. Nice of you to think of her.'

'Janey's brilliant. Gave us a laugh on a terrible day.' I smile when she says this. 'Mrs Devine, would it be OK if I took her for ice cream or something? I live near Byres Road and there's a nice café there.'

'I'm sure she'd love that, sweetheart. Listen, my money's nearly up, so tell me quick what day and time. I'll put her on the bus, and you meet her at the Botanic Gardens.'

After the business with the Edgars, speaking with Heather fair cheered me up. What a wee smasher. I don't understand why, but Janey likes talking about Samantha Watson and this outing could be a help.

Chapter 27

87 days

I can't get to sleep. Tomorrow will be my first day out alone in months and my head is spinning with Heather. Wonder what we'll do? She might take me somewhere amazing like a gig, or, or a record shop and buy me something. Wonder what she'll be wearing? What should I wear? And I wonder how she knew where Nana worked? I never tell anybody that. Probably one of the old gossipers at the hotel.

Down on the street some big girls are laughing as a guy on a motorbike circles round them. Possil is never quiet. I decide to sort my newspaper cuttings.

The first is old and yellow.

Maryhill Miracle

Hero fireman pulls tot from gas explosion carnage

That's me. I'm the Maryhill Miracle. Aunty Angela gave me the cuttings when I was seven, and said it was important that I know. Nana was angry but let me keep them when I begged. There's a picture of the hero in his fireman helmet and our tenement all wrecked like a pile of black Lego. You can see a broken sink lying on the street, and a man's glove. I'd like to know if it's my dad's glove but Nana doesn't like talking about it. Another paper's got Mammy and Dad on their wedding day, and Donna in her First Communion dress. I've got the same black wavy hair as Dad and Donna and the same wonky teeth as my mam. We look like a family but I don't remember any of them.

Body Found

The unidentified body of a woman has been found in North Glasgow. The discovery was made on Saturday morning by a local dog walker. Police are refusing to comment further.

That's me too, but this time, they weren't allowed to print my name. It's the law even though everybody knew. There's no more mentions of me in any of the Samantha stories after that.

Then, it's the report about the funeral.

Shocking Scenes at Funeral Reception

Following reports of a serious assault, emergency services were called to The Western Hotel on Thursday. Horrified mourners watched as James 'Skinny Jimmy' Edgar (31) was carried to a waiting ambulance during the funeral reception for local murder victim Samantha Watson (22).

Witnesses say Edgar did not appear conscious and had facial injuries. An elderly woman was also treated at the scene for shock. A spokeswoman for Glasgow Royal Infirmary described Edgar's condition tonight as 'comfortable'.

A police source today refused to corroborate speculation that the attack is linked to previous criminal activity but confirmed they are following definite lines of inquiry.

I'm one of the 'Horrified mourners' and Nana's the 'elderly woman'. I wonder if she's seen this. Bet she'd be chuffed at being elderly instead of old. There's a photo of Jimmy Edgar and, according to Nana, he's home now and all better, which is good.

When the police questioned everybody at the hotel, they kept Nana longest cos they thought she'd collapsed after seeing the fight. They got that wrong because Glencoe Suite windows don't look out to the car park. I did what Lulu said though, and kept my mouth zipped. The police took Mr Watson away, which was pure rotten. While Nana was out for the count, Heather and Uncle Hugh came to help me. They had to tell me about ten times what was happening, it was like they were speaking Klingon.

In films, they drink milk to help them sleep. But when I go in the kitchen a big shadowy demon crawls out from under the sink. I open my mouth to scream but feel his nose against my leg. Stupid Sid, he scares everybody. He is really massive with black spiky fur, a scabby bald patch on his belly, and a sticky-out fang that makes him look angry all the time.

I think about the day two years ago when we brought him home. At the Cat and Dog Home, I was jittery with excitement and wandered past every cage. Finally, finally I was getting a dog. It was very smelly and some dogs were barking and howling, others just lying about looking sad. Nana got fed up because I was taking so long to decide. I kept going, 'That one. No, this one. Wait, that one.' One of the workers brought out a new puppy, white with brown patches, a wee girl dog. She wagged her tail and licked my face and if somebody asked you to draw a perfect puppy, you would draw her. Nana said that one seems friendly enough, let's take it and get home before my feet start. Then we saw him, in a cage hissel because it was time for him to get put down. It was the way his eyes were, not like he was begging me to rescue him, just that he hoped I would. His eyes were full of hope. Next day, there was a picture in the paper of the Sex Pistols messing about in front of Buckingham Palace. Nana held it up beside the new dog and said, 'Who does that one with all the studs remind you of?' I still liked shitey Abba then, but I knew Sid Vicious was the perfect name. His original name was Lucky and that was just taking the mickey.

I sit on the wobbly stool in the dark kitchen. There's no milk but this is our most boring room and maybe that'll make me sleepy. And, I never see Samantha in here. Sid starts pushing his bowl around like it's feeding time, he never gets anything right, stupid dog. Can't even train him.

When Martin's big brother goes to the pictures, me and Martin always ask him to tell us about it. Neil is brilliant at describing films, doing the voices and actions, and it's as if you saw it too. When he did *The Hills Have Eyes*, we were shitting ourselves for weeks. Last year, Neil went to see this film called *The Boys from Brazil*. It's about a Nazi hunter and this boy, Hitler's son or clone or some mad thing, who sets his Doberman Pinschers on an evil scientist. Neil acted out the fight where the dogs tear the baddie to pieces, and Martin said, 'We should teach Sid Vicious to do that. In case any Nazis attack us. Or the Fleeto.' We used the same code words as Hitler-boy and pulled a big smelly teddy out the bins and dressed it up as the baddie. We tried for a whole week but Sid kept using the Nazi scientist as a pillow and we couldn't move for laughing.

Sid might look scary but he's totally useless as protection, especially against a murderer. When the murder slides back into my brain, all the excitement about Heather vanishes. I wish I could time travel and go back to that day we had a pure laugh with the teddy scientist. Or go way back, to the day at the Cat and Dog Home. It wouldn't matter about being babyish ten again, I would choose the lovely puppy and everything would be different.

Chapter 28

I'm no sure if it's the dream or a noise that wakes me but I'm glad of it. Takes ten minutes of deep breathing and prayers to shake the panic that he's come back and waiting for me, belt at the ready.

A long time since Donald Devine haunted my sleep.

After tracking the scraping sound to the kitchen, I tell Sid Vicious to leave his bowl and get back to sleep. Then I keek in to make sure the telly is switched off, costs a fortune in electricity when I forget. And there's Janey asleep on the couch with my jacket over her. The wee soul, if anybody knows about nightmares it's her.

I sit to watch her sleep. Her wee feet are sticking out and I notice a cluster of red bites on her ankles and marks where she's been scratching. No doubt it's midges at this time of year. But as if he knows what I'm thinking, Sid Vicious wanders in and starts biting at his tail. Fleas. That's all we need with the price of flea powder. Janey mumbles and turns, her face anything but peaceful.

I think about the day ten years ago, when I brought her home. At Yorkhill Hospital, I was jittery with grief and wandered the corridors looking for her. How many days after the accident was it? That time is still no clearer in my mind but I do remember

Social Services turning up to say Janey was ready to leave hospital and there was no one else to take her.

Vinnie's parents wanted nothing to do with the baby and were going back to Italy. At the funeral, they couldn't even look at her. Maybe they saw her as too big a reminder, or maybe they blamed her for living, I don't know. Vinnie's brothers kept in touch for a couple of years, visiting now and again, but one by one took their families to Pisa too. You never really know what's in anybody's mind, but it felt like abandonment to me.

I went to the hospital and found the ward where they'd been treating Janey for a cut to the hand. They said it was likely a result of the fireman pulling her free, the only injury to show for an entire tenement collapsing around her. She was in a cot with bars that looked like a prison and she put her wee arms up for me to lift her out. But when the nurses came to wave her off, the wee soul was all confused and brought the place down to be taken from them. To be honest, I felt like crying myself. A baby was too much, too much on top of my pain.

What would have happened if I hadn't taken her that day? No doubt somebody would've adopted a bonnie wee girl, but what about me? Without Janey . . . without Janey I would be long gone.

Chapter 29

88 days

It's exciting being on a bus yourself but when it's near your stop it's a pure panic you'll miss it. The rain's teeming down and the bus windows are boggin but I get it right.

Heather is standing at the Botanics' gate, wearing army trousers and a pink jumper, and holding a giant stripy umbrella. Don't like her jumper but army trousers are the best. She sees me and runs across the road.

'Hey, Janey,' she goes, 'how you doing? Your gran OK now? I'm glad you came. Man, trust me to bring you out on the pishiest day of the summer. Lucky I've got this monster, c'mon under.'

I squeeze in tight and she takes my arm. She's no too much taller than me so the umbrella covers us both. She's dead chatty and says my new haircut is cool like Joan Jett. I can't decide whether to say anything about Lulu. Does Heather know her secret boyfriend stabbed somebody?

The watch she gives me is red with black hands and just a bit scuffed. The strap's too big but Heather says that's an easy fix.

'Man alive, I wish I had delicate wrists like you. Mine are like tree trunks,' she says and holds one out for me to see. It's no like a tree trunk at all.

If you've got a watch, there's no excuse for coming in late, but since I'm never out playing now, I'm happy to have it. I put it in my cagoule pocket for safety.

'How about we just go round to mine?' Heather says. 'My bedsit's not far and it'll save getting soaked.' This sounds better than a café, I love seeing where people live. I nod, and in a mumbly voice, she goes, 'Thank God.' She must really hate the rain.

'What is a bedsit?' I ask.

'Bedsit is another name for midden,' she says. 'Nah, it's actually when your whole house is shoved into one room. Bed, cooker, sink, chairs, everything.'

'Even your toilet?'

She laughs at this but no cos I've said something stupid, just cos it's funny. We talk about how mad it would be if your lavvie pan was in your living room, and as we walk, I pretend that Heather is Donna. We are best pals, no like Asha and her sisters, and one day I'll live with Donna in the bedsit. Guess that's daft.

'Cheese and onion, or salt and vinegar?'

We're in Goodies, which is the best shop name ever. Heather is going to make us rolls and crisps, which Nana never makes. She also buys Penguins, Sugar Puffs, coffee and cans of Coke, and that's going to be my shopping when I leave home.

The bedsit is right across from the shops, in a big old grey building that's no like any of the Possil houses.

'It's a bit of a pit, Janey, I'm not good with housework,' Heather says. I tell her it's OK, I've been in the Smelly Kellys' house.

The main door has a glass panel and four locks. Then a gloomy hall with a bunch of old chairs and wardrobes at the far end. Wardrobes are my favourite furniture cos one saved my life. There's a smell of cooking but not anything nice. Heather's bedsit is the middle door out of six, and it's got a cracking nameplate, drawn with felt-pens and cut-out pictures of mushrooms. Hope she doesn't put mushrooms in our rolls, they taste like snotters. She puts her key in, then stops.

'We're friends, aren't we?' she says.

I feel a bit proud. 'Aye, for sure.'

'Then you'll forgive me. Just, just don't freak out.'

It must be something more than mess. She starts turning the key, and there's a noise inside the bedsit. Heather grabs my sleeve then opens the door.

Lulu is standing there, holding a hammer.

'Jesus, what you playing at? Give us that,' Heather says and snatches the hammer.

'Cannae be too careful,' Lulu says, keeping his eyes on me.

'You OK, Janey?' Heather asks. I don't know if I am. 'Come in and we'll explain. C'mon, don't stand out here, the neighbours aren't nice.'

I don't want Lulu putting me over his shoulder again so I go inside. I'm no even slightly excited to see a wee black and white cat sleeping on the bed.

Then I realize what Lulu must be wanting. 'It wasn't me that told the police, I didn't grass, Lulu. I kept my mouth zipped like you said, honest to God—'

'It's OK, it's OK. Nobody thinks that, we—' Heather says.

'Fucking Skinny Jimmy grassed,' Lulu goes. 'Before he was even out the hospital, cunt was boo-hooing to anybody that would listen. Even the fucking polis. That bastard deserves another tanking.'

'Go and stick the kettle on, you. Let me and Janey have a talk. Coffee's in the bag, and butter the rolls for us.' She's pretty bossy and Lulu goes to an alcove that is also a toaty kitchen.

Me and Heather sit on the bed cos the couch is covered with clothes and books and records. I want to go home but can't help stroking the cat.

'Her name's Boo. Like Boo Radley, in the book. Not as good as Sid Vicious, that's class. Boo and Lu, bonkers, right?'

I don't laugh. Her hand touches mine as she rubs Boo's ears and I pull away.

'You probably hate me now,' she says, 'don't blame you. But I had to help him, Janey. Lulu's in big trouble. He's a wild bugger but that doesn't make him a killer.'

Skinny Jimmy isn't dead, he's fine. Does she mean Samantha?

Heather tries to touch my hand again. 'It was very snide to lie to get you but give us a chance, then, if you don't like it, you can leave and never see my stupid face again.'

Lulu brings a flowery plastic tray with coffees, Coke and rolls. Heather goes, 'And where's the crisps?'

Worrying about why I'm here makes my belly ache but the roll and crisps helps and Boo is ace. She's trying to catch the watch as I dangle it, and it's good to have something to do while Heather talks.

'Remember at the funeral I told you that me and Lulu were going together? Since then, everything's turned to shit. He's been hiding here with me since the thing with Jimmy Edgar.' That was nearly a week ago and I wonder if he brought clean pants and socks. 'That's one of the reasons we got you here. We trust you, Janey. You knew we were together but you've obviously not told anyone.'

Nobody would be interested in who's winching who, it's daft playground stuff. But I suppose Nana would have liked to know. She was saying we should keep an eye for Lulu.

'Lucky we hadnae tolt anybody,' Lulu says. 'Ah always said it, didn't Ah, doll? To keep things quiet. Polis would've been at your door, Eggman, fuck knows who else.'

'Now, here's the other reason we got you here,' Heather says. 'A while ago, Sammy told me about a guy who fancied her, one of Billy's team. He'd been in love with her for ages but Sammy knocked him back. After her first boyfriend, she was, she was a bit of a mess when it came to guys.'

Lulu's walking up and down, all lanky and jumpy, his head swivelling at every wee noise. He's like the tramp pacing about in the police station, with better trousers.

'It was Lulu who fancied Sammy. He was hurt when she said no and he did something. Something really, really stupid and really underhand.' Heather is talking loudly and slowly now.

'Aye, OK, OK. Me and you have done that bit. Just keep going,' Lulu says. Heather gives him a dirty look and stomps to the alcove to get the Penguins.

'Sorry about all that shite at the hotel,' Lulu says, sitting beside me, 'didnae mean to hurt you or nothing, hen.' He rolls a cigarette, making it massive like a fat cigar, and the tobacco reeks.

Heather comes back. 'OK, next bit,' she says, her mouth full of biscuit. 'Lulu took photos of Sammy. Polaroids.'

'What's so bad about that?' This is more stuff I don't want to hear.

'She was steaming,' Lulu says, 'right out her napper. Ah was at her house, and her da wis out a message. Samantha came back from the pub and started hammering to get in, couldnae even use her key. Then she fell flat on her arse. Made me fucking carry her up to her room. Singing, shouting, going—'

'Yeah, OK, I'm sure Janey gets the idea. When this big imbecile took the photos, Sammy was passed out on the floor, and worst part, she'd stripped off to her underwear after throwing up.'

Dead Samantha's underwear was all ripped and pulled off, her skin too bare and battered. My hand goes to my knee but I can't mess with my scab because of the daft bandage, then I remember the envelope in the jewellery box and the way Lulu snatched it. It must've been the Polaroids and I feel sick that I nearly looked at them.

'That's horrible,' I say, and shift up the bed so I'm no near Lulu. 'Can I just go now?'

'Look, it wisnae planned or nothing. Ah only went into her room to check she hadnae choked on her sick. And Ah was pissed off, know?' Lulu says in a whiny voice. 'When she knocked me back, Samantha made me feel like scum. Ah thought she was looking down her snoot at me. Ah was just gonnae shove the photos in her face and say, "See? See? You're just as bad as the rest of us." But Ah didnae, cos it, it wisnae right. Ah handed her the photos and tolt her it was a joke. And know the mad thing? She said sorry. Sorry she got in that state.'

'Women have every right to get wasted.' Heather is affronted. 'Sammy had nothing to be sorry for.'

'Ah didnae think in a million years Samantha would keep they photos,' Lulu goes, 'total shock when you found them, hen.'

Lulu lowers his head and Heather rubs his back. His quiff is just a floppy greasy mess and he looks less hard without his leather jacket. His leg is vibrating, shaking the whole bed, and he's wearing pink socks with parrots on them. Guess he didn't bring any spare. Heather looks different too. At the funeral, she wore bright make-up and now her face is just pale and empty. They both look younger, like they're still at school.

Heather has gone to see what a noise is. It's likely just her neighbour's synthesizer but Lulu jumped out his skin.

'Neighbour's a bam,' Lulu says, his ear at the door to listen. Boo is hiding behind the curtains, which are closed even though it's afternoon. Lulu's likely worried about people looking in and seeing him. I wander about a bit. The wallpaper's got brown stains like Jean's damp patches and the manky plates would give Nana a heart attack. I decide that me and Donna would not live in a bedsit, we'd have a proper house, with a room each and no smell. And it'd be right next door to Nana.

Even though I'd like to be in a silent huff, I ask, 'What was

Skinny Jimmy saying that made yous fight?' I had a fight in Primary 6, when I spread it that Jackie wore a wig. Probably not what was going on with Lulu and Jimmy.

'That bastard's been winding me up for years, cannae stand him. Total speed freak, you know?' I nod, but he didn't drive fast when he took me home. 'At the hotel, Eggman sent me and him outside to check that woman reporter wisnae back, or the polis wurnae sneaking about. By the way, you talk to the polis again?'

I say aye, then add, 'But I don't want to.'

Lulu spits. Right on Heather's carpet. 'Nobody likes a grass, hen,' he says and I get a wee shiver.

The noise in the hall stops and Heather comes back. She and Lulu sit on the bed again.

'Did you explain to Janey what happened with Jimmy in the car park?' she asks.

'Aye, that's what Ah'm doin. Me and Jimmy were checkin the car park when he started bad-mouthing Samantha. Ah know Ah was a cunt with those photos, but Ah really liked Samantha, liked her from the minute Ah saw her. Ah was shattered about what happened. And angry too, know? Thinking that if she'd been ma bird, she'd still be alive. My heid was fucked till Ah met Heather.' He touches her hair and she touches his hand and I look away. 'Anyway, this prick Jimmy was coming wide, going on about how Samantha always came to him to buy toke, always sniffing round him and what a ride she was—'

'That's enough, Lulu,' Heather goes, 'you don't need to repeat that filth.'

'Fair dos, doll. So, Ah lost the rag. Said Ah was gonnae tell Billy that Jimmy was dealing to his daughter. Fuck, imagine what Billy would do? But Ah'm no grass. No way. Ah've no even tolt Billy what the Edgars are planning with MacQuarrie—'

'We don't want to hear about that. Do we, Janey?' Heather says, but I wouldn't mind knowing.

'Anyways, Jimmy pulled a knife. A toaty wee thing like you'd use to sharpen a pencil and Ah laughed and stuck the heid on him. Fat boy fell and landed on his knife and when he saw his blood, he fainted. Out cold. Dead funny, so it was. He must've told everybody it was me, but see if Ah was going to stab Skinny Jimmy Edgar, Ah'd use a fucking machete.'

Heather shakes her head like she doesn't approve, but I see her wee smile.

'Obviously the Edgar brothers are looking for Lulu, and the cops too, and we're working out what to do about that,' Heather says, then goes quiet till Lulu nudges her. 'What we need from you, Janey, is to get us the Polaroids.'

It's still raining. Heather was going to take me to the bus stop but I wanted away from her. Now I'm lost cos I went the wrong way.

Old ladies are great and when I ask one where the Botanic Gardens is, she takes my hand and walks me right there. She's wearing scratchy woolly gloves and I have to listen to her crazy story about a giant rat called Toby that's been living with her since the bin strike. But it's still better than listening to anything those two said.

They want me to go to Mr Watson's house and find the Polaroid photos.

First Val, now Heather and Lulu. They must all think I'm an eejit, and I am for believing them. But I'm really angry too. All that pretending. It's worse than me sooking up to Andrea to get invited to her birthday party.

The photos are still in the pocket of Lulu's leather jacket. He left in a big hurry and the jacket's hanging on the second peg behind Mr Watson's front door.

'Billy's always on about what a wee sweetheart you are,' Lulu said, 'and what a decent woman your granny is. Yous could visit no sweat, say yous're worried about how he's doing.'

Then, while Nana and Mr Watson are talking, I'm supposed to ask to use the toilet and grab the photos as I pass. They're still in the envelope so I won't even need to look at them. Even if somebody sees me, they'll think I'm just dipping the jacket for money. No problems, easy peasy.

'Ah don't care what Billy does to me for Jimmy Edgar, but, fucking hell, Ah don't want him thinking Ah killed Samantha. Ah don't want anybody thinking that, specially when Ah've no even got an alibi. Have Ah, Heather?'

'If anyone sees those photos,' Heather said, 'there's no hope. They'll say Lulu's a sicko. And he's not, Janey, he's not. He didn't kill Sammy, I swear he didn't.' She started to cry then.

'You owe me this, hen,' Lulu said, poking his finger in my face, 'doin your nosey, finding they photos. Your fault they're even in my pocket.' I started to cry then too.

When she came to see me out, Heather said sorry. Sorry for everything. She said I'm clever and lovely and don't deserve any of this, and when this is over, we really will go for ice cream. Then she said if I decide not to go to Mr Watson's, that's understandable, but she truly hoped that I would.

A woman at the bus stop says there's an 18 due at ten past four. I don't know how long that is, cos I shoved the watch under Heather's bed. Boo can have it.

Chapter 30

There's one day in the year worse than all the rest. Birthdays are bad of course, but it's 16th July that brings me to a standstill.

This morning, I went upstairs to use the Khans' phone. Mrs Khan was away to her bed after nightshift, and it was Mr Khan who let me in. It's weekends he works, with a brother in Shawlands. According to Janey, the Khans are saving for a bought-house over that way. There's some nice places in the Southside, and with the name-calling the family gets from some of the dirty bigots round here, I hope they manage something soon.

'I was wondering if I could use your phone again. Just for a wee minute,' I said when he opened the door. Mr Khan's a thin wiry man, a bit swamped by his own beard, with a much stronger Indian accent than his wife. He ushered me in and offered tea and breakfast if I wanted. Then he chased his girls out the living room to give me privacy.

Right away, Angela knew why I was phoning.

'Can't believe they're gone ten years. I keep thinking about the day of Neil and Donna's First Communion. Member that?' The Khan girls' school photographs crowding the coffee table are making this conversation even harder. 'We were all together that day, every one of us, and the sun came out just as the weans were leaving the church. It's like yesterday. Ten years, Maggie, it's no real.'

She had a plan ready for Janey. Usually in the summer holidays, Janey would be at their house, but today they'll come and collect her for a trip to the pictures. What would I do without Angela?

Then I phoned Tottie-Heid. He was ready to get tore in when I said I wouldn't be in, but shut up sharpish at the mention of 'women's problems'. It's a fair number of years since I've been troubled by that and it shows the ignorance of the man when he accepted it as truth. Glaikit so-and-so.

Mr Khan wouldn't take any money for the call, but he did ask me to sign his latest petition. He campaigns for road safety. You see him with his wee group at yon terrible junction on Hawthorn Street waving placards, or outside the post office collecting signatures. The shameful thing is, some ignoramuses refuse to sign. It was Mr Khan got a lollypop lady for their weans but they don't like the colour of his skin. Makes you sick.

As he saw me out, the youngest daughter appeared behind him, sneaking along the lobby on her tummy. Mr Khan's face lit up, he knew fine well she was there, but when she grabbed his ankles, he pretended a big fright. Then he swooped her up, the two of them struggling to keep their joy quiet for fear of waking Mrs Khan.

I walked Sid Vicious to keep him going till Gibby collects him, then stopped at Jean's to say I wouldn't be at dominoes. Angela and Martin arrived after lunch with a big story about Kirsty not wanting to stay with Neil and throwing a terrible tantrum. Going to the pictures is Janey's favourite, and I felt bad that she wasn't as excited as usual.

When they left and I was alone, I wished for a minute that I had a nice wee man like Mr Khan. A soft sort of man that would see me through this day. No often I feel that need.

I go into Janey's room and look at the Rothesay photograph. She's made a frame for it, using all her colours to draw hearts and write their names. I sit on the bed and let the wound open.

I know there's nothing special about grief, and like everybody in the war years, I had plenty of experience. But there's a different kind of suffering for those who lose a child. After the accident, I had to keep functioning for the baby, but it was such a mighty, bottomless heartbreak that it broke me, broke everything I was. All that was left was guilt and hurt, and for a time, that suited me fine. I certainly deserved the guilt.

It was Janey that saved me, of course. If I'd stayed in that bad place, I would have dragged her in there with me and that's no on. You have to stand up to grief, kick against it and put something of yourself back together. My mother managed it after the loss of two sons, but my poor father did not and his own life was shortened by a world that held nothing but his dead boys.

Even when you make the stand, you're never the same. Pieces of me were lost under the rubble of that tenement in Maryhill, lost forever.

Angela guessed that I wouldn't bother eating and brought me a hot bridie.

Martin is talking ten to the dozen. 'You need to go and see it, Maggie, it's mental. The baddie is going to drop poison gas on the whole world and that big massive guy with the metal teeth's in it and—'

'It's Aunty Maggie to you, cheeky wee devil,' Angela says, 'and let her eat her dinner in peace.'

'Yeah, but Aunty Maggie likes James Bond. Don't you? Don't you?'

'Course I do, son. You and Janey come and tell me all about it.'

Janey knows the date and knows I'm no at my best, so tonight she tidies round a wee bit. When I was her age, I already had to cook and clean up after my brothers and my father and I always swore I'd never ask the same of my daughters. Different times then, things are better for lassies now. Some things.

She gives me a right long hug before bed and I see tears in her eyes too.

The other day, she asked if we could go and visit Billy Watson, just to see if he's OK. I told her no but today I changed my mind. If Billy's agreeable, we'll drop in for half an hour. Regardless of what he does for his money, there's something about the man that I like. And when you're bereaved, it's wee things like people's kindness that get you back on track. Janey's compassion puts me to shame sometimes.

It's funny the things you remember that you aren't expecting. When Angela mentioned the First Communion, it came to me that Marie had a right sore foot that day. Tonight in bed, I hear her voice, clear as if she's in the room.

'Took the bin out in my slippers, Mammy, stepped on a broken bottle. You know what I'm like, never look where I'm going.'

Imagine that coming back. Maybe everything's still there.

Chapter 31

94 days

Wee kids are mad. They laugh at anything.

'Say it again, Janey, say it again.'

'Keech, Bum and Toley Fart, all went to Springburn Park.'

Me and Asha are looking after her wee sister, Jinky. That's no her real name but it's what everybody calls her. They'd better sort it before she starts school or she'll be Stinky Jinky Khan for her whole life.

Tomorrow, Asha's thirteen and she's allowed to get her ears pierced. She's been wanting it for years and years, and we were supposed to go today to get it done at Robin Hood. But we have to babysit instead.

We sit outside on the spare ground that's full of dog shite, and there's a few people here to sunbathe. I've never worked out why Possilpark has that name when there's no park. Nana made me bring Sid again and I've tied him to a pole. Asha wanted to tie Jinky too but I don't mind running about after her. Wee kids never pretend to like you just to get something.

Like Heather.

I wasn't going to help Heather and Lulu. I wasn't going to help till the guy in the lift. The other day after the visit, it was still lashing and when I got to the flats there was a man. He wore

Wranglers and desert boots so was definitely not old, but I couldn't see his face because he had an umbrella up. Indoors. When he got into the lift, he tilted it so I still couldn't see him. I stepped back and he caught the door as it closed. He was holding the lift open for me, and no even old people with nobody to talk to do that. My legs were numb and it was only the grinding clank of the door trying to shut that got me moving. I belted outside and ran into Gibby and Sid, both pretty dry so I don't think they'd walked far. Gibby was looking for a tap, and just to have somebody with me, I said there was a fifty pence piece down our couch. Umbrella man and the lift were gone but I was full of what-ifs. What if Heather's right and it wasn't Lulu? What if he got sent to jail anyway? And what if the real murderer is hanging about the flats?

Asha's put a blanket down for us to sit on.

'Jinky, get out the dirt and stop squeezing slugs,' she shouts.

When she first moved here, me and Asha loved playing in the dirt, digging holes all day at the Basin. Sometimes we hit red dirt, clay maybe, and I'd tell her it was Hell and we'd both run screaming and hide before Satan got us. That should be a funny memory but today it gives me the willies and I don't know why.

It's dead hot in the summer sun and I'm glad we're not in town. As well as Robin Hood, Asha wanted to traipse round cafés looking for a Saturday job. If you're fourteen, you can help with orders and wash the dishes. Asha can pass for fourteen, she got in to see an AA film and there was nudes in it. When we walk together, she likes to wrap her arm round my shoulder and I was desperate to be soft and pillowy like her. No any more.

'Can I give you your present now?' I ask. I bought earrings with Mr Watson's change, real silver studs and I don't know why I spent so much. Jinky runs over when I bring out the present, and Sid Vicious gets all excited at the sound of something being opened.

'Oh, Janey, exactly the ones I wanted,' Asha says and grabs me close. The heat of her. The chill of Samantha. She blushes when I shake her off and I feel rotten.

'Anything for Jinky?' the wee yin asks.

'If the van comes up, I'll get you something,' I tell her and she does a dance, a weird drunk Pinocchio dance. Me and Asha pish ourselves laughing, and everything feels good and ordinary and I wish it was this all the time.

'You sure this is right?' I ask, looking at the ice lolly.

'Yeah, it is. My cousin showed me, and she's pierced millions of ears.' Asha's decided that since she's got the silver studs, there's no point wasting her birthday money. You're supposed to freeze the ear and I'm using a chunk of Jinky's Strawberry Mivvi.

Asha's big sister, Reeta, had got off the bus and told us to bring Jinky in out the sun. In the flat, they had a fight about the babysitting, a strange quiet fight cos their mum's sleeping after nightshift. Asha eventually bit her sister's leg and now we don't have to babysit. And Reeta had to take Sid too.

I rub Asha's ear with melting Mivvi. She sits on the bed, one towel wrapped round her shoulders and another covering the mirror because she's scared to watch. The needle, the fat kind for darning, is still a bit warm from the cooker. You need heat to get rid of germs.

'Count to three, then shove it in,' she says.

The needle slides easily into Asha's skin, like a spoon going into ice cream. Like a knife going into a tummy. I pull it out and she does a brave closed-mouth scream. A blackness comes and Asha's voice sounds different, as if she's running in and out the room.

'Janey, is there a big hole? Is my earlobe hanging off?'
In and out. Stab. Stab. Stab.

'Told you,' Reeta says. She's kneeling on the floor holding my feet in the air. 'Told you she's not dead.' Her grip reminds me of something else, something bad, and I kick at her.

Asha is patting my hand and crying, the towel still around her shoulders. I must have fainted like Nana at the hotel. I sit up and Jinky puts her arms round my neck. Sid Vicious is here too, snuffling at my face, and the bedroom feels crowded and hot, shimmering like cartoon electricity.

'I— I'm going to go home now,' I say.

'No. Stay till my mum wakes, let her check you over,' Asha says.

'I'm OK, honest.' I stand and call Sid. He looks at me and wags his tail and everything tumbles in again.

I hear barking, not in Asha's bedroom but far away down the Dummy Railway, and Sid is barking because I'm touching a dead woman.

Chapter 32

The journey to Billy's was a lot easier when I came in the taxi. Three buses and then the last driver wouldn't let us on with Sid Vicious – there's no even any rabies in Scotland. A woman sitting near the front called him a hard-hearted so-and-so, and I was able to thank her when he threw her off. She was wearing a floral chiffon scarf that would have looked nice on somebody half her age. I've a cheek to talk in my lilac twinset. No that I'm wearing Sunday best for Billy Watson, it's just manners to make an effort.

There's no much effort in Billy's appearance, unironed trousers and a jumper with a bean stain. His hair seems whiter too but I may be imagining that. The house is still clean and tidy so he's not too far gone and he's genuinely pleased to see us.

'See what I found for you, wee darling,' he says, handing Janey a ball. 'I bet you're great at netball. The hoop's on the side of the garage, see and have a shot.'

Janey frets the dog will burst the ball, Billy says no to worry. We watch her at the window for a while. The ball's not going anywhere near the hoop but she's no giving up.

'That was good of you, Billy.'

'Good of yous to come all this way. I'm a social pariah since the funeral. Likely folk don't know what to say but it's no use being on your own.'

'You've still got all your thugs with you though, your wee criminal gang.' This is out of my mouth before I can stop it.

'Aye, I'm still up to neck in hoodlums.' Billy smiles, and I'm relieved he saw it as a joke. His terrible raw intensity seems to have gone, or maybe he's just hiding it better. 'Mon sit down, Maggie. I'll get your tea. Then you can listen to my proposition.'

The sound of the ball stoating in the driveway is very agreeable. It's always been my wish to have a garden, even a teeny bit of grass and dirt. During the war, my mother and I helped with the vegetable plots and I got right fond of planting. I suppose if you tried that now, your carrots would be pinched before fully grown. You can't blame people for that kind of theft, no when they're in need. Same with the ones that steal your washing. Colette-with-the-cat was in a right stooshie when she caught Wee Morag wearing the polo-neck that went missing from her line. Poor Morag, it was the first decent thing she had to wear in a long time.

Funny that, me thinking about thieves just as Billy Watson offers me a job.

'The taxi dispatchers split the shifts to suit their selves,' he tells me, 'and it's afternoons they need somebody. A couple of hours, the odd weekend and better money, guaranteed. What do you say?'

I'm taken aback, to be honest. The minicab office is just five minutes from the flats, and I imagine sitting calling for drivers would be a damn sight easier than cleaning The Glen. But it's no that straightforward. For one thing, why is Billy doing this for me? I've no known him long and it's no like we're friends. Another bigger thing, do I want to be working for drug peddlers?

'Well, eh, I'm no too sure the now, I, eh,' I say, busying myself with scone crumbs. Soft and buttery it was, I'd guess M&A Brown rather than City Bakeries. 'Thing is, Billy, eh—'

'No like you to be lost for words.'

He's at the window again, watching Janey, and his face is lighter now.

Earlier, he'd lost his composure when telling me that he thought he saw her. Samantha. A lassie in a shop with books under her arm, same haircut, a dress like one she wore. He'd gone racing across the road full of joy. When I told him that I still catch glimpses of women that might be Marie, of girls I'm certain are wee Donna, he was relieved to know it wasn't just him. It's a nasty deceitful trick your mind plays.

'So, you don't want the job, then?' Billy gives me a sour look. 'Worried about working somewhere dodgy? Is that it? Because it is legit.'

'That's no what *The Sunday Mail* says.'

'Christ almighty, woman. You believe all that fucking gossip? You do, don't you?'

He sits, looking disappointed rather than angry.

'Duncan Edgar is a hard bastard, you have to be in the private hire business, but all that Eggman shite? He laps it up, loves the legend, makes him feel like his da. I wouldn't be surprised if half the nonsense in the papers comes from Duncan hisself. But Ashfield Cabs is in his wife's name and there is no a penny goes through the books that is no earned. There's drivers signing on but that's their look-out, no ours.'

'Aye, and the band played.' I gesture around his beautiful room. 'You don't get all this from a few taxis in Possilpark. Don't insult me.'

Billy sighs. 'Do you want to know about the money? You sure? Right. I assume you know not to repeat any of this. You've got too much to lose if you do.' He nods towards the window, towards the sounds of Janey and Sid Vicious, and I'm no sure I do want to hear now.

'It's motors, stolen motors. The boys knock them, drive them to Newcastle and I see to it that they end up in Poland. That's the money and the truth.'

'Poland? Poland? Ach, away, the Communists would never stand for that.'

'It's the Communists that are buying the cars. The country's on its fucking knees, I hear there's no even enough to eat in some places. Party officials see to the paperwork and the cars get shipped as tractors and farm machinery. See when your John Paul visited Warsaw the other week? I bet he was driven about in a Cortina lifted in Castlemilk.'

I can't help laughing. 'Actually, he had a special Popemobile,' I say and Billy laughs too. 'So, how did you get started in this? I mean, you don't go to the Labour Exchange for that.' I'm picturing yon spy film with Richard Burton.

'Have you ever done one wee thing that changes your life, Maggie? Fixes your path?' Just at that, Janey's ball hits the window, and it's the fright that reminds me what my own 'wee thing' was.

Nancy Smedley, 1937. There was a fog, a pea-souper we called them, and I'd got off the tram at the wrong stop. I walked right into Nancy, who I hadn't met since school. She was on her way to a place in Govan that was hiring, something to do with the shipyards. Nobody cared what the jobs were, you tried for whatever was going with whoever employed women. 'You should come an all,' Nancy said. And that led me to Donald Devine.

Billy offers me a half, but I'm sticking with the tea today. I need to watch myself with the drink.

'When me and Helen first started going out together, I was an apprentice joiner,' he says, which explains his magnificent shelving units, 'and one day her father asked me to fix floorboards at his warehouse. That was it, simple as that. Norman Kelman was one of these upstanding businessmen, you know the type – charity work, Orange Lodge, shaking hands with the Lord Provost. Called hisself an importer of quality goods but in reality very little of his business was above board. Norman took a liking to me, taught me a new trade, and we made a good living. He died no long after Helen was hospitalized and that's when I started working for the Edgar brothers. The contacts for the cars were ready and waiting, and I had to do something to secure Samantha's future.'

Billy's quiet for a few minutes, likely deciding whether to say more. He pours a second whisky and downs it in one. Drinking at this time of day, a sin for him so it is.

'Early January, the brothers got into something, something more big-time than usual. And I keep wondering, did they over-step the mark? When a couple of cabs got smashed up, I put it down to the usual territorial shite with the other taxi firms, but maybe, oh fuck, are the polis right? Was Samantha my fault?'

He does lose it now and turns away from me, his shoulders heaving with the pain. He gets another drink.

'I'm sure this is no on you, Billy. I'm sure the police just have to look at every possibility. You can't blame them for making connections when you're photographed with the big men with the reputations.'

When his wave of hurt has passed, he says, 'I thought I was clever getting seen with them, showing up at some cunt's trial or funeral. Thought it would make the CID look in the wrong places. Was just trying to confuse them.'

'I can see that would work,' I say.

'Maybe I was being too fucking clever and now they're ... But listen, I'm sorry to disappoint you. Sorry that I'm no dealing heroin lollypops, or, or running a brothel staffed by nuns or any of that. I never have been, Maggie.'

He holds his palms out to show he's finished, he's come clean.

'I appreciate you telling me all this and I'll never breathe a word of it, but one other wee thing, Billy. Why you offering this job to me? I don't get that bit.'

Billy goes to stand next to the photograph of Samantha. The candle has gone but her lovely smiling face still dominates the room.

'Because maybe I can help you take care of your wee lassie. Fuck knows, I failed my own.'

I excuse myself and my bladder and sit in the bathroom to think it over. Do I believe Billy? Would he have any reason to lie? His story certainly has the ring of truth, although if I was selling heroin lollypops, sure as hell I'd pretend to be just a glorified car thief. But do I believe enough to take the job? Imagine being rid of Tottie-Heid, imagine no more cuts from broken glass, no more mopping up diarrhoea. Ach, I don't know, I just don't know.

I'm at the top of the stairs when the doorbell goes and I hear Janey.

'Mr Watson, Mr Watson, the dog ran in your neighbour's garden and won't come out,' she's shouting.

'Don't worry, hen, I'll go.'

I make my way downstairs and, God in Heaven, what's she up to?

'Janey Devine.' She's rummaging in the jackets hanging at the door. The colour drains from her face and it's obvious she's been caught in the act. I hurry over and grab her wrist and I'm tempted to slap her hand because it looks very much like stealing. I prise open her tight wee fist but it's empty. Anger flashes across her face and I'm shocked. Then it passes and her eyes tear up.

Just then, Billy appears with Sid Vicious.

'It's OK, Janey, hen, I got him. See?' Billy says, mistaking her expression for concern about the dog. I need to get to the bottom of this so I ask Billy to put some water in a dish, Sid Vicious's muzzle is yellow with pollen from the neighbour's lilies.

'Mon get a drink, son,' Billy says and takes him to the kitchen.

'Right, missy, what were you playing at?' I pull Janey into the living room and speak in a whisper.

'I was, was, I thought I saw his leather jacket.'

'What leather jacket?'

'Lulu's. And, and I thought if his jacket was hanging up, maybe Lulu is hiding here.'

'Here? Why in God's name would he— why would you even want to know?'

'It's just, just,' her wee cheeks turn beetroot and she's biting her lip, 'I'm a bit worried about Lulu. I kind of like him, Nana, and the police are after him. I just thought if he was here, I could say hello and, and tell him I'm on his side.'

'Janey, sweetheart, the police are looking for Lulu for good reason. Remember that man at the Wake, Skinny Jimmy? Remember the state of him? He's Mr Watson's friend. Lulu wouldn't be here, Mr Watson wouldn't want him here,' I say as gently as possible. She's awful naïve about this whole business, the wee lamb.

'Can you ask him? Can you ask him where it is? I mean, not it, him. Lulu.'

Billy comes back with juice and an empire biscuit for Janey. Whatever else he is, Billy is certainly well mannered.

'Was it OK to give the dog a lamb casserole?' he asks.

'Sid Vicious eats anything.'

'Christ knows how he got in there. That one's paranoid about keeping the gate on the snib, so she is.'

'He jumped right over the hedges, Mr Watson,' Janey says, her face still red, 'I'm dead sorry.'

'No worries, no worries, Janey. So, how did you get on with the netball? It's hard, isn't it? I've never got a single goal.'

Billy and Janey chat and it's obvious he would've been good with his daughter. Some men have no idea what to say to weans, even their own.

Near time for our bus, I remember to ask about Lulu.

'Janey and me were talking about him the other day,' I say. God forgive me.

'Have yous heard anything?' Billy sounds eager.

'Not a peep. How about you? Any news?'

'Nothing,' he says. 'Mind you, the polis can't be having any luck either. Showed up here with a warrant. You believe it? Turned the place over and took everything Lulu had left. As if I'd be harbouring that big cun— big dafty.'

'Everything? They took all his stuff?' Janey asks. Billy and I look at her. You never know how a wean's mind works sometimes.

Chapter 33

100 days

It's one hundred days since I found the body. I don't know why I'm keeping track, is there ever going to be a last day?

'Hello, Janey,' says dream Samantha.

'Hiya.'

'I like your outfit, you look great in black.'

'I like it too. What you doing here?'

'Was wondering if you wanted to come a walk with me? To my bedsit.'

'Are you OK for walking? You've still got your bare feet.'

'I'm fine, Janey, thanks for asking. You are so much nicer than horrible Val.'

'She is horrible, I hate her guts. Oh, Samantha. I shouldn't mention guts in front of you. Sorry.'

'You can say what you like, we're pals. Where's your other pal? Where's Sid Vicious?'

'He's at home, howling.'

'Just me and you then. And the guy following us. On the way, we'll stop and buy some tiny sandwiches.'

'What guy? Who is he, who's following us?'

'You know, Janey. You know.'

'I— I— don't. Wait a minute, you're taking me the wrong way. This is the path to the Dummy Railway. Samantha, stop. I don't want to go there again. Stop.'

When I go into the kitchen to look at the clock, Sid wakes and wags his tail.

'It's still night,' I tell him, 'beat it.' But I let him into my room, because Samantha won't leave. He spots a half-eaten piece'n jam and I toss it out the window. 'No jam for bad dogs that find dead bodies.'

He trots over and pushes his head into my hand. I try to clap him but the feel of his fur reminds me of tugging at it to stop him snuffling in Samantha's blood. His big eyes are all hurt when I push him away. Idiot dog, if I didn't have him, none of this . . . It's like one of those dot-to-dots when you suddenly see what the picture is.

At Mass, the priest once said that God has a plan for everyone. Maybe Samantha was always meant to get killed and everything leading up to it was just part of His plan. Knowing that might help Samantha rest in peace, so I put the big light on and start a list.

Stuff that doomed Samantha Watson:

1. I choose Sid Vicious – No Sid, no finding a body.

But Samantha would still have been there, all herself till somebody else came along. That goes for me finding the firework and for Martin going to the Botanics that morning, nothing I did made any difference to Samantha being dead. So this list needs to be Samantha's. I rip that page out the binder and rummage about to find the notes I made at the funeral. The napkins are a bit squished but I can still read what Samantha's pals said. Maybe these are the reasons she was killed.

Stuff that doomed Samantha Watson:

1. Carlos the Jackal finds rhubarb.

I don't know who Carlos is and I don't know why he would want Jackal for a nickname because they are hideous according to *Wildlife on One*. But the party at Hillhead happened because Carlos makes beer and wine that is 'rancid and lethal and blows your napper off'. He'd found a pile of perfectly good rhubarb in a skip and the party was to celebrate the wine being brewed.

2. Heather is too wee.

Samantha, Tony and Heather were meant to be at a gig that Friday night but Heather got a knock-back. The bouncer said no way was she eighteen and he didn't care that she was in last week and he was this close to losing it if they didn't bugger off.

3. Samantha's new dress.

Samantha wanted to go somewhere because she was wearing a lovely summer dress from Virgo. Tony suggested the party because at least the wine would be free.

4. Rubbish music.

The records at the party were driving them bonkers, it was folky stuff about Maypoles and forest sprites and Tony wasn't surprised that Samantha left.

The list isn't long enough so I think up a couple more:

5. Samantha and Nino split up.

I'm pretty sure about this one. If she had stayed with Nino, she would have got married, had babies and likely lived happily ever after. It's dead sad to think about that.

6. Samantha decides to go to college.

Mr Watson told me that Samantha couldn't wait to become a social worker. She learned about it at school Career Day and was 'passionate'. So even if she and Nino got married, I bet she would have kept going to Glasgow Tech. Nino might not have liked her new pals but Samantha would've just laughed. Like the way she laughed when her pal Tony borrowed money or when Frizzy-perm forgot about meeting for a curry and left her sitting alone in the Shish Mahal.

7. Samantha didn't like pollution.

Even though her dad was going to buy her a car of her own, Samantha said no because of oil wells and air quality and mad stuff like that. If she had a car, she wouldn't have needed a lift home and . . .

This is getting daft. There's too many random things that made a difference. And that must be the same for the murderer – what if a traffic light was red instead of green, or Samantha left the party five minutes later, maybe she couldn't find her bag, or needed the toilet?

This isn't any big holy plan, just a pile-up of teeny things that make no sense. I slam the binder shut and go back to bed.

'Sorry, Samantha,' I whisper, 'sorry I can't help.'

Chapter 34

It wasn't really anything Billy said that convinced me to take his job. It was Samantha. Whatever is going on with the police and their investigation, the fact remains that some bastard, and I allow myself to call him that, took her life and is still on our streets. And here's me with a chance to be at home more, a chance to keep a proper eye on my Janey. How could I turn that down for some high-minded principle that might be misguided in the first place? With Secondary school on the horizon, I need to be more vigilant, and no just because of the murderer, it's all the danger facing teenage lassies.

So, I phoned Billy to thank him, and Duncan Edgar to accept the job.

He told me to come in to see what's what, so I popped along on Saturday after the Co-op. Ashfield Cabs stands alone on the corner near the rent office, a whitewashed concrete box with one front window. There's barbed wire on the roof but God knows why, it's no more than a pokey waiting room with a disgraceful couch. The whole place is in need of a good mopping, to be honest.

Eggman wasn't there – ach, I need to stop this Eggman nonsense now he's my boss.

Duncan wasn't there, and a friendly brown lad showed me

around. He was right busy with customers coming in and the phone going, but he took time to chat and even showed me how to work the microphone thingy. He mentioned some of the other controllers, Bert, who is longest here, and Nightshift Mary, who works late cos of her man's bad back, and they all prefer it busy because time goes quicker.

It's always a worry starting something new at my age and this is very different from my past jobs. By the time I got up the road, I'd forgotten what I'm supposed to say to the drivers and what buttons I need to press. Daft old so-and-so.

When I told Cathy I was leaving, she arranged a wee farewell do at her place. Stuart was there and the two lads that do busy nights and Saturdays. And a grand surprise when Jean arrived with the domino women. Cathy had made a real effort, which touched my heart.

Janey was talking to Cathy's lassie, Cheryl. They're about the same age and the two of them looked right fed up. The two wee sons were running a-savvy, knocking over drinks and plates, so Cathy handed them bubbles and sent them all out to play. They're on the ground floor and their backcourt is gorgeous, urban regeneration or whatever the Corporation is calling it. The boys were blowing the bubbles and Janey was tearing around with Cheryl trying to burst them. I was worried Janey might be pushing her too fast and was about to chap the window, but Cathy's husband intervened.

'Don't trouble them, my lovely,' he said, which made me smile because I've not been called lovely in donkeys' years. 'The path's safe enough for the wheelchair and it's only proper that Cheryl gets to play too.'

Right enough.

Cathy's man is English, which you'd think she would have

mentioned before now. He was in charge of the food and even baked the cakes himself. This modern world where men cook and wash dishes, Jeez-oh. After the food, he played his banjo and Cathy did Dusty Springfield. What a performance, she had all the actions and my ears were ringing. Everybody agreed she's wasted as a barmaid. It was nice to see Stuart join in without going anywhere near the lager.

They'd all chipped in to get me a wee gift.

'So you always remember the Snotterer,' Cathy said. It was a green glass ashtray and I laughed and laughed. A beautiful thing, though.

It was a rare afternoon, and at prayers that night, I asked God's forgiveness for ever thinking that Cathy was a torn-faced moaning minnie.

Now, I've four more shifts till I'm done. No doubt I could leave right now but I want paid for the week. There's a cheerful glow inside me as I think of the things I'll say to Tottie-Heid when I walk out on Friday. He's the only one that doesn't know yet.

Stuart sits for a rest after wrestling the one-armed bandit out the Gents. How they managed to sneak it in there and break it open without anyone noticing is a mystery. He watches me scrape something vile and grey from under the big table.

'Be the last time you do that,' he says.

'Any idea what this is?' I ask, holding up my cloth. 'It's got a face.'

'Fuck sake, Maggie, burn that,' he laughs and comes to help me up off my knees. 'We'll miss you, so we will.'

'How you gonnae miss her?' Tottie-Heid moves surprisingly softly for such a midden of a man.

'Just, just—'

'I was telling Stuart that I'm no getting any younger,' I put in quickly, 'and I'll no be much longer on God's good earth.'

'It's always God wi you fucking Fenians,' Tottie-Heid says. I catch Stuart's wink and return it, grateful again to Billy.

It's twenty minutes past opening and a group of off-duty police are getting hammered. I recognize the beardy one that everybody loathes and talks about. Tottie-Heid is in his element, sooking up to big men, grovelling at their table and shouting at his staff.

'Ah tolt you to leave those glasses and see to this order. Are you deaf as well as stupid?'

Cathy loads a tray with pints and whispers that she wishes she was coming with me. A few months down the line I might be able to put in a word for her. And for Stuart too, get him driving and away from temptation.

Then I notice Stuart is talking to Taxi Alex. First time I've seen Alex in The Glen and it seems like AA business. Stuart is leaning on the table, his eyes closed while he talks and talks, and Alex is nodding, no saying a word. Maybe I misjudged him, it takes a good heart to be a sponsor.

As I go to put my bucket away, Tottie-Heid stoats over. It's a miracle that man still stands at the end of the night.

'Here, c'mere,' he slurs, 'you'll no know anything about this yet, but Ah'm trusted. Trusted, see?'

'Is that right?'

'It is fucking right, so less of your cheek. They've got him, lifted him in the West End.'

'Who's that?'

'That big bastard, Lew— Lewish— McLuney or something, the wan that chibbed Skinny Jimmy,' he says.

'Lulu McLure?'

'That's the one. And get this, they . . .' He tails off, distracted by something stuck to the front of his shirt. 'What was I saying?'

'About Lulu.'

'Aye, so it is. The const— contunble there tells me, no a word

188

mind, he tells me they've no just got him for Jimmy. It's for the lassie. They're gonnae charge him for killing the Watson lassie. A blackmail gone to fuck, he says. Dirty photos, see. So there you go, Ah'm trusted.'

When I get outside, Taxi Alex rushes out too.

'What a day, what a bloody great day,' he laughs, 'I'm off the hook.'

He takes my hands in his but I shove him away. Wee nyaff must've been eavesdropping. He is right about being off the hook though.

'Now maybe the Big Darlins will get back to normal, and wifey will stop her moaning.'

'Big Darlins?' I ask.

'Aye. That murder business fair wrecked my takings,' Alex says. 'Friday, Saturday nights I used to pick up at least five fares from Possil, Milton, Ruchill. And bring them home again when the dancing closed. Now I'm lucky to get one group of big lassies, and they all ram in together claiming they're too scared to go alone. My arse they're scared, they're just trying to save a few quid.'

I'm no in any mood for Alex's rubbish, and start walking home. It's a nice mild afternoon and I go the long way, past the Callaghans'. Janey allowed Lorraine in the other day and I can't help thinking that's a good sign. It warmed my heart to hear the two of them chattering away.

I know Janey said she likes Lulu but once she knows what he did, she'll be glad to see him locked up. I'm glad, very glad. Those Edgar brothers will be disappointed no to have got him first, more than disappointed, but the police have got their evidence.

I pray to God the police have evidence.

Chapter 35

103 days

Martin got monkey boots. They are really cracking but he's too show-offy about them.

'I'm allowed to wear them to school, Angela says so.'

That's another annoying thing about Martin these days, calling grown-ups by their first name. Bet he stole it off somebody on TV, that's where he gets all his ideas. We've been taking photos with the big camera and now we're heading up to mine cos Martin's dad is home. George gets drunk a lot when he's back and he's always mad angry with the boys but dead nice with Aunty Angela and Kirsty. I told Martin he still shouldn't hate his da because what if he fell off the oil rig and drowned. Martin says that would suit him fine cos there's life insurance.

We reach the flats and Martin stops to take a photo of a burst bin bag. He kneels to get closer and gags at the stink. Everything stinks in the summer. Out the corner of my eye, I catch someone rush at us then my arm gets grabbed. Lulu grabbed me like that, and, and who else? But I don't have time to remember cos my face slams into the rough knobbly stone of the wall.

It's Heather.

'It was you, you daft wee fucker,' she screams, sweat running down her face, 'nobody else knew, rotten lousy shitbag.'

She's angry about Lulu getting arrested. My cheek feels grazed and I'm pure stunned but I look right at her and say, 'I never grassed. Honest to God, I swear on my nana's—'

Heather's no listening. She's shaking me and I can't even hear what she's saying because she's so shouty.

There's a thing you do when you're dummy fighting with boys who get too wild. If you knee them between the legs, they'll shout, 'My baws, my baws,' then fall over and take deep breaths. I try that with Heather, making it really powerful because she hasn't got those soft bits.

'Jesus fuck,' says Martin, 'that looked sore.' He's moved back a few steps, either to get a better view or avoid getting hurt. Heather is on the ground, no shouting any more. Mr Burns from upstairs passes and tells us not to mess about but he doesn't stop.

'What's all that about?' Martin asks, staring at Heather.

'She— I— it's cos I told everybody who she fancies.' It's lucky Heather looks young, and Martin's no interested in girl business.

'Can you go to Jean Jarvis's and collect Sid?' I ask him.

'You gonnae get Sid to set about her?'

'No. We just need to talk.'

Heather's stopped crying and is staring at the ground. I had to help her up and now we're sitting on Pigeonshit Wall.

'How long were you waiting for me?' I ask. She pulls pink tissues out her pocket and honks her nose.

'Hours,' she says in a much teenier voice, 'two hours. Lulu told me you live around here. Before they took him away.' She slings me a right dirty look.

'Aye, and that was nothing to do with me. Nothing. Me and my nana went to Mr Watson's but his jacket wasn't there. The police already searched the whole house and took everything of Lulu's. Ask Mr Watson, ask—'

'The police have it? Oh no. No, no, no.' She starts getting all worked up and I shift along the wall a bit. 'Janey, that means, oh no.'

'They must've seen the Polaroids. They think he killed Samantha.'

Heather starts wailing again. 'Oh, shit. What if Lulu tells on me? What if he tells them everything?' she goes. 'My mates are already furious and they don't even know the half of it.'

I don't feel even a wee bit sorry. Martin arrives with Sid, who scares the crap out of her. Sometimes it's worth having Sid.

'You done?' Martin asks. 'I'm starving and *Hong Kong Phooey*'s coming on.'

Heather is standing on the wall to avoid Sid and as we walk away she shouts, 'If I find out it was you that told on us, I'm going to—'

'You won't do anything,' I say and stick two fingers up at her.

Lulu's arrest was on *Scotland Today* and in the newspapers. A 'twenty-one-year-old male' they said, and it's daft they keep names a big secret when everybody knows. He's been done with Skinny Jimmy's stabbing and, according to Nana, about to be charged with Samantha's murder. Nana claimed she was first to find out but I bet she was just saying that. She always wants to be first with news and once had a hairy fit when somebody forgot to mention a stupid baby getting born.

I wasn't sure what to think about Lulu. I stuck the arrest story in my scrapbook, then I ripped it out. Just cos he battered Jimmy doesn't mean he murdered Samantha. Then I stuck it back in because what if he'd been kidding on about his stupid mistake? What if he really did take the Polaroids cos he's the maniac? What if he did kill Samantha and I was trying to help him? I was worrying about it all night and couldn't stop.

Then at breakfast, Nana says, 'This arrest is a blessing in more ways than one. Since I heard Lulu might be hiding in Possil, I've been up to high doh wondering whether I could be doing more. Maybe chapping on doors, searching the streets. Should I have reported him when he was nasty about poor lovely Samantha? Well, it's out my hands now, it's all down to the police and the courts, thank God.'

One time in school we had this special test. We were in groups and if yous didn't finish by the end of the week, there'd be no trip to Edinburgh Zoo. I really wanted to go to the zoo but the Green Group were rubbish and we got stuck on the last maths problem. Snobby Andrea and the Yellows were finished by Wednesday and we were still working on Friday. A student-teacher was in our class watching over the test, and near time for the bell, she came and sat with us. And she finished the maths problem. Edinburgh Zoo was great, and dead funny when a penguin ate a fag, but know the best bit? The best bit was when the student-teacher took over. We sat back and she fixed it and it was like a holy miracle.

When Nana said that about the arrest, it was the same. The police fixed it and now I don't need to care about Lulu or Heather. Or even the bad thing.

Chapter 36

The racket is apparent the minute the lift doors open.

Dominoes was cancelled, half the team's down with a tummy bug and after The Glen, I'd had enough of pubs. In the end, I didn't tell Tottie-Heid what I thought of him. It was enough to see the colour drain from his nasty bigoted face when he heard I'd be working for the Eggman. I left with my wages and my dignity.

'What's going on in there?' I ask Sid Vicious. His tail's wagging ninety to the dozen so he likely hears something I don't.

'Maggie! It's Maggie and Sid,' Martin shouts when we walk in. He's bouncing on the couch and the music is blaring. Mrs Khan's lassie comes running over.

'Janey, turn it down for your grandma. Sorry, Aunty, I told them it's too loud,' she says and I'm that chuffed to be called aunty. The cassette-tape-thingy's in the middle of the living room and Janey's clumping around in big boots, singing along to some horrible song filled with swear words.

It's the best thing I've witnessed in a long time.

She takes my hand and pulls me onto the rug. 'We're all having a shot of the monkey boots. Try them on, Nana. Have a wee pogo,' she says, her eyes shining.

'Give me the boots, then,' I say as Sid Vicious leaps onto

the couch to dance with Martin. 'Now, what's the words to this tune?'

I'm no sure how long it was before Mr Burns chapped down but it must've been a hellish noise because he's deaf as a post.

It was worth it anyway, I had a right good birl with the three of them. Asha was fine when she saw she wasn't in trouble and we were all singing and clapping and spinning like billy-o. Martin explained the song is about The Troubles and it wasn't a bad wee tune considering the singer's sore throat. Every time I joined in with the F-word, the weans roared and stamped. Surprised nobody else complained.

It'll be weeks before my feet recover from those boots right enough.

We walked Martin home at ten but I didn't go in. No harm to Angela, just didn't want that miserable so-and-so George spoiling our mood. Being out with Janey, talking about nothing serious, lifted my spirits even further. This week seems like a fresh start. No just the murderer being caught and the new job, it feels as if Janey might be getting over her ordeal. No, not getting over it, who can say if that'll ever happen, but she is coming back to her self and even that worrying twitch seems to have passed.

You can't help marvel at how resilient children are.

Chapter 37

105 days

'Did your mother get her good shoe back?' Nana is in the living room talking to Gibby. 'Come in, Janey, lamb, and I'll get us all tea.'

Since she jacked in The Glen, Nana's been dead jolly. Last night was a laugh when she swore with Stiff Little Fingers then fell over Sid. It was strange to feel happy again, like it was a new invention but one that doesn't seem so great any more.

I think Nana's glad about the new job too. Wonder if she'll bring anything home? It was tumblers from the pub and years ago the broken doughnuts were brilliant, but what could she get from a taxi place? Maybe those wee dangly trees that smell nice, that would be ace.

Sid is really pally with Gibby, jumping on him and licking his face.

'How you doing, boy?' Gibby says, doing the ear scratch Sid loves. I notice Gibby's rubbishy tattoo, blue and smudged, and wonder if it might be Rangers. He sees me looking.

'Army. Royal Scots,' he says, holding his thick arm out. 'Ah seen bad stuff too, you know. Northern Ireland.'

I wish Nana would hurry up and come out the kitchen. I don't want to be talking about this.

'Do you see her in your dreams? The dead lassie?' he asks.

I nod. 'Every night.'

'Aye, it's rough right enough. Like having worms living in your belly. Good they got the bastard that did it, shame it was you that found her but. All sliced up, that dirty word on her face. Fucking shame.'

Nana comes back with custard creams. 'Take two, son,' she says, handing the plate over Sid's head.

I make it into the toilet and slam the door before the sick comes out. Vomit all over Nana's good towel with the roses on it.

Thing is, nobody in the world knows about the word on Samantha's face. Nobody but me and the person who wrote it.

I wasn't scared when I saw her, not at first. She was lying face up and her legs were apart but at weird angles. You could see right away that she was dead. I knelt down beside her and a wee bit of glass went into my knee.

Her dress was all bunched up, so I fixed it nicely.

'That's better,' I said and took her hand. 'You're freezing, so you are. But I'm here now.' Sid started barking. 'Don't worry. He won't bite you, I won't let him.' I picked up a stone and hit him with it.

Then, to cheer her up a bit, I started to sing.

'Wee chookie birdy, toe-loh-loh . . .' That's when I noticed the word.

Samantha's face was a mess of grey, black, purple and the word on her forehead was in red lipstick. It was the really bad swear. I got a piece of toilet roll from around the firework and did a bit of spit on it, like Nana used to do for sticky cheeks.

'There, there, wee lamb,' I said, rubbing and rubbing till only a toaty bit of the C was left. But then the bluebottle was on her teeth and I was running and running and I was screaming and I was in The Screke.

Chapter 38

I didn't like leaving Janey sick in bed but what would Duncan think if I didn't show up on my first day? Poor Janey, but I'm sure it's just this stomach bug that's going about. At least the Gibson boy's coming to take Sid Vicious off her hands.

I'm being shown the ropes by Bert Something-or-other, who I recognize as a customer in The Glen. He's a dour, humourless man in his fifties and I'm counting my blessings we won't need to work together. No even two minutes in the door when he says, 'What makes you so special that we all had to rearrange our hours? You family?'

'I'm no related, and I'm awful sorry yous had your shifts upset. I asked for school hours, see, to be home for my granddaughter.'

'Aye, well, we've all got things we need home for. OK then, come on in and we'll get this done quick. Jacket on the peg and stub that out. I'll have no smoking near me, no with my nostrils.'

Feel like a wean on first day at school, even sitting at the front counter with Bert standing over me like a teacher. The stink of man-sweat doesn't help my concentration and he's a mouth breather which makes me think of my husband. To get Donald Devine out my head, I look closely to see if Bert's nostril problem is visible but they're well hidden under a thick moustache. Deliberate, no doubt.

Bert talks me through the controls twice and when a real phone call comes in, he makes me take it and do the shout-out on the microphone for a driver. What a mouth on him when I get into a fankle. Then, to crown it, I let out a squeal when the cupboard door flies open and a man steps out. Nobody told me there was a room for the drivers to sit, and now the two of them are having a laugh at the daft old woman.

They shut up sharpish when Duncan comes through the same door and shakes my hand.

It's a terrible long afternoon. Bert left me to it after just ten minutes and forgot to explain the procedure for a customer coming in. What a relief when the first one in is the priest's housekeeper and she tells me what I need to do. Since I'm not bothered by their smoking, I can leave the door open to the Break Room and shout through if there's a driver in there. The housekeeper is a regular at Ashfield Cabs because her poor mother is in a place in Kirkintilloch. Dementia and only seventy-two. What would become of Janey if that's on the cards for me? It doesn't bear thinking about.

Around two o'clock, one of the drivers, a young lad in very thick glasses, takes over to let me get a break. Bert Thingy told me I'd have to be quick learning the drivers' names but he'd better no hold his breath for that. The Break Room has a kettle and tea bags but I'll bring my own cup, the mugs are a disgrace. I sit for fifteen minutes and have a blether with a loud-voiced driver from the Milton. He's friendly enough but cadges two fags.

As the afternoon goes on, I feel more confident and apart from hanging up on callers, there's no major mishaps. Duncan reappears, this time with his bonnie baby in a pram, and his brother, Skinny Jimmy, who is still walking funny. Stabbings take an awful toll.

They sit in the Break Room and I hear cans being opened. There's another fare for a hospital appointment, a lot of these, and I shout to the cigarette moocher to take it. When they're alone, the Edgars start talking about Lulu and I listen. There are times when nobody would blame you for being nosey.

'Taking too long for my liking,' Duncan says, 'he needs sorting.'

'You know how tight Bar-L is, man,' Jimmy says. 'But Ah'm moving on it, he'll no say nothing to naebody.'

At this point, baby Duncan wakes and most of what they're saying gets drowned out. But it seems they're trying to get in touch with Lulu in the jail, possibly arranging a delivery for him? I wonder if that means they don't believe he's the killer. Maybe they know something the police don't.

Chapter 39

107 days

Ever since talking to Gibby I've been trying to remember if I told anyone else about the swear word. Not on Dummy Railway Day, that's for sure.

When the police arrived, I led them to the dyke and pointed. They wanted me to walk down the embankment and show them exactly where Samantha was but I couldn't move.

'That bush, there,' I said, all croaky because of the screaming. One of the police rushed down with an ambulance man or maybe he was a doctor. Pointless anyway. Taxi Alex was standing with us too, holding Sid's collar. I don't know how he got Sid.

'I hope you didn't go near the deceased,' a big fat policeman said.

'I— I just touched her—'

'You what? Oh, bloody hell. Robert. Robert,' he shouted, 'this wee diddy touched the body.' He put his face right in front of mine and all the sun was blocked out. 'You're going to be in the shite for this, stupid wee clown.'

There were sirens now, like more shouting, and I started to cry. Taxi Alex took my hand and squeezed, his hand all leathery and rough.

By the time they got me to the police station, all the strength was sucked out of my muscles and a policeman had to lift me out of the car. I couldn't even get up onto the examination table when the doctor-type person had to do important things with her swabs. My voice got so teeny they could hardly hear when I answered their questions. Then when Nana arrived and kicked up a fuss, I didn't need to say another damned word to any of them.

When Baldy and Val came to ours a couple of days later, I'd had a chance to think. If the police were raging that I touched Samantha's dress, what would they say about me cleaning that word away? You see it on TV, the way they study the crime scene and use special Alsatians to sniff out evidence and every teeny thing is important. So, no way was I going to tell Baldy that I wrecked a clue.

I couldn't trust any of my pals, they would have blabbed to some grown-up.

In Confession, I said I did something wrong but didn't give details. You can do that when the priests are no really listening.

How could I tell Nana, when she's always got everything to worry about? How could I do that to her?

And I definitely didn't tell Gibby.

It could be that he found Samantha earlier and didn't let anybody know, but why would he do that? Nobody could see her and just go away and forget it. Another thing, you had to be really close to see it was a word. It looked like a smudge of blood unless you were sitting down, looking right at her, maybe holding her hand. So how did Gibby know, unless he wrote it?

I just wish that I hadn't listened.

When I was a wee girl, six or seven, we used to visit this big family who lived in Cadder. I can't remember why we went there but I totally worshipped the biggest sister. She was the best runner and a brilliant climber and always in charge of our games. I followed her everywhere and was dead proud when she gave me the nickname Wee Fido. But one day she did a terrible thing – she told me how babies are made. She had some kind of health leaflet and showed me the horrible, horrible pictures. For ages, I prayed that one of the saints would perform a miracle on my brain so I could go back to not knowing.

It's like that now with Gibby, only worse.

Today is Nana's first day at Ashfield Cabs. I don't want her to go and won't get up.

'Hurry up for God sake, lassie, you're going to make me late,' she shouts.

I tell her I'm still sick, and that's nearly true. Inside my brain is like a broken TV with everything crackling and fuzzy.

Nana sits on the bed and puts her hand on my forehead. Her skin is thin and rough like old trees but I love the feel of it. When I had chickenpox, she stayed with me for days. We watched *Mr Benn* together and drew our own funny costumes for him. Nana makes everything better and I wish she could do that now.

'You've no temperature, you could walk round to the Gillespies' and sit with Aunty Angela. No? Well, I'll leave a tin of tomato soup, nice and light on your tummy. I need to run, sweetheart. Gibby'll be here soon to take Sid V—'

'Gibby? No. No. He can't, I mean, I mean, I'll take Sid out. I don't want Gibby here,' I say in a too-loud voice.

'Calm down. It's only Gibby, and you don't need to bring him in, just pass—'

'I won't.'

'What's got into you? Look, we'll sort this later, but that dog needs walked whoever does it. Now, give me a wee kiss and make sure you have that soup.'

Her Nana-smell, soap and Embassy Regal, makes me want to cry.

A noise like the school fire alarm wakes me. I shake under the blanket till I realize it's only stupid Sid, howling.

'Shut up,' I shout and get out of bed to show him he's not in alone. He nearly knocks me over with joy. What am I going to do? Should I just not answer when Gibby comes? But then Sid will pish all over the place. Or worse. I'm going to have to walk him and hope Gibby arrives while we're out.

I think I'm being sneaky going down the back stairs and totally crap myself when we walk right into a man. But it's only the guy from the seventeenth who can't use the lifts. He got trapped in one overnight and doesn't go out much now.

At the scrubby bit of grass outside, I tell Sid to hurry up. 'C'mon, stupid dog. Do your pee.' He only sniffs around and we have to go further.

By the time we reach the canal, I'm starting to feel a bit better. Who cares why Gibby knew about the swear word? Tonight, I'll tell Nana that he plays the flute in the Orange Walk and I won't need to speak to him ever again. I'm dead tired and sit and stare at a pink flower that is way too pretty to grow here. Sid has a good old chase with a rat.

'Yo. Wee yin, 'mere a minute.' It's Gibby. 'Matter with you, hen? Ah was just up at yours,' he says, bending to say hello to Sid.

'I didn't see you. I'm sick,' I tell him. Is he looking at me funny?

'Is that right? Still sick, eh? See the other day when you ran to the lavvie, Ah thought it was me that made you boak.' Gibby laughs at this and my hand starts to shake. 'You shouldnae be out yourself if you're no well. How about Ah come an all? We'll take a wee donner wi the dog?'

He reaches for Sid's lead and I imagine his hand slamming into Samantha's face and a wee scream comes out my mouth. Now he is looking at me funny. I do the scream again, turning it into a kid-on sneeze. Don't let him see that I know, please, please— Oh, fuck. He's touching me, his big smelly work glove on my bare arm and my eyes are glued to it.

'Aye, right enough, hen,' he goes, 'you do look sick. Ah'll take Sid.'

'I walked him already,' I say, and I can't stand being near him a minute longer. I don't care if it makes me look suspicious, I run. I run into the flats, the sound of his boots behind me. Gibby's following me.

I kick Sid right into the lift and hammer the button. Hammer it again, and again, and there he is, standing watching. Finally, the lift door grinds shut but I still hear Gibby, laughing again.

Chapter 40

I'm visiting Jean to see if she's recovered from this tummy bug. I'm no that concerned to be honest, she has the constitution of an ox, but Janey's been sick and is getting worse instead of better. She hasn't been over the door in two days.

'Right nice of you to come round, right nice,' Jean says and brings me in. Jean and her husband try their best with this place, forever cleaning and painting, but the dampness always wins. It's no just the smell, it's the mould. There's a new growth on the wall like a big dirty waterfall spoiling the nice Artex. These are good flats, roomy with modern bathrooms, and it's a disgrace the Corporation don't see to it.

'I was a bit peely-wally over the weekend but I'm fine now,' she tells me, 'a fry-up last night and I've kept it down. Maybe the wean just has a bad dose of it, you know what these things are like.'

'Ach, I hope so.'

Jean puts buttered bread on a plate and pours the tea. She still uses tea leaves, boiling them for hours to make stewed brown tar. Gorgeous.

'Now then, what do you make of the news?' she asks.

'I heard it on the wireless. Imagine that flaming Thatcher

blaming the Marxists for all this unemployment. Jeez-oh, it made me—'

'No that. I never listen to anything that bugger says. I'm talking about the murder. Have you no seen this?'

She hands me the paper.

Samantha Slaying – Man Arrested

Police confirm a local man has been charged in connection with the death of Samantha Watson (22). A murder investigation was launched in April this year after Miss Watson's brutally battered body was found on an abandoned railway line in the city's Lambhill area. Officers today thanked members of the public for support in what they described as 'a challenging investigation'.

The 21-year-old suspect is due to appear at Glasgow Sherriff Court on Monday 6th August. It is believed he is from the Possilpark area, with sources claiming police had him in custody on a separate charge of assaulting a member of a Glasgow crime family.

The father of the murdered woman, Billy 'The Ghost' Watson (63), was not available for comment today. Watson has previously been linked—

I stop reading. I know what they have to say about Billy.

'It's that Lulu one, isn't it?' Jean says. 'And Possil's name blackened again.'

'No doubt about it. I expect they'll identify him in court.' I don't mention that I already know all this. 'It makes me nauseous to think that I even spoke to that Lulu. What must Billy Watson be feeling knowing he brought the killer into his home? What must the McLure family be going through? Do you know them?'

'Fruin Street, the high-backs.' Jean's face seldom registers anything but disappointed weariness, but her chins quiver with disgust.

People always find somebody to look down on, and in Possil we've got The Jungle. It's just a few streets, the same closes and flats we all live in, but the Corporation seem to have sent every anti-social tenant in Glasgow there. It's a no-go for taxis and Heaven help anybody that actually needs a policeman. Last time I was in Sloy Street, a couple of families were knocking lumps out of each other over ownership of a three-piece suite that was sitting in the middle of the road and everybody else just casually going about their business.

'There's still a lot of decent families up there,' I say, 'and no even The Jungle is an excuse for taking a life.'

'This assault mentioned, that'll be the attack on yon Jimmy one, then? Do you think it's all tied in with a crime clan feud?'

'I've no idea.'

'Ach, away and raffle your doughnut,' she says, shaking her head. 'You're cosy enough with that shower to know exactly what they're up to. Imagine you taking their job. Nobody good should be around the things going on in Ashfield Cabs. You know the taxis got all smashed up, with hammers they say.'

'Who made you judge and jury, Jean Jarvis? You, with your two pensions coming in. I'm scunnered with people giving opinions—'

Thank goodness for Sid Vicious. It's at this point he decides to investigate the bin and stops me saying something I'd regret. It takes Jean and myself working together to wrestle the chicken carcass from his mouth.

Once we've cleared the floor of rubbish, she asks me to take him up the road. 'Susan's bringing the grandweans and you know how he scares them.'

'It's a shame that, because Sid Vicious is very gentle with wee yins, aren't you, son?' I notice he's still crunching something, but let it pass. 'How is your Susan? No seen her at Mass in a while.'

For the second time today, Jean's face changes.

'She lost the baby, Maggie,' she says. 'Eleven weeks. Shattered, so she is.'

I put my hand on Jean's arm and we're still for a while. Sometimes there's just nothing you can say.

Walking home, I can't get Jean's daughter out my head, or my own lost baby.

Donald Devine and I married in 1939, right at the start of the war. He had a reserved occupation so it wasn't the looming call-up that made me accept his proposal, it was my age. Twenty-six and already I was being called a spinster. Nancy Smedley had two weans in her teens, and even my mother was dropping hints. There had been boyfriends, I loved dancing and I loved a good dancer, but Donald was a serious man, older than myself and well respected in the factory. While we were courting, he was quiet and polite, a nice contrast to my rowdy brothers, and he was generous with money and good to my family. All the things I imagined would make a decent husband and father. His true self started to appear early in the marriage but I was making excuses for the slaps because they were infrequent. Then I was pregnant and happy.

That Christmas, though, Donald got harder. He tore down and trampled the wee decorations I'd put up and cut my housekeeping so there would be no presents. And then there was no baby, only a boot-sized bruise on my stomach. If he was sorry, he never showed it. When the next baby was conceived, and I can't even let myself remember that night, I invented a reason to stay with my mam and dad. With God's grace, Marie arrived safely.

My heart breaks for Jean's lassie, but those babies are never really lost, you carry them forever.

*

The fish van is parked on Carbeth Street so I get a couple of breaded fillets to try and tempt Janey. Yon doctor would have apoplexy to hear how little she's eating. The fishmonger throws a handful of fish heads over the counter for Sid Vicious. No problem with that brute's appetite.

'Hello, Mrs Devine.'

The lassie looks familiar but I can't place her. In her twenties and dressed liked a plumber but with one of these hats the French wear. What is it you call those wee hats again?

'Heather, Samantha's pal,' she says. 'From the funeral. Me and Janey met up. Remember?'

'Course I remember,' I say. These youngsters think everybody over forty is doolally. 'Yous went to a café. Nice to see you, hen. How are you doing? Getting over things a bit?'

'A bit,' she says. She's started walking alongside us, now that the fish heads are gobbled up.

'What you doing up this way? Have you come with that watch? Janey said she went away and forgot it.'

'Yeah, that is why I'm here. Lucky I bumped into you because I don't know your flat number. Janey just said Westercommon.'

'She's no been very well these last few days, hen. Maybe seeing you will be the tonic she needs.'

'I'm sure I can sort her out,' Heather says.

Chapter 41

108 days

'What have I told you about using glue in your bed? Put it away right now. Somebody's here to see you anyway.'

'Nana, no. I said nobody's to get in. I said this morning—'

'Hiya, Janey. It's only me.'

Heather. I can't believe her showing up again. I'm totally raging at Nana but at least I lose my panic about it being Gibby.

'Stand there a minute, Heather. I'll bring the stool through for you.'

'Don't go to any trouble, Mrs Devine. I'll sit on the bed beside Janey.'

'That is cosy right enough. I'll go and put this fish away. Janey, remind me later to tell you who came in for a taxi today. Remember her that used to take the Brownies? Always wore big platform shoes and— ach sorry, yous are wanting to chat. I'll away.'

'You here to fight me again?' I say. I'm not happy about Heather sitting on my bed and I'm not happy about her seeing me in bunny pyjamas. Makes me feel wee and weak.

'Bloody hell, even I'm not that stupid,' she smiles, but I don't smile back. 'I came to say sorry. Really and truly, sorry. I'm mortified about the way we treated you.' She's fiddling with her fingers, peeling bits off her purple nail varnish. She's wearing her make-up again but her eyes are all puffy.

Suddenly, I realize the Samantha scrapbook is right beside Heather's bum. I was adding a clipping about Lulu getting charged with murder. Poor Lulu. I keep thinking about how he was when Heather was crying and how he was nursing Boo the cat like a wee baby. And then I think about Gibby and the swear word.

'You been to see Lulu in the jail?'

'No, and I hope I never see him again. Janey, Lulu killed Sammy, I know it now.'

I can't believe she's changed her mind, especially after hiding him. 'How come?' I ask.

'The police convinced me. All that time I helped him,' Heather says, 'all that time McLure pretending to be the tough guy with a heart of gold when really he's a killer. I never even knew about his horrible past convictions, how could I know?'

While Heather's waffling about what a shame it all is for her, I move nearer the binder.

'It was unforgivable the way he made me treat you. And the way he dragged me into this horror with the cops.' She stops and I freeze. 'Janey, are you OK if I talk about this? I mean, I know you're twelve but you're the only other person I know who's caught up in this. And my mates are still giving me the cold shoulder. Is it OK?'

'Aye, it's fine,' I say because I'm not really listening, I just want to get the scrapbook out the way.

'When I got taken for questioning, this detective was shouting at me, accusing me of helping a murderer. Lulu and I had planned what to say if he was arrested. He must've stuck to it because they believed I didn't know his real name and that we only met at Sammy's funeral. But the cop started asking if I helped with the blackmail thing.'

'What is the blackmail thing?' I ask and stop inching the scrapbook away.

'They wouldn't explain but I've read blackmailers sometimes kill their victim to keep them quiet. I'm guessing they think Lulu demanded money for the Polaroids, then killed Sammy when she wouldn't pay. Or, or because she threatened to tell Billy. I don't know. But I keep wondering this, Janey, was I the next victim? Oh, man, it's like a bad trip. I barely sleep and if it wasn't for Mum and Dad's support, I don't— oh, is that the Ancient Egyptians? I did that at school too. Did you make papyrus?'

I try to shove it under my blankets but Heather snatches and opens it at a random page.

'What is this?' Her face goes pure white and even her lipstick loses its pinkness. 'What the hell is this?'

'Here we are, girls.' Nana comes in carrying a Tennent's Lager tray. 'I wasn't sure what you like, hen, so I've brought diluting orange. There's Clubs as well but let me know if you're not fussy for the fruit ones.'

Heather is breathing very loudly. She looks at me and I do a toaty wee shake of my head, hoping she gets it. Hoping she knows to keep her stupid nosey face shut.

'Are you all right, hen? You're very pale. Will I open a window in here?'

'I'm— I'm fine, thanks, Mrs Devine,' Heather says and slowly closes the scrapbook. 'Actually, could I get a coffee, please? If you have it.'

'I'll pop the kettle on. And call me Maggie.'

When Nana's gone, Heather flicks quickly through the pages, then goes back to the start.

'Man alive. You've got it all. From the very beginning.'

I don't know what her face means. Is she angry? Grossed out? Does she think I'm mad? She comes to the photo booth picture.

'Oh. I never saw this report. I remember that day. Sammy and me were meeting Tony at Central Station and his train was late,' she says and wipes her nose on her sleeve. She's crying.

The scrapbook is, what's that word the priests use about sins? Shameful. It's a shameful thing that I've made and Heather can't bear it.

'This bit, this bit you've written underneath the photo, how did you know someone was making Sammy laugh?'

'There's a lot of made-up stuff like that. Just crap really. I was, I'm try— it's to—'

'Is this so you never forget what happened to you? Or is it, is it to do with Sammy? Are you trying to make her feel more real? Is that it?'

'Not real, just, just not murdered. Not the thing she was at the Dummy Railway.' Heather stares. I slide under the blanket to hide myself.

'Janey. What you saw, what you've been through, to do this. This is brilliant.'

'What?'

'Making this book to help and doing it all by yourself, a bloody brilliant idea,' Heather says and lunges at me. I flinch but she's only wanting a cuddle and a cry. I let her, even though her mascara is going on my pyjamas. 'I've been so caught up in the murder recently, I'm forgetting about Sammy. But you aren't. You aren't. God, I miss her, Janey, I miss how she was. See those policemen? Once they believed that I wasn't helping Lulu, they started to infer things about Sammy. They asked terrible questions, how she behaved around men, was she leading anybody on at the party, wearing anything sexy—'

'I heard yous talking about the party when we were at the funeral,' I say.

'I didn't even want to go. I'd been up the night before finishing my Sociology assignment and was really narky when Sammy suggested it. But she got us a cab from her dad's place, and that tosspot Jimmy Edgar picked us up.'

'I got a run from Skinny Jimmy too. He kept talking about chocolate.'

Heather laughs. 'Chocolate? Seriously? That night he was trying to wangle an invite to the party. Man, he's about forty. Anyway, when we arrived everybody was wasted and the music was crap. Sammy danced anyway. At least I stayed awake long enough to join in, at least my final memory is spinning around, laughing together. After that I crashed out in Carlos's bedroom till Saturday afternoon. If I'd been awake, I wouldn't have let Sammy leave alone, that's for sure.' Heather starts crying on my neck again and it makes me want to cry too.

Nana barges in, with toasted cheese this time. 'Ach, look at that. Good pals.'

Me and Heather eat while Nana yaks for ages about how well brought-up students are nowadays, and how admirable they are protesting against the Tories.

I start wondering if it was a good thing that Heather found the binder. It's supposed to be top secret but now she knows, and says nice things about it, would it be OK to tell her the other stuff? Would it be OK to tell her about Gibby?

We are looking through the pages together and Heather says it has inspired her to write something about Samantha, a memoir of their friendship maybe. Kind of proud now.

'My favourite thing has to be the drawings. I knew this was Sammy's bedroom right away. And this gonk, love it. I remember winning one too, brown it was, a shite-brown gonk.' Heather laughs. Then she looks serious. 'This stuff you got from Nino, I'm not sure. We didn't know him well, not our kind of mate, but we certainly didn't turn Sammy against him. There was a painful break-up, and then she barely mentioned him. There was a night though, Sammy told me some bad memories of the guy but she was that half-pished, mad weepy way. You'll know all about that mood one day soon.' She laughs again but I'll never get drunk, you act like a total tube. And lager tastes disgusting.

When we get to the page about Lulu, I ask what changed her mind about him.

'I told you. The police convinced me,' she says, her voice sharp and narky now. 'They've got evidence and there's more than just the Polaroids.'

Heather digs about in her pockets. I don't really like her dungarees but the zipped pockets are brilliant. She unfolds a letter. It's on lined paper and I think it's from a kid because the writing is huge and not even joined up. But it's from the jail.

'Lulu's been sending letters. Every one is the same – he admits stabbing Jimmy but swears on his mother's life he didn't kill Sammy. What a thing to do, swear on your mum's life. He talks about a miscarriage of justice and you should see how he spells that. Look at this, "you know I never hurt a bird". Bird. Jesus, how did I get taken in by that?'

'What's that bit there?' I say, pointing. 'Is that about the Hillhead party?'

'No, course not. It's a different party. One we went to ages ago.'

If they were boyfriend and girlfriend in secret, how could they go to a party? I'm about to ask when Heather pulls something else out of another zipped pocket.

'This time it's not an old one,' she says and opens the watch box. It's digital with a metal strap and it fits perfectly. 'I know this can't make up for what we did to you, or for me pouncing on you, but I hope it helps.'

It does help. Heather helps. She's a grown-up woman who believes it was really Lulu. And she says the same thing as Nana about police and evidence.

Gibby is likely just a creepy weirdo trying to frighten me.

Heather left me her phone number to call for a chat. Anytime, she says, and she promised to find some bits and pieces for the Samantha scrapbook. Maybe it's nearly finished anyway.

Chapter 42

I think I've made a terrible mistake. Things might have been bad at The Glen but I was never in any danger.

Earlier, Janey and Sid Vicious walked me to work. Having her out was enough to put me in good spirits and I'm sure she's softening towards the dog too. Bert was desperate to leave so he could put a certain horse on. Spends a lot of time in the bookies, that one. It wasn't a busy afternoon and I'd settled with *My Weekly* to read about Engelbert Humperdinck's tasteful country home, when three policemen marched into the office. I asked if they were wanting a car but they ignored me and one of them opened the wee door on my counter. I think of it as a stable door except with a snib. They were into the Break Room before I could even stand.

'You as well, missus, in here. Now.'

The Edgar brothers and the short-sighted driver were the only other ones in. Duncan was lounging with his feet on the desk but the poor driver was standing there shaking, his hands raised like a cowboy in a saloon shootout.

'Mrs Devine, wait and Ah'll give you a wee hand,' Jimmy said and ran to take my arm. He walked me to a chair like an invalid. But as he sat me down, he slipped something into my hand. 'Don't you worry yourself none,' he said, and gave me a look.

Dear Mother of Christ, it was the look I hoped I'd never

see again, the warning my husband used when he claimed I'd stepped out of line.

'Edgar, against that wall,' shouted a policeman.

'You'll need to be more specific there, pal,' Duncan said, no even shifting his feet from the desk. 'In case you didnae notice, there's two of us.' Well, he was smacked in the face for that. No surprise there, everybody knows no to be wide with the police.

'You as well, missus. Stand, arms out.'

It took a fair effort to get out the chair and when the policeman went through my cardigan pockets, I felt like scum, absolute scum. Then I was told to open my hands and show my palms.

'Leave her alone, ya cunt, she's an old woman,' Jimmy shouted and he got it in the face too.

I might be an old woman but I know what a drugs packet looks like. And I know that even an old woman would have been arrested if she hadn't hid that packet in her hanky. It was terrible nerve wracking when the policeman checked me over. He even gave me a final check down the back of my collar. Jeez-oh, I'd need to be a contortionist to plank anything down there.

'Do you mind if I use the bathroom now? It's the stress, maybe your own granny is the same.' I was desperate to be rid of those drugs. And desperate for the toilet too.

'Nobody goes nowhere till we're done,' the policeman said, 'but you can sit down, missus.'

When the men were made to lower their trousers, I fixed my eyes on the old slippers that Nightshift Mary keeps here. It must've been awful humiliating even for those bad brothers.

Finally, after ransacking the entire place, the police left.

I went straight back to the front counter and put on my anorak. My legs were barely holding me up and it was a struggle to take a full breath, but I wasn't staying there a minute longer. There was a customer still waiting and he looked disappointed to miss the end of the show when Jimmy arrived and chased him.

Then, Jimmy stood right in front of me. 'You no forgetting something?'

I pulled my hanky out from my sleeve and shook the packet onto the floor. It was like one of the wee bags of Persil her in the laundrette sells for the price of a full box.

'You're a sly old bastard, you,' Jimmy said, smiling and scooping up his filthy drugs.

'Jesus, Jimmy,' Duncan said and grabbed his brother's arm, 'fuck you up to this time?'

'Piss off, man. How did Ah know they'd search an old dear? The cunts.'

'You know the score. Never ever here. We're already on thin ice with that last fuck-up. Ah swear, if he finds out, Ah'm no putting my baws on the line. You're on your ownsome this time, pal.'

The young driver appeared at this point, and without a word to the brothers, he helped me outside to his cab. The drive home was only minutes but he let me sit in the car to get myself together. Neither of us spoke and I forgot to even thank the boy.

What the devil was I thinking, taking this job? Jean was right, nobody good should work for the Edgars. What would Billy Watson say if he found out there was drugs? Or maybe he knows. And who is this somebody that frightens the hard Eggman? Before all this, the only time I really encountered big lies was Tottie-Heid's version of himself, and Trisha McNulty's version of dominoes. Now, I'm finding it very hard to know who's telling the truth. Just what the devil was I thinking? Maybe The Glen's still needing a cleaner.

Chapter 43

109 days

Martin's coming up to get his Clash t-shirt and I can't find it. It's just a rubbish homemade thing and the paint comes off on your skin so I don't know why he wants it back. I can't see it anywhere and I'm fed up looking.

Me and Nana met him out with Aunty Angela, and he grabbed my arm and pulled me away so they couldn't hear.

'My da's going back to work,' he said. 'See, if he gives me money, want to come to the pictures? And can you, maybe, gonnae, maybe see if Asha can come too?'

Martin never usually bothers about girls but he definitely fancies Asha. When we were dancing about the other night, I saw him holding her hand and it wasn't just cos he was worried she would fall and mess his boots. Asha can speak three languages and she's kind and pretty. Martin doesn't believe in kangaroos – just very big hares – and he's a mad eejit with a beaky nose. He's got no chance.

'Sing like Johnny Rotten,' I tell Sid. All the peepholes were painted green when Celtic won the League so I can't see who it is. It's probably Martin so I open up, but it's Gibby.

'Your granny in?' he says as Sid barges out to say hello.

'Uh-huh, she, she's in the bath.' It's no Sunday night but it's the first thing that comes into my head.

'A bath? You sure, hen?'

I nod and he laughs. Gibby's laugh is not the kind you do when something's funny.

'Didnae know they had baths in that taxi place. Ah'll need to go in and get one next time Ah'm dirty. Talking about taxis, listen,' he says. I try to close the door but Gibby's carrying a bundle of long poles and he shoves one into the hinges. 'That's pure copper,' he says, 'a good couple of bob at the scrappy.' He doesn't say why it's jamming the door.

'I need to go in now,' I say loudly.

'Sure, hen, sure. But do you no want to hear my safety tip first?'

'Safety tip?'

'Aye. For you and that pal of yours. Is she your pal? She looks older than you, twenty-something Ah'd guess. Ah'm Ah right? Twenty-three? Twenty-two?'

'Heather?' I say, then wish I hadn't.

'Heather. Lovely name, lovely lassie. But she wants to start wearing nicer clothes. Dresses. Tell her she needs to wear dresses. You an all, you look like a wee boy.'

Gibby's boiler suit is covered in brown oily stains, his hair is brown and oily too, and his teeth. Nana wore a nylon overall to work in the pub, and even after washing, it stank of booze. That's how Gibby smells, he's totally gross. Or maybe I'm just imagining that. The big girls once made a shag list and all the Gibby brothers were on it so he's probably good-looking.

I try pushing the door again but it just makes a noise, like the scream that's inside me.

'Ho, watch it. The hinge'll break and your granny'll banjo you.' He pauses to make a roll-up and manages without letting go of the copper. 'Listen, you tell the lovely Heather to be careful. Tell her to watch getting into taxis. Know what Ah mean?'

Somebody's on the stairs and I know it's Martin cos he's playing a drum solo on the banister.

'Martin,' I shout. Gibby pulls the poles away but doesn't leave. When Martin comes through the fire exit, Gibby does the not-happy laugh again.

'Are you the boyfriend? Fucking shambles of a boyfriend, Janey.'

Martin looks at the ground, his ears bright red. Martin never knows what to do when people pick on him.

'Mon in, Martin. And bring Sid,' I say, and as soon as they're inside, I put the chain on.

'Member about my safety warning about the taxis,' Gibby shouts through the letterbox, 'and tell your wee boyfriend too, just in case.'

'George left me three quid so I can pay us all in. What about *Moonraker* again? I wouldn't mind, I'd watch it four times. Or the Odeon's got *The Muppet Movie*. What do you think Asha likes? Did you ask her to come yet? Did you?'

Martin doesn't say a single word about Gibby. It's like nothing happened, like if you don't talk about it, it goes away.

I lie on my bed while he rummages through the clothes on the floor, talking non-stop about how funny the Muppets are even though they're for kids. I want him to leave but I'm worried about him going outside.

What was that about with Gibby? Is he watching me? Why did he even mention Heather? I think he might've been threatening her. Was he? Or was he really just talking about being careful? I hate Gibby. Hate him.

'I'm taking this back too, by the way. Where the fuck's The Clash?'

'Can't find it,' I say and turn to the wall.

'You better find it, or I'm never lending— oh, fuck, Janey, it's just a t-shirt, you don't need to cry about it. I'm no even bothered. Look, you can keep this one. Here, keep it forever.'

Martin spreads The Damned gently over my legs then goes into the living room. I hear him talking to Sid about Kermit the Frog.

'Wake up, sweetheart.' Nana's shaking me and it feels like night-time. 'Are you a bit wabbit again? You weren't sick, were you?'

'What, what time is it?'

'It's no four o'clock yet. I finished work early, a bit wabbit myself to be honest. You know that Martin's in there, waiting to go to the pictures?'

'Can you say I'm no well? Please.'

'I'll tell him to come back tomorrow. Ach, who's this now? I wish to God they'd get the buzzers fixed so we—'

'Don't answer it, Nana.'

'Away with you, I need to see who it is. Janey, let go of my cardigan. Who is it, Martin?'

'A guy,' he shouts. I know it's Gibby, I know it. He'll be standing out there with some big chunk of metal thing and he'll threaten Nana.

I jump out of bed and run after her down the hall. I've been sleeping in my clothes and I'm boiling and I'm no actually running but walking like my legs are tied together. Nana only opens the door a teeny crack so I can't see who it is.

'It's nobody for you, away and play with Martin. Away,' she says in her angry voice. Martin's lying on the floor, watching Play School and messing with the camera.

'Was that Gibby at the door?' I ask.

'Bet it's the Round Window,' he goes, not looking up.

I'd like to kick Martin's stupid face in. 'Was it fucking Gibby?'

Now he looks up. 'You swore. Haha, I'm telling Maggie.'

I'm about to empty the ashtray over him when Nana comes in.

'Look out some clothes and pack them, hen,' she says. 'The wee blue holdall will do.'

Chapter 44

So much for the summer heatwave that was promised. The rain is stoating off the roads and the bus has slowed to a crawl.

We left Glasgow early and I was surprised at how enthusiastic Janey was to get moving, she's generally very sluggish in the morning. And I was surprised she didn't want to bring her pal, especially since they're close again. No that Finn will be sorry, he was nice enough to Lorraine but got weary of her questions about German spies. Too many films, that lassie.

Sid Vicious is awful miserable. The bus driver took one look at him and told us to sit at the back, and I'm sure the noise from the engine makes him worse. I didn't feed him in case of sickness and he's got the face of a condemned man. Ach, we'll soon be there.

Janey is breathing on the window, drawing happy faces. Just like her mother used to do.

The first time Marie and I made this journey, about a year after Finn settled and was ready to see people again, we were bursting with excitement. I had a bag full of square sausage in case you couldn't buy it in Fraserburgh, and Marie was carrying a special lucky feather for her uncle. It was just a dirty seagull feather but weans' minds work in marvellous ways. Finn's directions were useless and we ended up in Aberdeen and had to sleep in the bus station. Oh, it was grim, but Marie made it into a big adventure. She was a rare wee stick, and never lost her sense of fun no matter what life threw at her.

'How will Uncle Finn know we're coming?' Janey says.

'It'll be a nice surprise for him,' I say, and hope that's true. On bad days, Finn can't bear his own face in the mirror.

'See if he doesn't mind, can we stay till school goes back?'

'I wish we could, sweetheart, but I need to get home for work.'

'Aww. But I guess it was nice of Mr Eggman, I mean Mr Edgar, giving you time off when you just started,' she says.

'It was nice,' I say, because I can't say the holiday is a reward for keeping my mouth shut.

When Duncan Edgar appeared, my first instinct was to slam the door in his face. Although I'd been doing my best to hide it from Janey and Martin, I was still in shock. I've never been searched in my life, and it left me feeling dirty. Dirty and afraid.

'A quick word,' he had said.

'You might be my boss, Mr Edgar, but you're no welcome at my home. So make it very quick.'

'Ah want to make sure you know the score, is all. That deal you saw was just Jimmy's personal use, it—'

'Saw? Excuse me one minute. More than saw. I was made to conceal it,' I said.

'Ah apologize for that. My brother isnae the sharpest tool in the box and the fucking speed disnae help. To be hon—'

'Wheesht, the wean's here.' After I'd dealt with Janey, he started with the excuses again. 'Get to the point, please.'

'Right then,' Duncan said, 'you've no to say a word about any of this. To anybody. No your neighbours, no your family and no Billy Watson. You got it? Because if you do—'

'Don't you dare threaten me,' I said, trying to keep fear out my voice.

'Threaten? Ach, Maggie, you've got the wrong end of the stick. In fact, Ah'm here to square you up for your trouble. Just sorted the wee speccy driver out with a few quid, the same for yoursel?' He waved money in my face, the way these men solve everything. 'No? You sure? What about a bit of time off then? Put your feet up till, will we say next Wednesday? You fancy it?'

'Aye, but what would the other dispatchers make of me for deserting them like that? You can shove—'

'They'll no say a word cos Ah'll get Jimmy to cover your shifts. Stupid bastard, it's the least he can do. Here, make it paid leave.' I take what I'm due. 'Oh, and missus, if you do tell anybody, Ah'll find out.'

As we near the town, I reach for the bags but Sid Vicious is already on his feet. How do dogs know these things? Do they sense their owners' readiness, or do they actually memorize the bus stops? One of the great universal mysteries right enough.

The rain here is just a smirl and it's certainly milder. Finn should be finished work by now and we start the long walk to his house.

'Wait a minute, Janey. Hold Sid Vicious while I pop in here.' We're passing the pub and I have a feeling that turns out to be right. Finn's sitting at the bar by himself, nursing a half and half. The fish factory is laying off this coming winter, the Cod Wars to blame apparently, and as usual the old boys will be first out the door. I worry what Finn will do with himself without the job, when his routine goes.

'You're here then, Maggie,' he says as if my appearance in his local is an everyday occurrence.

When I see my brother the passing of time always shocks me.

Everybody thinks their mother is lovely-looking but ours really was. My father was ugly as sin and cheerfully admitted it, but Mam was all golden hair, film-star cheekbones and beautiful big smile. Finn and I were the lucky weans that took after her. Now, I'm a dumpy jowly granny with puffy ankles, and Finn's a scrawny, wire-haired insomniac with a stoop. And neither of us has much to smile about.

'Janey and the dog are with me. It's just till Tuesday, you don't mind, do you?' I ask, keeping a tight grip on my handbag. Right bad for thieving they are up here.

'Grand.'

'Sorry I didn't get a chance to write, I'll tell you all about it the night. Is the shop still open and I'll nip in for messages?'

'Open late on Thursdays,' he says, wiping his nose on the sleeve of a shabby jacket that long ago might have been part of a suit. Finn was once very dapper, his clothes ironed and shoes polished even for work. The family teased him about the time he spent getting ready for a night out but he'd just laugh and continue Brylcreeming his much-admired hair. The loss of that pride is sadder than all the wrinkles and ageing bones.

Rather than rush his drink, Finn gives me his keys, and outside, Janey is talking to two lads. They hurry away when I approach and when I ask if they're friends, her wee face goes crimson.

'They, they just stopped to clap Sid, I've no idea who they are,' she says. One of them definitely called her Janey but I say nothing. Boys are another sign of time passing that I'll need to get used to. I'm just pleased when she does anything normal these days.

By the time Finn gets home, I've put clean sheets on the beds, scrubbed the kitchen and got a big pot of soup on. It's no that the cupboard is empty, it's just no right for a man to be living on tins.

'Uncle Finn,' Janey shouts and runs to meet him. She knows no to hug him but he pats her head and the same for Sid Vicious.

'Soup,' he says, and goes off to his room.

It was Marie that started calling Finn's home 'the cottage' but it's very much not. A decrepit two-storey on the very outskirts of the town, it's the last one occupied in a row of old fishermen's houses. It has an outside toilet and hot water that depends on Finn's ability to keep the boiler functioning. The electricity is forever cutting out and the chimney is frankly a death trap. I'm always on about withholding the rent till the landlord gets work done but it suits Finn because nobody bothers him. Christ alone knows what he saw on the battlefield, but it put Finn off people for life.

Later, he came out for a walk with the dog, no saying much but pleasant enough. We walked an hour and didn't pass another soul. I know the air up here is healthy and the sea is stunning and all these good things, but it's no for me. There's never a day goes by in Possil when I don't meet somebody to talk to, and once Janey's grown and left, that's what will keep me sane. God willing.

Janey was a bit keyed up and I had a right struggle to get her to bed. If I hadn't told her there's no weasels this time of year, she would still be awake. God forgive me.

I brought a half-bottle and Finn and I are settling with cups that I had to sterilize. It's nice to have somebody listen to the events of the past three months without passing judgement. I'd already written about Janey finding Samantha Watson but when I go over the details, Finn weeps. Very easy to cry, for a man.

Finn's no likely to be spreading stories around Possil so I fill him in on what happened with the Edgars.

'Bastards,' he says, the whisky loosening his tongue, 'fair oot bastards.'

'They are that, but what do you think I should do? Would it be best to quit? Do you think that would be the safest option?'

Finn stares into the fire, our conversation forgotten. It's the flames, they burn like memories and you get lost. He should switch to electric.

I'm startled when suddenly he says, 'Keep your head down, Maggie. Keep your head down.'

Chapter 45

110 days–114 days

No Gibby for days. When Nana said we were going to Uncle Finn's, the dread inside me shrunk a wee bit. Maybe the Eggman got Divine Intervention to help me.

But now we're here everything is different. I mean, it is the exact same, but it doesn't feel right. It's like a fake Fraserburgh, as if I'm watching me and Nana on TV. When Andy and Fergie appeared, they were like actors saying their lines. Everything was so good before and now it's not. Since Dummy Railway Day everything's fucked. I'm even swearing. What if I never get back to normal? What if being scared and worried is normal?

It was better inside the cottage, better with Uncle Finn, because everything's familiar and broken and comfy. My bedroom is at the very top. You go up the wooden ladders then houk yourself through a trapdoor. Nana can't get up here any more so I'm sup-posed to be in charge of making the bed and tidying. Always looks fine to me. It's bigger than my room at home but there's no carpet and it smells of the paraffin heater even in the summer. The mattress on the floor is for Sid, and for Lorraine, and it's newish and soft. I sleep on the metal bed with the jaggy springs because it was my mammy's bed and one of her drawings is still on the wall next to it. It's a picture of the beach with a rainbow over the sea. I did one the same and it's so bad I'd rip it down if Uncle Finn hadn't stuck it to the wall with glue.

There's never any real dark in Possil, but even summer nights are black here and the quiet makes your ears go funny. When I hear the voices outside, it sounds like a football crowd. Just below the dirty wee window, I see Andy and Fergie on their bikes. Stupid Lorraine for blabbing the address, I'm no telling her Fergie's had a shave. I shut the curtain and hide under my blankets. The boys won't come in anyway, everybody's scared to chap Uncle Finn's door.

In a horror film, Uncle Finn would be the baddie. As well as his wrecked ear, part of his neck is raw, like when you skin your knee on the red ash pitches. His hands are covered in fish-gutting scars and he's only got two vampire teeth but doesn't bother getting falsers. And sometimes he talks to hisself. Mad thing is, in horror films, handsome guys like Gibby and Lulu would be the goodies.

There's no TV at Uncle Finn's. That's why Martin never visits with us and why I'm trying to find the news on the big radio that Nana calls a wireless. It looks kind of sci-fi with lights and dials and valves, but is spoiled by the daft brown cabinet. Today is Monday, the day Lulu goes to court, and the only crime story in the local paper is about a man arrested for urinating off the pier. Nana is still resting her feet after the long walk to Our Lady Star of the Sea yesterday. Uncle Finn never comes to church and Nana says it's a tragedy that he lost his faith.

At Mass, the creepy feeling came back. The altar looked like cardboard and when the doors opened at the end, I expected the wind to blow the crucifix over and send paper altar boys flapping to the roof. I was going to do Confession and this time confess about destroying evidence, but the priest looked like a bad drawing.

The radio hits a squeal of static.

'What in hell?' Nana shouts and sits up like somebody slapped her head.

'Sorry.'

'Ach, Janey, can you no give me five minutes' peace? Just for once.'

'You've been sleeping for an hour,' I say in a quiet, crabby voice.

'What are you fiddling with that thing for anyway?'

'Nothing. Nothing,' I say, 'but maybe you can try so we hear what happened to Lulu.'

'Lulu? You woke me to listen to her?'

'Lulu, Nana, Louis McClure. It's his day at court.'

'Oh God, so it is. But nothing's going to happen. It's just the plea. They only ask his name and if he's pleading guilty or not.'

'Yeah, so? I want to know.'

Nana fiddles with the dials, but keeps moaning, 'You need to stop thinking about this business, it's no good for you. High time you let the police get on with their job.' The only station we get is some posh guy talking about tractors and she falls asleep again.

Dinner was from Uncle Finn's work, fish with heads still on. The staring glassy eye made me think of Samantha and I fed the whole thing to Sid when nobody was looking. Nana and Uncle Finn both get annoyed if you leave even a toaty scrap of food. I think it's to do with the war.

We walk into town but there's no Glasgow newspapers so I have to wait. Lulu's not going to say he did it unless he's been hit by a thunderbolt like St Paul. Stupid Fraserburgh with no proper news. Me and Sid go to the beach and it's a relief there's no Andy or the others, I can't be bothered with a boyfriend any more.

The dunes make you pure knackered so I go up to bed early. Sid tries to follow. His paws miss the rungs and usually I shove his bum to help him but tonight I don't and he falls. I wonder if I'll ever like Sid again?

Everything creaks in the cottage and Uncle Finn knows I'm behind him. He's sitting in front of the fire but I don't think my scream woke him because he is always awake, even if you sneak down really early to snoop.

He stirs the fire with the bent poker and flames spring up.

When you do a painting of fire, you use red and yellow, but in real life there's flashes of blue and green and white. When he doesn't have any coal, Uncle Finn burns an old shoe from his pile and the colours are wild. Smell is rancid though.

Uncle Finn points to Nana's chair with the poker. There's no couch and I usually sit on the floor. Nana's left her cardigan and I bundle myself into it. Angora, doubt it.

'Bad dream,' he says. It's no a question but I nod and try not to stare at his ear. You can't help it.

'Sorry if it was me that woke you up,' I say.

'Sometimes,' he says, then is quiet for a bit. 'Sometimes, you need to let them in.'

'Let who in?' I ask, but kind of know.

'The dead. The ghosts. Your murdered lassie.' His voice is deep and creaks like the floorboards and it makes me think of the horror film again.

'Have, have you got a ghost, Uncle Finn?' I don't like other people talking about Samantha's dead body but I want to hear this.

'Three. Out of the many, just the three come back. It's because

242

I saw their faces, because I'm their witness. Most of the time, I shut them out, tell them to get away. And they go, they go. You've got that power, see? But it only works if you let them in. Just now and again, mind.'

'What do they . . . do they, do they talk to you?'

'No, no words, just the memories. That's what they want, for somebody to relive the last day for them, that's enough,' he says and blows his nose on a man-hanky. Uncle Finn cries a lot, even more than Stevie Baw-Jaws.

'If I relive it for Samantha, will it stop the dreams?'

He looks up from the fire. 'No, hen, she'll always be there in your dreams, always. But you're the boss, tell her that this night, you're busy. Then promise the lassie that you will remember it. Just now and again, mind, that's all she needs, for you to look at her face.'

Remember. That's what I have to do. No matter what it is hiding in my brain, no matter how shit-scared I am, I need to find it and help Samantha.

Uncle Finn gets up and hurries into the kitchen like he's left a pot boiling. Even though I'm completely still, there's a moving shadow behind me that might be a dead soldier. I'm pretty sure Uncle Finn's ghosts will be soldiers, maybe he saw them getting shot or blown up or something. Maybe it was him that shot them. The soldiers wouldn't be interested in me but the fire cracks and suddenly there's another shadow.

I'm in The Screke and the shadow is solid. I can smell smoke behind him and feel his fingers tight round my wrist. There's something about him, something that's not a man. Not a man.

Then, I'm back in the cottage and Uncle Finn is here, with the Big Spoon.

'Gas meter?' he asks.

When the gas runs out you have to put a ten pence piece in the meter to get it back on. One time, when we had none, we ate cold spaghetti hoops for breakfast, lunch and dinner. Brilliant. Uncle Finn fixed the meter so the Big Spoon slides inside, through a gap behind the padlock. His hands are too old to do it now but he taught me, and before I go back to bed, I scoop out a whole load of ten pences. To keep.

We never tell Nana about the Big Spoon. And I've no to tell her about my ghost either, Uncle Finn says she's got a bad one of her own.

Chapter 46

The minute I walked into Ashfield Cabs, the humiliation of the police search hits like a ton of bricks. But I'm keeping my head down as Finn advised, and God willing, things will settle.

It was Bert on dispatch and he didn't waste a minute.

'I've worked here from day one,' he said, 'and I've no so much as taken one extra day off, never mind getting Jimmy to cover for me. What is with you, eh? You know something you shouldn't? Been sticking your nose in, is that it?' he said.

'I just asked is all. Family emergency. Duncan was very good about it, speak to him if it bothers you so much,' I said, trying to hide my disgust at his ridiculous wee tennis shorts. There should be a law about men and shorts.

'Family emergency. Aye, so it is,' he muttered. 'Hurry up and get yourself sorted. Real boss is in today so at least pretend you know what you're doing.'

As soon as he left, I lit a fag and opened the door to the Break Room. I was expecting to see whoever it is that scares the bejeezus out of the Edgars, or maybe Mrs Edgar, the real boss even if it's only on paper. But it was just Billy Watson, who gave me a slight nod, and went back to his paperwork. Billy's no the boss of anybody, he's just the one with Communist connections.

'Ashfield Cabs. Can I help you?'

'Maggie, it's me. Did yous have a nice wee break?'

'Angela, hello, sweetheart. Aye, we did, thanks. The weather wasn't the best but—'

'Have you seen yesterday's paper?'

'I haven't, no. Why, hen? Is it—?'

'I'm going to nip in,' Angela says. 'I need to go to Galls for underwear anyway, God knows where Kirsty hides her pants. See you in about ten minutes.'

You'd think after everything going on, nothing would faze me, but the sweat on my hands has turned cold. It's always bad news these days.

'Free,' I say, and cross myself, 'Samantha's killer, free.'

Angela leans across my counter, keeping her voice low so the woman waiting for a cab to Clydebank doesn't hear.

'Just hours before he was due in court. Murder charge dropped, McLure walks,' Angela tells me. 'The reporters were all waiting and what a show of hisself he made on the six o'clock news. Swearing and shouting that the polis framed him, calling the officials all the names of the day. Right scandalous. He's still to appear for the assault but he'll no serve time for that. Nobody cares about Jimmy Edgar.' She gets distracted by the wean. 'Kirsty, leave that woman's messages alone. I'm awful sorry, missus, here's your onion back.'

'Here, cheeky face. Draw me a wee house.' I give Kirsty my notebook then look at the newspaper. The front page is taken up with an unpleasant photograph of Lulu lunging at the reporters.

Angela speaks with one eye on the wean. 'Ali in the Red Shop heard somebody came forward with an alibi. And that they were paid to do it.'

'Ach, I wouldn't put creid in anything Ali says, he's got a big mouth.'

'But he got it from that hard case tally man. Des Grey, is it?'

'Big Des?' I say. 'What does he know about Lulu?'

'You wouldnae ever go to that robbing bastard, would you, Maggie? You know to come and see me if you're skint and—'

'You're a blessed saint, hen, but don't you worry about me. Now, I need to get back to work and you need to get to Galls. If Kirsty hides any more, tell her the Pants Fairy is watching.' As they leave, the wean hands me a drawing that you'd swear was a loaf.

The drivers at Possil Bus Depot are staging a wildcat and it's pandemonium this afternoon with everybody and their granny needing a cab. But at every quiet moment, I think about Lulu and about Des Grey's tale. A shiver goes down my back when I remember the Edgars discussing Lulu. I wouldn't put anything past that Jimmy, filthy wee so-and-so, but would he pay for a false alibi? Who would get a murderer freed just for their own revenge? I don't know if Lulu is the killer or no, it's no up to me to judge, but he did manhandle Janey into a car and now he's off scot-free.

I finish my shift just as Billy's leaving and he offers to carry my messages.

'It's five minutes,' I say, 'I'll be fine.'

'You sure? You've a lot of bags.'

There was barely a thing in after being at Finn's and I had to do a big shop. 'Ah, well, if you don't mind then.'

We pass a lassie on her bike and Billy tells about a Christmas when Samantha got a Chopper. She loved it so much, she kept it right next to her bed. It tore the wallpaper one time, and Billy would give anything to take back the row he gave her for that. I get the feeling he doesn't get many chances to talk about his daughter. Maybe he does with his wife, but who knows what that poor soul understands.

It's when we reach the flats that he finally mentions Lulu.

'Do you believe in karma, Maggie? It's probably no something the Catholics go for, but this feels like karma.'

Maybe karma would explain why I lost my family, maybe I got what was coming. 'What's karma got to do with Lulu?' I ask.

'There couldn't be any better comeuppance than my daughter being killed by a boy I treated like a son.'

'Karma's nonsense, Billy. And if you were that close to Lulu, you should know if he did it.'

'Aye, maybe, you're right, maybe I should trust myself,' he says. 'The Edgars say I've lost the plot but two things about Lulu don't add up. Even when she got into the women's lib and all the rest, Samantha still loved her jewellery. The bastarding killer stole everything, all her rings gone, earrings ripped off, the necklace from Helen, cunt took every penny out her purse. And that's no Lulu. See, Maggie, I test everybody that comes to work with me, a wee set-up with cash, and Lulu's the only one that never skimmed. Didn't take so much as a ten pence piece. Money wasn't his thing, know? Lulu wanted to, to . . . he's got a shite family and he just wanted to be part of something. And that rules him out doing it for a rival team. Nah, it doesn't add up.'

We stand in the lobby and I'm no sure whether to ask him in for a chat. No that I'd get a word in anyway.

'Then there's the way he is round lassies,' he says. 'Always getting his heart broke, always protective. If somebody as much as raises their voice to a woman, Lulu'll wade in, even if it means getting his head kicked in. Maybe down to having to look after his wee sisters, no that we ever talked about it, mind. It's no I don't believe he could do serious harm, but to hurt a lassie? To hurt Samantha?'

Billy carries the bags into the kitchen and I put the kettle on. Only polite to offer. He helps me put the tins away, asking after Janey and how I'm finding the job and if the money is enough. I notice he's finally out the black tie, smart in tan slacks and clean pullover. It's no much, but a good sign.

Before he leaves, I ask about Lulu again. I can't get this out my head.

'Have you seen him since he got out?'

'Nobody's seen him. Vanished. Cannae blame him with the Edgars on his case. I just wish to fuck it had got to trial so I could see what the polis have on him. But now,' he says and slams his fist on the wall, 'ah, fuck.'

He hasn't got the peace he was wanting. Even if every court in the land had found that lad guilty, there would still be no peace for Billy Watson.

Chapter 47

116 days

Lulu's out of jail.

When we got back from Fraserburgh, Nana went right to sleep but I was desperate to see what happened at court and sneaked out to find a newspaper. Nobody knows why the Witchy Sisters leave their newspapers outside their front door, they just pile up and pile up till somebody takes them for a bonfire. During the day, the Sisters wear thick lipstick, white face powder and dark cloaky things that are called ponchos, but when they opened their door wearing short frilly nighties, it was even freakier. Totally shat it.

'Are you all right there?' the tall one said. Her eyes were very sleepy.

'I just— just, is it OK if I take an old newspaper? I— I need it for a school project.' It felt like I'd been caught robbing their stash of secret cursed gold or something.

'Help yourself,' she said. Then the wee one brought out Tuesday's *Glasgow Herald* and held it out for me. She didn't say a word. Honest to God, I was shaking when I got back in, shaking. I don't know where they were going at midnight in those nightgowns and I didn't want to imagine.

Then I read about Lulu and the Witchy Sisters were nothing any more.

Since listening to Uncle Finn talking about reliving that day for Samantha, I've been thinking about Val's 'wee flashes' of memory. If the flashes are real and no just a dream, then I saw somebody on Dummy Railway Day. And that somebody saw me. This isn't just about getting rid of Samantha any more, this is about the murderer.

I need to start remembering pretty quickly.

I can't let Gibby near me, that's for sure, at least Martin's agreed to walk Sid – if I get Asha to come to the pictures.

We are at the library to find her, and it's a relief that Martin's not all fake and papery. That got left behind in Fraserburgh.

'Member, Janey, don't make it like it's me that wants Asha to come,' he says, 'just pretend you're desperate to see *The Muppets*.'

Martin's handing back *The Big Book of Scary Tales*, and it's Nino on the desk.

'Hello, you,' Nino says, which likely means he can't remember my name, 'long time no see. How's your knee?'

I show him. I'm wearing the denim shorts that Nana made out of some old pair of bellbottoms. She frayed the ends and they look shop-bought, which is pretty good work for Nana. My knee is nearly better but it would bleed if I started on it again. Nino comes round the desk for a closer look and my face goes red when he touches the scar.

'You've been through so much,' he says. 'Hey, I'm just stopping for my break. Can I show you something?'

Martin shoves me from behind, but Nino just gives him one of the nice smiles and takes me to the staff room. On the walls are a couple of Book Owl posters, and warnings to guard your belongings, and with cups and cigarette burns on the couches, it looks just like the school staff room.

'Have a seat,' he tells me, then talks to a woman worker who leaves. 'It's Janey, isn't it? Janey Devine.' He did remember. 'How are you? Things any better for you yet? Heard anything from the police again?'

I've only told Nana about Val taking me down the Dummy Railway but I tell Nino because he's interested.

'Christ.' He looks annoyed. Val annoys everybody. 'And did it work? Did you remember anything else?'

'Wee bits.'

'It's better to forget horrific details, there's a reason you're blocking it out. That policewoman might've caused serious damage to your mind. It's fucking harassment, so it is.' Nino sits beside me, his voice loud and his face angry. Then he smiles. 'Don't look so worried, honey, I'm not annoyed with you, just the bloody police. That reminds me, I dropped in to the legal advice charity on Saracen Street. As a minor, you should be protected during police questioning. Would you like me to set up a meeting with their advocate? She's very nice, does great work around here.'

Nino's voice is confident and he looks right at you. It feels like he's in charge but not in a bossy teacher way. And he's the first person to say I should be protected.

'I'm no sure,' I say. Don't know if I want any more official people near me, snooping and finding faults with Nana.

'That policewoman should never have tricked you,' Nino says. 'It sounds like the pushy cow who interviewed my Uncle Callum.'

'Did the police hassle him too?'

Nino nods. 'Hauled us both into the station, which really upset the old soul. My alibi is airtight but the police are still coming into the library, "just a few more questions, Mr Hogg. Won't keep you long, Mr Hogg." ' Nino does a stern police voice that's pure spot on. 'We shouldn't have to put up with it especially when they let the killer walk free.'

'What's your alibi?' I ask.

'Well, that's when you prove you were somewhere else when a crime was committed.'

'I know the word, I just wondered where you were.'

'You're a real character, aren't you? Well, Detective Devine, on Friday 13th of April 1979, I was with my uncle. I arrived home at four p.m., gave him medication, and we watched a film until late. On Saturday morning, I went to the local shop and bought bacon, then at one p.m. I began work at Possilpark Library. My uncle and co-workers will corroborate my statement.' I laugh because it does sound like he's talking to the police. 'Am I off the hook, Detective?' he says and I laugh again.

Nino stands and stretches like he's just out of bed. His sore leg is stiff when he walks and I bet his burn is sorer than my cut. He fixes the elastic band in his ponytail.

'My hair's too long, isn't it?' Nino says when he sees me watching. 'Should I get a punky spike?' He hoists the long strands above his head and it looks totally stupid. 'You're right,' he goes, 'I'll leave the cool haircuts to you. Really suits you, by the way.' He ruffles my hair and smiles.

I'd like to stay here talking but I remember Martin and the pictures.

'Before you go, this is what I want to show you.' Nino opens a big plastic bag. 'I made this.'

It's a wooden cross. It has red hearts painted all over, with 'Samantha' in gold in the fanciest letters and 'Always mine' underneath.

'Oh, beautiful,' I say, and touch her name. 'You should've brought that to her funeral. It's way nicer than the flowers.'

'It might sound soft coming from a guy, but I was too heartbroken for the funeral. I wrote to Billy and Gran Kelman because I couldn't face it.' He turns his head and takes off his glasses to wipe tears.

Nino's dead nice and I feel sorry some people don't like him. Heather didn't tell me any of the bad stories about him, but maybe Samantha was exaggerating. When the guy in the café chucked Jackie's sister, she spread it that whenever they went drinking, he shat his trousers. Nobody went in the café for a long time.

Nino runs his hand over the cross. 'What I want is to leave this at the spot where she died. There should be a marker. You could come with me and show me exactly where. Will we put it there together?'

'Ehm, maybe,' I say, 'but I'd have to ask my nana.' No way am I going back down there.

'Surely you can do one thing without asking?' Nino's suddenly narky but then his big smile. 'Sorry, Janey, I'm just constantly on edge when I think about Samantha. Speak to your gran about coming with me, and see how she feels about the legal protection. You deserve someone on your side.'

Martin was pretending to browse, and went quiet when we sat with Asha. She was reading a book from the Big Library and no even cos somebody was making her.

'I wouldn't mind going,' Asha said, 'but not *The Muppet Movie*. I don't think they're funny.'

'Neither do I, they're crap,' Martin said. Closet.

When we asked Asha's dad about the pictures, he gave us crisps and cartons of Um Bongo. And Nana got one of her drivers to take us.

Now, we're on the way to The Salon and we're in a minicab and Martin is acting pure dolly.

'I'm giving the driver a Spicy Nik Nak for a tip,' he whispers, and spits a half-chewed lump into his hand, 'this one.' Asha's laughing at everything he does so maybe his beaky nose won't matter.

The film is called *Escape from Alcatraz* and it's an AA.

'Nobody's going to give us a knock-back, it's too empty,' Martin says, and he's nearly right. He and Asha get their tickets but when I try, the usherette goes, 'Come back in five years, toaty.' Five years? In five years I could see an X.

'I'm not leaving you alone,' Asha says, taking my arm. Martin's behind her, miming walking a dog.

'It's fine. I don't even want to see it,' I say and that's true. A film about prison would've made me think about Lulu. Martin actually skips when they go in together. Asha says we can meet up later but I've got something else to do.

The Salon is near Byres Road, and once I find Goodies, the bedsit is easy. When Nana goes visiting, she takes something nice, so when Heather opens her door, I hand her a packet of Quavers. She's surprised to see me.

The piles of manky clothes and records and books are all gone, just furniture and some cardboard boxes in a corner. Heather is getting ready to leave.

'Where's Boo?' I ask.

'Already at my parents'. They've been on at me for ages to come home so at least somebody's happy.' She's wearing an old-fashioned flowery skirt and her purple hair is now the colour of a squashed mouse.

'Will you still go to college?'

'I dropped out. I've no mates there now and obviously won't be going into social work with Sammy.' She kicks at the bed. 'This place isn't fun any more, I can't stand that Lulu was here.'

'Were you his alibi?'

Heather drops the Quavers. 'How the hell did you know that? Nobody's supposed to know that.'

'You tell lies, Heather. About how long yous were going out

together, about the party in Lulu's letter. I'm no a diddy, he was obviously writing about the Hillhead party. Did you say he was there? Was the alibi a lie too?'

Heather sits on the floor and closes her eyes. 'I got together with Lulu in December, at Sammy's house. The relationship would have to be secret to keep me safe, he said. But it was nothing to do with his criminal connections, he just didn't want Sammy finding out. He was convinced she'd eventually give in to him. And know what? Know what, Janey Devine? I didn't care, I didn't give a flying fuck that Lulu was using me. I was crazy about him, and he was crazy about her. How sad is that?'

I sit on the couch and get a big memory of Lulu looking under the cushions for a teaspoon, and I wonder where he is right now.

'On the night of Carlos's party, I heard Sammy phoning for a lift home,' Heather goes, still keeping her eyes closed. 'She was using that giggly drunk voice and I knew she was talking to Lulu. Fucking knew it. When she went into the kitchen to wait, I slipped outside. I stood freezing on the street at two a.m., and when Lulu drove up, I persuaded him to sneak back into the party and into the bedroom with me. How low is that? How pathetic and snide and bad is that?' But Heather doesn't sound like it is a bad a thing, she sounds raging.

'It's your fault she got in the fake taxi.'

'Shut the fuck up, you. You don't know everything. I fell asleep again and when I woke Sammy was gone, and so was Lulu.'

'So, you told the police Lulu was in the bedroom?' I ask.

'Lulu told them, told them I was his alibi. Not long after I visited you, they lifted me at my parents' house. This time the interrogation was even more awful, and this time I told the truth. But the police didn't pass my new statement to his lawyers. When—'

'How no?' I say. 'How did the police no let Lulu go right away?'

Heather opens her eyes and scowls. 'Why you asking me? I'm

257

only telling this cos you got caught up in it, so shut up and stop interrupting.'

I stomp past her to the door. No way will I leave but Heather can't boss me about.

'OK, OK. Don't go in a huff,' she says. 'I think the police were desperate to find a link between the murder and Billy's criminal activities, and that link was Lulu. It was just before the court appearance that Lulu's lawyer got his hands on my statement. I don't know for sure but I imagine the PF had to drop the murder charge because of police obstruction, and because I lied in the original interviews. But guess what?'

I'm lost, I can't guess anything.

'I fell asleep, I don't know when Lulu McLure left that party,' Heather says. 'He might've been with me till nine a.m. like he said, but he might've followed Sammy right out the door. His car might've been the fucking fake taxi.'

'Why did you try to help him then?' I think she's lying again, this makes no sense. 'Why did you make me look for the Polaroids?'

'Because I was scared everybody would find out what I did that night. Imagine what newspapers and TV would say about me? They'd make me out worse than the killer.' Heather finally starts big loud crying. 'And deep down, deep down I was scared of Lulu.'

Something bad just occurs to me. 'Oh, shite, that's why you're leaving. You think he's coming to get you.'

And if it was him I saw on Dummy Railway Day, Lulu's coming for me too.

Heather wipes her face on the yukky skirt then goes to the wee kitchen bit. 'My mum made fairy cakes. Want one? She put loads of icing on them.'

'But, but what about Lulu now? Where is he? Do you think he really killed—'

'Stop it, Janey, fucking stop,' she looks at me, eyes like hard wee stones, 'you need to let go. For your own sake, for your well-being, let Sammy go. Burn that scrapbook, forget Lulu McLure, be a girl again.'

After that, Heather tells me about the tree in their garden for Boo to climb; her new job in an office; the nice clothes she'll have to buy. I want to shake her and shout that I'm scared too and that we still need to help Samantha.

But I just eat cake and listen to Heather talk rubbish.

Chapter 48

The last time Janey and I were in this bit of town was the interview with those flaming policemen. What a mood she's in but still an improvement on that frightening silence.

'Does it have to be stupid Stirling Stevens? Their school stuff's garbage,' Janey says, 'and I'm no wearing a skirt, that's for sure.'

She was at the pictures yesterday and we had a bit of a row. Instead of the film and her pals, all she would talk about was the murder and that big Lulu, and I know I shouldn't have lost the rag but I'm scunnered hearing about it. Coming into town for the school clothes was supposed to take her mind off it but it's no working. Nothing's working, and the nights when I can't sleep are filled with a terrible feeling that I'm missing something, something that's been there since the start.

'I know all about the skirt and the trousers, Lorraine's mammy told me. And aye, it does have to be Stirling's since you said no to the catalogue.' Paying up a Stirling Stevens account means I'll definitely have to stick it out at Ashfield Cabs, whatever they're up to.

Could not believe it when Nightshift Mary told me that when Lulu walked from court, the Edgars had a party. She says it was nothing to do with him being innocent, Jimmy was celebrating for his own self. Singing a song about how the C-word was going to get what he deserved and that anybody messing with the Edgar boys gets the same. Duncan shouted that Lulu will no be grassing to anybody now and mimicked a throat cutting with the butter knife. Mary speculated about the grassing thing. 'The Edgars are tied to the killing and the boy knows it,' she said. In my mind it'll be the dirty drugs, although I keep my mouth shut on that. What we are both sure of is Lulu's no safe around here, and those brothers are bad devils. It's no surprise they support the Rangers.

Even at this time of the morning, the school department is mobbed, and the price? I nearly fall on my back. And that's no including shoes. When I ask if they stock the monkey boots, the lassie brings a t-shirt with a chimpanzee's face on it. Janey laughs, so I add it to the account. She says she likes it but now I'm wondering if it's a bit young for her.

By the time we get to the bus stop, I'm worried about being late for work.

'Is that a 47 now?'

'It's a 61. Can we no get a taxi? I'm boiling,' Janey says.

'A taxi? After what I just spent? If you would stop your complaining, you'd feel better.'

'I'm starving too, how can we no get chips?'

'Will you just wheesht and—'

'Ho. Yous want a lift?' somebody shouts. A motor with different-coloured doors has pulled in and everybody in the queue is straining to see if it's for them.

'Is it us, Janey? Can you see who it— oh, it's Gibby. Mon, sweetheart, we're getting a run.'

'Gibby? I'm no getting in his car, no in a million—'

'Bring the bags, I'm not in the mood for your nonsense, lassie.' But the wee besom stays where she is and I have to grab her hand and march her to the car like a wean.

It's two of the Gibson brothers and the one we know jumps out, opens the back door and puts our shopping in the boot. Far better than a taxi and I'll make it home in fine time now.

'I never knew you could drive, son,' I say to Gibby.

'Army taught us. Fixed the motor up masself.'

'The army? Well, I didn't know that either. Were you in long?'

'Naw. Went in at sixteen but couldnae hack the discipline. And they made us do stuff that fucks you up. Glad they kicked us out.'

'Got any fags?' the brother asks. He's talking to Janey but I pass him my packet.

'Help yourself, son. Sorry I don't know your name.'

He looks at me as if I'm glaikit. 'It's Gibby,' he says, pocketing two Regal, which is a downright cheek.

Mrs Gibson's sons are very alike. I couldn't swear on the number but I think there's five of them – all with faces like baby rabbits, and all with muscles like baby gorillas. Aye, they're well sought after around here.

Our Gibby twists right round to face Janey. 'How you, doll?' I'm gripping the seat because we're in right busy traffic and he's only got one hand on the wheel.

'Good of you to ask. She's fine, aren't you, Janey?' She's in a right funny mood, squirming about and fiddling with the door handle, and after all the moaning about wanting a taxi. 'Fixing cars is a good skill, you should see if they're looking for mechanics at the bus depot,' I say, since Janey's obviously no going to talk to him.

'Nobody takes you if you no got papers. But Ah've plenty going on anyways,' he says, which makes his brother snigger.

'How's your daddy these days?' I ask.

'Far as Ah know, he's still six feet under, Mrs Devine,' our Gibby says. And the two of them roar with laughter.

'Oh, boys, I apologize. I'm a stupid old so-and-so.' For Heaven sake, what am I like? I knew their father was dead. A terrifying man he was, kept his family living in dread. When the cancer finally took him, you could hear the celebration in our block, the sons were on the lash for days. Just last year that was.

The Gibbys talk all the way to Possil, mostly about other drivers, but I join Janey in her silence. I've been assuming it's the trouble with her and the dead lassie that has been disturbing my memory, but what if it's no? The priest's housekeeper said her mother can't remember her own name, can't even fasten a button. What if that's for me, that place in Kirkintilloch with locks on the doors to stop the poor old souls wandering?

'If you drop us at Saracen, that'd be grand. I need to pick Sid Vicious up from my neighbour,' I say, and Janey's hand goes straight to the car door.

'No sweat. You wanting me to take Sid, by the way? Could do the morrow afternoon.'

'No,' Janey shouts.

'Thanks for the offer, son, but you've done plenty, and I wouldn't want you missing your flute practice.'

'Flute? Fucking flute practice,' Gibby's brother says. And the two of them are in hysterics again. I could have sworn Janey said he played flute in an Orange Band.

Seems I'm just a laughing stock now.

When I get into work, I get a cuddle of the baby. It's always the son that Duncan brings to work, never the daughters. Maybe you need to start hardman training early. Oh, that's no funny, I'm glad I never said it out loud.

Duncan's got something to ask. 'Some guy was in last night asking for work. He said you would vouch for him, Maggie.'

'What was the name?' I'm in the middle of wiping the wee man's chin. Even a baby's sick is a nice thing.

'It's, fuck sake, what's that word? See Jimmy's writing. Aye, it's definitely Alex, Alex something. Says he knows you, says he's been on the black hacks but cannae give a reference cos of "a wee spot of bother". You know him, then?'

Taxi Alex. No him again.

'I know him very slightly. He certainly did have a taxi, let me think, at least till June.'

'Good enough. Long as he can drive, and knows Partick from Pollock. He a Tim, by the way?'

I think of the photograph of the two sons in Celtic strips but say, 'No idea.' Then I wonder what kind of bother Taxi Alex's got into in just six weeks.

Chapter 49

118 days

'So, do you think if I put them in Kirsty's hair, she'll get nits?' Me and Martin are out with Sid and he's talking about the Lice Palaver. Everybody in the whole school got them, no just the one time, but over and over. The stink of nit shampoo was everywhere and the boys all had skinheads and the girls tight ponytails. It was the Smelly Kellys but we weren't allowed to blame them because Jesus would've forgiven anybody that gave him nits.

Martin kept some eggs in a matchbox.

'They're likely dead,' I say. 'Why do you want to infect Kirsty anyway?'

'She ate my fucking Caramac,' he says.

Some days, the only thing in the world that feels real is murdered Samantha, then Martin comes along talking shite, and everything is ordinary again. I guess I'm lucky he still hangs about with me.

'What does an Avenger look like?' I ask.

'Is that a superhero? Cos I only read *2000 AD*. American comics are for morons, except *Uncanny Tales* and *Creepy Worlds* but you only get them in—'

'It's a car, numpty. A Hillman Avenger.' The car Samantha's killer drives.

*

It was a torture being in Gibby's car. Him and his rancid brother, stinking of lager, laughing and taking the mickey out of Nana. I kept imagining Samantha in that car after the party, sitting in the same seat as me, on the way to the Dummy Railway. Did she notice something wasn't right? Was the driver scaring her? Or was she fine right up to the very last minute?

There was a crumpled hanky on the back seat, and I imagined it belonged to her. It was just a hanky but I didn't want to be near it and I jammed myself right against the door in case my skin touched it. When Gibby turned round to talk to me, I nearly jumped out and ran. If Nana hadn't been there I would have.

When we were home, I got out the scrapbook, Heather was totally wrong about burning it. The newspaper report said a dark-coloured Avenger picked Samantha up. Gibby's car is dark, it's jobby-brown apart from one dented white door. But he could easily have switched that.

'How do I know what an Avenger looks like?' Martin says. 'Motors are crap.'

Martin's useless with boy stuff. He was pure depressed when Asha said she's waiting till she's sixteen for a boyfriend, then he cheered up because he won't need to bother fancying anybody for three years.

'Neil knows about cars,' he says, 'he's getting one to go down to London.'

'Is he in? Can we go to yours?'

Martin's brother Neil is eighteen, Donna's age if she was alive. I'm the same age as Martin and I wonder if women can plan babies, I wouldn't even know who to ask about that. Neil is saving to go to London and has lots of jobs. At night, he works in a warehouse, in the morning, delivers ginger on the Alpine lorry, and on weekends, washes dishes in a fancy café in town.

Aunty Angela thinks he's going to London to train as a chef, but it's really to get away from his dad.

Today, he's getting paid to babysit Kirsty, which is a bit rubbish cos he should do that for nothing. When we go in, Bob Marley's on, and Kirsty is jumping around like mental. Neil grabs Sid's front paws and they dance too.

'Sid Vicious joins the Wailers,' he shouts, and it's funny cos Sid really is wailing.

Martin takes the record off to watch TV, and I play with Kirsty for a while. She's all red and hot from jammin, and keeps shouting that she wants a coal-carry. I make her sit down with the Weebles. George got her a massive new set-up with a tree house that cost way more than the three quid he gave Martin.

The money isn't the main reason the brothers don't like their dad – it's cos whatever they do, George says it's crap. One time, Martin got a Gold Star in a spelling test, and George said he must've cheated. And when Neil passed his driving test, George said the instructor was likely blind. Then he pretends it's all just a wee joke.

'Do you know what a Hillman Avenger is?' I ask when Neil finishes tidying up the ornaments that Sid knocked over.

'The antelope's horn is off, that needs wood glue,' he says. 'What's that about an Avenger?'

'What does a Hillman Avenger look like?'

'You giving up those mad bands and getting into cars then?' Neil sometimes slags me and Martin about punk, but compared to other big brothers I've seen, Neil is OK.

'It's just, just something for school,' I say. You can say that for anything cos nobody's interested.

'Aye, the Avenger's a decent car, and you can pick them up cheap. My mate got one at auction with radio-cassette, leather seat covers, an engine—' I stop listening because it's very boring. Then I remember the camera.

'See if I bring a photo of a car, will you know if it's an Avenger?'
I ask.

'Aye, sure. But this sounds right mad for a school thing, specially in the holidays,' Neil says. Luckily, Aunty Angela comes home and asks me and Sid to stay for dinner. She doesn't notice the antelope even though it's stuck together with sellotape.

It's fish fingers then Arctic Roll cos they've got a freezer. Aunty Angela is pleased that I eat everything and she'll probably make a special visit to let Nana know. But that's OK, now I've got a plan.

Nino said he'd get somebody from a law place to help, so I can tell the police about the word on Samantha's forehead and they won't be able to shout or arrest me or poke about in Nana's business. A photo of Gibby's dark-coloured Avenger would be good to show them too. And if Lulu comes back, I'll make a new plan about him.

Heather might be giving up but I'm no. Even if I can't remember enough to relive the day like Uncle Finn says, I'm still going to help Samantha.

Chapter 50

When I worked at The Glen, Friday was just the day before the long rotten Saturday shift. Now, it's payday, dominoes and the weekend to look forward to. It'll need to be the shops for school shoes tomorrow, still no quite as bad as fishing fag dowts out the urinals.

'Hullo, Maggie.'

'Jeez-oh, I jumped out my skin. What you doing here?'

Taxi Alex has aged ten years. His cheeky-boy face is covered in ginger stubble and his freckles are drowned in the greyness of his skin. Even his false teeth are suffering.

'I'm starting work the night,' he says. 'Somebody's showing me the car later, but I wanted to see you first, say thanks, ken.'

'Thanks for what?'

'I was told that you spoke for me. Much appreciated, Maggie. When Stuart said you were working at Ashfield, it felt like a lifeline to a drowning man. A lifeline.'

'Alex, what happened? Where's your real taxi?'

I'm due my tea and I take Alex to the Break Room. All his frantic energy has gone and he sags like a three-pound bag of potatoes. I put his tea in one of the filthy mugs, it's no like he's fussy any more.

'I try no to blame my wife,' he says, 'she's a lovely, lovely woman, but when she walked out with my two laddies, I wanted to strangle her. Hand to God, I would've killed her if I wasn't too drunk to stand.'

'You're drinking again?' Oh, that's tragic.

'It was the stress. The police pulled me in nearly every day for a month, a whole bloody month. There was never anything straightforward, just insinuations. Nasty, filthy insinuations, sometimes for hours. Even after they lifted Lulu, they tried to make out I knew him and that I was in on some scheme to get money. At the end of July, I lost my taxi, then I lost my family.'

'You weren't drinking and driving, were you?'

'I couldn't fucking sleep, woman. Drink was my only option,' he says, and I don't like his tone. The man's on the very edge.

'Does Duncan know this? Driving with a drink is no right, you need to—'

'He knows. And he knows I'm nine days sober. Stuart will back me up on that. Nine days might seem like nothing but let me tell you—'

'Well, Duncan obviously doesn't have very high safety standards if he's taking you on. And I'm not saying that to be rotten, it's the plain truth,' I say.

'Before you fall off your high horse, think on this. The state I'm in, with no job and no family, that's all down to your granddaughter. Remind yourself about that bairn of yours wandering about on the road, all blood and pish, and I was the only one that stopped, the only one.' His voice is getting higher as it gets louder, and the other drivers are staring. 'Then she sent me down that railway looking for her eejit dog. Left my footprints at a crime scene, saw what she saw. Saw that, that abomination. And you know what, Maggie Devine, I wish to fuck that I had just kept driving.'

Alex slams the mug down and strides out. Everybody is looking at me and my face burns with shame. I never thought.

*

Later, I go to the off-licence for a quarter-bottle, then stop in to tell Jean I'm too tired for dominoes. Janey must've waited at Angela's for dinner and that works out well. It does me good to sit alone and mull over what a self-righteous midden I've been.

All their faces come to me, all the lives touched by Samantha's murder – Billy and the Watsons, Alex and his two wee ginger nuts, the college pals, Skinny Jimmy with a stab wound, Lulu and his family. And of course, Janey and myself. Even big ugly Sid Vicious losing Janey's love. Talk about ripples on a pond. And right at the centre of it all, the devil who killed her.

'Marie, is that you, pet?'

I don't know where I am.

'It's me, Nana. You were dreaming,' Janey says.

'Dreaming?'

'You were saying sorry, over and over.'

'When did you get in, lamb? Have you had your dinner?'

'I'm fine. Just go to your bed,' she says, 'it's night.'

When I stand, I actually hear something inside me creak. The noise of an old door. Christ. In the bathroom mirror, I stare at the new hollows under my eyes and the dream comes back. I know who I was apologizing to. But sorry will never be enough because it was my fault that my family died.

No directly my fault, which was obviously the Gas Board, and no my fault if you believe that God has predestined death dates for every one of us, which seems like a nonsense. But it was another of those ripples and it was me at the centre.

Marie and her family were living in a pokey room and kitchen with rowdy neighbours and a crumbling unlit stair. Marie, always one to make the best of things, never complained, but Vinnie's parents were worried and offered them a place to stay. The last of the Rizzo sons had just got married and they had this big house in Cathcart with two extra rooms and a garden. But I didn't want my family on the other side of the city, I wanted them near enough that I could speak to my daughter and play with my granddaughters every day. So, I warned Marie against living with her in-laws and talked her into putting her name down with the Corporation. A couple of months later, they took the flat in Maryhill.

So it was me, me being selfish and foolish and bad. And, God help me, they aren't the only deaths I have on my conscience.

Chapter 51

119 days

Saturday is when men go to the pub so I thought tonight'd be a good time to look for Gibby's car. The camera was all set and ready when Lorraine showed up. Nana brought her in and gave us cakes so it'll need to wait. I'm getting that way where you know something bad is coming but you want it to happen soon.

As Nana left, she told us to try on our uniforms, but Lorraine decided to practise her smoking and we're on the way to the Red Shop for a single. Lorraine's got her own lighter. I never smoke, I can't take a chance on anything stunting my growth.

We meet Jamesie from our class, and he's got five Players.

I don't like Jamesie. One time at school dinner, me and Jackie were sitting beside him and he poked one of my badges with his custardy spoon. 'Is that another of your daft made-up bands?'

'The Buzzcocks are punk,' I told him.

'Cocks,' Jamesie said and did that rude thing with his pinkie finger. A couple of people at the table laughed.

'You know nothing,' I said and flicked a mandarin skiff at him.

'See her?' Jamesie was shouting now. 'She's only into punk cos Martin's into punk. You say you like those bands just to copy your cousin, Janey Devine.' More people laughed, and Jackie laughed the loudest and that's when I went off her too.

Jamesie was talking shite. Before I made Martin listen to *Streetsounds*, the only record he liked was The Smurfs.

'Ah'll gie you a fag,' Jamesie tells Lorraine, 'if you come round the back of the Askit Factory.' He puts his arm round her waist and winks, which looks insane with his skellie-eye. Even in the holidays, Jamesie wears a trampy school jumper that smells of meat so no way should he be getting wide with Lorraine.

'Piss off,' she says, 'and mind the hair.' Lorraine is way too fussy about her hair, it's in a layered wedge and needs brushing every two minutes. With a special brush.

'Mon a wee while,' Jamesie says, then lowers his voice, 'Ah'll show you the hatchet we found.'

'What the fuck would I want to see a hatchet for?' Lorraine is getting annoyed.

'Ask her,' Jamesie points at me, 'she saw the deid woman. They did her with this hatchet. We saw two guys planking it down a stank.'

I don't want this, I don't want to know any of this, but still ask, 'What did the guys look like? Did you tell the police?'

'Aye, right. Two big cunts wi a hatchet. Like we'd run to the polis.' Jamesie rolls his squint, then squeezes even closer to Lorraine. 'Me and Kendo and Fat Scobie jumped the Askit wall with the bad-wire and we saw—'

'Bad-wire? Bad?' Lorraine laughs. 'It's barbed, stupid face.'

Jamesie gets a pure beamer so crashes his fags to distract us. Lorraine's dead showy with her lighter.

'What happened with the hatchet but?' she goes, and Jamesie huddles in again.

'Right, so. They gets out this BMW, black, pure class but. They had scarves right up their faces and aw we could see was their eyes and black gloves and clothes. Like big kung-fu ninjas. They were scoping out the whole place but they didnae see us or nothing or they'd have done us an all. Then that tube, Fat Scobie, sneezed and we—'

'How'd you know it was the killers?' I ask, in the voice of a toaty baby.

'Cos of the hatchet.' Jamesie draws on his fag like he's a man, holding the smoke in till even Lorraine is impressed. 'Polis can guess the weapon by the shape of the wounds. Ah bet that body was hacked to bits, sure it was? See in that film *Psycho* that big slice on the guy's coupon when—'

'You never saw *Psycho*, you wee liar,' Lorraine says.

'Aye, Ah have. Yous coming or no? Cos Ah can go in for Jackie.' Jamesie starts walking and Lorraine runs after him.

Do I want to see the hatchet? I don't know, I don't know. Maybe it could be something else to tell the police when I take my clues, another thing that helps Samantha. The two ninja guys might've been Gibby and his brother, or Lulu and one of the crime gang. But do I want to look at a hatchet and wonder if it made the mess of Samantha's body?

In the end, I run after them because I don't want to be left alone.

Saracen is mobbed, all the pubs loud and mental. Jamesie stops to watch two women fighting outside The Standard. They are slapping and kicking at each other in a lopsided drunk way. Men at the pub door are laughing and one steps out. It's Skinny Jimmy, in a cream-coloured suit that doesn't look like his own. He grabs the youngish woman, the other is Nana's age, and pulls her close. Then he starts kissing her. She's trying to wriggle away but Skinny Jimmy's got a hand up her blouse. It makes me feel woozy and sick and I don't want to go and look at the hatchet any more. The older woman falls and Lorraine and Jamesie start arguing about whether it's a sin for her or no.

I watch their mouths moving but my ears have stopped working. Something's floating about in the air. Smoke.

'Janey, Janey. Wrap it in, people's looking.'

I'm sitting on the kerb, head low with my hands over my ears. Sirens are screeching and there's blue lights that make me think of Christmas. Lorraine has her arms around me and I feel like a dick when I pull away.

'You're OK,' she says, 'it's just fire engines.'

'Fire engines,' I say, and spit acidy sourness onto the pavement. Lorraine watches the crowd running towards the smoke, Jamesie already following.

'Mon we'll go,' she says, pulling me to my feet, 'mon see what's burning.'

We don't have to walk far to see Ashfield Cabs on fire.

Chapter 52

I've left Janey in with Aileen Callaghan to try on their new school clothes. A nice ordinary wee evening for her. Aileen? No, that's no right. What is it with that wean that I can never get her name? It's, it's . . . ach, nothing there but a dod of empty space. It was a delight to see her anyway and I left them a box of Mr Kipling that— Lorraine. It's Lorraine. Thank God.

Sid Vicious and I are taking another box to Angela's dad. Mr Kipling were half-price in the Red Shop and the dented packets hardly noticeable. Ali is still repeating the story he heard from Big Des, Lulu was alibied by somebody wanting to get at him and there were plenty of candidates. To stop him talking, I complained about the price of his beans. I hope the McLure family never gets to hear, imagine knowing your son is in that kind of danger.

It's near nine and the weans are still out playing kerby, they get wild near the end of summer. I wind the lead tight around my hand, Sid Vicious is notorious for bursting footballs.

Angela moved her family here from Maryhill right after the explosion. She was heartbroken and in shock and very lucky to get one of the nice two-in-a-block houses in Auckland Street. It wasn't long after that her parents got a mutual exchange, moving in right round the corner. See, that's what I should've done, followed Marie and Vinnie to the Rizzo house on the Southside, got myself a wee place close by. A snippet of some poem comes to mind, something from school. I can hear the teacher reciting in his Highland lilt, and Nancy Smedley giggling because I said his head looked like a chimney pot. The poem was about the road not taken.

You could drive yourself to an early grave thinking about roads not taken.

Angela's mother, Bernadette O'Shea, opens the door. She's carrying a rosary, on her way to say a Novena for the leg. Very devout, so she is.

'He's struggling, Maggie. We've had to put him in the living room.'

A big lassie in an overall and sturdy shoes appears. Burly would be a fair way to describe her, with a hard-working rosiness to her cheeks. 'Are you a home-help?' I ask.

'Fiona Hendry, trainee SRN,' she says, shaking my hand. I remember Angela mentioning the posh nurse, and she shows me in as Bernadette leaves for St Teresa's.

Bernard's bed takes up most of the living room. Bernard and Bernadette, and always the wee joke about how their names brought them together. Awful nice couple, very caring parents and very well liked. Bernard has suffered with the bad leg for donkeys' years but never to this extent.

On the display unit, there's a photograph of the whole family in wedding finery, next to Bernard's medals. Angela has no idea what the medals are for; they never tell, those men. Never.

'This is a rare set-up, you can watch the telly from your bed, Bernard.'

'You know, apart from Bernadette, you're the only person left that calls me Bernard. Last ones standing so we are, and no for much longer either,' he says.

'Away. We've years ahead of us.'

'I'm sixty-eight in October, if the Lord spares me.'

Sixty-eight isn't old but he might be right about not seeing it. The air in the room is sour and medicinal with a hint of wound rot. No wonder Angela's worried.

'Have you seen much of your boys?' I ask. There's two O'Shea sons still in Glasgow and a third, well, I don't rightly know where he is. He gave up priest training and ran away with the anarchists. I don't expect he's visited.

'Peter was in Friday, Dermot and his lot on Sunday. But they don't stay long,' Bernard says. 'A blessing I have my Angela. Daughters are a gift from God.'

There's never a truer word spoken.

We blether for a while until a French Fancy takes him by surprise. Nurse Fiona moves quickly to stop him choking then he falls asleep with the exertion. She makes herself comfortable on the pouffe and counts pills into a plastic dispenser. I don't think I've ever met anybody with such vibrant grey eyes. Or such small teeth, like a hamster when she yawns. When I see any nurse, there's always a wee twinge of, not envy exactly, more a kind of longing, because nursing was what I had set my young heart on. In the twenties, my Aunty O'Connell spent her final months in a TB sanatorium and I just loved going to visit. It wasn't to see the poor aunt, who I barely knew, it was to watch the nurses. Those women moved through the wards like they ruled the world. When I left school though, my father said no. It was fair enough for my brother to study as a clerk but to waste college on a daughter was a nonsense. And what your da said was law. Maybe it's just as well, who knows what the war would have done to a young nurse.

Watching Nurse Fiona work with the same confidence, I start wondering if Samantha would have made a good social worker.

'Angela was telling me that you went to school with Samantha

Watson, God rest her.' I shouldn't bring this up but it's out my mouth before I can stop it.

'I did, yes, I did,' she says. She has a beautiful speaking voice, warm and reassuring, and even if she was amputating your arm, you'd feel at ease. 'As training goes on, I'm getting used to losing patients, but I'll never come to terms with Samantha's death, never.'

'I'm no being nosey, hen, it's just that it was my granddaughter found the body. We feel connected, you see.'

'Angela told me about Janey, what a shocking experience for her. And for yourself of course,' she says, then after a pause asks, 'Mrs Devine, have you had any bother with reporters?'

I mention yon scunner at the funeral and Fiona tells me what happened in July. 'My mum's getting on a bit and when the reporter came to our door, she thought it was something to do with the drains. When I got home from work, they were having tea together. The reporter took some time to come to the point and—'

'Was it a woman? Gayle Something, with big glasses?' I ask.

'It was a woman, although I don't think she gave her name. No idea where she got my details but she claimed to be writing an article about the real Samantha Watson, something to redress what had been printed in the gutter press. Personally, Mrs Devine, I would have shown her the door—'

'Aye, and the toe of your boot,' I say.

'Exactly. But Mum is a quiet, trusting person and she reminded me of the lovely Samantha memories that could be included in an article.' Fiona smiles as she remembers but the pale eyes are tearful. 'I know I sound privileged, Mrs Devine, but my dad's a farm labourer and I only got a place at Bishopbriggs Academy because Mum fought hard. Money at home was tight and the school had ridiculously high standards. It was Samantha who noticed, and helped. It began with a blazer – she said she'd been given an extra one and would I like it? Every term she'd pass on something and always without a single soul knowing. I don't know why at that age, but Samantha understood the embarrassment of being poor. She understood friendship.'

The more I hear about Samantha Watson, the more I like the lassie.

'But that's no what the reporter was wanting though,' I say.

'No, it wasn't.' Nurse Fiona's lovely voice has an edge now. 'When all I could say about Billy Watson was how friendly he'd been, the reporter's questions turned to boyfriends. "Love-life" was the phrase used. Samantha had a reputation at school, were there many boyfriends? Men? Did she see grown men? Any indication of an unwanted teen pregnancy?'

This would make you weep, so it would. Samantha was a child.

'Said she was going to write the article anyway and wouldn't I prefer it to be the truth. When she had the effrontery to offer money I sent the parasite packing.'

'It's a damned disgrace, so it is,' I say. But then, something occurs to me. 'You're right to be protective of Samantha but what about him with the name? The ex-boyfriend that treated her badly. Maybe he should be shamed in the papers?'

Bernard wakes up at this point, ready for another chat. He used to be a right funny man, full of the jokes, even looks like Eric Morecambe. Now, everything's about Bernadette and the good works she does. He's turning her into a saint, poor woman. I admit I do that with Donna but at eight years old, it's the truth.

Nurse Fiona has to see to his leg, but she takes me to one side and it's obvious she's already considered the librarian thing, maybe even talked it over with quiet trusting Mum.

'Apart from teachers, no one at school liked Ninian Hogg. He was one of those kids that know exactly what adults like to hear, a suck-up I guess. God knows what Samantha saw in him but the other boys tormented him. I generally avoided him but there's a day . . . Samantha and I had been to a netball match and Hogg arrived in his uncle's car to drive us home. He always seemed to show up when Samantha was out on her own. She was different around him, all her spark gone, and we drove in complete silence. Suddenly, the car slammed hard into a van stopped at a junction. Hogg very calmly got out, signalling to Samantha to do the same, then whispered in her ear. The van driver was storming but Hogg ignored him. He marched Samantha to the car window. "Tell her, Samantha," he said, "tell your friend." She looked at me, tears running down her face. "Sorry," she said, "I'm very sorry, Fiona. I distracted Nino and made him crash." He made her repeat it to the driver and that poor girl had not done a single thing wrong. Oh, you've never seen such humiliation.'

Fiona breathes deeply to calm herself. I do the same because I'm back in a single-end in Maryhill.

Donald Devine was drinking with a couple of his cronies. 'C'mere, Mags,' he said, grabbing my arm as I passed. Then he lifted the back of my skirt and held it high. Right in front of those men. 'See, tolt yous,' he said and the three of them roared with laughter.

Aye, I know about humiliation.

'The problem is,' Fiona says, hurrying now because Bernard's needing the bed pan, 'the problem with mentioning Ninian Hogg to the newspaper, it wouldn't be him that suffers. It had already happened at school, that's what the reporter meant about Samantha's reputation. She was . . . talked about. Going out with an older boy made everyone assume she was sexually active and the media would make the same assumptions. Hogg hurt Samantha in life, I can't let that continue in death.'

Apart from Janey, I rarely cuddle anyone, but I wrap my arms around that big lassie. 'You're a credit to your pal, hen.'

'I suppose it will all blow over once they catch the murderer,' she says. But I have a feeling it'll be a long time before the papers let go of this story.

I'd let Sid Vicious wander around the backcourt and he comes when I shout. Well, he comes when he hears me open the potted hough that Bernadette left for him.

'Just eat it here, son, it's going off,' I say. 'Look, red sky at night. Nice day tomorrow, Sid Vicious.' But a fire engine goes tearing by, then a police car, and the weans are chasing after them. Suddenly my legs won't carry me.

Chapter 53

119 days

It's mostly smoke puffing out of Ashfield Cabs, like a big storm cloud landed in the street. All the flames and heat are in the back car park where a minicab is blazing.

'Oh, nice, look at it burn. I'm going to get a scream going.' Lorraine loves a good scream but I drag her along the street towards Mr O'Shea's house, doing all the Hail Marys, till we see them. Nana and Sid.

'Nana,' I shout, 'we were coming to get you, the—'

'—a big fire, Mrs Devine, and—' Lorraine says.

'—it's at your work, Nana. Ashfield Cabs is burning.'

'Sweet Mary, Mother of God,' Nana says and crosses herself. Me and Lorraine take a hand each to hurry her along, and I grab Sid's lead and drag him. They're the only ones that don't want to go and watch.

'We knew you weren't on fire but,' Lorraine tells Nana.

'I was a bit worried,' I say and squeeze her hand. 'You maybe popped in to see your boss or something.' It was more than worry. I got it in my head that I was meant to die with my family and that Nana was in there burning to make up for it.

The crowd at Ashfield is getting bigger, everybody ignoring the firemen's shouts to stand back. There's police too but they're no doing anything. Somebody's handing out Jaffa Cakes and

Mrs Craig is using a tennis racket to keep the wee kids from getting too close. Nana says she's got to get Sid home but I know it's her that wants to go, I know what she'll be thinking about.

Lorraine is talking to Jamesie and some of his pals, so I wander over to watch the burning car. The windows are caved in and the paint is blistered, springs show through the melted seats and it stinks of burning rubber. I try never to think about how Mammy and Daddy and Donna died, if they were crushed or burned, but this brings a picture of them scorched and shrivelled and huddled together. I turn away quick, and there's Taxi Alex. He's sitting all by hisself on the pavement, in a state, and I feel sorry for him.

'Hullo,' I say, 'it's me. My nana said you worked here now. Is that your taxi on fire? Are you OK?'

'You,' he says, 'and here I am thinking the night couldn't get any worse. Do you think I'm OK? Do I look OK?' His squeaky voice is loud, more like a squeaky shout. 'Have you no done enough? Just get tae fuck out my sight.'

That's rotten, I'm only trying to be nice. He's lucky Nana didn't see. When I don't move, he stands and shoves me and I stumble backwards into Mr Burns from 9B. Now he's shouting at me too. I run to Lorraine and try to concentrate on the embers floating about in the sky. They're like toaty red butterflies. At least it's easy to pretend it's just the smoke when she asks if I'm crying.

I don't get it. Taxi Alex was nice on Dummy Railway Day. Maybe he thinks I know who lit the fire. Maybe he thinks it was my pals, or, or me even. People think everybody round here is mental. Or maybe he knows that I stuck him in to Val and he's been getting police hassle. Another thing that's my fault.

Chapter 54

See, this is the nonsense in films, when something bad happens they all race towards it. Even old yins like John Wayne run like billy-o when the shooting starts. But you can't, when the fear hits you, you can't move. Me anyway. But then I saw them, Janey and what's-her-name, racing along Auckland Street and my guts went back to normal. I know I should've been concerned about my workmates and about customers and firemen being harmed, but all I could think was, if Ashfield burns to the ground, how am I going to pay the rent?

The firemen are trying to stop a small but fierce blaze spreading from the back door and one of the cabs is well alight. Half of Possil has gathered, the rest watching from windows. There's a lot of drinking and the weans are dancing about like these ancient pagans you see in films. Funny how religion uses flames as both the torment of Hell and as the comfort of the Holy Spirit, like the Popes can't make their minds up.

Janey is with her pals and I tell her no longer than an hour. A fire is too sore for me to watch but I'm old and slow and the past catches me anyway.

*

Right after the explosion, the woman from Immaculate Conception nailed a blanket over my kitchen window so I wouldn't see the rubble. It was a week before I was fit to go outside and I had Janey by that time. There was nothing left belonging to her, no even a spare nappy, and her pram was a ramshackle old thing that a neighbour had handed in. The wheels squealed as we walked to Maryhill Road, a terrible ordinariness about the day with the reek of lingering gas the only hint of death. In those days, safety was a flimsy wire fence strung around the accident site and a couple of big lads were climbing about in the debris, 'lookin for luckies', they said. What surprised me was how small the pile was. A four-storey tenement reduced to a wee hill of blackened wood and broken stone. Reminded me of Clydebank after the air raids and the streets strewn with brick and furniture and people's lives. The pile was still smoking in places, the teenagers cheerfully ignoring the smoke and embers, when suddenly a huge blue bolt roared up behind them. It frightened baby Janey but I barely moved. One of the lads laughed. 'There's still gas trapped, missus,' he said and went back to poking about with his stick.

Funny that, the fire smouldering all that time and then bursting out.

Sid Vicious and I squeeze through the crowd and suddenly the heat hits my face.

Did they feel it? My wee family sitting at their kitchen table – did they feel that heat before the fireball took them?

The dog tugs at the lead but I haven't the energy to move. I lay a hand on my chest to try to slow my heartbeat and gasp to stop the faint coming. And then she's beside me. Mrs Khan.

'Let me take your arm, Mrs Devine,' she says, and I feel her strength and kindness and it's enough.

'Now, we all go together,' she says, and I notice Wee Morag

latched tightly to her other arm. We hang on like weans as Mrs Khan guides us to the back of the crowd and stops to let us get our bearings.

'This is not a sight for you. Bad memories,' she says quietly when I thank her.

Wee Morag is rummaging in the dirty plastic bag she carries everywhere. 'They've been at it again,' she says, 'this is their handiwork, so it is. I'll need to put it in the book.'

It's difficult to say what age Morag is. It's assumed she's middle-aged because of the constant headscarf and heavy coat, and because she's no the full shilling, but looking at her in the glow of the flames, I'd swear she's only in her twenties. Her thin hand shakes as she opens the jotter filled with offences. I've always wondered who it is she takes umbrage with – the ones who supposedly stick bible pages to her door, who play bagpipes in the night, who shove stolen polo-necks through her window even though she's on the fifteenth floor. I wonder if Morag knows.

'Are we ready to walk again?' Mrs Khan asks, surveying the route like a tank commander.

'Missus, missus.' Somebody tugs at the back of my cardigan, his voice making the three of us jump. It's a man, a young lad, in one of these sweatshirts with a hood like a boxer. There's something familiar in his height.

'Lulu, is that you, son?'

He looks around then pulls the hood down. 'Aye, it's me, Mrs Devine, but gonnae keep your voice down.'

'Where's your hair?' I say. His clothes are dirty and I can smell him even above the smoke, but it's the cropped stubble that bothers me most.

'Should I intervene?' Mrs Khan whispers in my ear. I'm surprised, but comforted, she believes she could go ahead with big Lulu.

'We'll wait and see what he's got to say for hisself,' I say loudly.

'Ah've no got any time to talk,' Lulu says, eyes swivelling, 'gonnae just lend us a couple of bob?'

'Money? You're no going to tell me what's going on, but you're wanting money?'

A police car is parked a few yards behind us, but with the weans squealing, would they hear if I shouted? I don't know what to do here.

Lulu steps closer. 'It wisnae me, Ah swear on my sisters' lives, it wisnae me that killed Samantha. It wis—'

He stops as the firemen sound the siren to stop a couple of lads trying to lob a Calor gas canister into the flames. The crowd boos and there's going to be disappointment if the firemen put it out too quickly.

'Mrs Devine, please. Ah'm begging here.' Lulu's eyes barely leave the police. Or is it the Edgar brothers he's watching? 'Ah need to get to Bishopbriggs to tell Billy what Jimmy's been up to. And about MacQuarrie.' His voice cracks now, the hardman gone. 'Ah, Ah'm starving an all.'

At this, Mrs Khan produces a huge leather purse and Wee Morag scrabbles about in her bag.

'Nobody should be hungry,' Mrs Khan says, handing him a pound note. Wee Morag finds a couple of ten pence pieces, that wee soul barely feeds herself. I feel ashamed and give him the silver from my purse.

'Cheers,' Lulu says, 'yous are good women. There's no anybody good on my side.' Then he pulls up the hood and sprints away towards the Cross. If the police decide to look for the arsonist, my guess is he'll be in the chippie.

With Mrs Khan leading, we start moving towards the flats.

'The fire,' Wee Morag says, and I see her shrink into herself, 'it's spreading.'

'No, no, the firemen are doing a grand job,' I say. 'You'll be safe soon, pet.'

'We're never safe,' she whispers.

I look back to where the Edgar brothers are shouting and waving their arms at a yawning policeman, and the drivers in an edgy huddle, and Taxi Alex sitting on the kerb, weeping into his hands. And I think about Lulu, still around after all.

Maybe Wee Morag is right, maybe we're never safe.

Chapter 55

121 days

Even two days later, I still taste smoke in my mouth. It makes me think of The Screke and I don't know why. What, what was burning? The smell of smoke in the darkness and somebody was . . . it's vanished again.

Nana went down to Ashfield early this morning to see what's happening about her job but it was all locked up. Most of the damage is at the back where their Break Room is. She said her front counter looks fine, but it's a shame the couch survived. She's praying to St Jude that it might open again soon. He's patron saint of hopeless causes.

After lunch, she asks me to nip down too.

'Just have a wee look, see if anybody's there yet. If it's Duncan or Jimmy, don't say anything, just come and get me,' she says.

She makes me take Sid, which feels like I'm dragging one of those things prisoners wear in *The Beano*. A ball and chain, that's it, Sid's my ball and chain. At least I'm no by myself.

Ashfield Cabs is usually whitewashed and now it's a big mess of manky smears, and already spray-painted. Nobody would paint 'IRA' and 'Provos' if Eggman was in there. Rubbish from last night is scattered right up the street, chip pokes and cans and Mrs Craig's tennis racket. The burnt-out taxi is still in the back car park and wee kids are playing in it. One of the Smelly Kellys is the driver, throwing his pal out for no paying the fare. Somebody must have been inside because there's a pile of smoke-blackened stuff – chairs, cups, kettle, a lavvie pan. I kick a mug that has 'World's Best Wife' on it and Smelly Kelly boy comes over.

'Oh ah, cha, cha, cha,' he says, 'a big man told us no to touch nothing. You're gonnae get leathered.' He's happy about that. The sooty rust makes him look like a wee chimney sweep from the olden days and he's the one that'll get leathered when he goes home like that. I kick the mug again, and when nobody comes, he does the same. Wee copycat.

Even at the Red Shop, I can hear him and his pals smashing the lavvie pan. I brought gas meter money for a Super Duper Mr Frostypop. And because the shop is empty, Ali lets me take my time choosing for a 10p Mix-Up.

Dogs are allowed in but not Sid cos he once stood on his hind paws and ate all the iced buns off the counter.

The shop fills with the smell of car oil and lager, and my heart starts hammering.

'Half-ounce Golden Virginia,' Gibby says, standing close beside me. 'Some fire last night, Ali. Know what Ah think?' I grab a bunch of jelly eyeballs and try to give Ali my money and leave before Gibby says what he thinks. 'Ah think it was a warning, know? A warning to somebody no to open their fucking stupid mouth.' He leans forward, close to my ear, and I know he's not really talking to Ali.

I dump my ten pences on the counter and squeeze against the big fridge to get out without going too near Gibby. I slam the door even though there's a sign that says not to.

Me and Sid run like mental along Bardowie Street. I don't know if Gibby's chasing us, I'm no slowing down to check. But Sid stops suddenly and I get jerked to the ground. Sid is likely strong enough to pull a tank, and I always wonder why he just doesn't go where he wants all the time.

'What you doing?' I say, looking up at him. The knees are out my denims, and my wrist's grazed.

It's Colette's cat.

I wish that cat had a name, even Tabby would do. Maybe Colette gave it a name but keeps it secret because it's so daft. Like the woman at Mass who had to change Pussy-Wee-Man to Boab.

Sid is no moving. He's crouched, doing a low growl and there's slabbers dripping over his fangs. The lead vibrates as he gets hisself ready to attack. Colette's cat doesn't move either. It's just sitting there, fur sticking up like the spiky grass on Fraserburgh sand dunes. Suddenly, I'm raging. Raging at the two of them.

'Get away, cat, get safe,' I shout and hiss at it. When it finally runs, I smack Sid's nose with the Mr Frostypop. 'Don't you dare, you stupid bugger dog. Don't you dare.'

And then Gibby arrives.

'C'mere, you. Up,' he says and lifts me by the hood. It's strangling me. I make a muffled noise but Gibby does scissor fingers to his tongue, like he's cutting it off. Then he does his no-funny laugh, brushes me down and goes, 'Watch yourself, hen, running away like that. Gonnae get hurt.'

Nana catches me before I can get to my room.

'Lucky it didn't start the sore knee bleeding again,' she says, when I tell her I fell. 'Take your trousers off and I'll sew them.'

'It's fine, I'm fine, just leave us alone.'

'You need to wash that cut. Toilet, now, and change the trousers,' she shouts, then more quietly, 'Did anything else happen? You're awful upset for a wee fall, lamb.'

'It was the stupid dog. I hate him, hate him.' I pull my cagoule off and something falls out the hood. It's the monkey t-shirt Nana bought me in Stirling Stevens. I thought it got left at the bus stop but it must've been in Gibby's car. My hands shake when I see what he's done – the happy chimp's mouth is ripped off and his googly eyes are poked out.

Nana stares. 'Did you cut that up for yon daft punk rock? You should've said you didn't like it and saved me wasting money. Honestly, Janey, you would try the patience of a saint.'

'It wasn't me, I didn't do that, it was Gi—' Crap. I nearly said it, I nearly said his name.

'It was who? Who cut that up?' She's still angry.

'Nobody,' I say. If Gibby is the killer, he'd kill her too.

'Janey, what the hell is going on with you?' She snatches the t-shirt, saying it'll do for cloths, then she says in a softer voice, 'You would tell me if there's anything, wouldn't you? It's no good to keep things to yourself. A secret is . . .'

But she doesn't say what a secret is.

When she's watching *Coronation Street*, I get the camera ready. Tomorrow I'm taking the picture of Gibby's car. Then I'll write everything down – about the swear word and the hatchet and Heather no knowing when Lulu left the party and Gibby's threats. Then I'll ask Nino to get his law helper and we'll all talk to the police together. I need this to be done.

Chapter 56

Secret. I was about to tell Janey that a secret is a lonely thing, but she would have asked about mine and I've never told a soul. Not even the Confessional priest, because that would mean asking forgiveness and I'm no sorry. I'm no sorry.

On yon *Star Trek* that Janey loves, the handsome captain has part of his memory destroyed by some alien gizmo with flashing lights. If they ever invent a real machine to do that, I'd use it to take Samantha Watson from Janey. And I'd take 6th January 1943 from myself.

It was a terrible cold night, there was ice on the inside of our windows and the streets were treacherous. Donald Devine had still managed a session in The Vaults though, and was sleeping it off. I was doing my utmost not to wake him, which wasn't easy after eating bad clappy-doos from a seafood stall. Marie was just turned two and usually slept without a peep, the wee sweetheart. Cross my heart to God, never a day passed that she didn't bring me joy. But something woke her that night, maybe it was me rushing out to the toilet on the landing, maybe the cold, or just a bad dream. The second I got back in, I could hear the wrongness of her cry, a jerking gasp like a backwards scream.

Marie's bed was in the kitchen alcove, and in the light keeking under the blackout blind, I saw a wee sock lying on the lino. Marie had laughed and laughed getting those socks on, because we had Little Piggy Went to Market. The sock was off because he was shaking her, Donald Devine was shaking my child like a wet rag. I grabbed him, tugging at his pyjamas, tugging at his hair, desperate and screaming until he let her go.

'Keep your fucking wean quiet,' he said, as casually as he would tell me to bring his tea. Then he went back to bed and was asleep in minutes.

The next morning, I stood up to him, warning that if he ever laid a hand on Marie again, I'd tell my brothers and they would take him apart. Dear God, I can still hear Donald laughing when I said that. All the courage that took, every ounce of my strength and he laughed and said nobody would believe me. Nobody.

I'd use Captain Kirk's memory wiping machine on this next bit too. Or would I? I can't honestly be sure.

I'll never know what wrecked Donald's lungs. Our factory switched from shipyard parts to making something for the Navy, and he was one of the skilled workers in a locked room off the main floor. If he knew what it was they were making, he certainly never told me, but there was a dust, and they breathed it in. He wasn't the only one from that locked room to suffer but at least somebody was paying the doctors' bills. When Donald's coughing fits got worse, the hospital gave us a special hypodermic. I can't remember what the drug was, but a nurse came to the house to show me how to inject him in a crisis.

A month after her father's assault, Marie's bruises were finally fading. I'd taken to sleeping in the kitchen next to her, and was getting my nightdress on when Donald started banging on the wall with his shoe. It was usual for him to cough when he lay down, but when I went in, he was sitting on the edge of the bed. It had reached the stage where he was too weak to cough and was struggling for breath. The greyness of his lips was the warning sign and I rushed to get the syringe. As I prepared his arm like the nurse showed me, I noticed the rip. The rip in his pyjamas where I had dragged him off, the rip from the night I had to stop him killing my baby. A calmness filled my mind, a clarity as bright and lovely as the blessed Holy Ghost, and I walked slowly to put the syringe back in the drawer. Then I watched. I watched the anger and hate in my husband's eyes turn to fear.

'Mags,' he gasped, even now using the name he knew I disliked, 'need . . . Ah . . . ma . . .' For a man with such a vicious tongue, Donald was surprisingly coy about bodily functions. With shaking hand, he pointed at his trousers. 'T . . . toilet, ma bowels.'

And that's when I left him to die.

Chapter 57

122 days

I've been looking since morning but still haven't found Gibby's car. At least Sid's had a long walk, and a chance to bark at a man on a bike. He never barks at kids or women on bikes, just men. Eejit dog.

At the maisonettes, some big boys are drinking super lager and singing the Soldier's Song. They're the ones who crushed a giant snowball in my face and got an extra laugh when snow went down my throat. I was only nine.

I switch direction so they don't see me and there's the car, the brown car with a bashed-in door that doesn't match. Martin's been messing about with the camera and there's only two left on the spool. It's tricky to get in focus so it's a while before I take the car photo. Then I notice Gibby. He's waiting outside a house, his arms folded, watching me. He comes towards me, then changes his mind and goes back.

I pretend to fix Sid's collar, then walk away slowly so it doesn't seem suspicious. Heel segs clack on the street behind me, closer and closer then the hand on my shoulder.

'What you up to now?' Gibby says. He looks different. He's wearing a big-collared shirt that's clean, high-waisters and shiny brogues. Crappy disco clothes.

'I'm no doing anything.' I turn away, then nearly fall when he tugs me back.

'Ah know what you think about me,' he says. 'Why don't you just say it, hen?'

'Wha— what do you mean?'

Gibby comes so close that I see the zoo animals on his shirt. I keep my eyes on a teeny lion so I don't have to look at his face.

'Mon now, stop playing wee lassie games,' he says in a whispery voice, 'tell me what Ah did.' Then he just walks away, back across the road to the same house. I stand and stare because I can't move yet. A woman comes out and he puts his arm around her and it's Samantha. Gibby is with Samantha. I thump down hard on my bum and I want to scream but nothing's coming out.

It's no her, course it's no. When they come closer, I see her hair isn't short, just tied back, and her face is thinner and her mouth smaller. But she is wearing a summer dress and she is blonde and she is getting into his dark-coloured Hillman Avenger. I'm scared for her. She sits in the front and fiddles with her necklace, a heart with a teeny green stone in the centre. Aquamarine, the birthstone for March.

Somebody is shouting at Sid Vicious. I must've let go of his lead and he's peeing on a pram. I make myself stand and call him. The Avenger does a noisy U-turn and zooms past, Gibby leaning out the window, waving and smiling at me.

There's no time to wait for Nino's law person, I need to do an anonymous phone call right now. I run home for the wee card Detective Alistair Baxter left. On TV, people disguise their voices with hankies over the receiver but Nana's hanky drawer is filled with big bras, brassieres she calls them, and other underwears that give me the willies. Gibby will never know who grassed anyway cos I'm no giving my name and I'll use my fanciest words and poshest voice. With your pals, you have to be careful about the words you use in case you get called a swot, but grown-ups like all that.

I wonder what Samantha's voice was like? Heather is posh, so is Nino, but Mr Watson isn't. Would she speak like her dad or her pals? All this time and all the stuff I've found out about her and I'll never know what Samantha sounded like.

I walk miles to the phone box near the swings at Parkhouse. There's nowhere to tie Sid so I let him off the lead. Who cares if he gets lost?

Suddenly, I feel nervous and a bit worried, what if—

'He— hello— ehm, can I please speak to Detective Alistair Baxter, please?' I say. 'It's urgent.' – 'Urgent' is a good word. 'No thank you, I do not want to give my name, and it concerns the murder of Samantha Watson. Thank you.'

They're putting me through. My tummy feels tight.

'Detective Baxter's desk,' a woman says. It might be Val, she's got the same snooty accent but I'm no sure. It's no him anyway.

'I want to give Detective Alistair Baxter information about the murder of Samantha Watson. This is an anonymous phone call, by the way.'

There's a big sigh. 'Detective Baxter is on annual leave, I'm taking messages. But if this is a wind-up, we'll—'

'It's no, it's no a wind-up, honest . . .' I forget my posh voice. 'The information concerns the murder of Samantha Watson, on 14th April 1979.'

'I'm familiar with that case, but I need your details first.'

'I'm not giving details just information about the murderer.' Oh man, this is totally nerve-wracking. I thought it would be easy but I'm shitting myself.

'What information?' Might-Be-Val sounds more interested now.

'The murderer is likely Gibby. He lives in Westercommon flats and drives a dark-coloured car that might be an Avenger. Yous need to arrest him.'

'Right, now listen to me. If this is a prank, you are in serious trouble. If you have genuine information regarding this person, you can start by providing their full name and address.'

'His name is, is . . .' Shite-on-a-bike. What is his name? The whole family are just Gibby: the five brothers are Gibby; the dad was Gibby; they had a greyhound called Gibby. And what block does he live in? What floor, what flat number?

I hang up before they trace the call.

There's a bottle in the phone box and I stomp it so hard the glass breaks and stinky cider goes over my trainer. How did I not even think to find out his real name? What a diddy, total, utter diddy. Sid comes trotting up, carrying a bright new tennis ball. I can't even lose an idiot dog.

The rain has started and it's past lunch time, but I traipse about Possil trying to find out the Gibsons' names. There's hardly anybody out to ask, so I end up going in for people.

Speccy Kathleen thinks one of them is called Scott, 'wee Gibby,' she says. Is that height, or age? Is killer-Gibby the youngest, the wee-est? Ali in the Red Shop says their names are John, Paul, George and Ringo, and Boaby. No even funny.

Jackie isn't in but her big sister, Pauline, speaks to me. Pauline's wearing a massive smock because she's about to be a single mum. I think that would be nice, having the baby without bothering about being married.

Last year, Martin said that me and him would likely get married. We were playing at the canal and a man chucked a bag in the water. It was a decent-looking bag so we fished it out and three teeny kittens were in it, perfect and ginger and drowned. Martin cried first, then I started, and we held hands and that's when he said the thing about getting married. Then he goes, 'Right after the wedding, you get to see each other's nudie arse.' I burst out laughing and so did he. We put the poor kittens in an old basin and set it on fire for a Viking funeral. We said proper prayers too, in case the Viking thing was sacrilege.

Pauline says that the guy upstairs was at Possil Secondary with one of the Gibbys, and that Mrs Hickey up the next close goes to bingo with their mum. Pauline is helpful, so I tell her I hope it's a nice baby and that it comes out of her good and fast. I think that's what you say.

Jackie and Pauline live in one of the old tenements and every wall of their close is painted with Young Young Posso Fleet, the lights and windows are smashed and there's glue pokes everywhere. It's an utter midden and I have to go up the stair slowly and carefully.

'You wanting?' Possil Secondary guy says. He looks the right age for my Gibby, twenty-five or twenty-nine.

'Em, did you go to school with Gibby?'

'How?' Behind him in the lobby there's a stack of crates and a white statue like you'd see in a fountain. Voices come from one of the rooms and a woman is loudly doing 'One potato, two potato' and when she reaches 'more' there's a big cheer. Now, I've got that daft rhyme in my head.

'Just, just, can you tell us his first name? And maybe if you know his address?'

'Get tae fuck,' he says.

Mrs Hickey is nicer and her flat is all flowery patterns and smells of baking. She brings me in and gives Sid a bowl of Rice Krispies, which even he isn't sure about. I know one thing about Mrs Hickey – she sat on her budgie. She's got a huge bum and I try not to picture poor Blue-Boy. When I ask about Gibby, she says Mrs Gibson doesn't talk about her sons when they're at bingo. Then she goes on about the time she nearly won the Link-up, one number away, and certain people would know all about it if she had that kind of money. I'm glad Mrs Hickey didn't win, she'd likely have bought a new budgie.

I give up with Gibby's first name and head back to Westercommon to look for his flat. There's four blocks, each with nineteen storeys and I don't even know where to begin. Then Sid starts wagging his tail and tugging the lead. He's spotted Nana going in and I run to catch her.

'You're sodden, sweetheart, you didn't need to walk Sid Vicious all morning,' Nana goes. 'What do you say to toast and a hot baby tea, eh?' Baby tea is full of milk and sugar and is tops. 'Jean Jarvis saw workies in Ashfield Cabs so— ach, look at that, they've ripped the lift wires out again. Take my arm, hen.'

It takes us ages going upstairs. Nana keeps stopping to check on 'poor souls' who won't get out because of the lifts. She's got a list of messages to get them, but I bet it's me that has to go to the shops. No wonder Mr Watson catches up with us.

'You're fairly tearing up that stair,' Nana says.

'I'll walk yous up,' he says and takes Nana's arm. He takes mine too.

Nana opens her handbag. 'Do you know anything about venison, Billy? They were selling it off the back of a van, ten bob a lump, and I wouldn't like to think some farmer is missing a horse.'

Mr Watson laughs. 'Ah, Maggie, you're a stoater, so you are. I was going to chap your door to say Ashfield's nearly ready.' He leans close to Nana and whispers but I hear anyway and he's checking we're OK for money.

When we get to the eighth, Nana asks Mr Watson in. 'Check this meat and tell me if it's only fit for Sid Vicious.'

'No the day, no. I'm, eh, I've a bit of business with Des Grey. No doubt I'll see you in Ashfield.' He bows down and pats my cheek.

When we get in, Nana's turned crabby. 'Des Grey. What does he want with that big scumbag? And here I was starting to like Billy Watson.'

She's muttering away, forgetting all about my tea and toast. But I start wondering about Mr Watson. He's supposed to have a gang or something, and one newspaper said there's a 'vicious and violent feud'. What if I tell him about Gibby?

Chapter 58

Ashfield Cabs reopens today and I'm to start at my usual time.

Last night, I wanted to get Janey talking, that nonsense with the t-shirt doesn't sound right at all. So, I made a jelly, hoping if she relaxed, maybe a wee laugh, she might let me in.

The winter of the big strikes, was that 1974? '75 maybe? But one night when the blackout hit, I dropped a big bowl of lime jelly. Janey and I were crawling about in the dark, scooping it off the carpet with teaspoons. We laughed so much, neither of us could stand. When the lights came back on, she said, 'You look like a big giant snottered on you, Nana,' and away we went again.

But Janey didn't laugh when I reminded her. She didn't eat the jelly and stomped away to her room when I asked if she was still thinking about Samantha Watson. When I get paid, I'll try buying her a wee thing. Just no a t-shirt.

'At least you're back,' Bert says as a hello. He's in shorts again.

'Is no everybody coming back, then?' I ask. There's a smell of fresh paint but I make a mental note to wipe the smoke-stoor off the counter.

'Nightshift Mary's jacked it. Says she's feart. Fuck knows who's going to cover her shifts. You wanting any? Naw? Didn't think you'd help.'

At dominoes the other night, Jean told me something about Bert. Apparently, he's a known ladies' man, divorced twice, umpteen weans, and now shacked up with yon eejit Tory from the post office. I thought it was the wrong Bert till she mentioned the nostrils. None of us could work out the attraction, although Trisha is right fond of a big moustache. They're no after him for his knees, that's for sure. Or his manners.

I look in at the Break Room and there's nothing there but a stack of new plastic chairs. The desk has a big sheet over it so I can't tell if that survived.

'Where's the kettle? And the wireless?'

'Aye, you need to bring a flask till everything's sorted. A new lavvie's fitted but no sink yet,' Bert says. He stops to answer the phone and do a call-out, then says, 'That's the other thing, the phone's no been done right. We're getting all the incoming calls, even the ones meant for the extension. If you hear them talking on the other line, you need to press the switch. Naw, no that one, stupid, the grey one. Look, look what I'm showing you, for fuck sake.'

'Here's something I've been meaning to tell you, Bert,' I say. 'One of my neighbours was at work when somebody accidentally knocked boiling tea over him, and like yourself, he was in short trousers. Got a terrible scalding, privates like raw mince. So I heard.'

Ladies' man. No this lady.

What will I do for a cuppa later? I wish I'd known about bringing a flask. Right enough, I'm no sure about our flask, was it no leaking when we went to Ayr last year?

What a nice day that was, sitting on the beach, Janey digging a trench right down to the sea and then a donkey ride. It was comical when she dropped her wee windmill and tried to jump down and . . . oh, no, no. The donkey ride was Marie. Surely I shouldn't be confusing 1948 with 1978? Surely.

We didn't get away for the day this year. Ach, I'd better no start thinking about this summer, end up crying. It's good that school's back next week. Maybe if all this had happened in term time, Janey would've been too busy to dwell on things.

I've tried to imagine myself in her position, how I might have coped at her age, but those were different times. There was a family in our street, McGhee I mind was their name, and the landlord was called because of a stench in their close. Turned out both parents had died from flu and the weans hadn't known who to tell. An aunt came from Dumfries to care for them, but there was nowhere else for them to go and they had to stay in that same flat. Imagine, those wee mites sleeping in the room where their mammy and daddy's corpses had lain. In those days, there was no time to spare on anything but food on the table, but that's no to say their suffering was any less. It gets right up my hump when people say the working class were hardened to loss. And right up my hump when they still claim it now.

I know that nowadays there is more help, and I do regret no asking for one of these new psychological people from the social work. They would have known why Janey's head's still full of Samantha and why she's carrying guilt, they would've helped. I should've asked. Every time I think she's over the worst, away she goes inside herself again. Surely things will change when she's got all the homework and studying and new friends. But if not, I will fight to get her seen, and yon good-food-and-exercise doctor will know all about it if I have to read the riot act.

Impossible to get a minute's peace this afternoon, the back door is still boarded up and the drivers have to come through the front. Duncan and Jimmy are in and out like a fiddler's elbow. I say hello but they ignore me, their faces tripping them. The boy with the thick glasses stops for a smoke and a quick blether. Seems some of the drivers have been scared off too, and the ones left are on double-time. He doesn't know if Taxi Alex is coming back.

I don't get my break.

'Ashfield Cabs, can I . . .' I say when the phone goes. But it's the other line, like Bert said, and it's Billy Watson calling. I wish I could say I don't hang up because I've forgotten which button to press, but God forgive me, it's sheer nosiness.

'Duncan there?' Billy says.

'Aye, but what's the score, man?' Jimmy says. 'When we gonnae get—'

'Shut the fuck up, and put him on.'

'Awright?' It's Duncan now. Eggman, Mr Edgar. The man has too many names.

'No, I'm no all right, no by a long chalk, so tell me you got something,' Billy says.

'It was the MacQuarries right enough, you were spot on, and by the sounds of it, we got off lightly. Supposed to be a petrol bomb through the front window but daft prick came in the back way.'

'Fucking MacQuarrie, fucking knew it, that . . .' Billy calls him all the names of the day, and there's something different, a sharpness in his voice that I don't recognize. 'Right, listen. Go for the son.'

'Honk MacQuarrie?'

'No him. The other one, the one with the calliper.'

Now, that's something you don't see much of these days, callipers. Modern medicine is a wonder. Finn used to play with a boy in a calliper, what was his name? Ach, I'm away again.

'Sure you want him, Billy? Far as Ah know, Raymond's nothing to do with nothing. He's a plumber, fixed my maw's sink that time.'

'You questioning me here, pal? Eh? Cos—'

'No, you're fine, solid. If you say it, that's it, Billy. Always.'

I cover my mouth in case my shock bursts out. Billy is the Boss. The one that scares the Edgar brothers, the one in charge of all the dirty business, the one that's right now ordering a beating for a harmless man. My head feels light. What about the rest of Billy's claims? The car thieving and the dodgy Communists? The reason for offering me work? Does he even care about my Janey? Yon obnoxious loudmouth at the funeral claimed Helen and Samantha Watson paid the price for knowing too much about Billy's business – is that what this is? Is he making sure Janey and I don't know anything? Dear Mother of God.

The woman with the yappy Chihuahua comes in for a cab, and I'm glad of the interruption because I can stop listening.

When my shift finishes, I go to Duncan and hand in my notice. I can't afford to just walk away so I say that I'll stay till they find a replacement. Hopefully give me time to find somewhere else. A vein in his big thick neck pops as he gives me a shirikin. Do these men have no words but swear words?

'I'm sorry but I won't change my mind. Mary and myself are too old for this carry-on, and like her, I'm afraid for my safety.'

It's only half a lie because I am scared, just not of the arsonist.

Chapter 59

126 days

Aunty Angela, Kirsty and me are up the town in the shopping centre. I didn't want to come but Nana's on my back all the time now and I couldn't think of an excuse.

Kirsty had a hairy fit in John Menzies and we left because everybody was looking. You'd think she'd been skelped but it was just about getting a red lollypop instead of yellow. She's on a ride now, a dragon that goes round and round and makes fake roaring noises.

Aunty Angela bought me a load of school stuff – pencil case, a shoulder bag for all the books you have to carry, a pocket calculator. I wish I could be excited.

'You OK, Janey?' Aunty Angela says.

'What you meaning?'

'You're dead quiet, hen. No even a smile when Kirsty dropped her lollypop.'

'I'm fine.'

'Will I tell you something?' she says. 'Your dad was a thinker too. Marie loved that about him, but sometimes he went a bit too deep into hisself. Sometimes he never spoke for days and Marie didn't know how to make him better so she ended up feeling terrible too. You know what I'm getting at here, toots?'

'Did Nana say something to you? Did she make you say that? Cos I'm fine. People just need to leave me alone.'

Who cares what my dad was like? Or my mammy? They're no here.

'Maggie never said a word and I never meant anything, Janey. Just worried about you,' Aunty Angela says. 'Mon, I'll get Her Majesty off that dragon and we'll go to the Wimpy. Is that a wee smile?' She tries to put her arm round my shoulder but I wiggle away.

Aunty Angela walked me home, I didn't want to go to theirs for dinner. I hear Sid howling as soon as I get to our landing so Nana must be out somewhere. He bounces all over me and I give him a wee clap cos I feel like howling myself. There's a piece and corned beef in the breadbin for me and Sid cheers up when I put it in his bowl. I switch the TV on and stare at it, and it doesn't even matter that it's the boring news.

The buzzer goes and I jump out my skin, I didn't know they were fixed. It goes again and again but I don't answer. It'll be Gibby. Then there's loud chapping. Somebody else must've buzzed him in and you're no supposed to do that.

'Janey. Janey Devine.' It's a woman. Maybe it's the girlfriend who looks like Samantha. I stay very still and quiet but the chapping doesn't stop. Wish the peephole wasn't all green. 'I saw you come in. Open up, please, it's PC Wilde.'

Val. Horrible Val. I open the door in case the neighbours come out to do their nosey. Val's wearing police uniform again and there's another one, a man, with her.

'Can we come in for a quick word, love?' she says. I'm no her love and she's no getting in.

'I'm no allowed to let anybody in,' I say. 'Especially you, after what you did. Member? Going down the Dummy Railway without my nana's permission?'

Val steps back and speaks to the policeman. 'Eddie, do me a favour and let me talk to her privately. She's not good with authority.'

'Knock yourself out,' Eddie says. He's huge and walks away with his head stooped like he's used to bending down to get in places. 'Better check the car anyway, before it's stripped for parts.'

When he's gone, Val comes close to the door again.

'You're still no getting in.'

'Fair enough,' she says, 'but I know it was you who phoned. Want me to talk about it here? So everyone hears?'

My face is burning, I can feel it. 'I don't know what you're meaning, but you can come into the lobby.'

Val takes her police hat off and looks around with a worried face.

'Sid's in the kitchen,' I tell her.

'What is it you think you know?' she says. 'Who's this Gibby?'

'I have no clue what you're on about. I never phoned anybody. And I don't know a thing about Samantha's murder.'

'How did you know this concerns the murder? I never mentioned Samantha Watson.'

What a pishy trick. I bet they get taught how to be sneaky at police school.

'Look, I know this whole thing has had a devastating effect on you and I'm not surprised.' She pats her hair, checking her old-lady bun is nice and tight. 'But what you know could be very important, and truth be told, I have misgivings about the case myself. It's not that I actively participated in the investigation to a great extent but I did file the paperwork. And I read it all, Janey,' can't believe she's getting my name right, 'so if you have anything to add—'

'Don't know what you're talking about,' I say and look down. Sid's been biting the carpet and somebody's going to take a flyer over the raggy bit. With any luck, it'll be PC Valerie Wilde.

'How about I tell you what I know, then you tell me what you know? OK? Good.' Val walks into the living room and sits without being asked. 'Firstly, I always had doubts about Louis McLure. It seemed that his being charged was part of the keenness to link the murder with Billy Watson. Of course I wasn't allowed to take part in McLure's interrogation, but I transcribed the tapes. He owned up to assaulting Jimmy Edgar without hesitation, in fact he bragged about it. But when questioned about Samantha, his demeanour changed, becoming aggressive and evasive. He admitted to taking photographs of Samantha but vehemently denied it was for blackmail. When I saw the two Polaroids, I was surprised blackmail was being considered as a motive. One was so blurred, it could have been anyone, and the other was, well, I would have rated it as embarrassing rather than obscene. Then, at the end of a particularly long interrogation, McLure let slip that he knew something that could put him in danger. No names of course. Then when the Procurator Fiscal dropped the prosecution after he found that Sergeant—'

Someone else is chapping at the door now. Who's letting people in? Val is obviously waiting for me to open it. At least I'm safe with her here.

But no Gibby this time either. It's Nino.

'Hey, Janey. Is your gran in? No? Should I go then?'

'No, it's fine,' I say. I don't mind that it's Nino, just funny to see him outside of the library, and funny to see him in a hat.

'Great, I'll just come in for a few minutes and— Oh, Constable Wilde.' Nino steps back so quickly, he nearly trips. For a minute, he looks annoyed, nobody likes stupid Val, but then he shakes her hand, smiles and says how good it is to see her again. 'Any news on the investigation?' he asks.

'Nothing to tell, Ninian, sorry. I'm just tying up a few loose ends with Janey. She's been such a lovely witness,' Val is close beside me and it would be easy to stomp on her foot and pretend it's accidental, 'I will miss her when this case is closed. Oh, I'm sorry, Ninian. Samantha is more than a case, I know that.' She reaches out and pats his arm.

'So, what is it you're wanting?' I ask him, because the two of them are just standing smiling.

'Oh, yeah. It was to give this back to your gran.' He takes a pound note from his pocket. 'She must have been using it as a bookmark. I didn't want to wait in case she needs it.'

The pound belongs to somebody else. Nana knows exactly how much she has and never ever mislays money. But I take it because it's an honest mistake and not stealing.

'The things we find in books,' Nino says to Val, and she laughs like it's the funniest thing she's heard. 'Drop in soon, Janey. And tell Gran we've some new Mills and Boon.'

Nana hates Mills and Boon but Nino's just trying to be nice. As I close the door, he bends close to my face. I think he's going to kiss me, and mad thing is, I don't pull away. But he's whispering – his visit was to talk about the law charity, he just couldn't say in front of Val. I offer the money back and he just winks.

Val has gone back into the living room. Stinking snoop.

'That was very thoughtful,' she says, still smiling. 'Ninian and his uncle could not have been nicer during questioning. See, Janey, not everyone dislikes the police.'

I don't mention that Nino called her a pushy cow. 'Have you finished talking,' I say, 'cos Sid's scratching to get out?'

'Two more minutes,' Val says, pointing for me to sit. 'Now then, the second thing that bothers me is the student party on the Friday night. I helped take statements from the guests, and what a mess of contradictions. Estimates of numbers at the party ranged from "eight or nine" to "probably forty". Twelve statements were collected but there was the usual gatecrashers that couldn't be traced. No one was sure when the party started or finished, and only seven people were absolutely certain that Samantha was there. The witness who saw her leave in the car claimed he was watching the street from the kitchen, despite the kitchen having no window. It's very plain there was drug use as well as home brew.' Val starts pacing up and down, probably imagining she's a TV detective. 'So, what time did Samantha leave the party, and was she alone? One witness was outside and knows it was late because he'd come out to say hello to the moon. He saw a "pretty lady" talking to a man who had his arm around her, and although he couldn't identify Samantha from a photograph, he described her dress perfectly.'

'Does that mean, does it mean Samantha was talking to her killer?' I ask, desperately trying to think if Gibby and Samantha knew each other.

'Possibly, but the witness wasn't given much credibility because of his very poor English, and he was never asked to identify McLure as the man. So many crucial questions raised and so much unreliable information released to the press.'

Val stops and takes a big deep breath. Maybe this is the first time she's told anybody her ideas. Maybe I should tell her mine? Mine are way better. God, should I?

'So?' she says, looking at me. 'What do you think? Want to give me your information now?'

'Don't know what you're talking about,' I say, trying hard to swallow my crying because all I can think about is how easily Gibby would get to Nana. 'You need to go now.'

Val shakes her head and very quietly swears. She puts her hand on my shoulder. 'We can keep you safe. Whatever you are scared of, whoever you are scared of, the police will protect you.' Her voice is serious but concerned. 'Tell me what you know and I promise no one will harm you. Please, Janey, trust me.'

I believe her. For about three seconds. Then I open the kitchen door and let Sid out.

Chapter 60

No a wink of sleep last night, can't get Billy out my head. This bombshell made me realize what a gullible old besom I am. I went out early to ask Angela to keep Janey busy for the day, just to let me sleep in peace. She agreed and didn't even ask why. I don't know how to thank Angela, but no doubt there's a place waiting in Heaven. A place beside her best friend.

I lay down but couldn't settle and when Jean came by to say she had clothes for me, I was glad to get out of the house.

Jean has a tall slim build, which is a stroke of luck because when her short stout sister has a clear-out, the clothes come to me. A Primary teacher she was, shocking varicose veins but shops in Marks and Spencer. No like these modern teachers in clothes you'd be ashamed to give to a jumble sale.

It was a good-sized bagful but the real prize was a lovely pair of slingbacks.

'Try them on,' Jean said, and I sat beside her man on the couch.

Jean's husband is a great man for the reading. I like a book myself, a biography before bed is ideal, but I draw the line at keeping them in the house. There's bookcases on every wall, although that might be insulation against the damp. Today, he had the telly on for a programme about atomic bombs. When I sat, he made a point of turning the volume right up. Jean and I couldn't compete with the CND vicar and went through to the kitchen.

The slingbacks, white with a navy trim and sensible low heel, have very little wear, and with a bit of toilet paper stuffed in the toes they'll do a treat.

'Say thanks for me, these are grand. I'll try on the rest of it tonight.' Apart from the girdle, I'm no that desperate.

I'd brought magazines for her daughter since she's still not out much. No that anything could ever make the heartbreak of miscarriage any easier but Jean appreciated the thought.

'Thanks, Maggie, I'll pass them on. And will you drop a bag into the Foy uncle on your way home? It's just a loaf and a couple of tins,' she said.

So, I'm having to walk along Bardowie Street with two heavy bags. Ach, I don't mind for the Foy uncle, we all keep a wee eye on him. It's a relief when he answers his door, and a relief when he gives me a smile. He says he's fine, eating enough and remembering his medication, just no in the mood for Mass. He gives me another shy smile when I say we miss him at hymn time. Voice of an angel, the man.

He lives right across from Ashfield Cabs and who do I see going in but Billy Watson.

'Maggie, mon over, will you?' he calls, holding up a big plastic box.

'I'm in a terrible hurry, Mr Watson.'

'Spare five minutes,' he says and it's not a request.

I don't recognize the lassie on the counter, thirties with a well-cut pageboy, and by her hassled face, I'm guessing she's new. There's nobody else in the Break Room and Billy sets his box on a white table that's new as well. He unloads a kettle, cups and all the tea-making supplies. No before time – without tea, there wouldn't have been a driver left.

'Nothing for me, Mr Watson,' I say.

'What's with the Mr Watson? Am I no Billy any more? And what's with you handing in your notice? Expected you to have more bottle,' he says.

If I was sensible, I would politely apologize for being afraid, thank him for all his help, and shake his hand. And that would be the end of it. But like the silly old fool that I am, I let him have it.

'I've plenty of bottle, plenty. You're the coward round here. No even the courage to admit to my face it's yourself calling the shots with these lowlifes. The papers were right about you and your criminal empire.'

His face is completely blank, no a flicker of anger, surprise or even hurt. Nothing. Instead, he takes the kettle and fills it, the sink evidently working again, then waits calmly for it to boil. Maybe I should just walk out, but I'm rooted to the spot, waiting for him to boil too.

'Sit down,' he says, pouring tea. He even remembers I take it black with two sugars. 'You heard it from somebody here, didn't you? My own fault for giving you the job.'

I light a cigarette and sit across the table from him, unsure and more than a bit worried about how this is going to go. Anybody that orders violence done to a handicapped man would have no qualms about a mouthy old so-and-so.

'There's just never any fucking escape, is there? I'm no looking for sympathy here, I made my choices in life and live with them. But sometimes, sometimes it fucking grinds me down. I've nieces and nephews that are complete strangers because my brother cut me off. Moved to Corby, fucking Corby, and changed his name to escape association with The Ghost.' The blankness has gone from his face, anger and hurt blazing now. 'Whatever happens in my life, they never see past it. When my wife got knocked down, there she is, near death in intensive care, and I'm in a cell, polis desperate to pin it on me. And it was a fucking drunk driver. A drunk driver. Then there was a time when Samantha was six, playing with her Sindys on the stair and took a tumble. Big bruise on her forehead and the school notified the child cruelty. How many falls did your Marie have? How many has Janey had? Cruelty ever come to you? Didn't think so. How could they believe I'd batter my own daugh—'

We're interrupted by Skinny Jimmy, shouting, 'He's outside in the car, we got him—'

'Ho. Shut it,' Billy says and Jimmy looks confused. Then Duncan strolls in.

'Wee message waiting for you outside, Billy,' he says, 'no rush, like.'

'Let him go,' Billy says quietly. He's looking at his cup, no meeting anyone's eye.

'Aww, man, you tolt us.' Jimmy seems right put out.

'You,' Billy gets to his feet, 'away to fuck and do it.'

'Bags to drive,' Jimmy says, holding his hand out for the car keys, 'gonnae let us drive, man? That cunt in the back cracked me with his calliper, right in the baws.'

Duncan ignores him, and says, 'Ah'll just put that message back where Ah found it then. Right to his door, aye?'

Billy nods, then sits again. They're no the comfiest of chairs, these daft plastic things.

'Losing the plot these days. Since Samantha. Need to watch,' he says but to himself really. Then he looks at me. 'Right then, Maggie, that's us. I have to admit, I'll miss you. I appreciated the way you listened. You know what it's like to lose a daughter, and with you, I was just a grieving father.'

'Was it all lies? Even what you said about being grateful to Janey?'

'Ah, don't. Don't do that. You know what your Janey means to me. And it wasn't so much lies, as bent truth. The car export business is right enough, all in Duncan's name though, and it was my father-in-law got me into this. But what he taught me was how to take care of the money, and that's the one thing the reporters got right. It's no just for Tweedle-Dee and Tweedle-Dum out there either, I work with any cunt. No matter what they're selling, who they're threatening, what they're thieving, I make their money clean. If the devil hisself came to me with a good offer, I'd sort him out a wee barbers in Bellshill, no questions asked.' Billy is unable to keep the misplaced pride out his voice. 'The way the law is, as long as my own hands are clean, the polis can't touch me. And I've ended up with a power I was never after. All my clients, even the tosspots claiming they do it for a political cause, they all want to keep the money man happy.'

'If that's true, what do you need thugs for? If they want you happy, why would they kill your daughter? You're at it again with the lies.'

'Because at some point How Come kicks in. How Come Billy fixed it that I got a burger van, but he got a car showroom? How Come Billy got that bastard a pub in Tenerife, but got me a stall at The Barras? How Come? The big men are big weans and I found out long ago how jealous they get.' Billy rubs at his left thumb, the top of which is missing. All these months I've known him and never noticed that. 'And what if they imagine I'm actually thieving off them? How far do you think they'd go then? That's what happened in January, before, before Samantha. I got wind of some big mouth, going around claiming I was dipping his pockets, then the cars at Ashfield got smashed. Bastard comes from out Barlanark way, Mick M—'

'Stop right there. Don't you be telling anything about these people,' I say.

'Fair enough. All I'm saying is you need to watch your back

in this job and it's safer if you're no watching alone.' He leans back and looks me in the eye. 'So, Maggie, now you know, and if you decide to take everything to *The Sunday Mail*, well, I've had worse betrayals.'

'I wouldn't pish on that mob if they were burning in the pits of Hell,' I say.

'Aye, but I can see by your face what you think of me. Doesn't matter. I do want you to believe that I'll always be grateful to Janey, and meant well for yous both.'

He goes to sort papers at the desk, which has been surprisingly well cleaned. I finish my tea, but on the way out, I stop to say my piece.

'You'll understand that my conscience would never let me work for you, but anytime you feel the need to talk about Samantha, or just a blether, you're welcome to visit us,' I say, because even surrounded by all his men, Billy's got nobody. Nobody.

Chapter 61

131 days

I smell cooking but I'm no getting up. Aunty Angela's in and I hear whispery voices, talking about me. Always talking about me. For all I know, one of them is Gibby's spy. Maybe Gibby pays them. Maybe he threatens them. Tell me what Janey did today or I'll flatten you. Who was at her door? Who did she talk to?

'Up, right now, madam.' Nana barges in and pulls the bed-covers down. 'Clothes on and mon talk to Martin. I got your spool developed.'

When I go into the living room, Martin's got the photos set out on the floor. I'm no sure what to do with the picture of Gibby's car now. Val will have told her boss that I made a joke phone call with a made-up story and even Nino and his nice lawyer won't bother helping when they hear that.

Martin's dead excited. 'These are mental. Check this one I took of Sid doing a shite at the school gate. Sid, look it's your arse, and who's this mental halfwit behind you? Big coat with his hood up and it's boiling.' He throws me the photo and there's somebody in a black duffel standing alone in the distance. 'Here he is again, man, what a diddy.'

'Black-Hood No Face,' I say. The weirdo who scared wee Lorna.

'That's fucking brilliant. I'm stealing that for my punk name, "Tonight at the Apollo, Black-Hood No Face Gillespie".'

Martin finds the guy in four photos, always wearing the duffel coat, always with the hood up, always alone. Watching.

'It's Gibby,' I say.

'Gibby?' Martin examines one under the standard lamp. 'That's no any of the Gibbys. They don't wear daft coats.'

'It is. And it's me he's watching,' I whisper.

Martin looks scared and goes to sit in front of the TV even though it's not on. Aunty Angela tells him he can wait here for breakfast but he'll need to meet her at the Co-op to carry the shopping. Martin doesn't answer and as soon as she's away, he leaves too. Don't blame him, Nana's doing fried tottie-scones and they are like rubber.

Apart from taking stupid Sid out, I stayed in my room all day. I tried sleeping but kept imagining Black-Hood No Face Gibby reaching out the photos to strangle me.

I'm listening to my tapes now. This used to be one of my favourite 999 songs but when 'Homicide' comes on, I have to fast forward. Even music makes me think about Samantha.

Sid starts barking and Nana's talking to someone at the door. I turn the radio-cassette up to block them out.

'Janey, Janey. Get yourself in here.' Only Nana is louder than Crass. Her face is red, her perm flattened from a nap, and I wonder why she's wearing her jacket at ten o'clock at night. 'Put your shoes on quick,' she says, 'Martin's missing.'

The room spins.

'Missing? Missing? Nana, what—'

'That was Angela to see if he was here. He's no been home since this morning. She's up the wall, especially with this murderer . . . with things going on. Did he say to you where he was going, hen?'

It wouldn't help if Martin did say. Nothing will help if Gibby's got him.

Me and Nana and Sid head out to the Gillespies' house. I walk in front so she doesn't see my tears. How did I no stop Martin when he left? Those photos really freaked him out and I just let him go all hisself. Gibby knows that me and Martin are pals, maybe he's kidnapped him to get at me. Or maybe Martin is already lying down the Dummy Railway with his guts out.

'Can you no hurry up, Nana?' I say, tugging Nana's arm to make her go faster. The panic isn't just cos this is my fault, it's cos it's Martin.

Aunty Angela asked me for Logie's address and Neil's gone to check. Lucky Martin's no got a load of mates. She already phoned the police but it's still too early for them. When they do come, I'll tell them Gibby threatened Martin after a big argument about taking care of Sid. It's the best I can do without confessing everything.

'How long since Neil left?' Aunty Angela says, going to the window again. She's usually dead calm and I can hardly look at her.

'Just ten minutes, pet,' Nana says, fussing about with a duster. She's already washed every dish, hoovered the hall and cleared Kirsty's toys away. Nobody can stay still. 'I'm sure Martin's with his pal. Likely watching one of their telly shows.'

A Rezillos LP is sitting on top of the Amstrad. Nobody's allowed to touch George's hi-fi, but as soon he's away at work, Martin tapes all his new records. For me.

'Sure you don't want me to look for him?' I ask again. 'I know all the places he plays.'

'You're no going out on those streets at night,' Nana says. But Aunty Angela comes over and kneels beside me.

'Would you go, Janey?' She takes my hand and it feels cold and trembly.

'Angela. No.'

'Nana, please. Just a wee while.' I need out of here, my head is ready to crack open. 'I'll take Sid Vicious and only go as far as Saracen.'

When the phone rings and Neil hasn't had any luck and is going to check the canal, Nana gives in.

It's good being out of that house, even with Sid. The summer air has hardly cooled from daytime and there's a lot of people still around. Would Gibby risk being seen snatching Martin? I feel a teeny bit more hopeful.

Since Neil is checking places Martin might go, I'll check places where Gibby goes. The car he's been fixing is still parked at the flats. It doesn't look as ramshackle as before, with tyres on and the shattered windscreen replaced, and the doors have locks now. The wee boys that play tanks in it will be disappointed. I listen close to the boot but there's no sounds of anyone trapped in there. Maybe that's just in gangster films.

In Ellesmere Street, I sneak up the path to the house where Gibby's Samantha-face girlfriend lives. The curtains are open and a big colour TV lights the living room. There's a sudden movement at the window and Sid starts going nuts, barking and dragging me off my feet. My heart nearly bursts when I hear a shout from inside, a man. Then the window opens and, and a ginger cat jumps out and runs into the street.

A cat. Sid Vicious, you are such a total utter fucking closet. If he was any use, he'd be able to track Martin.

But I'm an idiot too. What am I doing keeking in random

people's windows? If Gibby has Martin, they won't be watching *Benny Hill* together. Deep down, I know the Dummy Railway should be the place to search but being down there again, finding . . . finding . . . oh, Martin. All I can think about is the excited-toddler face he makes when there's a punk band on *Top of the Pops*. How could he ever stand up to Gibby? Sid watches and whines when I throw up.

Every single step feels like a million and I don't think I can do it. I'll tell the police. Everything. What do they do with kids for messing up an investigation? If they find Martin, I don't care even if I'm sent to Barlinnnie.

Sometimes we play One Man Hunt in the church grounds and I'll have a wee check there so I can tell Aunty Angela I tried my best. I belt it along Saracen Street, through the stone arch and right up the driveway. If I slow down, I might think about Aunty Angela's face.

And there he is, sitting under headless St Teresa. Sid finds him and all my guilt and dread drain away. I yawn and Martin yawns back. It takes a lot of effort no to jump the wall and hug him.

'You better get home,' I say, 'your ma is going insane and Neil's out looking for you.'

'Gonnae no say you found me? No yet, eh?'

I can see he's been crying. 'You been here since this morning?'

'I was sitting in the church till that moany priest chucked me out. Fucking starving an all.'

I climb over and hand him the crisps Aunty Angela gave me. When he wipes snotters away to eat them, I see dried blood on his nose.

'Your arse must be sodden,' I say, sitting beside him. The big yellow flowers round the statue must've been watered today and the dirt is freezing wet. White pebbles mark the edge of the flow-erbed and I start throwing them at St Teresa.

'Is that no sacrilege?' Martin goes.

'Doubt God's watching,' I say, 'doubt God is even real.'

'Fuck sake, Janey.' He shoves Wotsits into his mouth, then quietly says, 'It's the dead body, isn't it? That's what made you all different.'

'It made everything different,' I say. But then Sid pees on St Teresa's feet and we start laughing.

'Sid's going to the bad fire an all,' Martin says.

'Is it cos of the murder that you're hiding? Cos of the photos and what I said about Gibby?'

'No really,' he says, standing to rub mud off his baseball boots. Martin gets all the best shoes.

'Well, did somebody scud you again?' I ask because he annoys a lot of people. There's times when you need to just zip your mouth and no answer back, but Martin never recognizes those times. He can't help hisself.

'It was one of the Campbells,' he says.

'Oh, man, that's bad. Cammy's a headcase, what did you say?'

'Wasn't Cammy. It was, it was his sister.'

'Sharon? Sharon Campbell?' I'm trying no to smile. 'Martin, she's only nine.' I get up and grab Sid who's started barking at a bush. 'There's nobody in there, diddy.'

Martin's sniffing again, his cheeks damp and smeared orange with crisps. 'When I was going home I saw somebody in a big duffel, like the guy in the photos. I didn't want him to see me so I cut through the Campbells' back.'

I let out a groan. The Campbell kids don't let anybody in their backcourt, even adults.

'I know, Janey, but I was all freaked out. Anyway, it was Sharon that caught me and whacked me with a bike pump. And, and she took Malkie-Boy off me.'

For years Martin's carried this plastic cat about, says it's lucky. He takes some slagging for it, no from me though. Malkie-Boy is weirdly nice.

I'm angry, no at Sharon though, at Martin. 'How did you let her do that?' I say, kicking at his leg.

'What was I supposed to do? Hit her back? I ran. And, and she shouted she's getting her big brother to me. Totally fucked so I am.'

Martin turns so I can't see his face and there's a white line on his neck between the sunburn and his terrible back-to-school haircut. I listen to his usual showy crying. Martin, who carries a teeny cat, who sings made-up songs in the playground, who draws dancing stickmen on all his jotters. Martin, who is going to get slaughtered at Secondary. It's a surprise how much this bothers me and I'm no angry any more, just glad he's a boy that doesn't hurt girls.

'Mon,' I say, climbing onto the wall, 'mon home.'

'What about Sharon? And Cammy? He's worse than my da.'

'They're no going to touch you,' I tell him.

We find Sharon sitting with a wee brother on their stair, eating cold pies. The Campbells get to stay out all night if they want. Martin waits at the corner with Sid, who's found a very interesting stain on the fence. I march right up to Sharon – one thing about knowing a murderer, other kids are nothing. Maybe Martin can't hit a girl but I can, and I pull her curls till she gives up Malkie-Boy. When she threatens me with Cammy, the daft wee brother goes, 'But he's away in List D school, Sharon. For chucking the bricks on the motorway, mind?'

Martin must be right about Malkie-Boy being lucky.

We stand at Martin's gate while he gets courage to go in.

'OK, I'm ready,' he says, but doesn't move. He looks at

me. 'When is all this stuff with the murder going to be done with?'

'It is done with. That stuff I told you about Gibby and Black-Hood, it was just a wind-up,' I say and wish it was true.

He smiles and does a bunch of soft punches on my arm. 'I knew you were kidding. And, and, Janey . . . I'm kinda glad Asha didn't want to be my girlfriend.' When Martin gets embarrassed only his ears go red, and they glow like streetlights as he runs to the door.

I hope Aunty Angela isn't too angry with him. Martin's an eejit but he's the best pretendy cousin I've got.

Chapter 62

See if I catch whoever it is pressing our buzzer, I'll skin them alive.

But here, it's Duncan Edgar asking to come up. I've still no found another job and I'm sure he's here to sack me after I sent a driver to Central Station instead of Queen Street. The angry accountant from Newcastle phoned to complain and what a mouth for such a respectable profession.

'A favour,' Duncan says, when I open the door, 'gonnae watch the wee man for a bit?'

'The baby? You want me to babysit? Have you nobody else?' I've got the doctor at four.

'Wife's up the town with the lassies. Ah'm no trusting him with any of the drivers, and Ah need to pick Jimmy up.'

'Could somebody else get your brother?'

'He's had an accident, the fanny.' Duncan's pushing the pram into the lobby before I even agree. 'Ah'll pay for your time, but gonnae just do it? Ah need to run here.'

'Aye, leave the wean with me but just till three at the latest.' With school shoes still on the horizon I need the extra money.

'Cheers for this, Ah'll be a half-hour, tops,' he says, handing me a bag with a bottle and nappies. Then he grabs my arm. 'Watch him. Seriously, if anything happens to that boy—'

'You don't need to worry, Duncan. You go and get your Skinny Jimmy and this wee angel will be fine.'

Baby Duncan is a wee angel right enough, but by God, he's got heavier since I last held him. He woke when the front door slammed and I nearly gave myself a hernia taking him out the pram.

'Here, here, what's all the noise about? Aunty Maggie's got you.'

It's funny how the songs come back to you, and I'm enjoying them as much as the wee man. 'Ali Bali', 'Too-ra-loo-ra' and 'Soul of My Saviour', because I know it would annoy his bigoted daddy.

But when I sing 'O, a lulla-lulla, lulla-lulla, bye-bye', I have a wee bubble to myself because it was Marie's favourite, and it's Marie I want in my arms. And of course, my daft brain makes the connection between Lulla and Lulu. He's been on my mind since I saw his mother yesterday.

I hadn't been in Miss Eveline's since a shampoo and set for the funeral and I was starting to resemble one of yon Bee Gees. Thursday afternoon in the hairdressers is busier than an Old Firm match but they squeezed me in. It's usually noisier than the football too, but when I arrived, there was absolute silence.

'Give us your anorak, Maggie,' Big Joyce said, 'and sit yoursel there.' She put a finger to her lips and pointed at a woman getting her roots done. 'Mrs McLure is just telling us what happened wi her son.'

It's no easy to see anything through the cigarette smoke in Miss Eveline's, but I actually recognized Lulu's mother. She and her husband were regulars in The Glen. No regulars exactly, just every Wednesday. Never any bother, never spoke to anybody, no even each other. Just drank in that very determined way until the giro money was gone.

The dryers were switched off and everybody was listening. Mrs McLure is early forties, must've been young when she had her weans, and thin enough to slip through the hole in a stank.

'. . . and they shoved him right against the cooker, wi' all the rings on full,' she was saying, and I was sorry to have arrived this late into the story. 'Ma Stephen's no a well man, he cannae take a doin. And two, two of the bastards against one.'

'You must have been very shaken up, dearie,' said Miss Eveline, who I've no seen in person since 1974 and had obviously come out the back-shop specially. 'And did your husband tell them where to find your son?'

'Too fuckin right he tolt them,' Mrs McLure says in the voice of a coalman. Pity anybody on the receiving end of a shirikin from her. 'He tolt them how Louis showed up and knocked all our food, tolt them he's sleeping rough up by the greyhound kennels. That boy has always been wild but Ah never thought Ah'd have heavy bams like that at ma door. Never.'

One of the stylists passed me and very quietly I asked, 'Is she talking about the police? Were the police looking for her son?'

'Wasn't the polis, was a couple of hardmen,' she whispered, 'kicked her door in, middle of the night. In her nightie, so she was.'

Jeez-oh. No wonder Lulu's slinking about in dirty clothes begging for money when his own parents gave him up.

Everybody waited to see if Mrs McLure would say more but all she did was light another fag. Miss Eveline heaved her huge self up and away back to counting her takings, and the talk switched to a christening that ended in four arrests and a dose of food poisoning.

But I couldn't take my eyes off Mrs McLure, the woman was bealin and I felt another twinge of sympathy for Lulu.

Then, the minute she was out the door, it started.

'Is it any wonder somebody's after her Lulu? There might be no justice in the courts, but there is in Possil.'

'McLure killt that poor big lassie as sure as the Pope's a Catholic.'

'Ah'll tell yous something. It's no surprise that boy grew up bad. Lamentable upbringing those McLure weans had. Left alone to see to theirsels, always dirty, always hungry. That wan has only hersel to blame.'

I've always known how mean-spirited they can be in that hairdressers but this was very harsh. Made me wonder what they said about me when I left.

I call Janey to see the baby, but she's in her bed again. I'm losing her and pray to all the saints this doctor is the answer.

Duncan's an awful good baby, falling asleep as I struggle with his nappy. You don't use a nappy-pin with these new-style paper things, just a bit of tape, and I end up with it stuck to my blouse. Maybe I could look after weans for a living? No doubt you need a certificate to be a babysitter these days, you need a certificate for everything.

Oh, that'll be the brothers back. I know which one of the Duncans I prefer and it's no the one at the door.

'Everything OK?' Duncan says, and hurries right in. Skinny Jimmy leans against the doorframe looking very dazed, a white hospital dressing on his forehead. I wonder if he's been in a fight again. Hard to feel sympathy for that man after he palmed those drugs onto me.

'Wee Duncan's fine and dandy, fine and dandy. You've got a beautiful son there,' I say, and for a wee minute, the Eggman looks like any other doting daddy. Two sides to everybody.

'Duncy, Duncy, man,' Jimmy says, too loud for a sleeping

baby, 'gonnae sort us out with another one of those pain tablets? My heid's loupin.'

'You're getting hee-haw, pal. And keep the fucking voice down,' Duncan says, grabbing hold of his brother and propping him against the hall table. I hope Our Lady of Lourdes doesn't fall again.

'Was it a bad accident?' I ask.

'Accident? He's the fucking accident,' Duncan says, laughing. 'Ho, Jimmy, show her.'

Jimmy lifts his t-shirt, reminding me I'll need to buy lard. I don't know what I'm supposed to be seeing till Duncan points to two blue squares scraped into his brother's skin.

'Dobber here was getting a tattoo, a big King Billy on his horse. It's no long started when he looks down, sees the blood and passes out. Whacked his coupon off the worktable. Ah had to take him to the Royal for stitches, whole fucking day wasted.'

'So, is that, is that the horse's hoofs he's got on his belly?' I forget about the baby and roar with laughter. 'Two toaty hoofs? Forever?'

'Shut up,' Jimmy says. 'Mind that it's only my own blood makes me faint. So shut the fuck up, both of yous.'

I end up having to make tea for Jimmy. Sitting with these two is not my idea of a nice afternoon, and I've still to get down to the doctors. I don't even know how we get round to talking about Lulu, probably me after singing that song.

'You know him, Duncan, do you think he's guilty of the murder?'

'Guilty enough to get put down,' he says, with a smile that makes me afraid. Would it have been him and Jimmy shoved Lulu's father against the hot cooker?

'So, somebody is out to get him?'

'That's guaranteed. That cunt chibbed my brother,' Duncan points at Jimmy, who has his smelly feet up on my footstool,

341

'and he's gonnae pay for that at least. And he deserves to get it for what he did to Samantha, for what he did to Billy and Helen. See Billy? Billy was great with that big Lulu, and I'm no just meaning with money and a job. Took him in when he was fifteen, got him clothes, taught him to drive, ach, you cannae imagine that kind of betrayal. Billy's . . . Billy's a decent guy. Loads of people, loads of families owe Billy Watson. And he does it all quiet like, never runs his mouth off about who he looks after.'

'You got any pills, missus?' Jimmy puts in. 'Any Valium? Tems?'

'I've nothing like that, and if I did, I wouldn't give them to you.'

Jimmy gets up, staggering. 'Can we go, man? She's doin my box in.'

Duncan gives me ten pounds, and for that, I'd look after twenty babies. I hand him Duncan's dirty nappy but apparently it goes right in the bin.

'See you the morrow, Maggie. And, listen. Just be glad Lulu's getting it. Your own lassie's safe now.'

How can Janey be safe in a world with men like the Edgars, men like Donald Devine?

Janey refused point blank to come to the doctors and I had to rush to make the appointment.

'A tonic?'

'She needs building up, Mrs Devine.'

I look at the clock on the wall behind her. Two minutes. Two bloody minutes is all the time she's let me speak.

'Dr MacTavish,' I say as calmly as I can, 'Janey's starting Secondary next week. How is a tonic supposed to get her through a school day?'

'Just make sure she's kept busy and gets a good night's sleep.'

'Sleep? The lassie is doing nothing but sleep.' It's me that's lying awake, going over and over things, trying to work out what's gone wrong between us.

Janey has always been independent, it's her nature. Since she learned to talk, it's always been, 'I'll do it myself, Nana.' From wiping her bottom to changing a plug, she can do it. Even when she can't. Eight years old when she asked for a door key, 'I don't need to go to Aunty Angela's after school, and I can get dinner all cooked for you.' She would've had a damn good try if I'd let her. See, I think that's the trouble now. I'm nearly blue in the face trying to get her to talk, but all she says is she'll get herself sorted. She has been trying, the wee lamb, but every time there's improvement, back she slips. And it's got to stop, I've got to put a stop to it.

Dr MacTavish is writing the prescription when I slap the details of the child psychologist on her desk.

'No, I'm sorry. I want this taken further,' I say, 'I've been told there's a unit at Yorkhill Hospital and I want Janey referred.'

Mrs Khan, God bless her, went to her consultant cousin to find the right department.

'As you wish, Mrs Devine, but believe me, young girls are prone to this type of nervous complaint. By the time a specialist appointment is available, your granddaughter will no doubt be right as rain. Do try the tonic.'

It's all I can do to stop myself telling her to shove her tonic right up her lazy big bahookey.

Chapter 63

133 days

Two things made me decide. First, it was Martin going missing. Then it was Eggman coming yesterday with his daft baby. The way Nana answered the door – she didn't ask who it was, didn't get Sid to bark, didn't put the chain on – just whacked the door wide open. And in my head, I saw Gibby pushing in. I saw a hatchet in his hand and I saw Nana grabbing at him, trying to save me. In my head, I saw the hatchet hitting her and it was like seeing the future.

So, it's got to be today. You'd think going to threaten a killer would make me scared but a weird bubble has grown around me and nothing's getting in. I go into my room and give Paddy Panda a hug; in the kitchen, I water the spider plant we got at the jumble sale; Nana's wee slippers waiting beside her chair don't even upset me. Perfect.

'Mon, Sid Vicious,' I say, 'it was you that started this, mon go talk to Gibby.'

Sid is panting in the heat, his tongue hanging out like a dod of wet spam. There's no shade at Pigeonshit Wall but it's a good place to be seen. And Gibby does see us.

'Where you been hiding?' he says, finishing his American

Cream Soda and chucking the bottle over the wall. I shrug and say nothing, the bubble making this easier than I expected. Gibby is his usual oily self with his honkin boiler suit and gloves.

'Time me and you had a talk, hen. How's about taking Sid to the Basin?'

'Aye, OK,' I say. My voice is loud and doesn't wobble, the right kind of voice to warn Gibby to leave us alone, to threaten him with Mr Watson.

This bit of the canal is usually busy and that's why I agreed. It's near the flats and littered with scabby furniture and tyres where people hang out. The path is just stomped-down grass and below the surface of the canal you can see shadows of rusting junk, dark jaggy shapes that were once real things. Years and years ago, a wee boy drowned at this bit, his ghost supposed to be bloated and green. Wee boy ghosts don't bother me.

Gibby is talking rubbish about a car he's been fixing, as if this is any ordinary walk. Sid is off the lead and when he spots a dead fox in the water, he goes mental with excitement. The fox is rotted and smelly with a bulging eye. The sameness of it makes me stop. Dread crawls up my back and suddenly the bubble bursts. I don't want to be here with Gibby, I'm no brave enough.

'Fuck are you greeting about?' Gibby goes.

I turn to face him. 'Please, please gonnae no hurt me.'

'What you on about? C'mere.' Gibby reaches out to grab me and I step back. His other hand is in his pocket. The knife, he's hiding the knife. I slump onto my knees, ready to beg for my life. My tears blur his movement as Gibby lunges towards me and I tumble backwards.

The shock of it. The shock of being dead. Gibby must've stabbed me. All around is thick murky cloud, no sound and no smell and no angels coming for me. This must be Purgatory for all my lies and for no helping Samantha, for being rotten to Nana, for stealing limeade from the Red Shop. I'll be hanging here in this nothingness for years and years. It's no so bad.

But there is a noise. Barking. There's no dogs in fucking Purgatory. A rush comes, like real Janey is blasting back inside me and I kick and kick. Breaking the surface, a new shock, the cold liquid iciness of the canal. I huff air, again and again even though it hurts. The bank isn't far away, I know I'm a good swimmer but something is tangled around my leg, dragging me back down.

Then I see him. Gibby in the water, splashing towards me. When I scream, septic canal water fills my mouth and I nearly boak. He's shouting and shouting and I'm punching and kicking. Then I run out of energy and his big muscly arm wraps round my throat.

Well, this is making it easy for him. Gibby just has to hold my head under and everybody will believe I fell and drowned. Easy peasy lemon squeezy.

'Fucking stupid stupid wee stupid lassie,' Gibby whines.

We are lying in damp weeds at the edge of the path. Everything is peaceful except Gibby wheezing and the noise of my heart. It thuds like Orange Walk drums then slows to teeny mouse feet. I stare at fluffy clouds and listen to its weird beat.

'Here, shove this on.' Gibby's clothes are in a dry pile and he tosses me his overalls. He sits and struggles to pull denims over wet legs. Wish he'd hurry. Even though he dragged me out the water, I don't want to see Gibby in his pants.

'Oh for fuck sake, look at this. Ma foot.'

Something under the water has pierced his skin and pink blood streams out when he moves. Sid has been cuddled in next to me, his doggy heat enough to stop my shivers, and he springs up and rushes to have a smell of the blood. His jaw is doing that excited thing, like Mutley sniggering in *Wacky Races*.

'Keep that fucker away from me,' Gibby says. He tries to get dry enough to make a roll-up, and the thin, red lines cut into his hands match the scratched circle around my ankle. It must've really hurt him to unsnag me.

My legs buckle when I stand, wet clothes weigh a ton, but at least I'm breathing normally again and the overalls make me a toaty bit warmer. I find Sid's lead where Gibby dropped it, years and years ago.

'What did you save me for?' I ask when my teeth stop chattering. He probably wants to slice me up, drowning would be too easy for a mental killer.

'Cos you were drowning, stupid,' Gibby goes. 'Fuck did you jump in for anyway?'

'I didn't jump,' I say, tasting rot again, 'you were going to kill me. Like you killed Samantha.'

'Kill Samantha?' Gibby stares at me, his mouth hanging open. 'It was that guy killed her, the guy that every cunt's after. Lulu. And kill you?' His voice is getting all fast like a cartoon. 'What is all this? Gonnae tell us cos Ah've no got a fucking scooby.'

'You killed Samantha. I know you did cos—'

'Ah robbed her, that's it, Ah swear. She was dead when Ah found her. Ah only robbed her.'

'Robbed her?' I say. 'What's that even mean?'

'Just, just took stuff off her body,' he says, looking at the ground. 'She was already dead. A right fucking mess of deadness. Ah just stole her stuff, Ah thought you knew that.'

'What, what you talking about?'

'That Saturday morning, Ah was down the Dummy Railway looking for scrap. And the lassie was lying there, all, all . . . Did you think Ah did that? She was disembowelled for fuck sake.' He looks at me and our eyes glue together. 'Ah still see it. The state of her. All the time.'

And I realize me and Gibby are a bit the same. I know Samantha is in his brain and his dreams and his bedroom, and I know he'll never get rid of her.

'Don't, don't talk about her body,' I say in a teeny voice, and he nods.

'Ah was gonnae get the polis, honest, but then I saw her purse. Know how much she had in there? Thirty-eight quid. Know how many giros that is? Then there was all her rings, bangles, a belter of a watch. Ah couldnae help myself.'

'You stole her nice jewellery? When she was dead?'

'Didnae even get to flog it, chucked it all in the Clyde.'

'Liar. I saw your girlfriend wearing her necklace.'

'Christ, what sort of wean are you? Aye, OK, Ah gave her that before knowing who the dead lassie was. Imagine that mad Billy Watson coming after you?' Gibby finally gets his roll-up lit. He coughs and grey canal sick, stinking of slime, goes everywhere. Sid tugs on the lead.

I wait till he gets his breath back. 'I know it was you that sliced up my t-shirt and stuffed it into my hood,' I say. 'You were going to cut my tongue off like the chimp. Or kill me.'

'You thought that? Fuck, no, that was just a warning to stop you grassing.' He flops onto his back again. 'Ah thought you'd saw me. Ah was wearing my gloves to stop fingerprints and it was taking ages to get her earrings off—'

'How could you do that? That is just so, so . . . wrong.' It's worse than his puddle of smelly sick, but Gibby just shrugs.

'Ah wis skint and she wisnae needing them. But that werewolf bastard,' he points at Sid, 'nearly ran into me, and then Ah heard you shouting. Ah legged it up the hill and watched yous for a bit. Felt rotten a wee lassie finding that but Ah couldnae risk the polis. Ah thought you'd saw me. When you threw up in your granny's, then went all weird, Ah thought it was cos you'd recognized me.'

I think back to Dummy Railway Day, to the bit before I walked around the itchy-coo bush, but Gibby isn't there. That shadow on the embankment when Val took me back, was that a memory of Gibby? Maybe I did see him. Doesn't matter anyway.

'I thought you were the murderer cos you knew about the swear word on Samantha's face,' I say. Gibby's mopping at his blood with a sock. 'And you were spying on me,' I say much louder. 'Hanging about at the flats in a duffel, and, and, threatening Heather about getting in your car. And—'

'Ah live in the flats, hen. A duffo? What's a duffo? And who the fuck is Heather? You talking about when Ah warned you and your pals no to get into any taxis? That wasn't a threat, that was real. Ah heard it was a taxi driver done Samantha, some nutjob bevvier wi orange hair. It was before the polis lifted McLure.' Gibby's voice is back to normal speed but still sounds different cos he's shivering. 'And spying on a wean? Fuck no. It was just a bit of the old mind games.'

'Mind games? Making me shit-scared?'

'You were winding me up too, no saying what you knew, no saying if you were gonnae stick me in. You went to my mate's door to ask my name and took photos of my Capri and—'

'A Capri? No an Avenger?' I say, and realize how weird I sound.

'Aye, a Capri,' Gibby looks confused but keeps talking, 'then that woman polis was back at yours. Ah was shitting myself. Had to make sure you didnae tell, see? Just wanted to freak you a wee bit, didnae think you'd be scared stupid.'

Two old men on the opposite bank have stopped to watch us.

'Bit nippy for a swim,' one shouts and the other laughs so much he drops his walking stick. Gibby swears and gives them the vicky and they walk on, still laughing. Sid pulls on the lead to have another smell of the cut foot. The blood is watery and the wound is puckered like a squashed snail. Bet that gets infected.

'Look, sorry, hen. Maybe Ah took it too far, but you're no gonnae tell on me, are you? Ah saved you, stopped you drowning. That's us square. No grassing, especially no to Billy Watson. Right? Right, Janey?'

The thought of Gibby taking her stuff makes me sick but I did the wrong thing too, I touched Samantha too. Maybe we both went a bit mental, maybe that's what happens when you find a murdered woman.

I tell Gibby I won't grass and he looks dead relieved. He manages to stand, then takes a step and tumbles. 'Fuck, Ah cannae walk on it. Gie's a hand, eh?' His eyes shine red raw from the canal water. Or maybe it's tears.

My legs are shaking like crazy and my brain feels like it's shaking too with all this new information. But no way am I going to help Gibby. No way, José. He could easily have stopped me from seeing Samantha, he just had to shout.

I walk away.

'Ah saved your life, hen,' Gibby shouts after me. 'Get one of my brothers to come with the motor. Gonnae? Eh, Janey?'

Walking back through Possil, I feel like I'm full of balloon gas. It could be nearly drowning, but it could be cos everything's over. Gibby is an utter bag of rancid shite, but he's no after me, or Nana, and he didn't kill Samantha. Maybe it was Lulu, or Taxi Alex like Gibby heard, or maybe just some random maniac. But I didn't mess up the investigation and not a single thing was my fault. Black-Hood No Face, Heather and Lulu, men in cars and men asking my name – all of it is just rubbish piled inside my head. If I wasn't holding Sid's lead, I might float away.

Ali's outside the Red Shop unloading stuff from his van and he shakes his head at my big overalls and dripping hair.

'No dogs,' he says.

'I'm no coming in,' I say, wriggling out the overall and kicking it towards him. 'This is Gibby's, the Gibby that fixes stuff for you. He, ehm, he fell in the canal and got hurt. Just near the Basin, he needs a hand.'

Maybe Ali went to help, maybe not. Don't care. Gibby won't be coming near me with his stupid mind games any more.

Chapter 64

There was a good turnout at ten Mass the day. With the schools going back, there's a brightness in everybody's spirits. That might be part of the reason for the change in Janey, but I'm sure it has more to do with the psychology appointment.

When I told her about it yesterday, it obviously made a difference. She was cheerful and obliging, even tried to help me with the washing. The spinner on the twin-tub must be on its last legs though, her clothes were still soaking and the smell from them was terrible. Maybe Gibby can fix it for me.

We watched a bit of telly and what a cuddle I got at bedtime, even a few tears. That'll be the relief. Janey's a clever enough cookie to understand how these mind therapies work and even if it takes time to get the appointment, knowing help is coming is a light at the end of the tunnel. For us both. We'll see how Secondary goes but if it's too much for her, I'll have no qualms about keeping her home and the authorities can take a run and jump. I just wish I'd pushed for this weeks ago.

Angela catches us up and Martin and Janey walk ahead, swinging Kirsty between them.

'Janey's looking more like hersel,' Angela says. Another new jacket, her George wasting money no doubt. 'You think she's stopped thinking about the murder?'

I tell her about the psychologist and she's delighted. Delighted.

'The end's in sight, hen,' I say.

'But is it?' she says, serious now. 'They've no caught the killer so the weans are still in danger. That was all I could think about when Martin didn't come home. I'll never forget Janey finding him and helping him down. He'd still be stuck up that tree if it wasn't for her.' Angela stops walking, and bites the edge of her thumbnail. She's had that habit since she was eight and it makes me suddenly aware of how long I've known her.

'Did I tell you I sent George back to work without any y-fronts?' she says. 'He got to Aberdeen and had to phone for the size, never bought underwear in his life. See, since Samantha Watson, I've been in a right bad place, Maggie. Cannae stop thinking about dying, about Marie and my daddy. It's like somebody poked my brain with a stick.'

I can't help give Angela a wee squeeze. If a young thing like her has been troubled, then maybe I'm no going senile.

'Nana, Aunty Angela,' Janey shouts, 'bands in Kelvingrove Park. It's today. Can we go?' She and Martin are looking at a poster stuck on a lamppost.

'What time does it start?' Angela says, grabbing a hold of Kirsty who's trying to tear it down.

'First band on at three,' Martin says, 'it's free, we don't even need money, and see them? They're punk, we need to go. Gonnae let us, Angela?'

'Let me see this poster,' I say. It's no that I don't trust them but the story about Martin being stuck up a big tree the other night sounded right fishy. 'The Vague, is that a punk band? I wondered when I saw it spray-painted all over the rent office. Aye, yous can go, long as you're back by seven.'

'I'll get Neil to pick them up, he's on the Alpine lorry the day,' Angela says. The two of them jump about, then talk all the way home about what to wear.

Definitely a brightness about this day.

Chapter 65

134 days

'That's me away,' I tell Nana. She's settling for forty-winks so doesn't notice me swiping her matches. I'm doing one thing before Kelvingrove bandstand with Martin, one last thing.

'Sorry, Sid, you can't come this time,' I say, shutting the door. This time I'm going to the Dummy Railway myself.

It was thinking about the Viking funeral for those drowned kittens that gave me the idea. Heather did say I should burn my scrapbook and if I put the ashes at the place where I found Samantha, it could be like a ceremony thing. A finish.

It starts raining when I get to the railings. The usual sicky feeling is building and I nearly turn back. But Uncle Finn said they need somebody to look at their face, so one last time then I'll tell Samantha no more.

The embankment is already wet and I get covered in green skid marks. Hope Martin can lend me another t-shirt for the gig. I'm shaking now, my heart bumping and ears buzzing, but I keep going.

There's a surprise when I walk behind the itchy-coo bush.

Nino's cross. He's put concrete at the base so it won't get kicked over. It'll be here forever and that makes me sniff a bit. It's so pretty, just like Samantha, a perfect place to sprinkle the ashes. A perfect finish.

The scrapbook never made anything better anyway, it wasn't the real Samantha. The stuff other people said about her, it was all just like my made-up stories.

It's taking ages to light a match in the rain and I start wondering how Nino knew exactly where the body was. It wasn't in any newspapers. Maybe he heard from one of the policemen or the doctor that came that day. Aye, that'll be it, that'll be—

Then, the world bursts and whirls around me. The force of it knocks me down and I lie in the wet dirt beside the cross and I remember. I feel like Samantha, torn apart with everything pouring out.

It wasn't scary hiding in The Screke, it was safe and black and I could see nothing. Lovely nothing. My skin was burning like I'd been sitting too close to the electric fire, and the slimy moss on the old stone felt cool and nice when I pressed against it. Just for a wee while, then I'd get somebody, just hide for a wee while.

I see now how quickly everything happened. I've been thinking I sat with Samantha for ages, hours maybe, but it was minutes. And it was just minutes before I realized somebody was in The Screke with me. And seconds after that I smelled the smoke.

The smoke was coming from the other end, the way out. I listened to the crackling of flames, and I listened to the movement behind me at the bend where all the light vanishes. I could stay with the breathing or go outside to the burning.

I wanted Nana. I wanted my Nana.

Very slowly, I crawled to the exit end. I crawled over stones and rusty metal and maybe skeleton bones, and I didn't make a single sound. I waited till my eyes got used to the light then keeked out. That end of The Screke is more wild and overgrown

358

and it was behind thick bushes that I saw a wee fire going. Then, I saw, no, please no.

I saw Satan.

He had a bright red face and red hands and his body was nude and hairy and he was throwing things on the bonfire. I saw Satan burning a pair of trousers and that's when I started screaming. And that's when I pished myself.

Satan looked up. There was a bin bag next to the bushes and, keeping his eyes on me, he emptied out clothes and shoes and a bright stripy towel like you use on the beach. When he put on the shoes, I was surprised he had feet and not hoofs. Then he kicked at the fire and lifted something from the ash. It was a long jaggy knife and he didn't burn his hand because he was the Devil.

He walked towards me. I wanted to shut my eyes to stop seeing his flesh and his horrible thing swinging about but all I did was scream. When he reached me, he put a finger to his mouth.

'Shhh, quiet now,' the Devil said, 'everything's going to be fine. Nice and quick with you, no bother with you. That's a girl, a bit closer.'

He held my wrist and dragged me out of The Screke and his hands were made of rubber. Not hands, gloves, and it was blood making them red. And blood on his face, and I can smell it now. I was on my knees and he was so tall above me, and he kicked me over and put his foot on my neck.

And that was when Sid Vicious came tearing out of The Screke. It was Sid in there, Sid staying close to me. And Sid that sunk big wonky fangs right into the Devil's leg. Satan fell and grabbed his leg and our screams merged together, echoing like crazy all through The Screke.

I ran. I didn't wait for Sid, didn't call him, didn't look back, just ran and ran. Up the hill onto waste ground and on and on till I couldn't catch my breath. I was on a street I didn't recognize and there was a boarded-up shop and I sat in the doorway for a long time. When I stood up, it felt like I'd been sleeping, maybe I was. Satan was just a bad dream and no even my dream. As I walked, everything faded till all that was left was Samantha Watson lying dead.

But it wasn't a dream and it wasn't Satan. It was Ninian Hogg. I remember now. Ninian's posh voice, the redness of the blood on his long hair, his nice smile when he kicked me over. It was Ninian Hogg who killed Samantha and who was going to kill me.

Chapter 66

I had to go out for matches, God knows where the other box went, and the heavens have opened. My lovely slingbacks will never be the same. The rain has flattened Sid Vicious's spiky coat and he resembles a panther, a right ugly panther.

We're both drenched by the time we get back. I'm puffing and panting up the stair and the dog is like an old yin himself, slinking up behind me. Flaming lifts.

Our front door's open. No wide open, but unlocked, and when I see blood on the door handle, all the organs in my body drop a foot.

'Janey. Oh dear God, Janey.' There's another streak of red on the wall in the lobby and I can't see her. I can't find her. 'Where are you, lamb?' My mouth is dry, the words barely audible. The dog goes shooting past and I follow him into the toilet and there she is. She's on the floor using the scrubbing brush on her knee, getting tore into the old scab, blood flowing down her leg. And, sweet Mother of God, her eyes are wild. Sid Vicious goes to her and licks her hand and I kneel and hold them both.

I don't know how much time passes. The dog eventually goes to look in his bowl and I stand too. My daft old legs have gone to sleep and when I stumble, Janey takes my arm and helps me into the living room. We cuddle in till her shakes ease and her teeth stop chattering, and I bring her a baby tea.

'Do your best to drink it hot, sweetheart,' I tell her. And then she tells me. Everything.

'The boyfriend? Oh for the love of Christ, sweetheart. Why didn't you say, why didn't you—'

'Can you just keep quiet for a bit? Can I just tell what happened?'

She talks in a voice I've never heard before, calm and adult, which makes hearing this all the worse. When she tells how the police treated her, the way they scared her, I'm bealin. Poor Janey, just trying to take care of the dead lassie and ending up terrified. And keeping it inside to fester like that scab on her knee. If those police had even shown an ounce of decency towards a frightened child, none of this would have happened.

When she reaches the point where yon Gibby starts threatening her, I lose it.

'Oh, my wee lamb, my wee lamb. No wonder you were in a state. And me thinking you were sick in the head. Oh, my wee lamb.' Tears are teeming down my face now but Janey doesn't even blink, it's like she's made of granite.

'I thought he was the murderer,' she says, 'I thought Gibby killed Samantha because he was talking about the swear word on her face. See, I cleaned it off. It was the C-word and it seemed worse than all her wounds. I wiped it away for Samantha and nobody knew about it. Nobody except me and whoever wrote it.'

'What were you doing keeping all this to yourself, sweetheart?'

But of course, I know why. It's my fault she's grown up secretive, learning from me to keep her suffering and her fear deep inside.

Well, that's going to stop. From this day on, I'll tell her about her lovely family, about their lives and their deaths no matter how much it hurts. And when she's a bit older, I'll tell her about Donald Devine because, by Christ, girls need to know.

By the time Janey reaches the end, I'm shaking so much, the fag falls out my hands. She picks it up and lights it for me. What in God's name was wrong with me that I didn't see what was going on? How will I forgive myself for this?

'It's OK, I'm OK,' she says, forcing a wee smile. 'It's just remembering everything is bad. It's all bad. Nana, what if Sid hadn't been there? What if he hadn't bitten Ninian Hogg?'

'That murdering scum deserves worse.' I'll be praying to St Olga for bacteria in his bite wound. 'Sid Vicious is a rare boy and he'll get a bag of pig's ears as a reward. But, Janey, you were wrong about Gibby, no totally wrong, damned filthy grave robber, so are you absolutely sure it was that librarian?'

'Totally sure. I looked right in his face. But then forgot. See, if I'd remembered, I would have told the police, honest to God, cross my heart hope to die, I would've told them everything.'

She's getting panicked and I lift the tea and make her drink. 'I know that,' I say, 'nobody would ever blame you. Your wee mind just couldn't cope and hid it away, and no wonder, my lamb, no wonder.'

'I think Ninian Hogg was looking for me, asking around to find my name. He didn't recognize me cos he wasn't wearing his glasses, they were probably on the bonfire with his murder clothes. Why didn't the police find all that evidence and go after him, Nana?'

I'm tempted to say it's either because they're incompetent idiots, or because they wanted to pin it on Billy. But truthfully, it would be down to Hogg himself.

'Men like Hogg are very sly, very devious. He would have left nothing to show he'd been there. Apart from you, Janey.' Oh, I shouldn't have said that out loud, terrifying to even think it.

'And it was me that told him who I was,' she says, voice quivering now. 'I walked into the library and told him I was the witness, right to his face. I'm so stupid.' I try again to hug her, this is too much guilt and blame for a wean, far too much. 'When I told him I'd forgotten stuff, he said it was better for me if I never remembered.'

'Better for him, the evil bastard,' I say. My swearing brings a real smile and that smile gives me hope.

'Then he started hanging about here,' she says, 'you can see him in our photos and he came to the door when you were out. That killer's been waiting to get me alone but I never was. Because Sid was always there.' It's now that she breaks, the stiffness in her body gone and the tears flowing. 'All that time I was pure rotten to Sid but it was him that saved me.'

Janey wraps her arms around his neck and holds onto the dog till she's cried her wee heart out. God, I love that Sid Vicious.

'Give me your wee hands. Big deep breaths. That's it. Now, did Hogg do anything else to you? Tell the truth,' I say, but I'm no sure I want any more truth.

'I thought he was nice and let him cuddle me. He touched my leg and now my skin's icky and dirty and it won't scrub off,' she says, and I'd like to take the scrubbing brush to my mind, picturing that filthy murderer touching my wee chooksy.

'This will make it all better.' I give her knee a kiss like when she was teeny. 'See? Nana's magic kiss.' She cries again and that's better than all the silences and all the secrets.

We are still for a long time, the two of us and Sid Vicious, all quiet together. And in the middle of all this suffering, all this horror, I yawn. I can't stop myself, I need to lie down and sleep for a thousand years.

Ach, give yourself a shake, Maggie Devine, you're no the one that needs anything here.

'How did I get everything so wrong?' Janey says eventually, swiping at her tears, anger in her voice now. 'I got tricked by that killer and by Lulu and Heather and Gibby and even horrible Val. I'm so stupid.'

'Don't you be thinking that. Ever. Being grown-up doesn't make anybody behave better, you'll see that soon enough. It's them that are the stupid ones.'

'But, it's no just being stupid, is it, Nana? Ninian Hogg was her boyfriend, he bought her a rabbit, how could he do that to Samantha?'

What a question.

Billy spoke about his daughter's final hours being filled with terror, and I try to imagine those hours. Hogg following Samantha to the party that night. Waiting in a car, or standing on the street, his West-Ender looks attracting no second glances. I imagine him offering her a lift, using his smarmy charm and sleekit smile to convince her their meeting is chance, and Samantha accepting because no woman wants to be alone at night. I imagine her panic when they reach the old railway and he holds the knife against her. I imagine the hours he kept her there, and the horror of her final minutes. And I try to imagine why.

He did it but didn't mean to go that far. He did it because he was jealous, because her dress was too short. He did it because something went wrong in his brain. He did it to stop her telling on him. He did it because she screamed, because she didn't scream.

He did it because he could.

'I don't know why Samantha was killed, Janey, but I do know there are some wicked men in this world. Very wicked.'

*

About three o'clock the door goes. We know it's Martin because he's shouting 'Sing like Johnny Rotten' through the letterbox. I tell him we're busy but he walks right in.

When he sees the state of Janey, he says, 'You heard then?'

'What you talking about, son?' I've got her cleaned up and into pyjamas but her wee face is raw.

'Concert's cancelled cos of the rain. Is that no why Janey's crying?'

'Aye, that's the reason, you're right, Martin. She's awful upset to miss The Vague, so you just go home the now.'

'Can I stay and watch TV? Please, Maggie. *Cartoon Cavalcade*'s on and I can't get peace for Kirsty running about.'

I let him put the telly on because there's something very urgent to be decided. I take Janey into the lobby and shut the door.

On the wee table, I lay out two phone numbers. Detective Baxter's number is printed on a Strathclyde Police card, Billy Watson's is written on the back of a sympathy card. It was Lulu who gave me it, that first night at Billy's. Poor big Lulu.

I take Janey's hand. 'You know that if we tell the police, it would be jail for Nimibus Hogg? Likely for a good long time.' She nods and says his name's Ninian. Like the saint.

'And you know what Samantha's daddy would do to him, don't you?'

She nods again. 'I'm no a baby, Nana.'

'If anybody's got the right to judge, it's you, hen. You and God almighty.'

How would it be for Janey to tell everything to the police? How would it be to tell Billy? With the police, Lulu's name would be cleared and Hogg would rot in jail for the rest of his miserable existence. But you hear of these clever lawyers that get murderers off. With Billy, Hogg would be tortured and possibly killed, and that could never be right. But then I think of Billy's pain and I know that pain and—

'Now that I've told you,' Janey's saying, 'it's already better. Sid's my pal again and you'll keep me safe and maybe I can get back to being real Janey. But see when I think about all them, the police and Gibby and Ninian Hogg, there's nothing. A big empty freezing nothing. Samantha's always going to be with me and that's OK, but the rest of them? I don't want them, and I don't want to decide what happens to them.'

I take her in my arms and whisper that it's all over, that nothing will ever hurt her again as long as I breathe. The lies you tell your children.

Then I shout, 'Martin. Martin, 'mere a minute.'

He comes out, leaving the door open so he can still hear his programme. 'What? Yous coming to watch?'

'I'm going out a message,' I say, and Janey smiles and squeezes my hand. My precious wee lamb. 'I want the two of yous to stay here with Sid Vicious. Don't open that door to anybody, hear me?'

'Aye, sure. But where you going, Maggie?' Martin asks.

'I'm going to get justice for Samantha Watson, son,' I say, and put both phone numbers in my handbag.

Acknowledgements

I am deeply indebted to my agents Euan Thorneycroft and Oli Munson, at A.M. Heath, and Transworld editor Finn Cotton for their unceasing commitment to *A Bad, Bad Place* and for the warmth and patience they have shown me.

Sincere thanks to the following:

To my family – without whom there would be no love and no book.

To the MLitt tutors at Glasgow University who gave me the skills and confidence to write, particularly Louise Welsh, who taught 'it is never just about the crime'. To my talented classmates for their encouragement, feedback and friendship, especially fabulous Lou, Cristina and the online group. I am also grateful to the trusts that provided funding for my studies – Glasgow Educational and Marshall Trust, Sir Richard Stapley Educational Trust, Scottish International Education Trust. And to Liz W, accountancy genius.

To early supporters Jo Unwin, Donna Greaves and Daisy Arendell; Open University; Bloody Scotland/Glencairn Glass and Moniack Mhor.

To all staff at the Queen Elizabeth Neurology Unit, particularly Professor B, Dr Maria F and specialist nurse Caroline C. I owe them my life.

To the good, good people of Possilpark and North Glasgow, including Icky with the best stories, and to all Glasgow Libraries staff.

And final thanks to my beloved swear advisor, Willy C, who picks me up when I fall.

Reading-Group Questions

Do you think the novel authentically captured Glasgow of the late 1970s?

Which of the main characters was your favourite and did you identify with either Maggie or Janey?

Do you feel the depiction of the police was fair and accurate?

The newspapers were quick to lay blame. Do you think the media has changed in its treatment of murder victims, particularly women, and their families?

Possilpark is a key location in the story. How did the author portray the community of Possilpark? Do you think Possil is a bad, bad place?

Did the mystery element and red herrings work, or did you identify the killer early?

How do you feel about the fate of Maggie's abusive husband? Was Maggie justified in her actions?

At the end of the novel, what do you think Maggie chose as justice for Samantha? Would you have made the same choice?

Do you think Sid Vicious is a good dog or not?

As a passionate advocate of lifelong learning, Frances was delighted to graduate at the age of sixty with an MLitt (Distinction) in Creative Writing from Glasgow University. In 2023, she won the Bloody Scotland/Glencairn Crime Short Story Competition, and the first chapters of her debut novel *A Bad, Bad Place* won Highly Commended in the Moniack Mhor Emerging Writer Award 2024.

Frances grew up in North Glasgow, and credits the people of Possilpark and Milton as her writing inspiration. She still lives in Glasgow with her family, and likes libraries and punk rock.